DREAMS REKINDLED

DREAMS REKINDLED

AMANDA CABOT

THORNDIKE PRESS
A part of Gale, a Cengage Company

GALE
A Cengage Company

LIBRARY OF CONGRESS CIP DATA ON FILE.
CATALOGUING IN PUBLICATION FOR THIS BOOK
IS AVAILABLE FROM THE LIBRARY OF CONGRESS.

ISBN-13: 978-1-4328-8737-7 (hardcover alk. paper)

Published in 2021 by arrangement with Revell Books, a division of Baker Publishing Group

Printed in Mexico
Print Number: 01   Print Year: 2021

For LeeAnne Patton, whose friendship
has brightened my life.
Thank you!
And thanks, too, to Richard for sharing
hundreds of his wonderful photos. I wish
we lived closer.

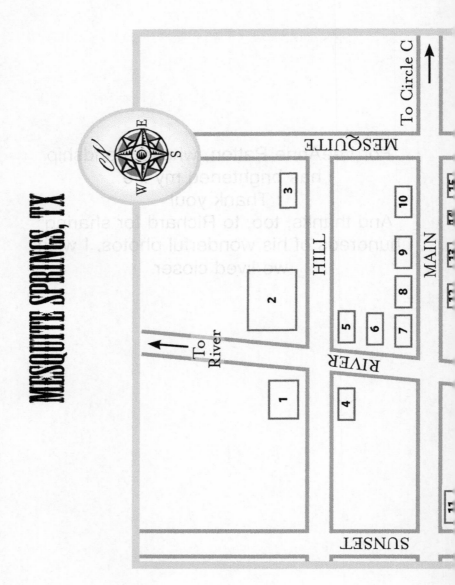

MESQUITE SPRINGS, TX

ALLEY

To Spring

SPRING

To Plaut Ranch

19 | 20 | 21

16 | 17 | 18

1 – Cemetery
2 – Park
3 – Widow Lockhart's House
4 – Downeys' House
5 – School
6 – Parsonage
7 – Church
8 – Mayor's Office/Wyatt and Evelyn's House
9 – Sam Plaut's Law Office (currently vacant)
10 – Dressmaker's Shop

11 – Saloon
12 – Mercantile
13 – Polly's Place and Dorothy's Home
14 – Post Office
15 – Sheriff's Office and House
16 – *Chronicle* Office and Brandon's House
17 – Boardinghouse
18 – Doc Dawson's Office and House
19 – Smiths' House
20 – Blacksmith Shop
21 – Livery

CHAPTER ONE

November 10, 1856

"You're the luckiest person I know."

She's wrong. Totally and absolutely wrong. Dorothy Clark tightened her grip on the fork as she continued to beat egg whites for today's raisin pie. She was not lucky, and this was not the life she wanted. Not even having her best friend back in Mesquite Springs could compensate for the boredom and the knowledge that this was not how she was meant to spend her life. Running a restaurant might fill people's bellies, but it did nothing to challenge their minds.

She doubted Laura would agree, so rather than rail at her, Dorothy answered as calmly as she could. "What makes you think I'm lucky?"

The pretty brunette who'd been her friend for as long as Dorothy could remember shrugged as if the answer were obvious. "Your mother lets you live here all by yourself. My mother would never agree to that."

Dorothy wouldn't dispute that. While she hadn't found it easy to convince Ma to let her leave the ranch and live in town, even temporarily, Mrs. Downey was more protective of her only child than Ma. Dorothy had been surprised — shocked might have been a better word — when the Downeys had sent Laura to an exclusive girls' school back East. Admittedly, Laura had not lived alone the way Dorothy now did, but she'd been more than a thousand miles from home.

"There's a simple reason Ma agreed," Dorothy told her friend. "We would have had to close Polly's Place otherwise. I may be over twenty, but Ma still doesn't want me riding by myself when it's dark outside."

Dorothy was the one who fired up the restaurant's ovens well before the sun rose and started preparing the midday meals she and Laura would serve customers. While she would never be a gifted chef like her sister-in-law Evelyn or as accomplished as Laura was now that she'd attended that fancy finishing school, Dorothy could get everything set out and ready before Laura arrived to prepare the more difficult dishes.

"Once Wyatt and Evelyn return," Dorothy continued, "I'll have to move back to the ranch." Unless she could find a reason to stay here. Having her own home, even if it was only a small apartment over her sister-in-law's restaurant, was wonderful. Though she loved Ma and hated to think of her being alone on the Circle C, Dorothy had discovered that she relished her independence. Here she was no longer Ma's daughter or Wyatt's younger sister. She was simply Dorothy, and that was good.

Laura looked up from the pastry she was fitting into the pie plates, a conspiratorial smile turning her face from pretty to almost beautiful. The intricate hairstyles Laura had learned in Charleston highlighted her hair, making the most of the blonde streaks in otherwise ordinary brown tresses, and drew attention to the eyes that Dorothy had always envied. Hazel was so much more interesting than her own plain brown. Her dark brown hair and brown eyes were just as boring as the rest of her life.

Dorothy lifted a forkful of egg whites, checking their consistency, as Laura said, "Maybe you'll be married or at least courting before they're home again."

Marriage. Laura was convinced that was the answer to every question, the solution to every problem. Once again, she was wrong.

11

"That'll never happen." Dorothy knew that as surely as she knew the sun did not rise in the west. She set the now-stiff egg whites aside and began beating the butter and sugar together.

At the other side of the long table, Laura frowned. "I don't think I'll ever understand you. Every woman wants marriage and children." Her normally sweet voice had turned steely with determination, and as she began fluting the edges of the first piecrust, her lips pursed as if she'd bitten into a lemon. "I wish I'd met the man of my dreams when I was back East. You know that's why Mother and Father sent me to the finishing school, don't you? They wanted me to find a husband."

Unspoken was the fact that while Laura had fancied herself in love with Wyatt, he had viewed her as nothing more than his sister's friend. Dorothy had suspected that the Downeys had sent Laura East to keep her from pining over Wyatt.

"But you didn't." Though the letters Laura had written during her year at school had been filled with stories of the men she'd met, each one had mentioned a different man, and each had made it clear that the man in question had serious flaws. One was too tall, the next too short. One's moustache made Laura laugh; the next one's smoothly shaven face made him look like a boy rather than a grown man. The litany of the men's shortcomings would have been amusing if Dorothy hadn't sensed Laura's growing desperation.

Laura shook her head. "None of them made my heart beat faster. I know I disappointed my parents, but I couldn't marry a man who didn't excite me." She set the pie plate aside and began to fashion the crust for the next one. "There's a man who's meant for me. I just need to find him."

If she hadn't found the right man in a city the size of Charleston, Dorothy wondered what hope there was for Laura here, but she wouldn't say that. Instead, she sought to encourage her friend. "Mesquite Springs is growing. Perhaps the man of your dreams is already on his way here."

That seemed to brighten Laura's spirits, for she smiled. "I hope so, but what about you? If you don't marry, what will you do?" Her smile turned into a frown. "You don't still want to be a writer, do you? I thought that was a passing fancy."

"It's more than that, Laura. It's my dream. The problem is, I don't know how to make that dream come true." The article she'd written earlier this year had excited her, and for a few days, Dorothy had felt as if she had accomplished something worthwhile, but now when she looked into the future that had once seemed clear, all she saw was a wall of impenetrable smoke.

"The one thing I do know," Dorothy told her friend, "is that I won't marry." The risk was too high.

Brandon Holloway nodded solemnly as he guided the wagon down the main street of what he hoped would become his home. The article he'd read hadn't exaggerated. Mesquite Springs was both attractive and apparently prospering.

The stone buildings gave it a sense of permanence, even though he knew the town couldn't be much more than twenty years old. Before he'd headed toward the Hill Country, Brandon had learned what he could about it, including the fact that German immigrants had established many of the communities starting in the thirties. While he saw none of the half-timbered houses that proclaimed other towns' European influence, he doubted Mesquite Springs had been here longer than the more overtly Germanic settlements.

And, if what he'd read was accurate, there were no slaves. Since the rocky soil and the hilly terrain weren't conducive to growing cotton, Brandon hadn't expected any, but he needed to be certain. If there was one thing he'd resolved when he left Xavier, it was that he would never again live in a county where men enslaved others.

As his eyes lit on a small sign, Brandon tugged on the reins. This would be his first stop. Ten minutes later, he emerged from the mayor's office, relieved that there had been no obstacles. Mr. McBride, who explained that he'd been mayor for decades and was now acting mayor until Wyatt Clark returned from his wedding trip, had confirmed that Mesquite Springs had no newspaper and — even more importantly — no barriers to starting one. He'd given Brandon a suggestion for a possible location, pointed him toward the town's only eating establishment, and told him that Widow Bayles had a vacancy at her boardinghouse.

As beginnings went, they didn't get much better. The only awkward moment had come when the mayor asked why Brandon had left Xavier.

"It was time for a change." That much was true. There was no reason to tell Mr. McBride that Brandon had lost everyone and everything he loved — first Ma, then Pa, finally his livelihood and his dreams. There had been no choice other than to leave. Even if he could have ignored what had happened to Pa — and he couldn't when he was responsible — Brandon had lost almost all his subscribers and every one of his advertisers. A man couldn't run a paper without them.

Life would be different here. Not only was the Hill Country different from East Texas, but Brandon himself was different. He would never again put others in danger.

In less than an hour, he had reached the boardinghouse, secured a room, and unpacked the things he'd need for a few days' stay. By the time he'd finished, his stomach had begun to rumble, reminding him that breakfast had been less filling than normal. It was time to see what the town's restaurant had to offer.

Brandon strode briskly down Spring Street, studying the well-cared-for buildings and the empty one on the corner of River that Mr. McBride had indicated might be a good location for the paper. It was large enough to accommodate the newspaper office and provide a temporary living space, and since it was on a double lot, he could build a home on the other half when the time came. The mayor was right. This building looked promising.

So did the rest of the town. The mercantile he passed on his way to Polly's Place had attractive displays in its windows, while the unexpectedly bright blue door of the restaurant not only caught his eye but seemed to welcome him. As he pushed the door open, the savory aromas made his mouth water.

"Welcome to Polly's Place."

Brandon had no sooner entered the dining room than a dark-haired woman of medium height greeted him. She wasn't the most beautiful woman he'd ever seen, but the warmth of the smile that extended to her caramel brown eyes made him feel as if he were a long-lost friend who'd suddenly returned.

"If you don't mind sharing a table, I can seat you right away. Otherwise, there'll be a fifteen-minute wait."

Her voice was low and clear, as welcoming as her smile and as difficult to resist. Though Brandon had wanted his own table, he found himself agreeing to her suggestion. "That would be fine, Miss . . ." He let his voice trail off as he waited for her to identify herself. There was no reason to be so curious about her; after all, this was a small town. Within a week, he'd know many of the residents' names. And yet, he didn't want to wait that long.

"Clark."

"Any relation to the mayor?"

"He's my brother." She started to lead the way to a table. "Please call me Dorothy. Almost everyone who eats here does."

"Thank you, Dorothy. I'm Brandon Holloway."

She smiled again, and once again, he felt the warmth of that smile. "Are you just passing through, or are you planning to stay in Mesquite Springs?"

"Staying. I'm a newspaper publisher." He shook his head when he saw the glint of interest and possibly admiration in her eyes. "That sounds pretentious, doesn't it? Actually, I'm the writer, editor, typesetter, and delivery man."

"A factotum."

"Exactly. If it needs to be done, I do it." And most of the time, Brandon enjoyed the work, even the mundane tasks. Most of the time, he found fulfillment in the knowledge that words were powerful. Most of the time.

Dorothy stopped at a table for four, currently occupied by three men whom Brandon guessed to be twice his age, all eating pieces of pie that, if their large bites were any indication, they found delicious.

"Mr. Holloway is planning to start a newspaper in Mesquite Springs," she said when she'd completed the introductions. "I'm certain you gentlemen have some suggestions for him." She glanced at their now-empty plates. "Shall I bring you more pie? You wouldn't want him to eat alone, would you?"

The man she'd introduced as Mr. Wilkins nodded. "Miss Dorothy, that raisin pie of yours is the best I've ever eaten." He smacked his lips as if to confirm his praise.

"You can thank Evelyn when she returns. All I did was follow her recipe." She continued addressing Mr. Wilkins. "Laura made the piecrusts. She has a light hand with them, doesn't she?"

As he nodded, the other two men placed their orders for a second slice of pie. "Can't let Chet and our newspaperman eat alone," one said solemnly.

Brandon matched the man's sober expression, though inwardly he was smiling. Miss Dorothy Clark was one impressive woman. Not only was she modest, refusing to take credit for the pie, but she was also the most persuasive person he'd met in a long time. She'd convinced him to share a table, and his companions now thought it was their idea to order more pie. All that in a pretty package. Amazing!

Phil Blakeslee reined in his horse at the top of the hill and grinned as he looked down at Mesquite Springs. Yep. It was just the way he remembered it. The spring to the west, the river to the north. River! He scoffed at the term the residents used. It was nothing more than a stream, but that was all Mr. K needed.

"Good job," the man had declared when Phil had returned from what Mr. K called his reconnaissance trip. Armed with a sketchbook and a thick journal to record his impressions, Phil had spent more than six months traveling through Texas, exploring the small towns as he searched for one that would meet his employer's requirements. When he'd first seen Mesquite Springs, he'd found it as close to perfect as he thought possible and hoped Mr. K would agree.

"It looks promising," his boss had said when he saw the sketches and read Phil's notes. "More than just a good location. The new mayor will be so busy learning his duties that he won't worry about anything else, and there's no newspaperman to poke his nose into anyone's business."

No meddling minister, either. Though Phil

hadn't included that in his notes, he'd talked to enough of Mesquite Springs's residents to know that the preacher was not one to condemn folks without good reason. "He's quiet, no Bible thumping," a rancher had told him. Phil had grinned. That was exactly the kind of minister Mr. K needed, one who wouldn't interfere.

Mr. K had studied the map Phil had made and jabbed his finger at the river. "Here's where I want you to start. You know what has to be done. Take that sketchbook of yours and get back to Mesquite Springs. If everything goes right, you'll be a rich man, Philemon Blakeslee. I have big plans for you and that town."

Even the memory of the man's use of his hated first name didn't make him cringe. Money — lots of money — made up for many things.

"C'mon, Dusty." Phil nudged his horse's flanks. "We've got work to do."

As she left the dining room, Dorothy pressed a hand to her chest, trying to slow her heartbeat. It was ridiculous the way it had accelerated while she was speaking with Brandon Holloway. Laura would say her reaction was a sign that he was the man Dorothy was destined to marry, but Dorothy knew better. Her heart wasn't pounding because Brandon was good-looking, though he was. The combination of blond hair and blue eyes was striking, and that square chin had caught her eye the moment he entered the restaurant. It spoke of determination, and that was something Dorothy admired.

But it wasn't the fact that Brandon Holloway was the most attractive man she'd met in ages that had excited her. No. Definitely not. His appearance had nothing to do with her racing pulse, nor did the fact that his voice was a tenor, as smooth as the caramel frosting she'd finally managed to perfect.

What intrigued Dorothy, what set her senses reeling, was the man's profession. He was a writer. As if that weren't enough, he ran a newspaper, which meant he had the power to shape people's opinions and to change their lives. Laura had claimed Dorothy was lucky, but Brandon Holloway was the lucky one. He was living the life she wanted.

"You seem flustered." Laura's eyes narrowed as she turned from the meals she was plating and looked at Dorothy. "Is something wrong?"

"No, no, not at all." She would never, ever tell Laura what had happened. They shared many things, but this silly reaction to the blond newspaperman was not something Dorothy would ever confess. Surely now that she was back in the kitchen, her heartbeat would return to normal.

"I need three more slices of pie for table four and a large serving of the stew. That's for a new customer, Mr. Holloway." Thank goodness her voice did not betray her agitation. Though Dorothy's heart had accelerated again when she'd pronounced his name, Laura didn't seem to notice. That was good. In another minute or two, she'd be able to forget her ridiculous response to the newcomer.

As she busied herself arranging everything on a tray, Dorothy made a decision. The best route to recovery was to avoid the cause of her distress. "Would you mind taking these out there? I think I'd better sit down for a while."

The furrows that appeared between Laura's eyes testified to her concern at Dorothy's deviation from their routine. Though Laura did the majority of the cooking and never failed to ask if there were something else she could do, this was the first time Dorothy had asked her to serve. "What's wrong? Can I get you something? A glass of water?"

Dorothy shook her head. "I just need to

sit." Maybe then she would be able to convince her heart that Brandon Holloway was simply another man and that there was no reason for it to race.

CHAPTER TWO

"He's the one."

Dorothy stared at Laura as she burst into the kitchen. Though she'd known her all her life, she'd never before seen Laura looking like this, with her face so flushed, her eyes sparkling more than a rare Texas snow.

"Who?" It was almost a rhetorical question, since Dorothy was certain of the answer, yet she knew Laura was waiting for her to ask it.

"Mr. Holloway." Laura confirmed Dorothy's supposition. "He's the one I'm going to marry."

There was no reason to feel as if a horse had kicked her. She wasn't the one looking for a husband; Laura was. And she shouldn't have been surprised by Laura's reaction. After all, Brandon Holloway would catch any woman's eye. Still, Dorothy couldn't deny the way her stomach roiled over her friend's declaration.

"How do you know?" Perhaps if she kept Laura talking, she'd regain her equilibrium.

Laura laid the empty tray on the table and smiled, obviously remembering what had happened in the dining room. "When I heard his voice, my heart started pounding, and then when he looked at me, I knew he was the one. No man's ever looked at me that way."

"What way?" As painful as the conversation was, Dorothy couldn't stop herself from asking for more information.

"As if I were the woman he's been searching for all his life." A contented sigh accompanied Laura's words.

Dorothy drew a deep breath and willed her stomach to behave normally. Even if she were inclined to flights of fancy, she would not have described the way Brandon had regarded her like that. She'd seen interest in his gaze, but nothing as dramatic as what Laura claimed.

It was probably only Laura's imagination. She had always tended to exaggerate, but even if it were true, it didn't matter. Of course, it didn't.

"You're two hours too late. I rented my last room this morning." The woman who was almost as tall and almost as thin as Phil shook her head and started to close the door.

This wasn't the way it was supposed to be. He needed a room, and Mrs. Bayles ran the town's only boardinghouse. For the first time, he wondered if he'd been mistaken about Mesquite Springs. *Nonsense,* he told himself. This was only a momentary setback. Furthermore, there might be a way to salvage it.

"Are you sure you don't have a place for me? The stars in this part of Texas are beautiful, but a man gets tired of sleeping under them." Phil gave the boardinghouse's owner a look that stopped short of pleading but left no doubt that he wanted to stay in her establishment.

As he'd hoped, Mrs. Bayles began to soften. "I hate to think of a nice gentleman like you gettin' cold, 'specially now that winter's a-comin'. Fact is, I have an empty room. I don't normally rent it out, on account of it bein' so small and up in the attic. It ain't got more than a bed and a chair. No fancy bureaus or curtains like the others. But it's quiet, bein' as it's the only room up there."

With each sentence, the room became more attractive. While Phil wanted a respectable address for his stay in Mesquite

27

Springs, he'd prefer to have no one close by. The fewer people who knew what he was doing, the better.

"I wouldn't mind that," he told his prospective landlady.

"You sure? A fine man like you must be used to better than that."

If she only knew where he'd lived! "I assure you that I'll be grateful for a roof over my head."

Though she appeared dubious, the woman nodded. "There's one more thing. The main staircase don't go there. You gotta use the back stairs." She led him along the hall and opened the door to the kitchen. "There they are."

The location would be perfect. Absolutely perfect, but Phil wouldn't admit that to her, not when they had yet to discuss the rent. "I'm sure it will be fine, Mrs. Bayles. I'll be closer to whatever delicious food you're cooking." He took a deep sniff. "That's making my mouth water."

Though she gave a little shrug, as if dismissing the compliment, Phil noticed the flush on her cheeks. "It ain't nothin' but chicken soup."

"My favorite."

"Well, then, Mr. . . ." She stopped, waiting for his response.

"Blakeslee, but I'd be honored if you'd call me Phil."

"All right, Phil. The room is yours. I won't charge you but half my normal rate, bein' as it's so small and all."

The day had just improved. "Thank you, Mrs. Bayles. The truth is, I was a bit worried about how I was going to afford to stay in such a fine establishment. It's not easy to make a living selling sketches."

Her eyes widened with admiration. "You're an artist! I ain't never had an artist staying here before." Her smile broadened. "Wait until Ida Downey hears this. A newspaperman and an artist all in one day."

The glow that had surrounded Phil faded. "A newspaperman?"

"Yes, indeed. A nice man. I reckon he's a few years younger than you. He's the one what took my last room. Said he's looking for . . ."

Though she continued to speak, Phil paid no attention to his landlady's stories as he considered the implications of her revelation. There wasn't supposed to be a newspaper here. Mr. K would not be happy, particularly if this man was like that son of Satan, Robert Monroe.

If he didn't hurry, he'd be late for supper,

and that would not please his landlady. When he'd rented the room this morning, Mrs. Bayles had told Brandon supper was served promptly at six, emphasizing "promptly." He had two minutes to get cleaned up enough that he would not offend the other boarders. With only seconds to spare, he entered the dining room.

"There you are, Mr. Holloway." His landlady greeted him with a smile. "Even iffen you're only here for a couple days, you'll wanna meet the others, seein' as how you're gonna be livin' in town."

She introduced him to four men whom he guessed to be around Pa's age. Three had lost their wives and hadn't wanted to live alone; the fourth had not married. "Never found a gal that suited me," he claimed. Though that might be true, the sorrow Brandon saw reflected in his eyes told him the man regretted his single state. Would he look the same way when he was the man's age? Brandon hoped not.

His musing was cut short by the introduction of the final boarder. "And this here is Mr. Phil Blakeslee. He's an artist." Mrs. Bayles seemed as proud as if she had Michelangelo himself under her roof. "I put you two young fellas together." She pointed to two chairs at the far end of the table. "I figger you got a lot to talk about."

Brandon gave his dinner companion an appraising look. Phil Blakeslee was perhaps an inch shorter than his own five foot eleven, with brown hair and vivid green eyes. While the eyes would catch most people's attention, Blakeslee's stature was the focus of Brandon's gaze. The man was extremely thin, making Brandon believe he had been deprived of nourishment as a child.

"I heard you're planning to start a newspaper here." Blakeslee's diction was good, telling Brandon he'd had the benefit of more education than many, with a faint accent that hinted he was from the East.

Neither of those surprised Brandon. What did surprise him was the hostility he saw in Blakeslee's eyes. It vanished so quickly that Brandon might have imagined it, but he knew he had not.

"I am."

"What are you going to write about?" It wasn't his imagination. Though the question seemed innocent, Blakeslee's tone was almost accusatory.

"The usual: local, state, and national news."

"Ain't a lot of things happening in Mesquite Springs," one of the older men announced. "Too bad you missed the election and the horse sale earlier this year. Them were the most excitement we ever saw."

Brandon made a mental note to learn what had happened. "Most towns have more things to report than you might think." That had been the case in Xavier. "I'll also offer personal printing — cards, stationery, posters for businesses."

"And you'll make your opinions known." Once again there was a tinge of hostility in Blakeslee's voice.

"My plan is to report the news and let my readers form their own opinions." That was the best way — the only way — to keep what had occurred in Xavier from happening here.

Dorothy's eyes widened in surprise at the sight of the woman entering Polly's Place. "Is something wrong?"

"That's no way to greet your mother." Though Ma's voice held the same note it always did when she was chiding her, Dorothy thought she saw a hint of sorrow in her mother's eyes that hadn't been there on Sunday.

"Sorry, Ma." And Dorothy was. The last thing she wanted was to cause her mother any more pain. She knew that her move into town, which left Ma alone at the ranch, had been difficult for her. Fortunately, though this was typically their busiest time, today they were experiencing a lull and had an open table. That meant Dorothy could spend a few minutes with Ma. She wouldn't probe — Ma would see through any questions — but if she let her mother talk long enough, she hoped she'd be able to determine why Ma had come into town.

"I didn't expect to see you today," Dorothy said as she led her mother to the table.

"You know Caleb does everything on the ranch." Ma set her reticule on the floor before sliding onto the chair. When Dorothy was seated where she could watch the door, Ma spoke. "I thought I'd treat myself to someone else's cooking and see what new things Ida has in the store."

It all sounded plausible. Ma was far from the world's best cook, and Ida Downey was her closest friend. Still, Dorothy couldn't dismiss the feeling that something was amiss.

"Are you sure you're all right?" She scrutinized her mother's face, looking for signs of an impending spell, but found nothing other than the faint shadows in her eyes.

"Of course." The acerbic tone was vintage Ma. "Besides, mothers are the ones who're supposed to worry, not daughters."

Perhaps that was true in the normal course of events, but their lives had not been normal, and as a result, Dorothy had spent ten years worrying about her mother. She wouldn't mention that. Instead, she forced herself to relax as she said, "We have chicken and dumplings and pot roast today. Which would you prefer?"

"The chicken." Ma glanced in the direction of the kitchen door as she said, "I want to see if Laura's dumplings are as light as Ida claims. I can't believe anyone can surpass Evelyn's."

"Spoken like a proud mother by marriage."

"I won't deny that I'm partial to Evelyn's cooking, but what do you think? You've eaten them both."

Though Ma might not like her answer, Dorothy wouldn't lie. "When she's not preoccupied, Laura's are as good as Evelyn's. I can't vouch for them today, though."

As she'd expected, Ma perked up. "Is something bothering Laura? She doesn't want to move back East, does she? Leonard and Ida would have a conniption if she did."

"It's not that. Laura's convinced she's met the man she's going to marry."

The way Ma tipped her head to one side

reminded Dorothy of a bird listening for the sound of worms beneath the grass. "That sounds like Laura. I remember when she chased after Caleb, and when he wasn't interested, she turned her attention to your brother. Who's her latest heartthrob?"

"His name's Brandon Holloway, and he's here to start a newspaper." Dorothy hoped Ma didn't notice the slight trembling in her voice. It was the paper — only the paper — that made her excited.

Laura had declared that Brandon Holloway's arrival was the best thing that had ever happened in Mesquite Springs, and Dorothy agreed. He'd opened new and tantalizing possibilities for her. If everything went the way she hoped it would, he would be an answer to prayer.

As the front doorbell tinkled and a man entered the restaurant, Dorothy's heartbeat accelerated. "There he is."

Polly's Place smelled even better than it had yesterday. Unless his nose was mistaken, they were serving pot roast and something with chicken in it today. Brandon's mouth watered at the prospect of either one. Even better was the knowledge that he would not be sharing a table with Phil Blakeslee. Though the man had appeared friendly at

35

breakfast this morning, encouraging every-one to call him by his first name, Brandon had been unable to shake the conviction that Phil Blakeslee did not trust him, and that bothered him. Why would a complete stranger take an immediate dislike to him?

Brandon's gloomy thoughts began to dis-sipate when he saw Dorothy sitting at a table with a woman whose resemblance left no doubt she was her mother.

"Welcome back," she said when she reached his side. "A table for one?"

At the same time that he nodded, the woman called out, "Bring him over here, Dorothy. I'd like the company." Her voice was a bit higher than Dorothy's, its light ac-cent telling him that she was one of the many Hill Country residents who'd emmi-grated from Germany.

The request seemed to have embarrassed Dorothy, making her smile appear forced. "Would you like to sit with my mother? You don't have to, of course."

"It's fine with me. Eating alone is no fun." And he'd noticed that the other tables were full, giving him no opportunity to meet more of Mesquite Springs's residents.

When they reached the table, Dorothy performed the introductions.

"Do you and Dorothy live here in town?"

Brandon asked her mother when he'd placed his order for chicken and dumplings.

Mrs. Clark shook her head. "No." She shrugged and continued, "Well, Dorothy does. She stays in the apartment upstairs, but I live on our ranch about fifteen minutes east of here."

She'd said "I" not "we," leading Brandon to suspect that she was a widow and probably lonely now that her daughter was no longer living with her. No wonder she'd sought his company.

"Do you raise cattle?" The more he could learn about Mesquite Springs and its residents, the easier his job would be.

"Horses, but I'd rather talk about you." Mrs. Clark gave him a surprisingly coy smile, almost as if she were flirting. "A widow woman's life isn't very interesting, but a newspaper — that definitely qualifies as interesting. Have you found an office?"

Brandon was still amazed by how much he'd accomplished in a little more than twenty-four hours. "Not only an office, but a home too. I moved into the Taylor place this morning." It might not be perfect, but it was as close to perfection as he could have hoped for.

"I've never seen the inside," Mrs. Clark

said, "but I heard it had fallen into disrepair."

"Not too bad. Some mice took up residence in the kitchen, but I evicted them. I should have the press and my office set up before nightfall."

He'd decided that the former residents' parlor would become the office, while the dining room would house the press and all the printing materials. Both of those rooms faced the street, making them well suited for a business. The kitchen and bedroom that occupied the back half of the house would give him a place to eat and sleep. That was all he needed right now.

"Then you're ready to write the first issue." Mrs. Clark's voice trailed off at the sound of approaching footsteps.

"It's good to see you again, Mr. Holloway." Brandon recognized the voice even before the woman who'd introduced herself as Laura Downey yesterday reached the table to lay the plates in front of him and Dorothy's mother. "I hope you and Mrs. Clark enjoy your meals. I've gotten a lot of compliments on the dumplings."

"I'm sure they'll be delicious, Miss Downey."

As she had yesterday, the woman whose coloring seemed a pale version of Dorothy's gave him a warm smile. "Laura. Please call me Laura."

Mrs. Clark seemed not to notice that Laura hadn't addressed her directly, or, if she had, she was amused by it, for she appeared to be trying to stifle laughter. "I didn't realize you served customers, Laura. I'm surprised you have the time." Mrs. Clark turned her gaze to Brandon as she explained, "Laura does most of the cooking, which is good for Mesquite Springs's residents. My daughter has many talents, but cooking is not one of them. Laura, however, is an accomplished chef."

Laura shrugged. "That might be an exaggeration," she said, "but I do enjoy cooking." She flashed another smile at Brandon. "I'll leave you to your meals now."

Though Brandon was certain it must have been accidental that Laura's hand brushed his as she turned away, Mrs. Clark's pursed lips said otherwise.

"It seems you've got yourself an admirer," the older woman said when Laura had returned to the kitchen.

But Brandon didn't want an admirer. He was far from ready to think about love and marriage.

CHAPTER THREE

Xavier. Phil frowned at the name of the town Holloway had reluctantly admitted was his last home. The way the man had bristled when Phil had asked had told him there was a story there, one the newspaperman didn't want to share, and that had made Phil all the more determined to discover what there was in Brandon Holloway's past that made him so secretive.

The problem was, Phil had never heard of Xavier. It was probably one of those towns in the eastern part of the state that he'd ignored, because Mr. K had said he was looking for a place farther west. Phil knew nothing about Xavier, Texas, but odds were good that Brother Josiah had been there. The man whose preaching had mesmerized audiences throughout the Lone Star State had been to almost every corner of Texas.

If anyone knew what had happened to Holloway in Xavier, it would be Brother

Josiah. That was why Phil was on his way to send him a letter.

"C'mon, Dusty. You can go a bit faster." It was a two-hour ride to Grassey, the closest town with a telegraph office. Ever cautious, Mr. K had warned him about sending mail from Mesquite Springs. "Go somewhere where no one knows you," he'd said. "You only need to check for mail once a week."

That made sense. Everything Mr. K did made sense. Even if he'd had doubts, Phil would have done whatever he said, knowing he owed complete loyalty and more to the man who'd been the closest thing to a father that Phil had had in decades.

"Where do you suppose Brother Josiah is?" It was probably silly, talking to a horse, but Dusty never seemed to mind, and it helped Phil sort through his thoughts. Right now, those thoughts were focused on the charismatic preacher he'd met in a small town east of El Paso. Phil had already dismissed the town as not meeting Mr. K's requirements, but since he'd had nothing else to do, he'd followed the crowd to the big white tent where Brother Josiah was holding a revival meeting.

It was a night Phil would never forget. He'd watched in awe and admiration as the man in the white robe held his audience

41

spellbound. No parson Phil had ever met had preached like that. After the service ended, he stayed to congratulate Brother Josiah and was shocked when the man invited him to join him for a drink.

"I thought I recognized a kindred spirit," Brother Josiah said when Phil explained that he was on a reconnaissance trip for his employer. "Both of us are looking for fruitful opportunities." He winked as he pronounced the word *fruitful,* then darted a glance at the baskets filled with tonight's offering. "If you hear of a town that might benefit from some good old-fashioned preaching, let me know. I'll make it worth your while. And if I can help you, here's how to reach me."

Though Brother Josiah had no permanent home, he explained that letters sent to San Antonio would be forwarded to him wherever he was. "I've got a good feeling about this," he said.

Phil had agreed. He and Brother Josiah were what Esther used to call peas in a pod. They both knew the value of money — lots of it — and of never underestimating the opposition. Brother Josiah was the right man to help Phil uncover Holloway's secrets, and when he did . . .

Phil chuckled at the prospect.

She was being as silly as Laura. Dorothy frowned as she placed the hat on her head for what felt like the hundredth time, tilting it ever so slightly to the left. It wasn't as if she were about to meet the president. All she was doing was going for a walk. There was no reason to fuss so much over her appearance.

Today was the fourth day since Brandon Holloway had come to Mesquite Springs, and it seemed that both he and Laura had fallen into a routine. Each day Brandon came to Polly's Place for his midday meal. Each day Laura kept peeking out the kitchen door, almost as if she didn't trust Dorothy to tell her when he arrived. And when he did, she insisted on taking Brandon's meal to him, returning to the kitchen with the same report: there was no question about it; he was the man she was meant to marry.

Finally satisfied with the angle of the hat, Dorothy secured it with two of her prettiest hatpins, then descended the stairs. Once a quick look confirmed that nothing in the kitchen needed her attention, she opened the back door and stepped out into the alley. There was still another hour before the sun would set, enough time for what she intended.

A sigh escaped her lips as she realized that she wasn't as silly as Laura; she was sillier. She would never marry, but no matter how much she tried, she couldn't stop thinking about Brandon. Not as a husband, of course, but as a man who intrigued her. He might be handsome; he might be charming, but that didn't matter. What mattered was that he was doing what she longed to do — changing the world with his words.

Laura viewed Brandon as a potential spouse; Dorothy saw him as a potential . . . She paused, not certain how to complete the sentence. "Employer" didn't sound right. She knew that most small newspapers were one-man shows, with the emphasis on "man." Women rarely played a role in the writing or printing process. That had been the reason she hadn't put her name on the article she'd written about Mesquite Springs and Wyatt's horse sale last spring. Since it had accompanied Wyatt's advertisement of the sale, the editors who'd printed it had undoubtedly assumed that Wyatt had been the author.

It was possible Brandon was like them, believing that women should confine themselves to the kitchen and the nursery, but though she hardly knew him, Dorothy did not believe that was the case. She sensed depths to him that she had not seen in other men. There was the courtesy he extended to everyone from the small child who'd bumped his table and spilled Brandon's coffee to the dowager who'd announced to the world that newspapers were a tool of the devil.

Other men were courteous. What gave Dorothy pause was the deep sadness she'd seen in his eyes. On the surface, he seemed cheerful, but something or someone had hurt Brandon Holloway. Laura hadn't mentioned it, nor had Ma, but Dorothy was certain she was not mistaken.

She crossed the narrow alley and checked the latch on the shed where Evelyn stored her extra supplies. Dorothy had suggested installing a lock to protect the contents, but Evelyn had insisted there was no need. She trusted Mesquite Springs's residents. So did Ma, though she'd insisted Dorothy keep the doors to Polly's Place and her apartment locked when she was there alone and had been adamant that Dorothy have a loaded rifle in the apartment. "You can never be too careful," Ma had declared.

Dorothy rolled her eyes as she emerged

from the alley. Ma was full of pronounce-
ments. When she'd returned to Polly's Place
after spending the afternoon with Ida
Downey, Ma had raved about Brandon, saying she understood why Laura was infatuated with him. And then she'd shocked Dorothy.

"Brandon's a good man, Dorothy. He'd
make you a fine husband," she had said as
calmly as if she were discussing the hair rib-
bons Ida had on display.

It was ridiculous. Dorothy wasn't looking
for a husband, and even if she were, she
wouldn't consider the man her dearest
friend wanted to marry. So, why was she
walking toward Spring Street, fully intending to turn left when she reached it rather
than heading toward the spring?

Curiosity, that's all it was. After all, she
had never seen a newspaper office. And
maybe, just maybe, there was a place for
her there.

Brandon grinned as he stepped onto the
front porch. All he'd wanted was a breath of
air. He hadn't expected to see *her,* but the
sight of her made him grin. There was no
mistaking her walk. While other women
minced, she moved with determination. It
was still a feminine gait, but more . . . He

paused for a second, searching for the correct word. Intriguing. That was it. Her gait was more intriguing than most women's.

His grin widened. Intriguing was a good adjective to describe not simply Dorothy Clark's walk but everything about her. Unlike her friend Laura, who fluttered her eyelashes and seemed to believe that scintillating conversation centered on the number of meals she had cooked, Dorothy challenged him.

She'd overheard Brandon telling a rancher that he didn't believe editors should voice their opinions in a paper, and she'd disagreed, claiming it was one of the responsibilities a man assumed when he started a paper. She'd looked directly at him and declared that while people might not listen to Brandon Holloway, the man, they would consider carefully what Brandon Holloway, the editor, had written. She was wrong, of course, but her arguments had been clear, concise, and compelling.

Dorothy appeared to relish challenging people. Look at the way she'd convinced him to try a piece of raisin pie, even though Brandon had told her he didn't like raisins. She'd insisted that Evelyn's recipe would make him change his mind, and she'd been right. It was delicious.

Brandon's pulse accelerated at the sight of her walking by his home, and he wondered whether it was coincidence or whether she'd come to challenge him about something. There was only one way to know. He stepped off the porch and approached her.

"Mind if I join you?" He considered inviting Dorothy inside to see the office, but it was such a beautiful late afternoon that the idea of strolling with her seemed more attractive.

When she nodded, he crooked his arm and waited until she placed her hand on it before he asked, "Did you come to place an ad in the *Record?*"

The way she lifted one eyebrow made him realize that his question was more than a little abrupt. When would he learn to hold his tongue? But her response indicated she'd taken no offense. "Is that what you decided to name it?"

"That sounds as if you disapprove." Brandon told himself he shouldn't care. After all, it was his newspaper, not hers. But the sinking feeling deep inside him gave lie to his brave words. He did care.

As she shook her head, he thought he saw a look of chagrin cross her face. "It's not my place to approve or disapprove, but . . ."

"You can be honest with me," he said

when she did not finish her sentence. "My feelings aren't that fragile." Or at least they hadn't been when others voiced their opinions. Somehow, Dorothy Clark's approval mattered.

"It's simply that . . . well . . ."

Brandon could hardly believe this was the same Dorothy who was so assured at the restaurant. He'd never seen her dither there.

"Don't keep me in suspense," he said as they proceeded east on Spring. "I value your opinion."

The way she appeared both surprised and pleased by his statement made him wonder if she was unaccustomed to having others listen to her. Surely not.

"Well, then." Dorothy paused for a second, as if still unsure, before speaking quickly. "It's only my opinion, but 'record' sounds stodgy to me. You're not stodgy, so why should your paper be?"

The spark of satisfaction that speared through him shocked Brandon with its intensity. He'd expected her to challenge him, and she had proven him right. But more satisfying than that was the rush of pleasure from the realization that she did not consider him stodgy.

"You may be right," he told her. "My last paper was called the *Record* and, while I wouldn't call it stodgy, a complete change is probably a good idea." Particularly after the way that venture had ended. "What would you suggest?"

"What about the *Chronicle?*"

He was silent for a moment while he considered Dorothy's recommendation. "The Mesquite Springs *Chronicle.* I like it." The name had a nice ring to it and, just as importantly, it carried no reminders of Xavier. "The *Chronicle* it is." Brandon gave her a quick smile. "Now that you've christened it, will you buy an ad, or better yet, agree to place an ad in each issue? I offer a reduced price for that."

As they passed the boardinghouse, he saw two men sitting on the front porch, smoking cheroots and seeming to enjoy each other's company, though they weren't engaged in a conversation. One was the single older man, the other Phil Blakeslee. They both waved, then returned to their silent companionship.

"I can't commit long term," Dorothy said in response to Brandon's question about putting ads in the newly named *Chronicle.* "Evelyn will have to make that decision when she returns, but I'll certainly place an ad in each issue until then."

"I'm not sure I understand." Brandon

suspected that his confusion was reflected in both his expression and his voice. "Evelyn's your brother's wife. Right?"

Dorothy nodded. "She's also the owner of Polly's Place."

"Oh. Now you have surprised me. I thought you were the proprietor." She'd certainly acted as if she were in charge of the restaurant.

"I'm just filling in until Evelyn and Wyatt return from their honeymoon."

Brandon wasn't certain whether he heard relief or uncertainty. He hoped he wasn't prying, but curiosity compelled him to speak. "What will you do then?"

"I'm not sure." And this time there was no doubt. Dorothy Clark was unhappy about that.

"Who's the gal with the newspaperman?"

Esther would have scolded him for saying "gal," telling him no educated man would use that word, but if there was one thing Phil had learned in the years since his sister's death, it was the importance of fitting in. John, the single man who rarely spoke at meals, would be far more likely to respond if Phil asked about a gal rather than calling her a lady.

"That there's Dorothy Clark."

"Any kin to the mayor?" As far as Phil knew, there was only one family named Clark in the area. When he'd been here on his reconnaissance trip, he'd learned that Wyatt Clark had turned over much of the daily running of his horse farm to the blacksmith's son and was now the town's mayor.

"Sister." John would never use two words when one would suffice.

"What do you suppose she's doin' in town?" More importantly, what was she doing with Holloway?

"Runs the restaurant now that Evelyn's away." John was becoming downright talkative, offering an almost complete sentence.

"Polly's Place?"

"Yep."

They were back to one-word responses, but Phil didn't care. He had the information he needed. Tomorrow he'd visit Polly's Place and make the acquaintance of Miss Dorothy Clark.

Though he'd given her an opening, Dorothy realized it was too early, not to mention totally unseemly, to suggest that she might write for the *Chronicle*. She had already been more forward than most women when she'd advised Brandon to reconsider the paper's name. Fortunately, he hadn't seemed to mind. In fact, he'd seemed pleased, but she wouldn't presume on his good nature again today.

What she needed to do was make him forget that she had aroused his curiosity. Since a man who made his living ferreting out stories wouldn't be satisfied with a superficial answer, her best recourse was to change the subject.

"Have you decided on your subscription and ad rates?" Dorothy hoped that her little laugh didn't sound as forced as it felt. "I should have asked about them before I so rashly committed some of Evelyn's profits."

"Ads will be a dollar for the first one, then fifty cents each time they're repeated."

Brandon didn't seem to mind that she hadn't continued the discussion, and that helped Dorothy relax. She did some quick mental arithmetic. "So, a year's worth of ads would be $26.50." That sounded a bit high to her, but her only experience with paying for space in newspapers had been the notice Wyatt had placed to alert readers to his first home horse sale.

Though she hadn't meant to sound critical, Brandon appeared to be considering his prices. "If someone's willing to commit to a whole year, I'd only charge $20. What do you think?"

What she thought was that it was wonderful that he cared about her opinion. What she said was, "That sounds reasonable, especially if you bill them quarterly." Even the Downeys, the richest people in Mesquite Springs, might be unwilling to pay $20 in one installment.

"What about the price for subscriptions?" she asked. This was a discussion Dorothy suspected few would find interesting, and yet it made her heart beat faster. It felt good to be talking to Brandon. It felt even better that he was treating her as if her views mattered, as if she were helping him make decisions.

"The going rate seems to be five dollars a year, so that's what I was planning to charge. Individual issues would be fifteen cents." He turned toward her, his eyes seeming to darken as he gazed at her. "Does that sound reasonable?"

"It does. And the yearly rate is a good incentive for people to subscribe rather than pay for individual issues."

They'd turned north on Mesquite and had reached the corner of Main. As he raised an eyebrow, silently asking whether she wanted to turn left toward Polly's Place or continue north, Dorothy pointed forward. This conversation was too enjoyable to cut it short.

"I was planning to offer the first issue free," Brandon said as they crossed the town's main street.

"That's an excellent idea." Evelyn hadn't offered anything free the day she'd opened Polly's Place, but a newspaper was different from a restaurant. Mesquite Springs had never had a paper, and until residents discovered how valuable one was, they would be unwilling to subscribe.

"I want it to be ready on the twenty-fifth." Dorothy visualized the calendar Evelyn had hung in the kitchen. "A Tuesday? How did you choose that day?" She was certain it hadn't been a random decision and wanted to understand how Brandon's mind worked.

"In my experience, it's the least eventful day of the week. Folks are done discussing the parson's sermon, and it's too early to get excited about anything that might be going on the next Saturday. My hope is that the paper will give folks something to talk about." He paused for her reaction. When she nodded, he continued. "I expect the local happenings column to be a major part, at least initially."

Dorothy wasn't surprised. "I've seen them

in other towns' papers, and I understand their appeal. Everyone likes to see their name in print."

"Most everyone." Brandon wrinkled his nose. "The Wanted section is also popular, but for the opposite reason."

They walked silently for a minute, and while Dorothy might have found silence awkward under other circumstances, this time it was comfortable. It also let her focus on the thoughts whirling through her mind.

"Have you thought about a name for the local news column?"

Brandon shook his head. "I didn't give it a title in Xavier."

So that was where he'd lived. Dorothy hadn't heard of it, but there were many towns in Texas whose names she didn't recognize.

"Since you asked, I'm guessing you have a suggestion."

She hadn't had anything in mind, but Brandon's statement sparked a thought. "What about 'sociable'?"

He slowed his pace, and furrows formed between his eyebrows. "Wouldn't 'social' be simpler?"

"I was thinking about the noun, not the adjective. An informal gathering. Characters in the books Laura sent me from Charleston were always going to sociables. That's where they learned what their friends were doing. Isn't that the column's purpose?"

When Brandon remained silent for a moment, Dorothy was certain he disapproved. She shouldn't have been so presumptuous, but he had asked. To Dorothy's relief, he nodded. "That could work, but let's call it 'The Sociable' so there's no confusion. Now, do you have any other ideas?"

She did. "What if we got people actively involved in the first issue?" Oh, why couldn't she curb her tongue? She should never have said "we." Even though he'd said "let's call it" rather than "I'll call it," the *Chronicle* was Brandon's paper, not hers.

"What did you have in mind?" To Dorothy's relief, either he hadn't noticed her use of the plural pronoun, or it didn't bother him.

"When you told me the date of the first issue, I realized it would be exactly a month before Christmas, and that made me wonder whether you'd have a Christmas theme for it." This time she was careful to say "you."

"You could ask the old-timers to tell you about early Christmases here. You know how folks like to talk about the olden days. You could write their stories. That way they'd be part of the paper." Dorothy stopped abruptly, conscious that she hadn't given Brandon a chance to express his opinion. Once again, she was being presumptuous.

Brandon didn't seem to mind. Instead, he laid his other hand on top of hers and gave it a little squeeze as he turned to smile at her. "That's a great idea. I wish I'd thought of it myself." A second later, he released her hand. "The only problem is, it'll take a lot of time. I'm not sure I can do it alone." He paused, slowing their pace again so that he could watch her. "Would you help? You wouldn't have to actually write the stories, but if you'd talk to some of the old-timers, as you call them, and take notes, I think we could make this an issue no one will forget."

Dorothy's heart skipped a beat at the realization that he'd included her in his plans. He'd said "we." Was there ever a more beautiful word in the English language? Even better was the fact that unbeknownst to Brandon, he was offering her a chance to make one of her dreams come true.

"Will you help me?"

Dorothy's pulse raced, and her heart beat so rapidly that she feared it might burst through her chest. This was what she wanted. This was what she'd dreamt of for so long. This was the culmination of the hope that had lodged in her when Brandon had said he was a newspaperman.

It wouldn't be difficult to get people to reminisce, especially since many of them came to Polly's Place and sought reasons to linger over their coffee. Dorothy would listen to their stories, but she could do more than that. She could write the articles. They wouldn't have the same impact as Harriet Beecher Stowe's book, but . . .

Unbidden, her sister-in-law's advice reverberated through her brain. "Don't abandon your dreams," Evelyn had said. "Life is too short to waste a single minute. If being a writer is truly important to you, you'll find a way."

"Yes!" Dorothy practically shouted the word. "Of course, I'll help you."

This was her beginning.

CHAPTER FOUR

"Welcome to Polly's Place." Dorothy smiled at the man who'd just entered the restaurant. Though she did not know his name, she recognized him as the younger man who'd been sitting on the boardinghouse porch when she and Brandon had passed it yesterday. He was taller than she'd thought, only an inch or so shorter than Brandon, with unremarkable brown hair. What was remarkable were his vivid green eyes and his almost painful thinness. She'd ensure that this man received larger than normal servings of whatever he ordered.

"Would you like to share a table, Mr. . . ." Dorothy let her voice trail off as she waited for his response.

"I'm Phil Blakeslee, and I'd be honored if you'd call me Phil. I've heard that most folks here call you Dorothy."

"That's true. Are you feeling sociable, Phil, or would you prefer a table by yourself?

I have to warn you that my only table for one is in the least desirable location."

"A single table is fine as long as I have a view of some of the other diners." Phil Blakeslee patted the book that he'd been carrying under one arm. "I like to draw."

Dorothy tried to mask her surprise. She'd told Laura that new people would come to Mesquite Springs, but she hadn't expected both a newspaperman and an artist to arrive the same week.

When she'd shown Phil to his table and recited the day's menu, she fixed her gaze on his sketchbook. "Would you show me some of your drawings?"

"Why, of course, Miss Dorothy. An artist can't make a living unless people see his work, can he?"

He flipped the book open. "What do you think of this?"

She gave a small gasp as she looked at the sketch of Polly's Place. Phil had captured the details of the exterior perfectly — the door half-open, as if inviting customers inside; the bench where people waited for a table on busy days; the window with "Polly's Place" stenciled on it.

None of those surprised Dorothy. What did was the sight of her face looking out the window as if she, like the half-open door, was welcoming patrons. It was uncanny and a bit eerie that a man she'd met only a minute before had, unbeknownst to her, studied her closely enough to capture her image that well.

He'd made a mistake. Something about the sketch had disturbed her, and now she was wary. That wasn't what he'd intended. Phil watched the direction of Dorothy's gaze and how she frowned ever so slightly when it rested on her likeness. That was the problem. She didn't like him drawing her.

"I heard the town is going to have a newspaper," he said, trying to make amends. "You probably want to place an ad in it, and I thought having your pretty face would attract more attention than just words."

She appeared slightly mollified. "I don't know whether Brandon is planning to have illustrations."

Brandon. It appeared he'd been right in thinking that Dorothy and Holloway were more than casual acquaintances.

"I can ask him," she continued, "but even if he agrees, it's not my picture that should be on the ad. It's Evelyn's."

John had said that Dorothy was filling in until her sister-in-law returned. "I doubt she's as pretty as you."

Though Phil had expected the compliment to please Dorothy, it had the opposite effect. "How could you draw me? We've never met."

Oh. That was what bothered her. "My sister used to say God had given me a special talent. She was a better artist than me, but she needed to have the model in front of her. If I see someone — even from a distance — I can usually create a good likeness. I saw you walking last night."

Dorothy's relief was visible. "That is indeed a special talent. Does your sister still paint or sketch?"

There was no reason to lie, especially since he wanted her sympathy. "Esther died when I was still a boy."

As he'd expected, Dorothy's eyes filled with compassion. "I'm so sorry."

Sorry didn't begin to describe Phil's emotion.

Brandon looked up at the sound of the front door opening. He'd had a number of visitors today, people curious about his plans for the *Chronicle* and wanting to see a printing press. A few had mentioned subscribing, and several of the proprietors had inquired about the cost of ads. None of those visitors had surprised him. This one did.

Brandon rose and extended his hand in greeting. "What can I do for you, Blakeslee?"

The man looked around, his eyes appearing to catalog everything in the office. "It's more of a question of what we can do for each other. Your paper could benefit from illustrations, and I could benefit from a little extra money." He patted his stomach. "Dorothy's not giving away those meals she serves." The hostility Brandon had seen at the boardinghouse had been replaced by a conciliatory expression, as if Blakeslee regretted their first meeting.

"It's a good idea." Brandon found himself wishing he could agree to it.

As if he sensed Brandon's vacillation, Blakeslee opened his sketchbook. "No one wants to buy a pig in a poke. Here's what I can do."

Brandon whistled. The drawing was more than good. It was excellent. "How did you get Dorothy to stand still long enough to sketch her?" In Brandon's experience, she was always in motion.

"She didn't have to pose. I saw the two of you walking, and that was enough. You could say she was etched on my brain."

Brandon had no trouble imagining that, because visions of Dorothy flitted through his brain at the oddest times. There was no question about it. Blakeslee was a talented artist, and the *Chronicle* would benefit from him.

"I wish I could hire you, but I'm not set up for woodcuts. Even if you could make them, it'll be a while before I can afford to pay anyone."

Blakeslee nodded, almost as if he'd expected Brandon's response. "Sorry to hear that, but when you're ready, the offer stands."

"Then you're planning to stay." Brandon had had the impression that he was an itinerant artist.

"Sure am. Mesquite Springs has more to offer than anywhere I've lived."

Brandon started to ask where Blakeslee had been before but stopped himself. The man was entitled to his privacy, just as Brandon was.

His first Sunday in Mesquite Springs. Phil tried not to scowl at the thought of what lay ahead — an hour, maybe more if he was unlucky, listening to people praise God, and the preacher drone on about some obscure

Bible verse, most likely one about God's love.

Phil knew all about God's love. It was a myth, just like the myth that ministers were shepherds, taking care of their flock. Pastor Selby had taken care of him and Esther, all right. When he'd read the article that meddling Monroe had put in the paper, Selby had denounced Esther from the pulpit, calling her a whore when she'd sold the only thing she still possessed to buy food for them.

And then, when the shame had been too much for Esther, that sniveling preacher who called himself a man of God had refused to bury her in consecrated ground. "The church forbids it. Your sister was a sinner." As if that sanctimonious man had never sinned!

Phil closed his eyes, willing the painful memories away. It had been two decades since the horrible day when he'd found Esther's lifeless body, two decades during which he'd managed not simply to survive but to thrive. If he did everything right here, by next summer, he'd be a wealthy man. He might even go back East and show that no-count Selby that the boy he'd driven out of the church had no need for him or his false piety. But first Phil had to finish his work here, and that involved going to church.

He would sit through the service that wouldn't be as entertaining as Brother Josiah's. He'd bow his head and pretend to be pious while he mulled over the people he'd met. For the life of him, he couldn't figure out why Dorothy wanted to spend time with Holloway, but the fact that she did meant that she might be useful to Phil. If Brother Josiah didn't know what had happened in Xavier, Dorothy might.

While the preacher was exhorting his flock to do something, Phil would figure out a way to ingratiate himself with Dorothy. Then, when the service was over, he'd shake the minister's hand and tell him it was a fine sermon. All those were part of the role he had to play. Afterwards, when the congregation made its way out of the church, he'd begin his real work by introducing himself to the three men whose land would house Mr. K's new home.

The Bosch, Sattler, and Link ranches had the best access to what the locals called a river, and that's what Mr. K wanted — a lot of land with a view of running water. It was up to Phil to convince the ranchers to sell.

"Welcome to Mesquite Springs." The minister smiled as he shook Phil's hand after the final hymn had ended. "I hope you plan to make this your home. There's no finer town in the Hill Country."

No finer town for Mr. K, but Phil would not say that. Instead, he merely nodded at the man who had — as Phil had predicted — turned a single Bible verse into a half-hour sermon.

"It's the shortest verse in the Bible," Pastor Coleman had announced, "but one of the most important, because it shows that while he was on Earth, Jesus experienced the same emotions we do. Jesus wept."

Phil had tried to ignore the rest of the sermon. According to the Bible, Jesus had wept when he learned of his friend's death, and then later, he'd raised Lazarus from the dead. A nice story and one that others might believe. Phil knew better. Where were Jesus's tears and his life-restoring touch when Esther died? He may have cared about his friend, but he didn't care about Phil or his sister. That story, like the rest of the Bible, was a myth.

What was real was what had been done to Esther. Phil touched the oilskin packet that he kept close to his heart. A stranger might find the contents ghoulish, but to Phil they were precious, the only tangible memories he had of his sister.

"My wife and I would be pleased if you'd join us for dinner today." The minister's words brought Phil back to the present. "We like to welcome newcomers to town, and this week we're blessed to have both you and Mr. Holloway. Will you join us?"

No! Absolutely not! It would be bad enough to have to endure a meal with the preacher, but Phil had no intention of spending any more time than he had to with the town's newspaperman.

Though he was tempted to shout his refusal, he said, "I appreciate the invitation, but I'm afraid that I have other commitments today."

"Another time then." The way Coleman looked at him made Phil suspect the man had seen beneath his excuse.

Another time? Not if he could avoid it.

"We're so grateful you're starting a paper here, aren't we, Jonathan?"

The smile Mrs. Coleman gave her husband reminded Brandon of the ones his parents had shared.

"Mesquite Springs needed one," her husband agreed as he helped himself to another serving of mashed potatoes.

The "simple Sunday dinner" he'd offered Brandon had turned out to be a feast, the table laden with platters of both chicken and ham; bowls of green beans, carrots, and mashed potatoes; plates heaped with fluffy biscuits, pickled beets, and a spicy cabbage salad. It was more food than Brandon had seen since Ma died and left little doubt why the minister was as heavy as he was.

"Right now, the town gets much of its news through the grapevine, and that's hardly reliable." Pastor Coleman frowned, as if remembering a particularly unpleasant instance of inaccurate reporting.

"The idea of asking residents to share their stories is a good one." Mrs. Coleman favored Brandon with a smile.

"I wish I could take credit for that," he admitted, "but it was Dorothy's idea." An even better idea than the name she'd suggested for the paper itself. People had begun to seek Brandon out to tell him how pleased they were that the *Chronicle* would feature more than state or national news. If this continued, his goal of making the paper a unifying force for the town would become reality.

"Dorothy's a fine young woman, and she'll make someone a fine wife," Mrs. Coleman said. "I don't know why she's not married yet. Maybe —"

"Now, Helga, I'm sure Mr. Holloway

70

doesn't need your matchmaking. He'll find the woman God intended for him in his own time."

If, that is, God intended Brandon to marry.

"Let's talk about other things," Pastor Coleman suggested. "What brought you here?"

That was a slightly better subject. "Ironically, perhaps, it was an article in a paper. The picture it painted made Mesquite Springs sound like a place where I'd like to live."

"That wasn't irony or coincidence. It was the hand of God." Pastor Coleman's voice resonated with the same certainty Brandon had heard in today's sermon. "We had a need. You had a need. He brought us together."

Brandon had certainly had a need — a need to escape the shambles he'd made of his life, a need to start anew, a need to prove that he'd learned from his mistakes — but he wouldn't share those needs with the Colemans.

"Mr. Holloway doesn't need a second sermon, Jonathan. Let him enjoy his meal." Mrs. Coleman gestured toward the platter of crisply fried chicken. "Would you like another piece?"

"Yes, I would. It's delicious, but please call me Brandon. Mr. Holloway was my father."

Mrs. Coleman nodded and pushed the bowl of potatoes toward him once he'd taken a drumstick. "You said 'was.' Is your father no longer on this earth?"

If someone else had asked, Brandon might have considered it prying, but this woman's interest seemed maternal, not meddling, and so he did not hesitate to reply.

"No, ma'am. He died two months ago." What he wouldn't say was that the pain was still almost as sharp as it had been that awful night. If only . . . Surely those were the saddest words in the English language. Brandon clamped his lips together, trying to control the guilt that assailed him every time he thought of that night.

"Jesus wept." This time Pastor Coleman spoke softly. "The Bible doesn't say it in these words, but I believe Jesus shares our sorrow. He weeps with us at the same time that he rejoices as another soul joins him in heaven. Helga will tell me this is not the time for a sermon or counselling, and she's right." The minister's lips curved into a wry smile. "When you're married, you'll learn what I have — your wife is almost always right. Remember, Brandon, if you ever want to talk, my door is always open."

"Thank you." But Brandon wasn't ready to tell anyone what he'd done . . . and what he hadn't done.

Only another mile to the ranch. Dorothy blinked in astonishment as she realized that she hadn't referred to the Circle C as home. Though she hadn't expected it, in less than two weeks, the apartment over Polly's Place had become her home. She reveled in the solitude, in the independence, in the knowledge that she could go anywhere she wanted without telling anyone.

It wasn't a matter of asking for permission. Ma wouldn't have stopped her from spending her evenings interviewing people and writing their reminiscences of early Christmases in Mesquite Springs, but Dorothy relished knowing that she didn't have to account for her free time.

Even more than that, she found herself exhilarated as she turned her notes into full sentences. The seemingly simple act of choosing the right word filled her with so much excitement that her heart would pound as if she'd raced up a hill, and when she reached the end of the article, she could hardly stop herself from rising from the chair and dancing a pirouette. Nothing she'd done before had felt so fulfilling.

When she reached the ranch, she slid down from Guinevere and looped the mare's reins over the hitching post. Wyatt might chide her for not turning the horse loose, but Wyatt wasn't here, and Dorothy wanted to see her mother. Ma had seemed distracted when she'd left the church, and while nothing about her distraction reminded Dorothy of the horrible year after Pa had been killed, she couldn't help worrying about her.

As she entered the kitchen, Dorothy stopped in midstride. Ma was wearing her Sunday apron. There was nothing unusual about that. She was stirring gravy. Nothing unusual about that, either. But she was humming as she stirred the gravy, and that was unusual. Ma never hummed.

"The roast smells delicious." Dorothy wouldn't comment on the humming, any more than she would mention the apparent distraction she'd seen in the churchyard.

Ma smiled as she inclined her head toward the pan of potatoes. "If you mash them, we'll be ready to eat." And then she began to hum again.

Glancing into the dining room as she reached for the potato masher, Dorothy blinked in surprise. Instead of the everyday dishes she'd expected, the table was set with what had been her grandmother's china, prized dishes that Ma had brought from Germany.

"Is today a special occasion?"

"No." Ma poured the gravy into the fancy gravy boat they normally used only on Christmas and Easter. "Something Ida said made me realize there was no reason to let the china sit around and collect dust. We ought to enjoy what we have while we can." She bent to pull the roast from the oven, hiding her face from Dorothy's scrutiny. "I'm not getting any younger, you know."

Distraction, humming, the china, now this. Fear assailed Dorothy as she considered the possibility that her mother was ill. "Are you feeling all right?" It might be nothing more than the realization that time was passing, but Dorothy couldn't dismiss the thought that something else was responsible for her mother's unexpected behavior.

"Of course, I am." The annoyance that colored Ma's response reassured Dorothy even more than her words. This was the mother she knew.

"Now, let's get the food on the table." Though it would have been easier to serve themselves here in the kitchen, Ma had always insisted that Sunday dinner be served family style, with everything in bowls and on platters even when there were no guests.

The meal was one of the best Dorothy could remember. Perhaps Ma was right in bringing out her china. Perhaps using pretty dishes made the food taste better. Or perhaps it was Ma's mood. She seemed almost playful today, and that was not an adjective Dorothy would have applied to her mother. If this was the result of something Laura's mother had said, she wanted to know what had caused such a transformation.

"What did Mrs. Downey say that made you think about the fancy china?" Dorothy had waited through most of the meal to ask, but she could wait no longer.

"Ida told me you're asking folks about their first Christmases here."

Dorothy could hardly believe that her plans for the first Sociable column had affected her mother this way. To her relief, Ma didn't seem annoyed that she'd heard the news from her friend rather than directly from Dorothy.

"I am. I was hoping you'd have a story to tell." She'd planned to ask this afternoon, though she hadn't been certain of the reception she'd receive. Ma rarely spoke of her husband, and Dorothy had feared that talking about the early years of their marriage might cause a setback. Those times when Ma retreated into some dark corner of her mind frightened Dorothy, because she never knew how long they'd last, and with Wyatt gone, she would have to deal with Ma's moods alone.

But there was no sign of that today. Ma was silent for a moment, stirring sugar into her coffee and staring at the cup as if it held the answers. Then she smiled. "It's a story I probably should have told you long before this. The first Christmas we were here, I was expecting Wyatt and was sicker than I'd ever been."

She took a sip of coffee, her smile growing rueful as she continued. "It wasn't only in the morning. The sickness lasted through most of the day. I couldn't cook, because the smell of food made me ill. Poor Wilson was at his wits' end."

Though Dorothy assumed that Pa had wondered how long he'd go hungry, since as far as she could recall, he was unable to cook a meal, Ma's next words dispelled that idea.

"He knew that I wanted our first Christmas together to be special. I'd told him how my family celebrated and how I wanted to cook a traditional German Christmas feast for him."

"But you couldn't."

"No, I couldn't, and your father couldn't either. Like most men, he had no idea what to do in a kitchen other than eat."

To Dorothy's relief, the reminder seemed to bring Ma pleasure, not distress. "So, what did you do?"

"It's what *he* did. He talked to every German woman in town, and each one agreed to give him a bit of her Christmas dinner. One gave us part of a goose with apple and sausage stuffing. Another made potato dumplings and red cabbage. Still another made a Christmas stollen for us. It was a true community effort."

Dorothy had no trouble imagining the townspeople helping Pa give Ma the meal she longed for. But, after what Ma had said, she had trouble envisioning her enjoying it. "How did you manage to eat it? I thought you couldn't bear the smell of food."

"I couldn't. That's why your father gave me the perfect Christmas present." Her smile widened as she recalled that long-ago day. "He carved it himself, then painted one side red, the other green. I don't think I'd ever seen him as proud as he was when I opened the package."

"What was it?" Dorothy had no idea.

Ma's smile turned into a chuckle. "A clothespin. Wilson explained that if I put it on my nose, I'd probably be able to eat, and he was right. It was a Christmas I'll never forget."

Dorothy laughed along with her mother and gave a silent prayer of thanksgiving for this day and the memories Ma had shared. "What a beautiful story!" None of the others could compare to this one. "I'm going to call it *The Gift of Love.*"

And what a gift it had been! Pa had given Ma a clothespin and a close-to-perfect Christmas, and in recounting the story, Ma had given Dorothy a new perspective on her parents' marriage. For over a decade, she'd seen only the aftermath of Pa's murder and how it had affected Ma. Now she had a glimpse into the love they'd shared and the happiness that love had brought them. All because of the Sociable.

CHAPTER FIVE

"Are you sure you won't stay for supper, Mr. Blakeslee?"

Phil smiled and shook his head. He'd spent enough time here today, sketching the area next to the river. There'd been more trees than he'd expected, and while the artist in him admired the brilliant fall foliage reflecting in the water, until he heard back from Mr. K, he would not know whether the trees were a problem or an asset.

"Thank you, Mrs. Bosch. I sure do appreciate the offer, but I reckon I better get back to town." He gestured toward the open area around the farmhouse. "This sure is pretty."

The rancher's wife, who was still looking at him as if she were certain a strong wind would knock him over, nodded. "Ed and me like it. I cain't imagine living any place else."

But they would. If everything went as

planned, the Bosches, Sattlers, and Links would all have new homes by next summer.

"I sure do appreciate you lettin' me draw your land. It's a mighty fine place." He turned his sketchbook so she could see the drawing he'd made of the land. When she nodded again, apparently approving the likeness he'd created, Phil pulled a sheet from the book. "This one's for you."

Her eyes lit when she saw the quick sketch he'd made of the modest building she called home. "That's mighty fine, Mr. Blakeslee. Mighty fine. Yer a kind man."

But he wasn't. Phil was a practical man, and soon he'd be a rich one, as long as no one interfered.

As difficult as it was to wait, Phil knew Mr. K was right. There was no reason to ride all the way to Grassey more than once a week. He'd wait until Wednesday to send the sketches, and then — if he was lucky — there'd be a response from Brother Josiah.

Two days. He could wait that long.

Dorothy paused as she approached the door. Should she knock or simply walk inside? She'd never visited a newspaper office before and was uncertain of the proper etiquette. Finally, reasoning that it was a business like Polly's Place or the mercantile,

81

she opened the door and found herself in a hallway that ran the length of the building.

To her right was what appeared to be the office, a room furnished with a large desk, two chairs for visitors, and a bookcase only half filled with books. Though the room to the left was dominated by the printing press, stacks of paper filled one side, while a table covered with shallow boxes and a large bottle of ink stood against the inside wall. All that was missing was the *Chronicle*'s editor. It was late afternoon, the time he'd said he was normally in the office.

"Brandon?"

He emerged from the back of the house, a mug of coffee in his hand. "It's going to be a long night," he explained. "Would you like some?" When Dorothy shook her head, Brandon ushered her into the office and gestured toward a chair. "I'm hoping those papers are your notes."

They were more than notes, but Dorothy wouldn't say that. She planned to leave the pages and let him discover that she'd drafted the articles. As much as she wanted to see his reaction, she couldn't suppress the fear that Brandon might hate them. It would be less embarrassing for both of them if he was alone when he read them.

"I'll have more for you on Friday, but I

thought you might want to get started with these." To her relief, her voice did not reveal how important these articles were to her. She didn't want Brandon — or anyone — to know how many of her dreams were wrapped up in those pages. They weren't life-changing like Mrs. Stowe's book, but they were Dorothy's second attempt to discover whether she was a writer, a real writer.

"I should have a chance to read them tomorrow morning." Brandon laid the papers on the desk. "Would you like to meet George?"

"George?" The question startled Dorothy. Brandon had been in Mesquite Springs for a week, and this was the first time she'd heard him mention George.

He chuckled as if he'd expected her confusion. "That's what I call my press. It's a Washington handpress, so George seemed like an appropriate name."

"It is." Dorothy liked this lighter side of Brandon. He was the only grown man she knew who'd give one of his tools a name. "And, yes, I'd like to meet him." She grinned as she stressed the final word.

Brandon pointed across the hall. "George is in there."

"I was surprised when I peeked at it,"

Dorothy said as they entered the pressroom. "It's smaller than I'd expected."

"He." Brandon winked as he pronounced the word. "George is big enough to do everything I need him to do and small enough that he's relatively easy to transport. That's one of the advantages of this particular model."

The way Brandon ran his hand over the curved top of the frame told Dorothy more clearly than words how much satisfaction he found in producing a paper. Did he know how fortunate he was to be doing something he so obviously loved?

"I've heard some editors set up shop in a tent or even under a tree in the open air."

That sounded like a tall tale to Dorothy. "I suspect those stories exaggerate. I can't imagine someone printing a newspaper in a field."

"Maybe not," Brandon agreed, "but it would be feasible to set type for stationery and print that there. For some editors, personal printing is more lucrative than their newspapers."

"We've never had a printer in Mesquite Springs, so I can't say how much business you'd get, but I certainly wish you'd been here last spring. My brother could have hired you to print posters when he ran for mayor." That would have been easier than handwriting them the way she and Evelyn had.

Dorothy continued to study George. The press was clearly sturdy enough to be used outdoors. Made primarily of iron, its frame reminded her of an upside-down U attached to two surprisingly graceful legs, each shaped like an inverted V. The four feet supported the majority of the press's weight, while a simple metal post held up the two rails that protruded from the press itself.

"How does it . . . er . . . he work?"

"I thought you'd never ask." Brandon gripped the handle of the large metal lever that attached the printing mechanism to the frame. With one easy motion, he raised the heavy square cover, revealing a smooth surface. "This is the platen," he said, pointing to the top portion of the press. "It holds the paper. Once the type is set, I place it on the bottom, and then the hard work of printing each page begins."

"Hard, maybe, but it must be rewarding to see your words in print." Dorothy knew she'd never forget the thrill she'd felt when Wyatt had shown her a paper with her article about his horse sale.

"It is. Now, let me show you the type." Brandon led the way to the table and gestured toward the shallow wooden boxes. "I use different fonts for the advertisements than for the stories themselves, and, as you can see, there are two boxes for each — one for uppercase letters, the other lower."

"Do you like setting type?"

"I do," Brandon admitted. "It sometimes seems like mechanical work, but I like the challenge of balancing the content of each column, hoping that readers will find both the appearance and the content pleasing. It's all part of telling the news."

She picked up two pieces of type, wondering how difficult it would be to arrange them in what he'd told her was called the composing stick. "How did you know you wanted to be a newspaperman?" she asked. "Is that what your father did?"

It must have been her imagination that Brandon flinched at the question, because his voice was even as he said, "Pa was a cobbler. He made the best shoes and boots in the whole county. I suspect he wished I'd follow in his shoes — bad pun — but from the first time I read a newspaper, I knew that was what I wanted to do. I wanted to tell the news and encourage people to think about what they read."

"You wanted to make a difference." Just as Dorothy did.

"That was my dream."

Dorothy shivered slightly as she descended the final step and saw that the back door was open. Had Laura arrived early and neglected to latch it? Dorothy was certain the door had been firmly closed when she'd gone upstairs to repair her hem, but now a cool breeze blew into the kitchen. If the wind had been stronger, she might have believed it could have blown the door open, particularly if she hadn't closed it completely, but the breeze wasn't strong enough to do that. Furthermore, she knew the door had not been ajar when she'd unlocked it for Laura.

"Laura!" she called. There was no answer.

Though it was not Laura's normal routine, Dorothy wondered if her friend had gone into the dining room for something. Ever since Brandon Holloway had arrived in Mesquite Springs, Laura's mind had been focused on him, not on preparing meals for Polly's Place.

The dining room was empty. Dorothy glanced at her watch and shook her head. Of course, Laura wasn't here. There was still half an hour to go before she normally arrived.

Returning to the kitchen, Dorothy strode

to the counter, determined to put the puzzle of the open door behind her. If they were going to have everything ready when the first customers arrived, she needed to start cubing the meat for today's stew. She shouldn't be wondering about open doors and what Brandon thought of the stories she'd given him. He'd said he wouldn't have time to look at what he thought were her notes until this morning, so the earliest she could expect to hear his reaction was when he came for lunch.

What on earth? Dorothy stared at the empty spot on the counter. The slab of beef that she'd carefully coated with the mixture of spices Laura had prepared was gone. The heavy paper remained, but there was no sign of the meat other than a faint stain from the juices. Though she hadn't heard anyone enter, it was clear that someone had come in, taken the meat, then left without closing the door. For the first time, Polly's Place had been robbed.

Dorothy clenched her hands in frustration, stopping only when she realized that her anger at the person who'd taken enough meat to serve several dozen people was accomplishing nothing. She and Laura had customers to feed. Since folks were expecting stew, there was only one thing to do.

Dorothy opened the icebox, pulled out another piece of beef, and began to cut it into cubes. Laura would be disappointed that it wouldn't have the special spices she'd prepared, but at least she'd be able to make a stew.

"Oh, what a wonderful morning!" Laura was practically bouncing on her toes as she entered the kitchen twenty-five minutes later.

"You might not say that when you hear what happened." Dorothy gave her a brief explanation, concluding, "I don't know who would have taken the meat. We haven't had any thefts in Mesquite Springs that I can recall, and I don't know of anyone hungry enough to steal."

Laura appeared as puzzled as Dorothy felt. "Maybe it was someone passing through town."

"If so, how would they know to come to the back door?" As she'd chopped the meat with more force than usual, Dorothy had tried but failed to make sense of what had occurred. "I doubt it'll happen again, but there's only one way to be sure. We'll have to keep the door locked unless one of us is here. As soon as we get everything in the oven, I'm going to tell Fletcher what happened." Fletcher Engel was the town's sheriff and, according to Wyatt, had been the first to encourage her brother to run for mayor.

"All right." As Laura donned her apron and tied the sash, her face took on the dreamy look it had worn so often in the past week. "I wonder what time he'll come."

There was no need to ask who "he" was. Only one man figured in Laura's thoughts and dreams. "I can't predict when, but I can tell you he'll be here. He told Ma he intends to eat here every day we're open."

"That's good. How is your ma?" Laura stopped measuring flour for the piecrusts and looked up.

"She seemed happier than usual when I was at the ranch on Sunday, but I know she's lonely now that both Wyatt and I are gone." That realization and the fear that loneliness might cause another of Ma's spells weighed heavily on Dorothy. Both Wyatt and Ma had told her not to worry, but she couldn't stop being concerned.

"Wyatt and Evelyn will be home soon," Laura reminded her.

"But not on the ranch." The mayor's office was across the street from Polly's Place and boasted larger living quarters than the apartment over the restaurant. When Wyatt had won the election and they'd started discussing marriage, both he and Evelyn had agreed that they needed to live in town so that Evelyn could continue running Polly's Place and so Wyatt would be closer to his constituents. The mayor's house had been the obvious choice.

Laura added salt to the flour and began to stir it. "But you'll move back to the ranch once they're here, won't you?"

That was the big question. "I'm not sure," Dorothy admitted. "Even though I worry about my mother, I like being here. The problem is, I don't know what I'll do when Evelyn returns." Dorothy gestured toward the pie plates. While she'd mixed fillings for Evelyn, she'd never made a piecrust. "She doesn't need two helpers, and you're much better at this than I am."

Laura smiled as if the answer should be apparent. "I won't work here forever. Maybe not even very long. Once I'm married, I plan to stay home."

"And raise your four children." For as long as Dorothy had known her, Laura had dreamt of a husband and four children, claiming that she'd have two boys followed by two girls. Dorothy wondered whether she'd shared that dream with Brandon, then chided herself. They hardly knew each other. Besides, it shouldn't matter. It didn't matter.

"Exactly." Laura reached for the lard. "Where's the nutmeg? I thought you were going to grate some this morning."

"It's right there, in the blue saucer." Dorothy reached across the counter for it, intending to show Laura the perfectly grated spice. That was one culinary technique she'd mastered. But the saucer was empty, the grains scattered on the counter as if someone had bumped the saucer.

"I don't understand." Dorothy looked at the saucer again, befuddled. "This doesn't make sense."

Brandon inhaled, enjoying the rich smell of fallen leaves. While Mesquite Springs lacked Xavier's tall pines, it had cedars and live oaks, as well as a few deciduous trees he couldn't identify. It was better to think about the changing seasons rather than the changes in his life. He'd wakened this morning to find his cheeks moist with the tears he'd shed while he slept, and the pall of sorrow had hung over him ever since. Though he'd intended to read the notes Dorothy had given him, he'd found himself unable to concentrate on anything other than his memories.

Today was the 18th, exactly two months since Pa had died. The grief continued to stab him when he least expected it, and the guilt had not faded. How could it when he began each morning with a solitary breakfast, so different from the ones he'd shared with his father? And, though the busyness of the day kept memories at bay, regret stabbed him each evening as the emptiness of his new home surrounded him. There was no one to talk to, no one to pray with. He was alone, and it was all his fault. If only he hadn't published that editorial.

Needing to clear his thoughts before he ate lunch, Brandon had decided to take the long way around the block. A brisk walk was what he needed. He would concentrate on the *Chronicle,* not on the mistakes he'd made in Xavier and their tragic consequences.

He'd spoken to several of the old-timers Dorothy had predicted would prefer to tell their stories to a man. As expected, some of the reminiscences had rambled and made little sense, but they'd had enough substance that Brandon could turn them into coherent anecdotes.

He'd also approached most of the business owners and had secured their agreement for ads in the inaugural issue. Today, if he had time, he would design his own advertisement, listing subscription rates and telling readers that he was available to do personal printing. It had been Pa's suggestion that he include an ad like that in every issue of the Xavier *Record*.

Pa. No matter how he tried to stop them, Brandon's thoughts returned to him. Oh, how he missed him. He hadn't realized how much he had counted on his father. Pa had helped with the work of putting out a newspaper, but he'd done more than that. He'd given advice whenever Brandon needed it. Had he taken him for granted? Brandon hoped that wasn't the case.

He swallowed deeply, trying to corral his thoughts as he approached the restaurant. He needed to tamp back his sorrow and focus on the future. That's what Pa would have wanted.

"We're not too busy right now," Dorothy said as she greeted Brandon with the smile that never failed to warm his insides. "Would you like a table to yourself?"

He would, particularly today when he feared he might inflict his mood on others, but that wouldn't accomplish his goal. He needed company and ordinary conversation to banish his doldrums. "I'd just as soon meet some new people."

He ought to tell her he hadn't had a chance to look at her notes — that was only common courtesy — but he couldn't find a way to do that without explaining why he was so sad today.

"Certainly."

Fortunately, Dorothy did not appear to expect him to discuss the *Chronicle* here. She was treating him as if he were nothing more than a customer, and that was fine with Brandon. More than fine. It was what he needed.

Dorothy looked around the room, then led him to a table with three men who were still strangers to him.

"Good morning, gentlemen," he said as he pulled out the empty chair. "I hope you don't mind my joining you."

"It's afternoon." The oldest of the trio fairly spat the words at Brandon.

"So it is. Good afternoon, gentlemen."

A man who looked enough like the grumpy one to be his brother shook his head. "Don't pay no mind to Pete. He's in a bad mood today, because Dorothy ain't got any oatmeal pecan pie."

"But I have pilgrim pie," she said, her voice as sweet as the dessert itself. "Some of our customers prefer it."

"How come?" Pete demanded.

95

"They think it has more flavor." She gave him a conspiratorial wink. "I'll admit that I'm partial to it."

Pete was silent for a second, considering what she'd said. "I reckon I could give it a try then."

Brandon bit back the laughter that threatened to erupt. In less than a minute, Dorothy had accomplished what the brisk walk had not. She had amused him with the ease with which she'd swayed Pete. "Make sure you save a piece for me," he told her.

The conversation was stilted at first, but when Laura arrived with Brandon's stew and stayed long enough for him to taste it and compliment her on the flavor, all three men gawked at her.

"I wish I was twenty years younger," Pete's brother announced. "I'd be settin' my cap for her."

"It wouldn't do no good. That gal only has eyes for Brandon here." Pete wagged his finger at Brandon. "You're one lucky fella. You know that, don't you?"

But he wasn't lucky. Not lucky at all.

CHAPTER SIX

Dorothy stared at the counter in disbelief. The ham she'd been slicing only a minute ago was gone. Yesterday had been bad, but today was worse. The thief had become bolder, entering the kitchen when she and Laura were only feet away. Even worse, it was too late to prepare another main course.

Forcing a smile that she was far from feeling onto her face, Dorothy returned to the dining room. Laura would be annoyed by the interruption, but it couldn't be helped.

"I need you back in the kitchen," she said when she reached the table where Laura was flirting with Brandon. She hadn't — and wouldn't — tell Laura that Brandon had said he wanted to talk to her when Polly's Place closed. It had to be about the stories she'd written. Laura knew she was doing that. In fact, her friend had encouraged her, but that didn't mean Laura would appreciate her speaking to Brandon. She'd become touchy where he was concerned, seeing every woman who so much as smiled at him as a rival. None of that mattered now. What mattered was the missing meat.

As Dorothy had expected, Laura's eyes flashed with annoyance, but she nodded. "All right." Turning her attention back to Brandon, she smiled sweetly. "I hope you enjoy the ham, Brandon. The sauce is a special recipe I learned in Charleston."

"I'm certain it will be delicious. Everything you ladies serve is." He was only being polite by including Dorothy in the compliment, but Laura did not see it that way. She glared at Dorothy and refused to leave Brandon's side until Dorothy headed for the kitchen.

"What's so important that you dragged me away from Brandon?" Laura demanded as soon as the kitchen door closed behind them. She stood with her hands on her hips, a scowl on her normally pretty face. "You know how I feel about him."

"And you know how I feel about Polly's Place. You may be the cook, but I'm the one who promised Evelyn I'd keep her customers happy while she was gone." Dorothy's words came out more sharply than she'd intended. It wasn't Laura's fault they had a problem.

Laura flinched. "So, what's wrong? We sell everything we make almost every day."

"That's the problem. Today's ham is gone." Dorothy pointed to the empty platter that was now so clean it looked as if the thief had licked it.

"He came back?" Laura's annoyance had been transformed into concern.

"Apparently. It must have happened while you were talking to Brandon and I was taking the meals to table number six. That's the only time we were both gone. When I came back, the door was open." Though they kept it latched, they didn't lock it during the day, because Dorothy had been certain the thief would not risk entering while they were there.

"Who is he and how did he know the kitchen was empty?"

That was Dorothy's question too. "I don't know. Fletcher didn't find any clues. He said there were no new people in town, and no one had seen anything suspicious." She frowned. "Fletcher thought it might have been a prank, but this doesn't feel like a prank to me. All I know is, this can't continue."

Phil whistled softly as he left Dusty at the livery. He'd gone to Grassey a day early, hoping for a response from Brother Josiah. Unfortunately, there had been none, but other than that, everything was going according to plan. He'd just returned from visiting the third ranch and, while Henry Sattler claimed that his land was everything he and his wife had ever dreamed of owning, Phil was certain he could be persuaded to sell. Offer a man enough money, and he'd do anything. That was human nature.

Since the Sattlers' land was not substantially different from either the Bosches' or the Links', there was no need to send Mr. K the sketches Phil had made. Instead, he'd start to work on the next part of the project: the location for the hotel.

Mr. K had liked his suggestion of the Lockhart place. Not only did it have the only triple lot in town, but it was situated next to the park.

"Some of my guests will be wealthy men and women," Mr. K had explained when he'd described his needs. "They'll expect luxury when they come here to learn about the investments I can offer them." And space was a type of luxury. That made Widow Lockhart's house ideal. Plus, it met another of Mr. K's requirements. He'd told Phil to be sure that whatever location he recommended was one where he could envision himself living. "If you like it," he'd said, "my guests will too."

When he reached the corner of River, Phil turned left and walked briskly to Hill, frowning as he passed the Downeys' home. He shouldn't have come this way. When he'd first visited Mesquite Springs, that building had been the one flaw in an otherwise almost perfect town. It wasn't anything he could share with Mr. K, but the Downey home, which everyone else considered beautiful, reminded Phil of the place he'd lived for the first ten years of his life.

It had been a good home for him and Esther. They'd been happy — some might say indulged, but certainly sheltered from life's unpleasantness — until Father had lost the house and everything else he possessed over a bad hand of cards. When he'd refused to pay, an angry creditor had shot him, turning Phil and Esther from pampered children into homeless orphans.

Phil clenched his teeth as he patted the oilskin packet that accompanied him everywhere. He wouldn't think about that. Those horrible years of cold, hunger, and fear were in the past, and he could not undo them. What was important now was the future.

He turned east on Hill, staying on the south side. If she followed her routine, Mrs.

Lockhart would take her afternoon walk in ten minutes. He intended to be in place, sketching her house when she emerged from it.

The drawing was more than half done when he heard her approach.

"What are you doing, young man?" she demanded, her diction as precise as he'd expected when he'd learned that she had once been a schoolteacher.

Phil looked up, feigning surprise at the sight of the petite gray-haired woman. He doubted she topped five feet, and though her dress had the flounces and furbelows that so many older women seemed to favor, it could not disguise that she was almost as thin as he.

"Oh, ma'am, you startled me. Is that your home?"

"It most certainly is. I repeat, what are you doing?"

Phil gave her the sheepish grin he'd perfected. "Why, ma'am, your house is so beautiful that I simply had to capture it on paper." He turned his sketchbook so that she could see what he'd done.

"Not bad, young man, but don't you know that it's rude to do that without asking permission?"

"No, ma'am, I did not. I apologize for my

rudeness. I assure you it was unintentional."

Her expression softened. "I suppose there's no harm done."

"Might I make amends by giving you the drawing when it's complete?"

She seemed taken aback by the suggestion. "Why would I need a picture when I own the house?"

Because, if I play this right, you won't own it much longer. "I thought you might enjoy looking at it on days when you can't go outside."

She nodded. "You're right. That would be nice. I'll accept your offer."

"Would you mind if I made a second one? I'd like a memento of this charming town when I leave."

Mrs. Lockhart fixed her gaze on him, as if assessing his motives, then nodded. "You may do that, but on one condition."

"What would that be?"

"Escort me back to my home and join me for a cup of tea. I'd like to get to know you better, young man."

"It would be my pleasure." The plan was progressing even better than he'd hoped.

Brandon smiled as he settled onto the bench in front of Polly's Place to wait for Dorothy. She'd told him that she could talk an hour after the restaurant closed and had suggested they meet here. Though he would have preferred the *Chronicle*'s office, he understood her wanting a public place.

Single ladies needed to be careful with their reputations. It was possible someone had noticed and commented on the time she'd spent at the *Chronicle* on Monday. Small towns, as Brandon knew all too well, thrived on gossip, but no one could look askance at an unmarried man and woman talking here.

His smile turned into a grin as he thought about the pages Dorothy had given him. She'd called them notes, but they were not notes. Instead, they were remarkably well-written complete stories. Brandon had chuckled at some and burst out laughing when he reached the end of Mrs. Clark's reminiscence.

Even now, almost a full day later, he was still marveling over them. Something about them seemed familiar, but though he'd racked his brain, he couldn't say what. But, thanks to Dorothy's help, the first issue would be a good one. Brandon could feel that in his bones. Dorothy's style was different from his and would provide a nice contrast to the stories he'd written. If he interspersed them, there was little worry readers would be bored.

"Is everything okay?" he asked when Dorothy joined him. "You seemed a bit harried today."

The light flush that colored her cheeks only served to highlight her eyes. Why hadn't he noticed that they were almost the same shade as the caramel icing on the spice cake she'd served him yesterday?

"We had a problem in the kitchen — nothing too serious, but it was annoying."

"I'm glad." When Dorothy's eyes widened, Brandon realized she might have misconstrued his meaning. "I'm not glad you had a problem," he said, trying to undo the damage, "but I am glad that it wasn't caused by the work you've been doing for the *Chronicle*."

"That's not a problem. I enjoyed collecting the stories."

And that led Brandon to the reason he was here. He wanted to tell her that she'd far exceeded his expectations and, by doing so, not only had she made his life easier, but she was making the *Chronicle* a better paper.

"You did a marvelous job. I wish you'd seen me when I read what you gave me. I think my jaw dropped in surprise."

Dorothy appeared uncomfortable, as if she

were unaccustomed to praise. Surely, she knew how well she wrote.

"There are good surprises and bad ones. This was a very good one." Brandon wanted her to have no doubt about what she'd accomplished. "I expected notes like the ones I take when I'm interviewing someone, but you gave me completed stories."

The flush returned to Dorothy's cheeks, only this time he suspected it was from embarrassment rather than exertion. "I figured you'd edit them, but I thought I might be able to save you some time if I drafted them."

Her words confirmed his suspicions and increased Brandon's determination to ensure that she knew just how talented she was. "You're being too modest. They weren't rough drafts. They were every bit as good as the ones I've written. Maybe better."

Her flush deepened, and he saw disbelief reflected in her eyes, confirming Brandon's suspicion that no one had complimented her on her writing.

"I doubt that."

"Wait and see what the readers say. I think you'll be surprised."

CHAPTER SEVEN

She had set a trap. Dorothy almost laughed at the thought that she was becoming a detective. Maybe she should apply to Pinkerton's, she mused as she sat quietly on the fifth step from the bottom. She'd heard they'd hired a few women. But, while the thought was momentarily intriguing, she knew it wasn't the right direction for her. The only sleuthing she wanted to do was right here in Mesquite Springs.

She had to catch the meat bandit. That was why she'd put a roasted chicken leg on the counter. She'd even left the back door ajar to make it easier for him to smell it. Now she was sitting on the staircase, waiting to see him when he grabbed the chicken.

If Ma had known what she was planning, she would have told Dorothy to have the rifle at her side. Intruders were intruders, she would have said, and they needed to be stopped. Instead, Dorothy was armed with an old umbrella. It wasn't much of a weapon, but she knew she'd never shoot a hungry man. Tripping him and giving him a tongue lashing seemed like a better approach. Wyatt might laugh, and Fletcher would probably chide her for not calling him, but Dorothy was convinced that her planned punishment would be enough to make the thief think twice before stealing more of her meat.

She didn't have to wait long. Though she couldn't see it from here, she heard the door open, followed by a clicking on the floor. How strange. Did he have cleats on his boots? Less than a second later, Dorothy's jaw dropped at the sight of her intruder. The thief was not a man but the mangiest, most pathetic dog she'd ever seen.

Tears welled in her eyes as she stared at the meat thief. He was so thin that the outlines of the poor creature's ribs were visible through his skin. His fur was matted, missing in spots, and so filthy that she could not determine the color, and the expression in those brown eyes melted her heart. In that instant, Dorothy knew she'd give him every bit of food she had.

"Hello, Bandit." She spoke softly, not wanting to frighten the mutt, as she descended the stairs. Though she'd thought he might try to escape, the allure of the food was too great. He cowered next to the counter, his tail between his legs, his eyes beseeching her.

"It's all right. You can have the chicken." Dorothy plucked it from the plate and placed it on the floor in front of the dog, then stepped away, wanting to assure the poor creature that she would not harm him. "It's all right," she repeated and took another step backward.

That was all the invitation the dog needed. He devoured the meat, then looked up at her, begging for more.

"Not yet. You need a bath as much as food." The stench of mud, neglect, and things she didn't want to consider was overwhelming. If she was going to keep this dog — and in her heart she knew she was — he had to be clean.

As if he understood and wasn't happy about the prospect, the dog headed for the door, and as he did, Dorothy chuckled. "I guess I can't call you Bandit, can I, girl? We'll find a better name, but first you're going to have a bath."

As she poured water into her largest kettle and started warming it, she continued to watch the dog. He — no, *she* — was medium-sized, reaching only to Dorothy's knees, and those large brown eyes whose pleading expression had won her heart seemed filled with wisdom.

A moment later, Dorothy discovered just how wise this homeless mutt was. When Dorothy approached the pantry, planning to look for towels and something she could use as a makeshift leash, in a movement so smooth Dorothy knew she had practiced it, the dog rose on her hind legs and pushed the door's lever down with her front paws. The mystery was solved. This clever animal had taught herself to open doors, probably driven by the desperation of extreme hunger.

"Smart girl." The dog was smart. The question was whether Dorothy was as well. Perhaps she should let the animal escape, but she knew that if she did, she would worry about its fate.

When the dog eyed the back door, Dorothy shook her head. "You need to stay here if you want more food." She tied a length of clothesline that Evelyn had left in the pantry around the dog's neck.

To Dorothy's surprise, the dog made no further attempt to flee but followed her docilely into the alley and submitted to her bath. While she didn't appear pleased by the process, something — perhaps fatigue, perhaps hunger, perhaps the realization that Dorothy would help rather than hurt her — kept her from trying to escape. She whimpered occasionally when Dorothy's scrubbing touched a sensitive spot but otherwise remained stoically silent.

"You need a name," Dorothy told the dog as she dried the now-clean fur with an old towel. With the mud gone, she saw that the animal was even thinner than she'd first realized, reminding her of Phil Blakeslee. Dorothy almost laughed as the thought popped into her head. The itinerant artist was unlikely to appreciate being compared to a mongrel.

The dog's fur was finer and longer than Dorothy had expected, and she suspected it would look almost fluffy when fully dry, making those floppy ears appear far larger than they actually were. Though still wet, the dog's coat had a reddish tint to it, reminding her of the spice the intruder had spilled the first day.

Nutmeg. The name was perfect. "That's it. I'll call you Nutmeg." Dorothy patted Nutmeg's head as she asked, "What do you think of that?"

The short bark sounded more like a warning than a response, causing Dorothy to turn toward the entrance to the alley.

"What is that?" Laura stopped a few feet away, her eyes wide with justifiable surprise.

Dorothy rose, keeping her hand on Nutmeg's head. "This is our meat thief. Her name is Nutmeg."

Laura continued to stare, then fisted her hands on her hips in obvious disapproval. "What on earth are you doing? You can't keep a dog."

"I'm not keeping her." Even as she said the words, Dorothy knew they weren't true. From the moment she'd seen Nutmeg, she'd known that she couldn't let her go, and when she'd felt the walnut-sized bumps in her belly, the determination to keep her only strengthened.

Dorothy had always scoffed when Laura spoke about love at first sight. Love was for others, not her. After seeing what love could do, she had resolved never to open herself to that kind of pain. Yet here she was, filled with an emotion that could only be love. It had been love at first sight, a totally irrational reaction. How ironic that her love was for a dog, a dog that, unless she was mistaken, was going to have puppies.

Laura shook her head. "You can deny it all you want, but I know you. You're going to keep that mutt. I see the way you look at her." The expression in Laura's eyes softened ever so little as she darted another glance at Nutmeg, but she kept her hands on her hips. "Be sensible, Dorothy. Where will you keep her? She can't stay in the kitchen, and there's no space in the pantry." Laura paused for a moment, her gaze moving to the shed next to their outhouse. "I suppose she could use that."

But Dorothy had no intention of leaving Nutmeg alone in an unheated shed. "I have plenty of room upstairs. She can have her puppies there."

"Puppies?" Laura's shock was evident in the way her voice rose. "What have you gotten yourself into? I thought you were the sensible one of us."

Dorothy couldn't help chuckling. "Apparently not where Nutmeg's concerned."

As he searched for the right word, Brandon glanced out the front window, his story forgotten when he saw who was walking down the street. The woman was Dorothy — he'd know her anywhere — but what was that with her? A dog? He rose and strode outside.

"I didn't know you had a pet." The dog with what appeared to be an old belt tied around her neck as a combination collar and leash was one of the homeliest animals

Brandon had ever seen. While her coat was clean, the missing patches of fur gave her a look that could have been rakish but was actually pathetic. Still, the way she watched Dorothy, as if she'd give her life to defend the woman at her side, made Brandon suspect there was more to this story than he'd thought.

"I didn't until this morning."

When he joined her and they began to walk slowly down the street, Dorothy recounted a tale of pilfered food and how she'd caught the thief. It was both amusing and amazing. What a resourceful woman she was!

"So, you adopted her."

Dorothy shrugged and gave her new pet a fond glance. "I'm not sure who adopted whom. All I know is that I couldn't leave Nutmeg to fend for herself."

"Of course, you couldn't. You have a kind heart." Brandon shivered. He'd been so caught up in the story that he hadn't realized he'd neglected to put on his coat until a gust of wind chilled him.

"I could never bear the thought of people or animals being abused," Dorothy explained, "but ever since I read *Uncle Tom's Cabin,* I felt as if I ought to do my part against injustice."

114

The chill that swept through him owed nothing to the wind. Brandon couldn't argue with Dorothy — he'd felt the same way when he'd been introduced to Harriet Beecher Stowe's story, because it encapsulated everything he felt about the evils of slavery — but he couldn't forget what had happened when he'd written about Mrs. Stowe's book.

"I didn't realize many people in Texas had read *Uncle Tom,*" he said as mildly as he could. "It's practically been banned." That had been one of the reasons he'd taken the stand he had, a stand that had had tragic consequences.

Dorothy had no way of knowing how painful even the slightest mention of the book was for Brandon. His reaction wasn't rational — he knew that — but he could not control it. With what seemed like an inordinately large effort, he forced himself to listen as she continued her explanation.

"Wyatt heard men talking about it when he took our horses to the big sale. He wanted to see what all the fuss was about, so he ordered a copy. I read it before he did."

When Nutmeg whimpered, Dorothy stopped to reassure her pet. Then she turned to Brandon, those caramel-colored

115

eyes filling with concern when he shivered again. "You're cold. Let's go back."

It was the sensible thing to do. He was cold, and he did not want to discuss the book that had created so much controversy, but Brandon found himself unwilling to be sensible. "I don't want you to cut your walk short on my account."

"And I don't want the town's newspaperman catching a cold on my account. Let's turn around." They'd reached the corner of Spring and Mesquite. "You can get your coat, and then we'll walk the other direction. I haven't been to the spring in a while."

"All right." Perhaps the change of direction would also change the direction of their conversation.

"Have you read *Uncle Tom's Cabin?*" So much for his hope that Dorothy would have forgotten they were discussing it.

"Yes." He wouldn't lie, but neither would he encourage her.

"Did you find it life-changing? I certainly did."

He had indeed found it life-changing, but that was something he wasn't ready to share with her or anyone. Still, he couldn't resist learning how the book had affected Dorothy. "In what way?"

As if she sensed her mistress's heightened

emotions, Nutmeg rubbed against her leg. Dorothy stroked the dog's head before she answered. "It made me want to be a writer so that I could influence people the way Mrs. Stowe did. Not everyone agrees with her, but her story has caused people to think about slavery in a new way."

"Some people." Others would never change their opinions. It was definitely time to change the subject. "It seems to me you're well on your way to accomplishing your goal. The stories you wrote for the *Chronicle* were excellent."

"I'm no Harriet Beecher Stowe." Once again, he heard the self-deprecating note in her voice, a reminder that Dorothy did not recognize her talent.

"No, you're not," he agreed. "You're Dorothy Clark, and that's equally important."

Through her writing Dorothy was helping him establish a new life, giving him hope that he might be able to rekindle some of his dreams.

"Thanks to you, the first issue of the *Chronicle* will be one no one will forget. The Christmas stories were your idea, and you've done half the work." Brandon paused for a second as a thought assailed him. "I ought to be paying you."

Though she'd been walking briskly, Dorothy stopped and turned toward him. "I didn't expect to be paid. I'm simply glad that I could help you get started here." Those brown eyes he found so intriguing were serious as she said, "Mesquite Springs needs a paper. I'd almost go as far as to say that every town needs one."

Nutmeg woofed as if adding her approval, and Dorothy responded by ruffling one of the dog's ears before she continued. "Since you brought George with you, I'm assuming there's no longer a paper in Xavier. That makes me wonder why you left."

Because he had no future there. Because he'd lost everyone and everything that mattered. Because the guilt was too overwhelming to be borne. Brandon wouldn't tell her that, but he owed Dorothy at least a partial explanation.

"After my father died, there was no reason for me to stay in Xavier. I needed a change, and the Hill Country seemed like a good place."

Dorothy's expression radiated more than sympathy. In her eyes, Brandon saw understanding. "It's never easy losing a loved one. My father died over ten years ago, and I still miss him." When Nutmeg, ever sensitive to her mistress's moods, licked her hand, Dorothy smiled at the dog. "I wish

118

I'd had Nutmeg then."

Brandon wished he could smile, but the memory of that night was so vivid that his knees threatened to buckle.

As if she somehow sensed his distress, Dorothy fixed her smile on him, and the warmth of that smile lessened his pain and made Brandon forget the cool wind.

"I'm glad you came," she said softly.

CHAPTER EIGHT

"We could serve sawdust today, and I doubt anyone would notice," Dorothy told Laura as her friend carved slices of roast chicken to place on top of the savory stuffing.

Though her statement was an exaggeration, Dorothy suspected that few diners were concentrating on their meals. Instead, conversation centered on the first issue of the *Chronicle,* which had been published this morning. As she'd told Laura before, it was all anyone could talk about. And that included her and Laura.

It had started when Laura entered the kitchen and found Dorothy seated at the table, reading the paper instead of chopping vegetables. Nutmeg lay curled at her feet, raising her head only enough to bark at Laura. Though it had been less than a week, the dog seemed to have adopted Dorothy as much as she'd adopted her and had become protective of her mistress. She barked at everyone, as if warning them to stay away. Everyone, that is, except Brandon. When he approached, Nutmeg would wag her tail and rush to his side to have her head petted.

She'd done exactly that when Brandon had knocked on the back door soon after six thirty.

"I know it's early," he said, "but I wanted you to be the first to see how our paper turned out."

He'd handed Dorothy a copy, pointing out that the front page contained two stories, one written by each of them. Though she'd looked at the paper, for a second Dorothy saw nothing. Instead, the words "our paper" reverberated in her brain. It wasn't hers, of course, but there was no denying the warmth that flowed through her at the realization that she'd played a part in creating it. Thanks to Brandon, her dream of being a writer was coming true.

He had stayed only a few minutes, telling Dorothy he needed to return to the *Chronicle*'s office, since he'd announced that the paper would be available for pickup beginning at seven, but during those few minutes, she had seen that the sorrow which never completely left his eyes had diminished. Wondering whether she'd find the reason somewhere in the *Chronicle,* though she should have been preparing vegetables for Laura, Dorothy had sat at the table, mesmerized by the stories Brandon had written and the way he'd interspersed hers with his, juxtaposing serious tales with more humorous ones, varying the lengths so that readers who had only a few minutes could still enjoy one of their neighbors' reminiscences.

"Where did you get that?" Laura demanded as she closed and latched the door a little after seven. Though this was earlier than normal for her to begin cooking, the roast chicken she'd planned to serve demanded extra preparation time, and she'd told Dorothy to expect her around seven.

"Brandon brought me a copy."

"Oh." Laura's eyes narrowed. "If he's making deliveries, I wonder why he didn't bring me one. I'm the one he . . ." She let her voice trail off. Though she'd made no secret of her fascination with Brandon and that she believed he was attracted to her and that it was only a matter of time before he asked to court her, something held her back this morning. "Let me see it."

It took only a few seconds for Laura to nod, a self-satisfied smile crossing her face as she said, "Now I understand." She pointed to a story that bore Dorothy's name. "He was thanking you for your help. It wasn't personal."

This morning's visit might not have been personal by Laura's definition, but Dorothy couldn't forget the look she and Brandon had shared as they'd spread the paper on the table and admired the layout of the front page or the way he'd clasped her hand to thank her and how he'd held it longer than simple courtesy demanded.

She wouldn't tell Laura about that any more than she'd tell her how Brandon had referred to it as "our paper." That would only hurt Laura, and Dorothy had no desire to do that. Besides, what she and Brandon had shared was not a romantic moment; it was the camaraderie that came from having worked together and the exhilaration of seeing the product of their efforts. Still, there was no denying that it had been a day to remember, and it was only noon.

Laura's chuckle brought Dorothy back to the present. "I'm not surprised that everyone's talking about the paper." She'd taken brief breaks to read a few of the articles. "The stories are wonderful, especially your mother's." Laura flashed a warm smile at Dorothy, her good humor restored despite her early morning petulance. "You have a way with words."

Words alone weren't enough. Dorothy needed ideas — big ideas — if she was going to change the world like Mrs. Stowe. But for today at least, she'd bask in the knowledge that she'd made a beginning, a good beginning.

"You did a fine job, Mr. Holloway." A woman with the brightest pink bonnet Brandon had ever seen approached his table. As he stood to greet her, she continued. "This is the kind of paper Mesquite Springs needs. You can count on Hyrum and me subscribing."

Her companion, whose hat was a more subdued navy, nodded. "Some of your stories brought tears to my eyes. I can't remember the last time that happened. Me and Jed are gonna subscribe too."

That was what Brandon wanted to hear and one of the reasons he'd come to Polly's Place earlier than usual today. He'd wanted to be available if customers had opinions, and oh, did they have opinions. He'd overheard a heated debate about which story was the funniest, while another foursome had argued over which tale was the saddest.

Laura, who usually waited to greet him until she brought his dessert, had hurried out of the kitchen the instant Dorothy had seated him, and had gushed — that was the only word he could find to describe the flow of compliments she lavished on him — about the paper. The praise had been welcome, and yet it hadn't touched him as much as the simple pleasure he'd seen in Dorothy's eyes this morning when they'd looked at the front page together and she'd admired the layout.

Pink Bonnet and Navy Hat left, and Brandon had no sooner sat down again and cut a piece of chicken than a man he'd yet to meet strode toward him. "I was sure I'd heard all the stories of the old times," he said, brandishing a copy of the *Chronicle,* "but it 'pears I missed a bunch. Matilda and me are gonna keep this here paper. We figger we'll read the stories again on Christmas morning."

One of the men seated at the next table chimed in. "Say, that's a good idea. My missus'll like doin' that."

His meal had been interrupted more times than he could count, leaving his food cold, but Brandon wasn't complaining. Far from it. The town's reaction to this first issue was critical to his ongoing success, and so far, it had been overwhelmingly positive.

When one of the few dissenters had complained that he hadn't been asked for his story, Brandon had countered his complaints by inviting him to stop by the office and suggesting that his tale might be published closer to Christmas. The man had left Polly's Place seemingly satisfied and saying that he planned to subscribe to the *Chronicle.*

"Would you like me to warm that up for you?"

Brandon smiled at the most welcome interruption he'd had since Dorothy had seated him at a table for two, promising to keep the other seat unoccupied. "You'll have visitors," she'd predicted, and she'd been correct. Now she was back at his side, her glance at his plate telling him she'd noted the now-congealed gravy.

"Thanks, but there's no need. This isn't the first time I've eaten cold food, and I venture to say it won't be the last."

"You've been so busy entertaining my customers that I haven't wanted to interrupt," she said, her voice low and conspiratorial, as if they shared a secret. Perhaps they did, the secret of satisfaction at a job well done.

"I imagine everyone's told you how much they enjoyed the *Chronicle,*" she continued. "It's all anyone can talk about."

"I'm pleased," he admitted, "and you

should be too. I couldn't have done it without your help."

Putting this issue together had been different from any of the papers he'd published in Xavier. Though Pa used to assist him with the mechanical aspects of creating a newspaper, helping to set type into galleys, then inking those galleys and feeding the paper through the press, Brandon had done all the writing. He'd never thought about sharing that task until he'd met Dorothy, but now that he had, he knew that not only did it lessen his workload, but it made the paper better.

She gave him one of those self-deprecating smiles that confirmed his belief that she wasn't accustomed to praise. "I was happy to help." A quick glance across her shoulder had her straightening her back. "It looks as if more of your readers want to talk to you."

Brandon listened to them, accepting their compliments but never failing to tell them that Dorothy deserved the praise too. Several nodded. One man did more. "I never knew she could spin a tale like that," he admitted. "She's a fine young lady."

She was indeed.

Phil folded the paper and set it aside, surprised that several of the stories he'd read had made him laugh. He hadn't expected that. In his experience, newspaper articles were either boring recitals of news or editorials like old man Monroe's, designed to ignite readers' anger. The *Chronicle* had neither. Oh, there'd been some state and national news, but Holloway had managed to make that seem interesting. That had been a pleasant surprise. The biggest surprise, though, had been seeing Dorothy Clark's name on so many stories. Phil had had no idea she knew how to write.

He leaned back in the chair, lacing his hands together behind his head as he considered the implications of what he'd learned this morning. Dorothy Clark wasn't simply the mayor's sister and temporary proprietor of the restaurant. She wasn't simply a woman who took an occasional walk with Holloway. It appeared she was working with him. That meant she would be privy to information about the man's plans for the paper. She would know if he was going to do more than report news and whether he would take it upon himself to investigate things like land sales or the investment opportunities Mr. K was going to offer to some of his guests.

The first issue had been a pleasant surprise, but the *Chronicle* was still a newspaper, and Mr. K had been adamant that there be no papers in what he'd referred to as his town. One way or another, Phil had to stop the *Chronicle*. Although he hoped Brother Josiah would have the information he needed and that whatever had happened in Xavier would be enough to get Holloway to leave Mesquite Springs, he was taking no chances.

It was time to get to know Miss Dorothy Clark better.

"That was the most delicious chicken I've ever eaten," Phil said two hours later. Though his stomach had protested the delay, he had waited until right before Polly's Place closed to enter the restaurant. He was certain Dorothy wouldn't turn him away, and if he ate slowly, which he intended to do, he would have the opportunity to talk to her when everyone else had left. That opportunity had arrived.

"I'll give your compliments to Laura. She's the one who roasted the chicken. I'm not much of a cook." Dorothy's smile was a wry one, designed to make a man chuckle.

"I suspect you're being too modest, but even if you aren't, you're something much better than a good cook. You're a great writer." Lavish praise, Phil had learned, was one of the best ways to loosen a person's tongue.

Dorothy flushed slightly, then shook her head. "Hardly that, but I will admit that I enjoyed telling our residents' stories. Perhaps you'd like to contribute something to a future issue."

No one here had any reason to know what his life had been before Mr. K discovered that he could do more than shine shoes and pick pockets. He'd been the one who'd paid for Phil's education, ensuring that he continued to dress, speak, and act like a gentleman. He'd been the one who'd given Phil a job when he'd finished his schooling and who'd trusted him enough to let him select the town for his hotel.

"I'm not sure how long I'll be staying." That much at least was honest. "It all depends on how well my drawings sell."

Phil patted his sketchbook. Mr. K would have everything he needed, thanks to Mrs. Lockhart's insisting Phil share a pot of tea with her. That had given him an opportunity to assess the interior of her house. It might not have the grandeur of the Downeys' mansion, but it could serve as the core of Mr. K's hotel.

"We could use a newcomer's perspective on the town." Dorothy was more persistent than Phil had expected.

"We'll see. As I said, that depends on my drawings." When she seemed sympathetic, he continued. "I need some advice and was hoping you could help me."

"What kind of advice?"

"Several things." Phil made a show of looking around the now almost empty restaurant. "I doubt this is the best time for you. Perhaps you could join me for a stroll later."

Sympathy turned to what looked like suspicion. Then she nodded. "I take Nutmeg for a walk when I finish here. You're welcome to join us."

"Nutmeg?"

"My dog."

So that was the mutt's name. Ever since one had bitten him, Phil had tried to keep his distance from dogs, but it appeared he had no choice today.

"I'm looking forward to that."

An hour later, the three of them were walking west on Main. The mutt had growled at him, but once Dorothy put her hand on its neck, the dog walked quietly on her other side.

"You mentioned wanting my advice. About what?"

Phil feigned chagrin. "My mother always

said it was crass to discuss money." He wrinkled his nose at the memory. Mother had had no need to worry about money. While she was alive, Father had been a respected businessman, earning more than they could spend. It was only after her death that he'd turned to gambling.

"I'd like to stay in Mesquite Springs," he said, "but the truth is, I haven't sold a single drawing." Selling sketches had never been part of the plan. Phil had proposed it to Holloway only to give him an excuse for seeing the interior of the newspaper office, but the more he thought about it, the more he liked the idea of being paid for his talent. Besides, sketching would give him something to do while he waited for Mr. K. The plan was for Phil to remain in Mesquite Springs at least until his employer arrived.

"Do you have any suggestions?"

Dorothy was silent for a moment, looking straight ahead as if she found whatever was on this block of Main Street fascinating. After what seemed like an eternity, she gave a short nod.

"I have two ideas. What if instead of selling your drawings, you were paid for your talent?"

"What do you mean?"

"I know Miss Geist — she's our schoolteacher — wants her pupils to learn more than the three Rs. She's mentioned that she'd like them to have music and art lessons. Would you consider teaching them to draw? I doubt it would pay a lot, but it would be steady money while you looked for other opportunities."

Phil could think of few things more disagreeable than attempting to teach young children anything. "I don't have the patience for that. Teaching requires talents I simply do not possess." Not to mention that if he had a regular job, folks might notice that he left town every Wednesday.

A light breeze rustled the leaves on the live oaks, the soft sound reminding him of the swish of Esther's skirts when she'd dressed for one of their parents' dinner parties. Phil had been too young to attend, but from the time Esther turned eleven, Mother had insisted that she was old enough to greet their guests and had ordered fancy gowns of silk and satin for her.

"Don't they sound nice, Phil?" Esther had asked as she'd twirled in front of the long mirror.

They had, but all too soon, the silks and satins were gone, sold to help pay Father's debts. And then . . .

Phil wrenched his thoughts back to the

present. "You said you had two ideas." Maybe the second would be less distasteful.

"I do. It's a temporary one, though. Christmas is only a month away."

"A fact no one in Mesquite Springs can ignore after reading today's *Chronicle.*"

Dorothy nodded. "Exactly. The *Chronicle* is part of my idea." She stopped and turned toward Phil, as if she wanted to ensure she had his full attention. This time she did.

"I heard people say they were going to keep this issue and reread it on Christmas. What if you approached relatives of the people whose stories were featured and suggested drawing a sketch to accompany the stories? If you framed the two together, it would make a nice Christmas gift."

The idea wasn't just a good one; it was brilliant. Besides giving him the opportunity to earn a bit of money, it would provide another excuse to get to know some of Mesquite Springs's residents. And when he learned what had happened in Xavier, it would give him the perfect opportunity to discredit Holloway.

"I like the idea."

Dorothy's smile widened into a grin. "Here's your first commission. I'd like a drawing of my mother."

"With a clothespin on her nose?" Phil was

certain Dorothy would shake her head, but she did not.

"Exactly. I want three copies — one for Ma, one for my brother, and one for me."

"Are you certain your mother won't mind?" His would have been furious if anyone had depicted her in such a ridiculous pose.

Dorothy gave her head a definitive shake. "She'll love it, and so will Wyatt and I. It'll be the best Christmas ever."

CHAPTER NINE

"Have you decided what you're going to give your parents for Christmas?" Though it had been more than twelve hours since her conversation with Phil, Dorothy was still smiling over the idea of combining her and Brandon's words with Phil's drawings. Together, they'd turn this into another memorable Christmas for many of Mesquite Springs's residents at the same time that they resolved — at least temporarily — Phil's worries about money. The only problem Dorothy could foresee was keeping the gifts a secret.

Laura shook her head as she stirred the chocolate tapioca pudding that would be today's second dessert choice. "I want to surprise them, but they're impossible to surprise. Even if I could think of something they don't already have, I'd have to ask them to order it. At least when I was in Charleston, I had places to shop." She stirred so vigorously that a blob of pudding flew out of the pan. "Look what a mess I've made, just thinking about finding something perfect for my parents. Do you have any ideas?"

Dorothy handed Laura a wet rag and waited until she'd mopped up the spatter before she said, "I do." When she finished her explanation, Laura's frown had turned into a grin.

"That'll be perfect. Are you sure Phil can draw them without them knowing he's doing it? I thought artists had to study their models."

"I thought so too, but Phil seems to be able to memorize a person's face and draw it later." The way he'd captured her likeness no longer seemed threatening now that she knew she hadn't been singled out. Phil's memory and his ability to draw were gifts from God, no different from Laura's ability to turn humble ingredients into delicious meals.

"And he can put both Mother and Father in the same drawing?" The story Laura's mother had recounted had featured both of them.

"Yes, although I imagine he'll charge you more."

Laura began spooning the pudding into

dishes. "That's only fair." She worked silently for a moment, but when the last of the bowls was full, she turned to face Dorothy. "He's perfect for you. You know that, don't you?"

"What do you mean?" Though she had known Laura her whole life, Dorothy was still occasionally puzzled by her friend's abrupt changes of subjects.

Laura's smile seemed to say that the answer should be apparent. "Phil, that's who. He's the perfect husband for you. Think about it, Dorothy. You're both artists — he draws, you write. Look at the way you're planning to combine those talents to make something special. I tell you, Dorothy, he's the one for you."

Dorothy almost sputtered in surprise. Marry Phil? Marry anyone? Risk having her children endure what she had? No! A thousand times no. Dorothy wanted to shout her denial but forced herself to smile as she asked, "When did you become a matchmaker?"

"When I realized the perfect man was right in front of you, but you were too blind to see it. Who knows? We might be able to have a double wedding. You and Phil. Me and Brandon. Wouldn't that be fun?"

Dorothy had to stop this before Laura got

any more nonsensical ideas. As it was, her stomach roiled at the image Laura's words conjured. It was wrong, so wrong. Once again, Dorothy feigned a calm she was far from feeling. "Have you forgotten that I don't plan to marry?"

"You don't really mean that." Laura slid the saucepan into the bucket of soapy water they kept on the corner of the counter.

"I do."

"But why?" Her friend's voice left no doubt that she was mystified. "Every woman wants a husband and children."

Dorothy wouldn't deny that she had thought about marriage and motherhood, particularly when she'd seen how happy Wyatt was with Evelyn, but she could not forget Pa's telling her countless times how much she was like Ma. And then there was what had happened to her mother when Pa had been killed. No one other than Dorothy and Wyatt knew how horrible that year had been, because they'd made a pact not to tell anyone what a toll the loss of their father had taken on their mother.

After the first month, Ma had somehow mustered the strength to attend church each Sunday, giving the appearance of normalcy. Only Dorothy and Wyatt knew that for the rest of the week, Ma remained in her room, so overcome with grief that she barely ate and refused to do anything around the ranch. It had been horrible to hear Ma's sobs, even worse that she'd rejected Dorothy's attempts to comfort her. "No one can help," she had declared.

Eventually Ma had recovered, and though there were relapses, they'd been brief, but the memory of that year was indelibly etched on Dorothy's brain. She would never, ever marry, because she couldn't run the risk of inflicting that kind of pain on her own children.

Dorothy wouldn't tell Laura the whole story, but she deserved an explanation. "I don't believe marriage is part of God's plan for me."

Laura did not appear convinced.

Brandon grinned at the sight of Dorothy walking down the street. He wouldn't make the same mistake as the other night. Knowing she was likely to be coming this way, he'd already donned his coat and was waiting for her.

"That dog is like your shadow," he said as he stepped off the porch and strode toward her and her furry friend. Though Nutmeg was no distinguishable breed, Brandon had to admit that he was beginning to find the dog attractive, especially now that her fur was starting to grow back in the bare patches and her ribs were no longer so prominent.

Living with Dorothy was clearly good for the mutt. And having Dorothy in his life was clearly good for Brandon. The first issue of the *Chronicle* had been a success, and the second was taking shape.

"Nutmeg's making up for the time I keep her tied outside," Dorothy said, resting her hand on the dog's head as she waited for him to reach them. "I can't have her underfoot while Laura's cooking, and she whines if I put her upstairs."

Brandon gave the mutt a pat, his grin widening when Nutmeg nudged his pocket. Ever since he'd given her a piece of cheese, she'd sniffed him each time she saw him in obvious hope that his pocket would contain another treat for her.

"Doesn't she mind being outdoors and tied to your shed? After all, she used to run wild." Dorothy had explained that she'd restrained Nutmeg to keep her from chasing the mercantile's deliverymen.

"It doesn't seem like it. I think she fancies herself my guardian." Dorothy smiled as the dog trotted a few feet in front of them, turning occasionally, as if to urge them to walk faster. "Ma claims that Nutmeg is practicing to be a mother and that she's protecting me the way she will her puppies."

Brandon couldn't help laughing at the image. "You're an awfully big puppy."

"Woof!" Nutmeg gave Dorothy a look of disdain at her comical attempt to sound like a dog. "I'm so grateful I found her," Dorothy continued. "I can't believe how quickly it's happened, but I can't imagine life without her. Even my mother, who's never particularly liked dogs, says she worries about me less now that Nutmeg's here."

Dorothy wrinkled her nose in a gesture Brandon found even more endearing than the adoring looks Nutmeg bestowed on her mistress. "Of course, that doesn't stop me from worrying about Ma. I worry that she needs more help around the ranch. The problem is, she's so stubborn — or maybe it's proud — that I doubt she'd ask for it."

Brandon knew a golden opportunity when it appeared. He'd wondered how he was going to introduce the subject, and now he didn't have to find a way to segue into it. Dorothy had given him the opening he sought.

"I'm not too proud to admit I need help. Putting out a paper is more than a one-person job."

Dorothy tugged on the leash to restrain Nutmeg, then slowed her pace so she could look at him. "Do you want me to keep helping with the Sociable column?" Before he could respond, she continued. "You know I see a lot of people at the restaurant, and almost everyone's eager to talk about themselves."

The day just kept improving. It was as if Dorothy had read his mind. Those caramel brown eyes that he found so intriguing narrowed ever so slightly as she said, "You can always edit them."

"I already know they won't need editing." She may not have had formal training, but Dorothy wrote as well as any reporter Brandon had met. "The truth is, I was hoping you'd be willing to take over responsibility for the Sociable."

This time her eyes widened, her surprise evident. "You mean, do all of the stories?"

"Exactly. I can't think of anyone more qualified." When he'd thought about Dorothy becoming a permanent part of the *Chronicle,* he'd identified only one problem. "Unfortunately, I can't pay you much right now. I need to see how many ads I can sell and how many people actually pay for their subscriptions."

Brandon had already agreed to take some

food in lieu of a cash payment, and he expected more residents to barter for their copies of the paper. As much as newspaper-men wished it were otherwise, that was re-ality.

Dorothy stopped and looked up at him, her expression earnest. "I didn't expect to be paid. I'm happy to be able to help a friend."

A friend. Brandon rolled the word around his brain, almost frowning when he realized it didn't feel right but that he couldn't identify the reason. Perhaps it was because he'd never had a woman friend.

"You're being very generous. Thank you, but I'll pay you what I can. Right now, all I can afford is 10 percent of the profits. If subscriptions increase the way I think they should, I hope to be able to offer you more in a few months."

Brandon grinned as he remembered the number of people who'd asked for a second copy of the first issue, saying they needed it for a Christmas gift and insisting on paying for it. When he'd learned the reason for the increased interest in that issue, his admira-tion for Dorothy had grown. She'd been able to help Blakeslee when he hadn't, and thanks to her idea, both Brandon and Blakeslee would benefit financially. The only one who wasn't profiting from the idea was Dorothy. That was one of the reasons Brandon was insistent that she share in the *Chronicle*'s profits.

"I'm hoping you have more ideas," he told her, eager to see if she did.

Nutmeg tugged on her leash again, obviously unhappy about the humans' slower pace. "She's always in a rush," Dorothy said. "I don't think she understands slow."

Brandon doubted Dorothy did either. Like her pet, she always seemed in a hurry, but for some reason, she was not in a hurry to answer his last question.

"Do you have other ideas?" Perhaps he shouldn't have pushed, but he was curious.

"Just one."

"So far." He couldn't stop himself from joking with her.

"So far," she agreed. "After seeing how everyone responded to the Christmas stories, I thought we might have themes for one Sociable column every month. The other weeks would be the usual notices of births, engagements, parties, and travels, but once a month there would be a unifying theme to the stories."

Unifying. Brandon liked the word.

"That sounds like a great idea. I want the *Chronicle* to be an instrument that unites the town, and you've suggested a way to do that."

Though Dorothy appeared pleased by his approval, she raised an inquisitive eyebrow. "Then you're not planning to have opinionated editorials that force people to take sides."

While Brandon was willing to experiment with new formats and content for the paper, editorials were one area where he had a firm policy. "Definitely not. Mesquite Springs is a peaceful town. Let's keep it that way."

"Amen."

"Any mail for me?" Phil asked as he entered the Grassey post office. Surely Brother Josiah would have responded by now.

The postmaster twirled the end of his oversized moustache, as if that enabled him to think more clearly. "Sure do. You've got a letter." Dave Flag handed him an envelope with unfamiliar handwriting.

"Thanks." Not wanting to arouse the postmaster's curiosity, Phil stayed for another minute, asking about Dave's family, although he had absolutely no interest in anything but opening the envelope and seeing what Brother Josiah had written.

"So, you're in Mesquite Springs," the letter began. *"That's one town where I haven't*

146

preached. What do you think? Is it worth my coming? I could use a new venue or two next year."

Phil let out an exasperated sigh. That wasn't why he'd contacted the preacher. He skimmed the next few paragraphs, all of which dealt with the logistics of a camp meeting and what Phil might hope to gain from one.

Holloway. Where was the information about Holloway? Ah, there it was.

"I've never been to Xavier, so it took a little while to find someone who knew what happened there. I didn't get a lot of details, but the gist is that Brandon Holloway was a troublemaker who was run out of town."

The letter continued, reminding Phil to contact Brother Josiah if he needed something and to be sure to tell him if the residents of Mesquite Springs seemed amenable to a camp meeting, reiterating that it would be mutually beneficial. Maybe so, but Phil didn't care. The information about Holloway's past in Xavier was all that mattered now.

Brother Josiah had given him a nugget; he could invent the rest.

Dorothy couldn't explain it. She had other people to visit in town, other stories to

147

write, and yet she'd felt an inexplicable urge to go to the Plaut ranch this afternoon. She could tell herself it was because she hadn't approached Mrs. Plaut for a Christmas story, but that didn't explain the sense of urgency she felt today, the small voice deep inside her that said, "Go visit Sam's mother." And so here she was, heading south on Mesquite, enjoying the warmth of the afternoon sun on her face.

"It feels good to be out again, doesn't it, Guinevere?" Like her brother, Dorothy often spoke to her horse when she rode. Neither one of them believed the animals understood all they said, but they still relished having uncritical listeners.

"Do you suppose she'll welcome my visit?" That was a question neither Guinevere nor Dorothy could answer. She hadn't seen Mrs. Plaut since her son went East after what Ma called "Sam's shenanigans."

"They were more than shenanigans," Dorothy told her mare. And, since they'd involved her brother and Evelyn, Dorothy wasn't certain Sam's parents would appreciate seeing her. Still, she couldn't ignore the feeling that she was supposed to visit Mrs. Plaut. Not only that she was supposed to visit her, but that she was supposed to visit her today.

It reminded her of the mornings she woke with the conviction that Brandon's father's death was weighing especially heavily on him. While his reaction was far different from Ma's, it was nonetheless severe, and so Dorothy did her best to cheer him, recounting amusing anecdotes or insisting that he take a walk when he claimed he was too busy. Nothing could end the grief, but she did what she could to assuage it.

She had no intention of talking about what had happened to Sam today. Few were aware of the whole story, and Dorothy wasn't about to reveal what she knew to anyone, not even his parents. That would only hurt them, and hurting two kind people was the last thing Dorothy wanted to do. The Plauts had suffered enough when their son had left Texas. Since then, they rarely ventured into town, and today their absence weighed heavily on Dorothy. Perhaps that was why she'd felt the need to visit.

When she reached the ranch house and knocked on the front door, Dorothy heard the sound of slow footsteps and a cane rapping the floor.

"Dorothy! What a nice surprise." Though the woman who was old enough to be Sam's grandmother gave her a welcoming smile,

Dorothy saw the pain in her light blue eyes. It could have been caused by the arthritis that twisted her fingers and forced her to use a cane, but Dorothy suspected that was only part of the reason for Sam's mother's obvious discomfort. Perhaps she knew more than Dorothy realized about what her son had done, but her smile was gracious as she said, "I was just about to make a pot of tea. I hope you'll join me."

Dorothy nodded and followed the silver-haired woman into the house. "I'd like that."

For a while, they chatted about trivial things while they sipped tea out of delicate china cups and nibbled a few cookies from the elaborately carved silver platter. The Plauts were not the richest people in Mesquite Springs, but they were far from poor. Still, all that money had failed to insulate them from tragedy. Dorothy could see the signs in the older woman's posture and the way her hands trembled. She appeared to have aged several years since Sam left last summer.

Dorothy could only imagine what it must have been like for Mrs. Plaut to have her only child involved in shenanigans. She and Ma both missed Wyatt now that he was on his wedding trip, but they knew he'd return soon. The Plauts had no such assurances.

"I read those stories you wrote for the *Chronicle*," Mrs. Plaut said as she urged Dorothy to take another cookie. "You did a mighty fine job. I could practically hear those other folks talking."

Though she refused the cookie, Dorothy nodded when her hostess offered to refill her cup. "That's what I was trying to do," she explained. "I wanted their voices to be heard."

"Well, you accomplished what you set out to do." Mrs. Plaut narrowed her eyes as she looked at Dorothy. "Your mother once told me you had a gift for helping people, and she was right. That's one of the reasons I wish you'd married Sam. You would have been good for my son."

But, even if Dorothy had planned to marry, she would not have chosen Sam. She didn't love him. Some days, she didn't even like him.

Oblivious to the direction Dorothy's thoughts had taken, Mrs. Plaut continued. "You cheered up an old woman by coming here. I don't know how you knew it, but I was in the doldrums today. Adam is out on the range, and I was feeling lonely, so your visit brightened my day. Thank you, Dorothy."

Though she was pleased to have helped

151

Sam's mother, Dorothy didn't want to accept undue credit. "I have to admit that my motives weren't all altruistic." The Plauts had been on her mental list to visit. "I'm going to be writing the Sociable column for the paper, and I wondered whether you had any news you wanted to share."

Mrs. Plaut shook her head. "No one would be interested in me." Perhaps it was only Dorothy's imagination that she seemed regretful. "I'm not going anywhere."

While travel plans, birthdays, and other social events tended to dominate the column in most papers, Dorothy wanted the *Chronicle* to have more than that. The themed columns would help, but variety was what would make readers eager to receive the next issue.

Brandon had told her she had free rein with the Sociable and could include anything she thought would interest subscribers. The question was, what would that be? As she looked at the bouquet of fresh flowers gracing a table on the other side of the settee, an idea popped into Dorothy's mind.

"You have the only greenhouse in the whole county." Though the Plauts had invited people to visit it soon after it had been built, Dorothy suspected few had seen it since then. "I'm sure readers would like to hear about what's blooming and how you care for your plants."

As she spoke, Dorothy saw that she had piqued the older woman's interest, so she continued. "Would you be willing to share some of your secrets?"

Her eyes now brighter than before, Mrs. Plaut gave a self-deprecating shrug. "There are no secrets. It's just common sense."

"Then would you be willing to share your common sense?"

Visibly pleased, the silver-haired matron nodded. "Of course. Would you like to see the greenhouse now?"

It wasn't Dorothy's imagination that Mrs. Plaut walked more confidently, that she held her head a bit higher. The woman's enthusiasm and the confidence with which she discussed her beloved flowers told Dorothy that she'd been right to come here today. She hadn't changed the world, but she'd made one woman's life a bit happier.

Perhaps Ma was right. Perhaps Dorothy had been put on Earth to help other people. And if that were true, perhaps she could find better ways to ease Brandon's sorrow.

CHAPTER TEN

"He's not the one."

Dorothy looked up from the meal she was plating, shocked by the change in her friend's demeanor. When she'd left for the dining room only a few minutes earlier, Laura had been smiling, and there'd been a saucy tilt to her head. Now her shoulders were slumped, and she was blinking furiously, as if trying to hold back tears.

"What happened?" Dorothy took the tray from Laura, laid it on the table, and wrapped her arms around her friend. There was no need to ask who "he" was. Only one man had figured in Laura's conversation for the past three weeks.

"He doesn't love me. All he talks about is the *Chronicle*. He didn't even notice that I'd done my hair differently today."

Although Laura had never liked the single braid Evelyn had adopted when she cooked, she had agreed that braids were practical

154

and had worn two braids coiled around her head. Today, however, she'd drawn her hair into a chignon.

"He was so busy discussing something that happened in Washington that he barely complimented me on the food." Laura's recital of Brandon's shortcomings continued.

Dorothy knew she shouldn't have been surprised. After all, when Laura had been at the Charleston boarding school, her fascination with a man rarely lasted three weeks. But Dorothy had thought this time would be different, because Brandon was different from the men Laura had met in Charleston. It wasn't simply that he was handsome. According to Laura, there had been handsome men in Charleston. Brandon was also talented, dedicated, a good conversationalist . . . . The list was endless, but it wasn't enough for Laura.

"I'm sorry," Dorothy said as she continued to hug Laura. "I know you thought he was the right man for you."

"But he wasn't." Laura moved out of Dorothy's embrace and headed toward the stove, where she finished plating the meal Dorothy had started. "When Mr. Holloway finishes his meal, you can take his pie to him. I don't ever want to see him again."

Though her voice was firm, a second later Laura's face crumpled. "What am I going to do? I want to be a wife and mother, but I can't seem to find the right man. What am I going to do?"

As her heart ached for her friend, Dorothy searched for the words that would comfort her. "You'll wait, and you'll pray," she said softly, "and then you'll find the right man."

"When?"

Dorothy had no answer.

Was a storm brewing? Ma had claimed that people's moods became erratic when violent weather was on the way. Perhaps that was why both Laura and Dorothy seemed different today.

Brandon hadn't noticed anything amiss when he'd entered Polly's Place. Dorothy had greeted him as cordially as she always did. But when Laura had delivered his meal and stayed to flutter her eyelashes and talk about the seasonings she had used for the pork roast, interrupting the discussion he'd been having over the latest news from Washington, she'd suddenly flounced away, prompting one of the men to say that something had put a bee in her bonnet.

And then, for the first time ever, Dorothy

had brought him his dessert. Brandon didn't mind that. Dorothy didn't flutter her eyelashes, and she'd never interrupt a conversation. But he couldn't help noticing that she seemed distracted, and that was unlike her. Something was definitely in the air.

When he'd finished his meal, instead of returning to the office and working on the article he'd started this morning, Brandon headed next door to the mercantile.

"Good to see you, Brandon. Are you starting your Christmas shopping?"

Brandon smiled at the heavyset man whose reddish-brown hair bore only a few strands of silver. He liked Mr. Downey, or Leonard, as the man had insisted Brandon address him. Though rumor had it that he was the richest man in town, with the exception of his residence, he'd never flaunted his wealth. To the contrary, he seemed to be a man of simple tastes. That made the marble and crystal that were reported to dominate the interior of the Downey mansion all the more perplexing.

"I hadn't really thought about Christmas," Brandon admitted. Ma had been the one who'd made it special, and though he and Pa had celebrated last year, without Ma it hadn't been much of a celebration. This year, Brandon had no reason to celebrate and no one to buy a gift for.

Leonard nodded as if he'd expected that. "First years are always hard." He paused before adding, "For some folks, every year is hard. That's why Ida and I invite people to share Christmas dinner with us. I hope you'll come."

It was a kind invitation and one Brandon suspected he'd accept, but after Laura's odd behavior, he was reluctant to give Leonard a firm answer. "Thank you, sir. Can I let you know in a couple weeks?"

Though Leonard seemed surprised, he nodded. "I hope your hesitation isn't because of my house. That was all Ida's idea. She wanted people to see what hard work could accomplish. And, make no mistake, we worked hard to earn it. When we built the house, there wasn't any place for folks to gather other than the church. Ida claimed Mesquite Springs needed a place for parties, so we gave them one."

While the house was far too ornate for Brandon, he could honestly say, "Your home is impressive."

"And so is what you're doing. I can't remember people as excited about anything as they are about the *Chronicle*. Most folks are talking about the Christmas stories.

Don't misunderstand me. They were good, but I preferred the way you presented both sides of the story about the squabble in Congress. From what I've seen, many editors use their papers to promote their own views and forget that there are always two sides."

Brandon had thought he'd presented both sides in Xavier, but the townspeople hadn't seen it that way. That was why he had resolved to be more careful this time and not let anything he wrote divide this town.

"I'm glad you approve of the *Chronicle,* sir." The piece Leonard had complimented had taken Brandon hours to write, because he'd agonized over his choice of words, determined to give his subscribers an impartial explanation of the argument in Congress.

"Leonard. Remember you're supposed to call me Leonard." The older man shrugged his shoulders. "I have no reason to disapprove, especially when my ad brought more sales. I thought folks knew everything we carried, but it appears they don't. Your idea of featuring different goods each week was pure genius."

"Hardly that. It just seemed to make sense."

As he'd walked through the mercantile

one day, Brandon had been impressed with the variety of merchandise the Downeys carried, but he'd noticed that most customers came in with a list of necessities and did not browse the shelves. Ida Downey confirmed that there were few impulsive purchases, and that started Brandon's mind whirling with ideas of how to change that. It appeared he'd succeeded.

"I like a man with both modesty and sense." Leonard gave Brandon an appraising look. "No doubt about it. You're an asset to Mesquite Springs."

"What do you think, Mrs. Dinkel?" Phil handed her the sketch he'd made of a young girl holding a goose made of plaid wool and sporting a large bow around its neck. "Will your daughter like it?"

It took the woman who'd commissioned the drawing only a second to begin nodding vigorously. "*Ja.* She vill. Olga vill love it. It looks just like her."

Phil breathed a sigh of relief. This was the only story he'd been asked to illustrate where he'd not seen the person he was expected to draw. Mrs. Dinkel's daughter had married a soldier and was now living at some fort in Dakota Territory.

"Everyone says she looks like me," Mrs.

160

Dinkel had explained, and so Phil had drawn a young version of the stout woman whose round face was dominated by large, expressive eyes.

"This is *gut*, Herr Blakeslee. *Sehr gut.*" Phil had noticed that the woman reverted to her native German when she was excited and took that as further approval of his work. Her story, recounting how her young daughter had made the mistake of turning the goose that was destined for the Christmas table into a pet had touched chords deep inside him. That was something Esther might have done.

According to her mother, Olga had begged that Goosie, as she'd named it, not be killed, claiming the family did not need the traditional dinner this year. But when she'd learned that Mrs. Clark had her heart set on roast goose but was too sick to cook one, Olga had insisted that Goosie be the Clarks' dinner.

Touched by her daughter's selflessness, Mrs. Dinkel had made a toy goose for Olga, a toy that Olga had carried all the way to Dakota Territory for her own daughter. That too was something Esther might have done if she'd been given the opportunity.

Phil wrenched his thoughts away from his sister, reminding himself that he had two reasons for being here. He'd delivered the sketch. Now it was time for the second part.

"That was a fine issue of the *Chronicle*," he said, adopting a nonchalance he was far from feeling. "I hope it doesn't turn out the way Mr. Holloway's last paper did."

As he'd expected, Mrs. Dinkel took the bait. "What do you mean?"

Phil feigned reluctance. "I probably shouldn't have said anything. Who knows how rumors get started, but this one seems real." He paused, as if waiting for Mrs. Dinkel's approval to proceed. When she nodded, he said, "I heard he turned into such a troublemaker that he was driven out of town."

"Nein!" A gasp accompanied Mrs. Dinkel's exclamation. "That cannot be true. Mr. Holloway is a *gut* man. That is a lie."

But it wasn't, and the sooner Mesquite Springs's residents knew that the better. Towns didn't drive anyone away without a good reason.

"I don't believe it," Mrs. Dinkel insisted.

Others would. Phil was counting on that.

162

CHAPTER ELEVEN

"What happened when your brother ran for mayor?"

Dorothy took a sip of coffee as she considered Brandon's unexpected question. They were sitting at one of the tables in Polly's Place, reviewing the items she had prepared for the next Sociable column, when he'd posed it. Though the mayoral campaign was a time she preferred not to recall, Brandon deserved an honest answer.

"The town was deeply divided, with half supporting Wyatt, the other half his opponent."

Brandon raised an eyebrow. "Sam Plow."

"Plaut," she corrected him. "He was a fierce opponent." She wouldn't say "worthy," any more than she would tell Brandon all that had transpired during the campaign. "He fought hard, but the people chose Wyatt."

"And now Sam is back East handling

some distant relatives' legal affairs."

Dorothy wasn't certain how to respond without sacrificing Sam's privacy, and so she said, "That's the story I've heard. Why are you so curious?"

Brandon appeared a bit abashed. "No real reason, I suppose. It's just that what I've heard tells me Mesquite Springs is not as perfect as some people would have me believe."

"I don't suppose any place is perfect. Wyatt and I used to think the town was boring. That's the reason both of us wanted to leave." Or at least one of Dorothy's reasons. There had also been times when she believed that if they moved to another town where they were not constantly surrounded by memories, Ma might have been happier.

Though she hadn't planned to share that aspect of her life with Brandon, Dorothy found herself asking, "Do new surroundings make it easier to put the past behind you?"

The tightening of his lips told Dorothy she had hit a sensitive nerve. "If you're asking whether I miss my father any less here than I did in Xavier, the answer is no. Not a day goes by that I don't wish he was with me."

Brandon stared out the window for a

second. "Pa never traveled more than ten miles from Xavier, so he never saw anything like these hills. When I look at them, I find myself wishing he could see how beautiful they are and wondering if he'd use the same words to describe them that I do. So, no, you can't outrun your past. At least I haven't been able to." Turning his gaze back to her, Brandon said firmly, "Let's talk about the next issue."

Though she tried to concentrate on the articles she'd proposed, Dorothy's mind continued to whirl with all that Brandon had said and what he hadn't said. It was only natural that his grief for his father was still fresh, but her instincts told her Brandon was suffering from more than simple grief. Whatever had happened in Xavier had left deep wounds. She wished — oh, how she wished — that she could help heal them.

Why had he done that? Why had he talked about outrunning the past? Brandon frowned as he realized that his pace was verging on a run. He'd thought he had better control over himself and his emotions, but clearly, he was wrong. He should have known better than to say anything about Pa, since even the slightest mention unleashed waves of pain.

Oh, Pa, I'm sorry. I never meant to hurt anyone, especially you. His father had done so much for him, giving his time, his energy, and ultimately his life for Brandon. And how had Brandon repaid him? He'd run away, abandoning the town his parents had loved so dearly. Now there was no one to visit their graves, to ensure that the man charged with maintaining the cemetery kept them free of weeds, no one to lay flowers on them on their birthdays.

He'd run away, and though he'd told himself that he had had no choice, Brandon could not dismiss the guilt that filled him every time he thought about that horrible night. He should have been there. He should have protected Pa. But he had not.

Brandon had been so caught up in his thoughts, his feet moving mechanically, that he hadn't realized how far he'd walked. Instinctively, he'd followed the route he and Dorothy took when they walked Nutmeg — east to Mesquite, north to Hill, then south on River.

If there'd been other people outside, he hadn't noticed them, but he couldn't ignore the woman who walked toward him. Laura. He hadn't seen her all week, though he'd heard her voice when he'd been at Polly's Place, so he knew she wasn't ill. The way

166

she shied at the sight of him today told Brandon she was uncomfortable; his mother's lessons told him it was his responsibility to mend whatever was wrong.

"I'm sorry I haven't had a chance to tell you personally, but I hope Dorothy has relayed my compliments on your cooking," he said when he'd greeted Laura. "This week's meals have been particularly delicious."

"Thank you." A slight flush colored her cheeks, telling him she appreciated the compliment. "Cooking is one thing I'm good at."

The frown that accompanied her words suggested she was thinking about an area where she did not excel. Brandon wouldn't pry. Instead, he said, "You're not just a good cook. You're an excellent one. I've never had such delicious food."

Laura nodded. "I guess we all have something we're good at. You and Dorothy seem to be good at writing. I'm glad about that, especially for Dorothy. She needs it."

Brandon's ears perked up at the mention of Dorothy. "Why do you say that?"

The look Laura gave him indicated the answer should be obvious. "Everyone needs something to do. Since Dorothy plans to remain a spinster, writing gives her a purpose."

Shock rolled through Brandon at Laura's unexpected and inexplicable announcement. "Dorothy a spinster? Why on earth wouldn't she want to marry and have a family?" That was the natural way of things.

Brandon struggled, trying to imagine why such a warm, loving woman would believe she was meant to become an old maid. The only answer he could find was that some man had broken her heart, but though he'd heard his share of gossip, Dorothy's name had never been linked with a man's.

He looked at Laura, waiting for an answer. If what he'd heard was accurate, Laura was Dorothy's closest friend. If anyone knew, it would be Laura. But Laura, it seemed, did not.

"Dorothy never explained why. All I know is that for years and years, she's said she won't ever marry."

So, it wasn't a recent decision. That made it all the more puzzling.

"I'm surprised." Shocked was a better word.

"So was I. I think Phil Blakeslee would be perfect for her."

Blakeslee? Brandon almost choked on the thought. He could not — would not —

picture Dorothy married to him.

"I told her so." Laura continued her story.

"What did Dorothy say?"

Laura frowned, as if the response was as confusing as Dorothy's original declaration. "She said some people aren't meant to marry."

That might be true, but Dorothy wasn't one of them.

"Mind if I join you?"

Phil looked up, startled by the sight of Pastor Coleman standing directly in front of him. He'd been so lost in his thoughts that he hadn't heard the man's approach.

Yes, I do mind. He was in no mood to talk to anyone, but he could think of no reason to refuse. This was what came from sitting in the park rather than returning to the boardinghouse.

"Not at all." Though it was a blatant lie, Phil moved closer to the edge of the bench, giving the minister plenty of room to stretch out. The man's bulk told Phil he'd never had to worry about where he'd find his next meal — yet another reason to dislike the pious preacher.

"You look troubled, son."

Phil was *not* his son. He was no one's son — not the man whose seed had given him life, not God's, and definitely not this man's. For years, his only family had been Esther, and then — thanks to a meddlesome newspaperman and a sanctimonious preacher — he'd had no one.

"I was thinking." About the way no one seemed the least bit worried about the rumors he was spreading about Holloway's past and about the letter from Mr. K that had been waiting for him in Grassey this morning.

Phil could not understand why the town's residents seemed so unconcerned by the story he'd concocted about Holloway printing such outrageous lies that he'd been driven from Xavier. Perhaps it was the approach of Christmas that had them feeling charitable. Peace on earth, goodwill among men, and all the other folderol that accompanied the celebration of a baby in a manger. Perhaps he should wait until January to renew his anti-Holloway campaign. Perhaps folks would be more receptive then.

According to Mr. K's letter, Phil had more time than he'd expected to get rid of Holloway. Mr. K had written to say that he would not begin work on the hotel until spring and that he hoped Phil still liked Mesquite Springs well enough to make it his home. The news about the timing didn't bother

Phil. After all, staying in Mesquite Springs a bit longer could be pleasant, particularly if he was able to sell more of his sketches. Besides, it gave him more time to ensure that Mesquite Springs did not have a newspaper when Mr. K arrived.

That was good. The man who was his mentor as well as his boss would praise Phil for running Holloway out of town and might not say anything about Phil's failure to tell him of Holloway's unexpected arrival. If he questioned that, Phil would explain that he hadn't wanted to bother him with a minor problem.

What bothered Phil was the part about making this town his home. In the past, he and Mr. K had worked together. Even though he didn't know all the details of Mr. K's business, he ran enough errands to feel as if he was playing a valuable role. This sounded as if he was no longer needed. That made him nervous, and so did the man seated on the other end of the bench.

Coleman smiled, but the expression in those gray eyes seemed to say that he did not believe Phil. "Perhaps you're thinking about some of the special people in Mesquite Springs."

Phil would hardly call Holloway or Coleman himself special, but there was no point in saying that.

Unfazed by Phil's silence, the preacher continued. "The Bible bids us care for widows and orphans. I know I speak for more than myself when I say that we care for Mrs. Lockhart. She and her husband were mainstays of the community, and now that Timothy is gone, the rest of us watch over her. We'd hate to see anyone hurt her or take advantage of her."

So, the preacher was thinking about the widow, not that blasted newspaperman. Good, because Phil had no intention of taking advantage of Mrs. Lockhart. Mr. K had told him to offer everyone a fair price for their land. There would be no swindling or cheating.

"I share your feelings," Phil said as calmly as he could when inwardly he was seething at the man's audacity. Why, he'd practically accused him of hurting — or planning to hurt — a nice old lady. "Mrs. Lockhart is a very kind woman, but she's also a lonely one. I've made it my mission" — though he used it deliberately, Phil hated that word, because it evoked memories of the preacher who'd declared it his mission to inform the congregation of what he called Esther's sins — "to ease her loneliness whenever I can."

"An admirable goal." Though the words

were benign, Phil knew that the minister was not convinced. Perhaps Holloway wasn't the only threat in Mesquite Springs. Perhaps Phil had been wrong in thinking that Coleman would not be a hindrance. Perhaps it was time to consider a different approach.

What was the word Mr. K used? Mitigation. That was it. He'd have to find a way to mitigate the damage the preacher might inflict.

CHAPTER TWELVE

"It's always the same."

The woman made no effort to lower her voice. Rather, Dorothy suspected, she pitched it so that everyone leaving the church would hear her. It wasn't the first time Dorothy had overheard Miss Jacobs complain, but it was the first time she'd seen the elderly spinster direct one of her tirades at the town's schoolteacher.

"I could give the sermon if anyone would let me use the pulpit," Miss Jacobs declared.

"Now, Charity, it's not that bad." Miss Geist was more than a schoolmarm. She was a peacemaker.

"Yes, it is that bad. We're wasting our money paying a minister who can't even write new sermons. The first Sunday in Advent, he always preaches about Joseph. The second Sunday is Elizabeth, the third Anna, and the fourth Mary."

Though Dorothy suspected she ought to

simply bite her tongue and walk by, her sense of fairness would not let her do that. "What you say may be true, Miss Jacobs. He does talk about those people every year, but each time Pastor Coleman gives us new insights. He brings the Holy Land and the people who were closest to Jesus's nativity to life for me."

The irate woman regarded Dorothy as if she were nothing more than an annoying insect. "I still say we ought to be thinking about getting ourselves a new minister, one who's more modern." She turned her gaze from the schoolteacher to Dorothy. "And you, Miss Clark, would do well not to contradict your elders. I, for one, intend to have a word with your mother. She should have taught you better."

Though Miss Jacobs did not approach Ma, perhaps because Ma was deep in conversation with Mrs. Plaut, she subjected her to the same glare she had fixed on Dorothy, then spun on her heel, effectively excluding Dorothy from the conversation.

Half an hour later, as she rode toward the ranch, Dorothy was still fuming. No matter how she tried to dismiss Miss Jacobs's words as nothing more than an angry woman's rant, she could not forget either her rancor or the way she'd blamed Ma for

Dorothy's outspokenness. Neither Pastor Coleman nor Ma deserved the woman's criticism.

"Do you think we need a new minister, Ma?" Dorothy asked as she helped her mother prepare the Sunday meal.

Ma turned from the potatoes she was mashing and stared at her. "No. Who thinks we do?"

"Charity Jacobs."

Letting out a disapproving cluck, Ma shook her head. "If there were ever a woman who was misnamed, it's Charity. I know I'm stooping to her level when I say this, but she always looks as if she's just drunk a cup of vinegar. I'm not surprised she doesn't approve of Pastor Coleman. The question is whether she approves of anyone. I, for one, doubt anybody could meet her standards."

Ma gave the potatoes a forceful mash, then gestured toward the dining room. "Let's serve dinner and talk about something more pleasant."

Phil grinned as he walked back to the boardinghouse. He hadn't expected it, hadn't even dared to hope something like this would happen, but it seemed that the mitigation was already underway. The loud woman had attracted a lot of attention, though some of the folks pretended not to listen. The way several nodded in approval at her suggestion that the town needed a more modern preacher told Phil his work would be easier than he'd anticipated. The coals were hot. All he had to do was fan them a bit. Then there'd be flames, and more importantly, smoke.

Before the good citizens of Mesquite Springs knew what was happening, the smoke would be so thick that no one would know how or where it had started. All they would care about would be getting beyond it, and he'd be at their side, ready to guide them.

Perfect. Now all he had to do was get rid of Holloway.

Brandon swallowed the last bite of the stew he'd made for his dinner. While his cooking would never compare to Laura's, he'd learned to make a passably good stew after Ma died. And though he rarely lacked for invitations to share Sunday dinner with someone, there were times when he preferred his own company. Today was one of those days.

Though he told himself that woman's diatribe was nothing more than the rantings of one angry person, Brandon could not

177

forget her words or the way others appeared to agree. Was this the beginning of a rift in Mesquite Springs?

The woman's opinion of Pastor Coleman was very different from Brandon's. He had been impressed with the man's knowledge of the Bible and his ability to make some of the more obscure passages meaningful for those who did not have the benefit of his education.

It was true Pastor Coleman was not flamboyant, but though he chose a gentle approach rather than preaching fire and brimstone, Brandon had no doubt that Mesquite Springs's minister would take a firm stand if he saw his parishioners heading in the wrong direction. The question was whether he would defend himself or whether he would let the situation either defuse itself or escalate. Brandon's heart ached at the prospect of escalation.

He needed to distract himself, and so when he'd dried the last dish, he returned to his office. He wouldn't work today — after all, it was Sunday — but reading wasn't work, especially the reading he had in mind.

Brandon reached into the top desk drawer and pulled out the article he'd read so often that the creases were starting to rip. Filled with information about the Clark horse ranch and how it came into existence, the article painted a vivid picture not only of the prize-winning horses but also of the charming town only a few minutes away from the Circle C.

At the time, Brandon couldn't explain why he'd saved the article. It wasn't as if he were particularly interested in horses or had any plans to visit the Hill Country. The newspaper that contained the article had arrived months before trouble broke out in Xavier, but when it did and he knew his only recourse was to leave, Brandon had recalled the almost lyrical descriptions. He'd read the article once more, then headed toward Mesquite Springs.

At the time, Brandon had told himself that he wanted to discover whether the town was as attractive as the author claimed, but now he realized there'd been another reason he'd come here. Even though he hadn't admitted it to himself, part of him had wanted to meet the person who'd penned the story.

He'd quickly discovered that the article had given an accurate portrait of the town. It was everything the author had claimed and more. As he reread the article today, Brandon began to grin. It seemed he'd also achieved the second part of his goal. Unless he was mistaken, he'd met the author.

"I'm sorry, but I don't have as many articles as I had hoped." Dorothy pushed the sheets of paper across the table, then took another sip of coffee. It had been a long day, since Nutmeg had wakened her, demanding to go outside an hour earlier than usual. She'd known there was no hope of getting back to sleep, so she'd started preparations for the restaurant's meals, then put the finishing touches on this week's Sociable column. And when Brandon had declared today's pie particularly delicious, she had suggested that rather than wait for her to bring the articles to him, he should return to Polly's Place for a second piece of pie as well as this week's articles.

"Mrs. Plaut was under the weather." Dorothy owed him an explanation for the short column. "And when I visited Mrs. Lockhart, she was too busy making supper for Phil Blakeslee to talk to me."

While Dorothy could have made mention of the frequency of Phil's meals at the Lockhart residence, she refused to include anything in the Sociable that hadn't been told to her directly. Gossip had no place in the *Chronicle,* even though other towns' papers seemed to include a good helping of it.

Brandon shrugged as he speared another bite of chocolate pie. "Fortunately, there's more news from around the state than usual. I can fill the space with that."

He'd given her the perfect opportunity to make another suggestion. "You could also start writing editorials. I'm sure our subscribers would like to know your opinions."

Dorothy had glanced at almost all of the newspapers that had come to the *Chronicle*'s office and had seen that the majority included an editorial column or, in some cases, a full page devoted to the editor's views on everything from the situation in Austin to a feud between two families. Surely the unpleasant comments about Pastor Coleman deserved a response from the *Chronicle*'s editor.

"That's not a good idea." Brandon's eyes turned steely blue.

"Why not?" Dorothy knew he felt strongly about many things, because they'd had more than one heated discussion, each trying to convince the other of the validity of one opinion versus another, but they had not discussed the absence of editorials other than the one time when he'd said he wasn't planning to write any. Perhaps he'd explain his reasons today.

"It just isn't."

Brandon's words left no doubt that the subject was closed, but the flash of pain she saw in his eyes told Dorothy she'd touched a sensitive chord. For some reason, the idea of making his opinions public distressed Brandon. That seemed strange, since he'd told her he wanted to both report the news and encourage people to think about what they'd read. Surely an editorial was the way to do that. Her first instinct was to ask him why, but she would not pry. He would tell her when he felt the time was right. In the meantime, Brandon deserved his privacy.

"I can hardly believe it's just over two weeks until Christmas," Dorothy said, deliberately changing the subject to something lighter. "Time seems to be going so quickly." Between interviewing people, writing articles, caring for Nutmeg, and worrying about what she would do when the puppies arrived, Dorothy had been busier than she could recall.

She took a sip of coffee, trying to think of another subject that would not upset Brandon. "It doesn't seem possible that Wyatt and Evelyn have been gone for more than a month."

"When are they due back?" The way

Brandon's shoulders relaxed told Dorothy he appreciated the neutral topic of conversation.

"Within the week. It sounds as if they're enjoying their travels, but Evelyn said they're looking forward to spending their first Christmas as a couple here."

Brandon forked the last of the piecrust crumbs as he asked, "Will you move back to the ranch once they arrive?"

It was a question that had troubled Dorothy for weeks now. "I'm not sure, but I won't go anywhere until Nutmeg has her puppies. It wouldn't be fair to move her to a strange place."

Though Brandon nodded as if he understood, he said nothing, perhaps because he realized Dorothy's reluctance to return to the ranch was based on more than her adopted pet.

"To tell the truth, I don't really want to leave town," she admitted. "I like living here."

This time he smiled. "Because it's a quiet, quaint, quintessential Texas town."

Dorothy blinked in surprise as she recognized the words. She'd spent the better part of an hour debating whether to use the alliteration or choose a simpler, perhaps less poetic, way to describe Mesquite Springs.

Ultimately, she'd decided to leave the alliteration as part of the story she'd written to help promote Wyatt's first horse sale at the Circle C.

"That's one way to describe it," she said slowly. It made sense that Brandon had seen the article, because she'd sent it to every paper in the state. But that he remembered the exact wording surprised her.

He reached into his pocket, withdrawing a piece of carefully folded paper. "Those words piqued my interest so much that I wanted to see if Mesquite Springs was as attractive as you claimed."

"Me? How did you know that I wrote that?" When she'd mailed the story, Dorothy had omitted her name, merely stating that the article was a true representation of the Circle C and the town.

"I didn't at first. I simply knew that whoever wrote it had a flair for words, but when I read the pieces you wrote for the *Chronicle,* I thought the style seemed familiar." Brandon gave her a self-deprecating smile. "I guess I'm a bit slow, because it was only yesterday that I put all the pieces together." He leaned forward, placing his forearms on the table. "How does it feel, knowing your words brought me to Mesquite Springs?"

For a moment, Dorothy was speechless as joy flowed through her. Pastor Coleman had once preached about how entwined people's lives were, how one act could have unexpected and far-ranging effects. He'd used the example of a row of standing dominoes, pointing out how if the first one toppled, it would cause all the others to fall.

Dorothy hadn't liked the example. When she and Wyatt had played that game, their goal had been to topple the whole line, so there was nothing unexpected about the falling dominoes. Though she still didn't like the analogy, today Dorothy understood Pastor Coleman's message.

She had written the article hoping to attract more people to Wyatt's sale, and she had. She had prayed that her words would help her brother, and they had. But they had done much more, things she could never have anticipated.

Her words had given Brandon a direction when he'd lost his father and his home. That had led to Mesquite Springs having its first newspaper. And though she would never have expected it, because of that first article, Dorothy now had the opportunity to write more stories. What an amazing answer to prayer.

CHAPTER THIRTEEN

"Anything for me, Dave?" Phil waited until the others had left the Grassey post office before he approached the man behind the counter. When he did, he fixed a friendly expression on his face, pleased that the postmaster had encouraged the familiarity of using Christian names. If Dave considered him a friend, he would be less likely to tell anyone about the letters he sent and received. Phil was taking no chances. It was inconvenient to ride all the way to Grassey to mail a letter, but the inconvenience was offset by the fact that no one in Mesquite Springs knew his business.

"Yes, indeedy." The postmaster fingered the ends of his long moustache before he turned to retrieve an envelope from the slot he'd designated for Phil. "I got a letter for you right here." He slid the thick envelope across the counter, grinning as he said, "That Mr. K sure writes long letters."

Dave didn't need to know that most of the envelopes contained one sheet of paper. What made them so thick was that they were filled with dollar bills.

"He doesn't have much else to do," Phil lied, continuing the fiction he'd created of a lonely, elderly man who'd been like a grandfather to him. "Not like you and me."

After the postmaster had bent his ear for five minutes, recounting all the chores his wife had found to occupy his spare time, Phil made his way to the hitching post. When he was out of town and away from curious eyes, he stopped under what had become his favorite oak tree, dismounted, and carefully slit the envelope.

"Proceed as planned. Get rid of any obstacles. Encourage everyone to sell."

The message was exactly the one he'd hoped for, proof that he'd pleased the man who held his future in his hand. Mr. K was happy, and so was Phil when he counted the money. This Christmas wouldn't be like . . .

Almost involuntarily, he reached inside his coat and fingered the oilskin packet, then shook his head. He wouldn't think about that.

If Pa could see him now, he'd probably

laugh at the idea of his son spending four hours in the saddle simply to buy Christmas gifts. Ma, on the other hand, would have approved. She was the one who'd told Brandon that the amount of money he spent meant less than choosing the right gift.

Though Leonard had insisted there would be no gifts exchanged on Christmas, Brandon had no intention of arriving at the Downeys' empty-handed. He wouldn't buy anything costly, but he was determined to repay the family's kindness in a small way.

Ma had been a firm believer that unexpected gifts were the best, which ruled out anything purchased at the mercantile. That was why Brandon was on his way to Grassey. He'd been told it was the closest town, but because it was situated southwest of Mesquite Springs, it was one Brandon had not seen on his trip from Xavier.

"Nothing compares to Mesquite Springs," Dorothy's mother had declared when she'd mentioned Grassey, "but it's not a bad town. They have a few things we don't, including a candy store."

The candy store had made the decision easy. Leonard's girth left no doubt that he enjoyed eating, and Brandon had yet to meet a woman who didn't enjoy a sweet or two. If the store had the variety he expected, he might even find something for Mrs. Clark as a thank-you for sending him in this direction.

Brandon grinned. So far, everything was going well. It was Wednesday, the slowest day of the week for him, and an unusually pleasant one for mid-December. When he reached Grassey, he saw that Mrs. Clark was right. The town was not as pretty as Mesquite Springs. The frame buildings on the main street could use a fresh coat of paint, and the street itself would benefit from a good sweeping, but the sparkling clear windows on the candy shop dispelled his concerns. This store, at least, looked promising.

Half an hour later, Brandon left the candy shop with four carefully wrapped packages in hand. He'd chosen chocolate mint fudge for Ida Downey, half a dozen chocolate creams with tiny rosebuds piped on top for Laura, peanut brittle for Mrs. Clark, and a new — at least to him — type of fudge for Leonard. One taste had convinced Brandon that this was the most delicious confection in the shop.

"What do you call it?" he asked the proprietor.

The gray-haired woman with light blue eyes shrugged. "Brown sugar fudge. Not everyone likes it, but some folks swear it's their favorite."

Brandon was part of the second group. The combination of brown sugar, butter, cream, and a bit of vanilla had tasted even better than it smelled, and that was saying a lot. Unless he was greatly mistaken, Leonard would enjoy it as much as he did.

All that remained was finding a gift for Dorothy. Brandon had already decided that he would not give her candy. Instead, he wanted something different from what he was giving the others and one that would last more than a few days. The problem was, he had no idea what that would be.

He stowed the candy in his saddlebags and began to stroll down the street, looking for inspiration. Clothing was out of the question. That was much too personal, but there must be something.

Brandon paused in front of the mercantile, gazing at the items displayed in the front window. Unlike the ones at the candy shop, these windows needed washing, the film of dirt from more than one storm making it difficult to see what the proprietor had placed near them to lure customers. In all likelihood, there was nothing suitable. But then Brandon's gaze landed on the far corner, and he laughed.

Perfect. The china figurine of a mother dog surrounded by three puppies would make Dorothy smile, and that was his goal. Perfect.

He was still smiling as he rode out of town. The day had turned out even better than he'd hoped, and the prospect of Christmas without Pa was no longer as daunting as it had been. Little by little, Brandon was rebuilding his life, creating a future that held promise and giving him the hope that one day he might be able to emerge from the shadows of the past.

Brandon was so engrossed in his thoughts that he almost didn't notice the man seated under one of the giant live oaks, apparently reading a letter. That was odd enough; even odder was the realization that something about the man was familiar. As he passed by, Brandon's eyes widened.

Why was Phil Blakeslee here?

"It was kind of your parents to invite us to spend Christmas with you," Dorothy told Laura as she poured boiling water over the raisins for today's raisin pies. "Ma's been down in the dumps ever since she received Wyatt's letter."

Instead of recounting amusing stories of their travels, Wyatt explained that Polly was ill. It wasn't too serious, he claimed, but it was serious enough that he and Evelyn did not want to subject Polly to the rigors of travel. As a result, they would not be home for Christmas.

Though she claimed that change was a part of life and that she and Dorothy would still have a merry Christmas, Ma had been unable to hide her worry that Polly's illness was more serious than Wyatt admitted. For her part, Dorothy worried that not having Wyatt and Evelyn here would trigger another of Ma's spells. The Downeys' invitation had been another answer to prayer, for Ma had accepted it gratefully and began racking her brain to find the perfect gifts for Laura and her parents.

"They have everything," she had complained.

"No," Dorothy had countered, "they don't." They did not have any of the beautifully crafted garments Ma made with what she'd nicknamed the Mechanical Monster, her Singer sewing machine.

It hadn't taken long to convince Ma that the Downeys would appreciate having unique pieces of clothing, and she was now happily sewing a shirt for Mr. Downey and fancy petticoats for Laura and her mother. The danger Dorothy had feared was past. It would be a happy Christmas, albeit an unusual one.

Laura laid the egg whites she'd beaten aside and began measuring sugar. "I'm sorry about Polly, but I'm glad you and your mother will be able to come. Father had already invited Brandon, and I was afraid that he'd be the only guest. That would have been so awkward." Laura frowned. "I can't believe how silly I was, thinking Brandon was the right man for me."

Unsure how to reply, since they'd already had this discussion multiple times, Dorothy remained silent.

"I'm not certain how many guests there will be," Laura continued, "but Mother has invited Phil and Mrs. Lockhart. I thought you'd be pleased by that."

Dorothy tried not to frown at Laura's latest matchmaking effort. Though she'd told her countless times that she was not interested, Laura paid no attention to her protests. Instead, she pointed to the amount of time Phil spent at Polly's Place and how often he joined Dorothy when she took Nutmeg for a walk.

Though Dorothy had done nothing to encourage him and Nutmeg continued to growl every time he approached, Dorothy had not forbidden Phil to accompany them.

Her heart ached for the man who'd lost his sister at such a young age. And so, while she had no intention of being courted by him, or anyone for that matter, she would not reject his friendly overtures. Everyone needed friends.

Dorothy mustered a smile for her match-making friend. "Ma will enjoy Mrs. Lockhart's company." Though Mrs. Lockhart was considerably older than Ma, the two women never seemed at a loss for words.

"And you'll enjoy having Phil there." Laura appeared to believe that if she repeated something often enough, it would become true.

"I know we'll all enjoy Christmas," Dorothy said, her heart beating oddly at the thought of sharing it with Brandon. That was ridiculous, downright ridiculous, but try though she might, she could not suppress her anticipation.

Brandon frowned as he turned the corner. He ought to be happy or at least content. The number of subscribers to the *Chronicle* increased each week, and several businesses had expanded their advertisements. While he wasn't wealthy by any means, profits were now high enough that he could pay Dorothy a bit more for writing the Sociable.

He had found Christmas gifts for everyone on his list, and he was — or he thought he was — coming to grips with what had happened in Xavier. So, why was he feeling disgruntled?

Surely it wasn't because he'd seen Blakeslee near Grassey. He probably should have stopped and spoken to the man, but Blakeslee had looked as if he wanted to be alone.

And, though Brandon knew Dorothy was disappointed that her brother and his family were unable to return to Mesquite Springs for Christmas, that wasn't the cause of his discontent. He wished the little girl weren't sick, but Brandon could not regret the fact that Polly's illness meant that he would be spending part of Christmas with Dorothy. That would make the day special and would ease the awkwardness of being with Laura.

Maybe it was simply the knowledge that he didn't deserve to be happy. Because he did not.

"You look like you're trying to solve every one of the world's problems."

A bolt of pleasure shot through Brandon. He hadn't expected to encounter Dorothy while he walked, but here she was, with Nutmeg on her leash.

195

"Not all of them." Even though the day was still overcast and damp, as if rain were imminent, Brandon's mood had improved dramatically. "You're out earlier than usual, aren't you?" Since Polly's Place had closed mere minutes ago, normally Dorothy would be helping clean up.

"It wasn't my idea," she said with a rueful look at her dog. "Nutmeg's been restless all day. She whined when I put her outside, so I left her in the apartment, but she didn't seem much happier there. Every time I checked on her, she was either grooming herself or wandering around as if she were looking for something."

Dorothy tugged the leash slightly, encouraging Nutmeg to keep pace with them. "I thought a walk might help."

As Brandon gave the dog an appraising look, he remembered the time a neighbor's dog had chosen his parents' back porch to give birth. "I doubt that it will. I suspect she's getting close to whelping." What an odd conversation to be having with a woman. Most women would have been horrified. Dorothy simply nodded.

"I hope it's that. I'm anxious to see her puppies."

So was Brandon. While he had no intention of adopting one of them, he was curious to see what they'd look like. Nutmeg herself had improved greatly from the first time he'd seen her.

"Think about how Nutmeg must feel. She's the one that's been carrying all that extra weight." As he gestured toward the dog's lumpy and distended midsection, Dorothy laughed.

"You're right. She's the mother. I'm only the . . ." She paused, apparently searching for the correct word.

"Honorary aunt?" Brandon suggested.

"That sounds good."

What sounded good was the laughter that accompanied her words. In just a few minutes, Dorothy had managed to dissipate his malaise. What a wonderful friend she was.

Christmas Eve was one of her favorite days of the year. Dorothy smiled at her reflection in the mirror as she began to curl her hair. While a simple style was better suited to her days at the restaurant, tonight she wanted something more elegant.

She tested the curling iron, then wrapped a lock around it. In little more than half an hour, she would cross the street to join her mother for the traditional service. Pastor Coleman would read the second chapter of

Luke while the congregation lit candles, turning the formerly dark room into a beautifully illuminated sanctuary, a reminder of the advent of the Light of the world.

"Perfect," she murmured as she released the curl. It wouldn't be a perfect night, because Wyatt and Evelyn and little Polly weren't here to share it with her and Ma, but still . . .

Dorothy touched the end of the iron, testing its warmth, then stopped when she heard whimpers. Heedless of her half-curled hair, she rushed into the room where Nutmeg had made a nest in a rag-lined crate. Dorothy had checked on the dog two hours ago, but though she'd wanted to remain with her, Ma's warning that animals liked their privacy when giving birth had kept her from doing more than peeking into the doorway since then. Now, however, the whimpering that had turned to an excited bark seemed to invite her back.

Gripping the oil lamp, Dorothy knelt next to the crate and stared at the wriggling mass. "Oh, Nutmeg, you did it." Her eyes filled with tears of joy as she began to count. "Four, five, no, six. You've got six puppies." The tiny creatures clustered next to their obviously proud mother were all clean and appeared to have only one thought: eating.

"Good job, Nutmeg. You're such a good mother." Dorothy stroked the dog's head, relief vying with sheer happiness as she realized the wait was over. Despite all of Dorothy's fears, Nutmeg had safely delivered her puppies and appeared to be settling into her role as a mother. "You clever dog, you picked the perfect day to have your litter." And Dorothy couldn't wait to share the news.

When Nutmeg turned her attention to her puppies, effectively telling Dorothy she was no longer needed, Dorothy rose. "I'll be back as soon as the service ends." She smiled as she finished curling her hair. "Wait until Brandon hears about this."

"Six?" he asked two hours later. "What are you going to do with six puppies?"

The service was over, and they stood outside the church while Dorothy waited for her mother, who seemed engrossed in a conversation with Mrs. Lockhart. Though Ma was planning to return to the ranch, despite Dorothy's suggestion that she stay at the apartment tonight, Dorothy wanted to tell her about the puppies and invite her to see them.

"I thought I might give you one," she told Brandon. "My mother always said that the perfect gift is something the other person doesn't have."

As his lips twisted into a wry smile, Brandon shook his head. "She was right about that, but a puppy is not what I want for Christmas."

Though his voice was light, Dorothy sensed an intensity behind it. "What is?"

He shook his head again. "A man's entitled to a few secrets. All I'm going to say is that it's not a dog."

His gaze moved from her into the distance, and for a second Brandon appeared almost wistful. Dorothy's heart stuttered when she saw the direction of his gaze. Laura was standing with her parents, laughing at something one of them had said.

Oh no. What Brandon wanted for Christmas was Laura, but she no longer wanted him.

CHAPTER FOURTEEN

"The goose is absolutely delicious." Dorothy laid her fork and knife on her plate and smiled at Mrs. Downey. She wasn't exaggerating. The food was superb; the house was filled with festive decorations; everyone seemed to be overflowing with the joy of the season. It was only Dorothy who felt no desire to celebrate. For the first time since that horrible year after Pa's death, she found herself without an ounce of holiday spirit.

Laura's mother returned the smile. "I'd like to take credit, but Laura's the one who cooked the goose. I would never have thought to use a honey-ginger glaze."

Helping himself to another piece of the succulent bird, Brandon said, "I agree with Dorothy. This is the best goose I've ever eaten."

Phil snickered. "Tell the truth, Holloway. This is probably the only goose you've ever eaten."

201

"You're right. It is, but that doesn't make it any less delicious." Brandon turned to Laura. "My compliments to the chef. And my thanks to all of you for making my first Christmas in Mesquite Springs a memorable one."

His gaze moved around the table, focusing on each person in turn. Mrs. Downey was seated at the head of the table, Phil on her right, followed by Dorothy and Brandon, with Mr. Downey at the foot. The opposite side of the table held Ma, Mrs. Lockhart, and Laura.

It was no coincidence, Dorothy was certain, that Phil had been placed next to her and that Brandon was as far from Laura as possible. Laura was in matchmaker and self-preservation mode, trying to limit her contact with Brandon.

To Dorothy's surprise, Brandon did not seem to mind being separated from Laura. He appeared to be doing his best to include everyone in the discussion.

"I understand you have six puppies. Whatever are you going to do with all of them?" Mrs. Lockhart, who'd been engaged in a lively discussion of Pastor Coleman's sermon with Ma and Mr. Downey, shifted her attention to Dorothy. "Surely you're not planning to keep them."

Dorothy shook her head. Though Nutmeg's pups were the highlight of the day, she knew their stay with her was only temporary. For a week or so, they would do little more than sleep and eat, but Ma had told her that once their eyes opened and they could hear, they'd become more active. While they were undeniably adorable and would only become more so, she could not imagine caring for seven dogs.

"I'll need to find them homes. Would you be interested in one?" Dorothy had no doubt that Mrs. Lockhart would be a good pet owner.

The former schoolteacher's gray eyes misted with emotion. "If I were twenty years younger, I would, but I'm afraid a puppy would be too much responsibility for me. Taking care of my house is becoming a bit of a burden."

"I'm surprised to hear you say that, Virginia." Ma leaned forward, lessening the distance between them. "Your home is always spotless."

"That may be, but it takes its toll on me." Mrs. Lockhart gave Phil a fond glance. "Phil has been good enough to help me move furniture so that I can clean behind it, but I can't expect him to do that forever. I don't want to be a burden."

That was twice that Mrs. Lockhart had used the word *burden.* Repetition of any sort was unusual for her, but perhaps the deep emotions connected to her home had caused it.

"You're no burden," Phil said firmly. "You know I enjoy your company."

Though the widow smiled, she wagged a finger at him. "You should be spending time with a young lady. A man like you needs a wife by his side."

Laura's father appeared to second Mrs. Lockhart's words when he said, "If you find a woman as special as my Ida, don't let her go." His gaze moved from Phil to Brandon. "Marriage is one of God's gifts."

Though Brandon remained silent, his expression revealing the same wistfulness Dorothy had seen last night when he'd refused to explain his Christmas wish, Phil was quick to respond. "I'll take your words under advisement, sir."

Mrs. Lockhart gave him a look that would have quelled a rebellious pupil. "Be sure you invite me to the wedding."

"You'll be the first to know."

"Surely you mean the second." Ma winked at Phil as she said, "Your bride should be the first."

As she'd intended, everyone laughed, and

the conversation turned to a discussion of plans for the new year.

This was what Christmas was supposed to be — family and friends gathered together to commemorate the greatest gift the world had ever received. It might be the darkest time of the year, but the light of the Savior's birth brought hope and the promise of peace.

Dorothy took a sip of water, trying to relieve the lump that had lodged in her throat. Why, oh why, couldn't she concentrate on the wonder of Christmas and the delight of seeing Nutmeg with her babies rather than the hollow feeling that had plagued her ever since she'd seen the way Brandon had gazed at Laura last night?

Somehow, she managed to keep a smile fixed on her face as the seemingly endless meal continued. But when they'd finished dessert and enjoyed a final cup of coffee, she turned to Laura's mother.

"If you're sure I can't help you clean up, I want to get back to Nutmeg. It's time to feed her." Dorothy hoped her smile didn't look as false as it felt. "I'm afraid what I'm giving her to eat won't be as delicious as the goose and dried peach pie."

The sound of laughter followed her as she retrieved her coat and left the Downeys' mansion. Surely, the rest of the day would be easier.

It had been a better Christmas than he'd expected. Brandon slowed his pace to a walk, telling himself there was no need to run and that the spring would still be there whether he arrived in five minutes or ten. What he didn't know was whether he would find the peace that usually settled over him when he reached the town's namesake.

Though he'd gone there numerous times since he moved to Mesquite Springs, Brandon had never been able to decide whether it was the sound of bubbling water, the sight of the tall trees that ringed the spring, or the soft, almost lacy texture of the ferns that encroached on the water that soothed him. All he knew was that this was the one place in Mesquite Springs where the burdens of the past seemed lighter.

Though the sun set early these days, he would still have time to see if the spring's serenity would calm his turbulent thoughts. Brandon had never believed he was an envious man, but envy was the only way to describe the emotion that had speared him last night when he'd looked across the churchyard and seen the Downeys. The way Ida had tipped her head to look at her husband as he'd placed a gentle hand on her shoulder had filled Brandon with a longing so intense his knees had threatened to buckle.

That was what he wanted: marriage to a woman he loved the way Leonard did Ida, a woman whose love was equally strong. But with that longing had come the realization that he would not be ready for a love like that until he was able to put the past behind him.

When he reached the spring, Brandon took a deep breath, inhaling the scent of fresh water and the less pleasant aroma of decaying leaves, then let out a chuckle that held no mirth. The scents of the spring were a reflection of his own life, the juxtaposition of his new, seemingly bright future and his murky past.

Settling on the spot he'd claimed as his own, he leaned against the tallest tree's trunk and stared at the water. Exposed tree roots and rocks made this a less than comfortable spot, but Brandon did not mind. The view more than compensated for the rocky seat.

Even at this time of the year, water tumbled over a small cliff, its splashes disturbing the edge of the pool, while in the center, bubbles marked the spring's emergence from underground. The volume of water would change with the seasons. What would not was the sense of timelessness Brandon found whenever he visited the spring. It had been here before he was born. It would be here long after he was gone. Perhaps that was why he found peace here.

But today that peace eluded him. His thoughts did not clear when he stared at the water. Instead, the memory of Leonard and Ida's smiles and the sense that though they enjoyed their guests' company, they would be glad when they were alone and could have a private celebration taunted Brandon.

And then there was Dorothy. Though he had no idea what could have changed in such a short time, the happiness and sheer relief she'd displayed when she'd told him of Nutmeg's puppies was missing at dinner. She had tried to hide it, smiling at all the right times, even joining in the banter, but her smile was as false as Widow Lockhart's teeth. Dorothy was unhappy on a day that should have been filled with joy.

Brandon shifted, and as he did, the small box he'd left in his coat pocket brushed against his side. Was that the answer? Though he'd intended to give Dorothy and her mother their gifts at the same time that he'd given the Downeys theirs, when he'd realized there were other guests, Brandon had held back the Clarks' presents. He didn't give a hoot about Blakeslee, but he wouldn't insult Mrs. Lockhart by excluding her from the gift giving. It was one thing to offer his hosts tokens of his appreciation, another to provide gifts for only some of the guests.

Brandon had waited until Blakeslee and Mrs. Lockhart had left, then as Dorothy's mother prepared to depart, he'd handed her the box of peanut brittle. Only Dorothy's present remained.

He pushed himself to his feet, filled with a sense of urgency. It might be flouting etiquette, but he would not let Christmas Day end without giving Dorothy her gift.

She wouldn't cry. She wouldn't. Dorothy blinked furiously, refusing to let the tears fall. This was silly. More than silly. It was ridiculous. She had no reason to be unhappy. She was here with six adorable puppies and one very proud mama dog. Surely, that was reason enough to smile. But Dorothy was not smiling.

"I miss him too," Ma had said after she'd admired the puppies, "but Wyatt will be home soon."

Dorothy had simply nodded. It was best Ma not know that Dorothy's melancholy had nothing to do with Wyatt, that she was upset because Brandon, the man who was her friend as well as her boss, was in love with a woman who did not love him.

Dorothy hated the idea that he would not find the happiness he deserved. That was the reason — the only reason — she had found dinner at the Downeys' so difficult. She had seen Brandon's occasional wistfulness and had wished she could assure him there would be a happy ending, but she couldn't. She couldn't tell Brandon that her own feelings for him were deeper than Laura's. That was something a lady could not do. It would sound as if she wanted to marry him, and she did not. Definitely not. Dorothy couldn't marry anyone, not even someone as wonderful as Brandon.

If she had had any doubts about that, the way she was feeling today would have erased them. Here she was, waging a war against melancholy, confirming her deepest fears. Pa had been right. She was just like Ma.

Someone was knocking on the back door, but Dorothy was so lost in her thoughts that it took a few seconds for the sound to register. Brushing away the tears that had fallen despite her best efforts, she descended the stairs.

"Brandon." Her heart began to beat far too quickly. "I wasn't expecting you."

The smile he gave her made her pulse continue to accelerate. "A very reliable source told me that you have half a dozen puppies here, and I wondered if could sneak a peek."

To Dorothy's relief, Brandon's expression held no signs of the yearning she had seen last night and during dinner. This was the Brandon she knew and lov —

As firmly as she could, she bit off the last word. Love had no place in her thoughts.

Without waiting for her response, Brandon continued. "I know it's unconventional, but I'll only stay a minute. The gossips will never know I was here."

So what if they did? At the moment, Dorothy didn't care. Even if it was only because of the puppies, Brandon had chosen to spend another part of his day with her. "I've probably already scandalized them by helping with the paper." She opened the door fully. "Come in."

As he followed her up the stairs and into the room where Nutmeg held court in the middle of the crate, surrounded by six squirming balls of fur, Dorothy was aware of the scents that clung to him. Unless she was mistaken, he'd been to the spring and brushed up against a few ferns.

"Here they are."

"I didn't expect them to be so cute," Brandon admitted as he watched the puppies vie for position next to their mother.

"I can't decide which is the most adorable." Even though Ma had warned her it was too soon to touch them, Dorothy needed a way to dissipate the tension that had risen with each step they'd taken. She and Brandon had been alone and unchaperoned when she'd gone to the *Chronicle* office, but that had been different. This was her home. Being here with Brandon reminded her that he was not only her boss and her friend, he was also a man. A single man. An attractive single man.

Dorothy picked up a puppy, nuzzled it for a second, then deposited it back in the crate. "I want to name them, but I'm afraid if I do, I won't be able to give them away. Right now, I'm just calling them One through Six." She was babbling. She knew that, but somehow, she could not stop. It felt wrong and yet right to be here with Brandon, and that was so confusing that Dorothy didn't know what to do other than babble.

"They deserve better names than that." He didn't sound as flummoxed as she felt.

"You could name them after stars or constellations."

"Polaris, Capricorn, Sagittarius." Dorothy tipped her head to one side, pretending to consider his suggestion. "No, I don't think so."

"What about authors? You could have Thackery and Dickens."

"Don't forget Harriet Beecher Stowe."

Brandon's frown broke the lighthearted moment and reminded Dorothy of the need for propriety.

"We should probably go outside. There's no need to give the busybodies anything more to talk about."

"I agree. The dogs aren't the real reason I came."

Once again, Brandon had surprised her. "What was?"

He shook his head. "Patience, Dorothy. Patience." It was only when they were seated on the bench in front of the restaurant that he spoke again. "I wanted to wish you a merry Christmas and give you this." Brandon pulled a small box from his pocket. "Merry Christmas."

She stared at it, practically speechless. While she knew he'd given Ma a box of candy, supposedly to thank her for recommending the candy shop in Grassey, Dorothy had not expected or even dreamt that he would have a Christmas present for her.

"I don't know what to say."

Brandon chuckled. "You don't need to say anything. Just open it." Though her fingers shook, Dorothy managed to untie the ribbon and remove the lid, revealing the contents. "Oh my!"

Slowly, almost reverently, she lifted the china figurine from the box, turning it so she could admire it from every angle. Though the mother dog bore little resemblance to Nutmeg, her protective posture and the way she looked at her puppies mirrored Nutmeg's behavior this morning.

"I don't know how to thank you, Brandon." This time, the tears that filled Dorothy's eyes were tears of joy. "You couldn't have chosen a more perfect gift."

Heedless of the dictates of proper behavior, she laid her hand on Brandon's and gave it a squeeze. "I'll never forget this Christmas."

CHAPTER FIFTEEN

It was time.

Phil grinned as he opened the door to
Polly's Place, inhaling the delicious aroma
of roast pork. No doubt about it: Laura
Downey was a mighty fine cook. The man
who married her would never have to worry
about vermin-infested biscuits or oatmeal
so thin it was little more than hot water.

It was a shame, a mighty big shame, that
he wasn't ready to marry, but Mr. K had
been adamant about that. "No personal
entanglements," he'd declared. "They slow
a man down or — even worse — they can
trip him up." Still, a little dalliance might
be . . . wrong. Phil completed the sentence.
He couldn't afford to be distracted, not now
when it was time to resume his campaign
against Holloway.

"Your usual table?" Dorothy asked when
she'd greeted him.

He shook his head and gestured toward

215

the table where three men appeared deep in thought. "I'd like to meet them." He managed a self-deprecating smile. "Maybe they'll be interested in a sketch or two. Christmas is over, but there's always Valentine's Day."

A commission for a sketch might be nice, but it wasn't the reason Phil wanted to join these men. He listened to stories of crops and cattle, feigning interest until there was a lull in the conversation. Then, as casually as he could, he asked, "Do you reckon there's any truth to the story that that newspaperman was driven out of his last town?"

"You're back!" Dorothy threw her arms around the tall, dark-haired man who stood in the doorway, a wide grin on his face, a blonde on either side of him. After what had seemed like an endless separation, her brother, his wife, and their adopted daughter had returned to Mesquite Springs. They'd missed Christmas and New Year's, but here they were on the first Monday of 1857. What a wonderful start to the year!

"We arrived about an hour ago," Wyatt said.

"But I didn't want to come while Polly's Place was still open," his wife chimed in.

"She thought that might distract you."

"I didn't want us to be an interruption." As Evelyn continued the explanation, Dorothy's smile widened. Her brother and Evelyn were already sounding like an old married couple, finishing each other's sentences.

"There's so much to tell you," Evelyn said. For the first time since they'd all entered the kitchen, Dorothy's adopted niece spoke. Even though it had been less than a minute, that was a surprisingly long time for Polly to remain silent. Once she'd realized that she was safe in Mesquite Springs, she had become a chatterbox, at least when she was with either Evelyn or Dorothy.

"I was sick, but Papa Wyatt let me have candy on Christmas," Polly announced, her pride evident.

Evelyn rolled her eyes. "I told him he was spoiling her, but he won't listen."

"I listen. I listen lots." Polly cocked her head to one side as if trying to distinguish a sound. "What's that?"

"It sounds like a dog." The look Wyatt gave Dorothy said he didn't believe what he was hearing, even though Dorothy had told him about Nutmeg's arrival and the fact that she would have puppies.

"Actually, there are seven," Dorothy said, watching her brother's expression change

217

from disbelief to amusement. "Nutmeg had six puppies on Christmas Eve."

"Puppies!" Polly clapped her hands and headed toward the stairway. "I want one!" She raced up the stairs, leaving the adults to trail her.

"Look, Evelyn!" Polly cried when everyone had reached the apartment she had once shared with Evelyn. "They're in my room." She stood in the doorway, staring at the crate where six wiggling animals crowded around their mother.

It was only in the last few days that the puppies had opened their eyes and appeared to hear Dorothy's approach as well as smell her. They were sleeping less than they had at first, but most of their waking time was still devoted to eating. Now, with nothing but food on their minds, they paid no attention to Polly.

"It's not your room anymore," Evelyn reminded her. "We have a new house."

Polly wrinkled her nose and began to pout. "But we don't got puppies. I wanna stay here."

Before Dorothy could stop her, the child raced to the crate and reached inside, obviously wanting to pick up at least one of the puppies.

"No, Polly." Though Evelyn's warning

218

went unheeded, when Nutmeg growled and bared her teeth, the child shrieked and jumped backwards.

"They're still babies." Dorothy took Polly's hand and led her to the doorway. From here they could see into the crate but were far enough away that Nutmeg would not be distressed. "She doesn't like strangers touching them."

"I'm not a stranger. I'm Polly. I won't hurt them." The words spewed from Polly's mouth as she vented her frustration.

An image of herself at the same age flashed before Dorothy. She'd been determined to climb into the stall with a newborn foal, convinced the baby horse was the perfect size for her to ride. Fortunately for both her and the foal, Pa had caught her before she'd gotten into the stall.

It had strained her six-year-old patience to wait, but eventually Pa had let her join him when he cared for the mare and the foal. Even now, years later, Dorothy smiled at the memory of how proud she'd been the first time she'd patted the foal's velvety nose. Polly deserved a similar experience.

"Nutmeg needs to get to know you before she'll let you hold them." Dorothy gave Evelyn a questioning look. "If Evelyn agrees, you can visit the puppies every day after school. When they're old enough, you can help me take care of them."

Her face beaming with anticipation, the little girl tugged on her adopted mother's hand. "Can I, Evelyn? Can I?"

Wyatt and Evelyn exchanged an amused glance, as if they'd expected this reaction and were becoming accustomed to the idea that their family might soon include a small dog.

"Yes, you may," Evelyn said, "but right now we need to leave the puppies alone with their mother."

When they were once more in the kitchen, Wyatt turned to Dorothy. "I imagine you and Evelyn have some things to discuss, and you don't need me for that. I'll take Polly home." He gave Evelyn another of those glances that married couples seemed to use for wordless communication, then smiled at Dorothy. "I might stop by the newspaper office tomorrow morning. I want to meet the man who's publishing my sister's stories."

Unbidden, a blush stained Dorothy's cheeks. Oh, how she hoped no one noticed. It was ridiculous the way just the thought of Brandon made her so flustered. "Brandon. His name is Brandon Holloway."

Wyatt's grin left no doubt that he'd seen

her blush. "I know. You must have mentioned him a dozen times in every letter."

"I did not! You're exaggerating."

"All right." A shrug accompanied Wyatt's words. "Maybe I am exaggerating. It might have been only eleven." Before Dorothy could react to his teasing, he chuckled and ushered Polly out the door. "Goodbye, sister dear."

Even Evelyn was laughing as she poured water for tea into the kettle and set it on the stove to boil. "Thanks to that brother of yours, I've laughed more in the last year than I did in the rest of my life. I'm so thankful I met both of you." She reached for a teapot and spooned the fragrant black leaves into it. "There aren't enough words to thank you for keeping Polly's Place open while we were gone."

"I was glad to help. You know that."

Evelyn nodded and set two cups and saucers on the table. "That's what I want to talk about. But first, tell me about that porcelain figurine I saw upstairs. I know it wasn't here last fall."

Dorothy felt herself blush again. "It was a Christmas gift."

Evelyn nodded as if she'd expected that. "From whom?"

"From Brandon."

"I see."

But Dorothy did not. She was still puzzled by the gift and why, though Brandon had given everyone else candy, he'd chosen something more permanent for her. It made no sense. If Laura was the woman he loved, surely he would have given her something more special, but he had not. And, though she had been watching carefully, Dorothy had seen no further evidence of the longing that had been so evident on Christmas Eve. Had it been nothing more than her imagination, or was Brandon like Laura, falling in and out of love quickly?

"We need to talk about Polly's Place." Evelyn's words wrenched Dorothy back to the present and sent a sinking feeling to her stomach. Though she'd known they would have this conversation, she hadn't thought it would be this soon.

"I know that running a restaurant isn't how you want to spend your life. Judging from your letters, you're much happier writing for the *Chronicle* than you are working here."

"That's true." Dorothy wouldn't lie. What she liked best about Polly's Place was the apartment. Living in town gave her an independence she'd never experienced and one she relished. If she no longer worked at the restaurant, there would be no reason to stay here.

The furrows that formed between Evelyn's eyes told Dorothy she was choosing her next words carefully. "You've been a big help to me. I couldn't have gotten Polly's Place established without you, but . . ."

"You don't need me, because you have Laura. She's a much better cook than I am, so it only makes sense that she should be your assistant." Until she marries. Though the words were on the tip of Dorothy's tongue, she bit them back. If Laura wanted to share her hopes with Evelyn, she would.

"I wouldn't have phrased it quite that way."

"That's because you're a lady. But you're right. I'd rather be visiting people to get material for the Sociable than serving meals to customers."

Evelyn poured the water into the teapot and brought it to the table before she spoke. "Wyatt and I talked about this, and we wondered whether you'd like to stay in the apartment. I'm sure your mother would prefer you return to the ranch, but you're welcome to live here if that's what you want." She paused for a second. "You'd be doing us a favor. Even though there's little crime in Mesquite Springs, the restaurant would be safer if you were here."

Another prayer had been answered. Feeling as if an enormous weight had been lifted from her shoulders, Dorothy smiled. "You're right. Ma won't be pleased, but I'd like to stay. It'll give me more time to interview people and write the articles."

"And more time to spend with the *Chronicle*'s editor."

"He's my boss." Dorothy said, hoping her response did not sound defensive. The truth was, she looked forward to every minute she spent with Brandon. They didn't always agree, but their discussions were always exhilarating. And though she was an employee, not a true partner, Brandon never treated her as anything other than his equal.

Ma still viewed her as a child, Wyatt as his little sister, but Brandon acted as if Dorothy were an adult. An intelligent adult with opinions worth considering. That was wonderful.

"I suspect he's more than your boss." The smile that hovered on Evelyn's lips told Dorothy she had not succeeded in deflecting her friend's questions. Like Wyatt, Evelyn seemed to believe Dorothy's relationship with Brandon was more than she'd admitted. They were wrong. Of course they were.

"Brandon and I are friends. Just friends."

Evelyn shook her head. "You can say what you want, but I know what I see. You're a different woman from the one you were when I left Mesquite Springs. Your eyes sparkle more, your cheeks are rosier, your lips are softer."

She paused to check the tea's steeping before she delivered her final salvo. "You can try to deny it, but everything about you tells the truth: you're a woman in love."

The sound of the front door closing carried into the kitchen, where Brandon had just finished making another pot of coffee. It had a been a long night, printing the *Chronicle,* but he'd met the deadline. Now he needed more coffee to get through the rest of the day.

He grabbed a second mug along with the pot, planning to offer it to his visitor. When he strode into the front room, Brandon blinked in surprise at the sight of a man with an unmistakable resemblance to Dorothy. He hadn't heard of his return.

"Welcome back, Mayor Clark." Brandon put the mugs on the table and shook Wyatt's hand.

The man who topped Brandon's height by an inch or so shook his head. "You've got that backwards. I should be welcoming you to Mesquite Springs, but it seems I'm several months too late to do that." He held up the latest issue of the *Chronicle.* "From what I hear, you've already made your mark on the town."

Brandon wondered how long Wyatt and his family had been back and what he'd heard. "A friendly face is always welcome," he said as noncommittally as he could.

Wyatt accepted the coffee and took a long swig. "I wanted to thank you for hiring my sister. You're making one of her dreams come true."

"And she's helping make mine a success. Besides being a good writer, she has a way with people. I've seen her smooth over difficult situations and calm folks who were irritated. She's very good at that."

Wyatt nodded slowly. "Our father used to say she was a peacemaker, but I have to admit I never saw that side of her." He chuckled. "Most of the time, she was just my pesky little sister, and I was doing my best to stay away from her. I'm glad everything's working out for Dorothy and the *Chronicle,* but she's not the reason I came today." He tapped his fingers against the paper that he'd laid on the table. "I wanted to tell you what a great job you're doing.

I've read a number of papers, and this is the best-written. It also has one of the best layouts I've seen." Wyatt drained the mug and plunked it onto the table. "I don't want to keep you from your work. Once we get settled, Evelyn and I hope you'll join us for supper some evening. I'd like to get to know you better."

"Thanks. I'd like that." As the door closed behind the mayor, Brandon grinned. Even though the visit had been a brief one, it had shown him that Wyatt Clark was someone he wanted as a friend.

CHAPTER SIXTEEN

"If you're looking for another story," Mrs. Downey said when Dorothy entered the mercantile, "we're all out."

Because it was the beginning of the year, she had chosen beginnings as the theme for this month's special Sociable column. The Downeys had given her several amusing anecdotes about the mistakes they'd made when they established the mercantile, and the Smiths had shared their fear of failure when they'd decided to open a livery in addition to the blacksmith shop. Dorothy needed only one more and was hoping that Mrs. Lockhart would provide it. Although so far the widow had been unwilling to contribute to the paper, perhaps this month would be different.

"That's not why I'm here," Dorothy assured Laura's mother. "Mr. Downey said he'd be willing to sell copies of the *Chronicle*. I wanted to talk to him about that."

"Ah yes. Leonard mentioned that." Mrs. Downey stressed her husband's first name. Though they'd both suggested Dorothy address them by their Christian names, she found it difficult to be so informal with people her mother's age.

"I wouldn't do that if I were you." Miss Jacobs, who'd obviously been listening to the conversation, interrupted. "I'm planning to cancel my subscription, and you can be certain that I will tell everyone I know to do the same."

Dorothy stared at the woman, unable to believe what she'd heard. For some reason, Miss Jacobs had transferred her disapproval from Pastor Coleman to Brandon.

"Why would you do that?" Dorothy asked. Surely it wasn't because she had not been featured in either the November or December themed Sociable. Though Dorothy had invited her to share a story, she had refused.

"I should think that the reason would be self-evident." Miss Jacobs squared her shoulders and glared at Dorothy. "I will not support a man who used his newspaper to spread lies. As for you, Miss Clark, you should know better than to associate with someone who was driven out of his home. We don't need people like that in Mesquite Springs."

By now, the other customers had abandoned all pretense of shopping and were listening to Miss Jacobs. Dorothy couldn't — wouldn't — let her continue.

"I don't know where you heard that story, but I assure you, it is not true. Brandon left Xavier because his father died and the memories were too difficult for him." He hadn't actually said that, but Dorothy had seen his sorrow each time he mentioned his father and knew that — not lies — must be what had driven him from Xavier.

"Brandon is an honest man. He would never print lies."

"Brandon, hah!" Miss Jacobs scoffed. "I'm surprised your mother approves of such familiarity. I thought she raised you better than that." With an angry flounce, Miss Jacobs turned away from Dorothy and faced the other customers. "Don't be fooled by what you've read so far. That man is a liar and a troublemaker who deserves to be run out of town. Cancel your subscriptions, ladies."

Though Mrs. Downey had attempted to defuse the situation after Miss Jacobs stormed out of the mercantile, telling the other women that she and her husband had complete confidence in Brandon and his integrity, Dorothy knew the damage had been done. The story of the older woman's accusations would spread through town before the sun set. There was nothing Dorothy could do to stop it, but perhaps if Brandon were forewarned, he could mitigate the damage.

"What's wrong?" Brandon asked when she entered the *Chronicle*'s office. "And don't try to deny it. Your face tells me you're upset."

"I am." Dorothy had no intention of denying anything. "Charity Jacobs is spreading some vicious lies about you and urging everyone to cancel their subscriptions. I think you should print a rebuttal."

"I won't do that."

"I don't understand. Why won't you? You don't even know what she said."

"It doesn't matter." Brandon gestured toward the two chairs visitors normally occupied. "Let's sit down."

He waited until Dorothy had settled in one chair, then took the other, leaning forward ever so slightly as if he wanted to close the distance between them. "Tell me what she said."

"She claimed you were driven out of Xavier because you printed lies in the *Record*."

Brandon was silent for a moment, and those blue eyes that Dorothy had seen warm with humor and compassion now darkened with pain, leaving her dreading whatever Brandon was about to say.

"Part of that is true."

"No!" Dorothy refused to believe him. This man was not a liar, and while it was true that he'd left Xavier, she was certain it had been of his own volition.

"I don't know where she heard the story, but there is a grain of truth to it. I did not print lies, but I printed an editorial that angered the townspeople so much that they did things that forced me to leave."

Brandon paused. "I'm surprised she didn't tell you that I killed my father."

Dorothy gasped. The whole idea was preposterous. If Brandon's goal had been to shock her, he'd succeeded. "Why would she say that? That's the biggest lie yet."

"Not really. There's more than a grain of truth in that too." Brandon's voice was as somber as the subject. "I told you I left Xavier after my father died, but I never told you how he died or that I was responsible."

This was the most bizarre conversation of her life, the subject so unthinkable that Dorothy might have believed she was having a nightmare. But the smell of ink and burned coffee and the feel of the smooth wooden chair arms she was gripping so tightly told her this was no dream.

"I don't believe you."

It was impossible that the man she'd come to know so well, the man who'd shown such kindness to everyone, could have killed his father or even contributed to his death.

"Believe me. It happened." Brandon's voice was harsh, filled with anger, anger that he'd directed at himself. "If it weren't for my actions, Pa would still be alive."

The words formed complete, grammatically correct sentences, but they made no sense. Though it was clear that Brandon believed them, Dorothy did not. "What happened?"

He inhaled sharply, then forced his lips into a smile that held no mirth. "It all started with that book you admire so much."

"Uncle Tom's Cabin?" Dorothy could not imagine what role the story of Uncle Tom, Eliza, and the others could have played in Brandon's father's death.

"That's it. Mrs. Stowe's masterpiece or the most despicable piece of prose in the English language, depending on your point of view."

Brandon rose and walked to the window, as if he sought an answer from the street.

When it was not forthcoming, he turned and faced Dorothy.

"You know that Xavier is in the heart of plantation country, so you can imagine how most people felt about slavery. I'd grown up surrounded by it, and even though in my heart I knew it was wrong — that no one has the right to own another person — I didn't do anything about it. When I read *Uncle Tom's Cabin,* I knew it was time to take a stand. That's why I used it as the basis for an editorial. That was going to be my first step toward actually denouncing slavery. As it turned out, I didn't have the chance to take the second step."

"Had anyone read *Uncle Tom's Cabin?* Wyatt said it was hard to find a copy."

Brandon shook his head. "They hadn't read it. That was the point I made. I recommended people read it if only to understand how Northerners perceived what some have called our peculiar institution: slavery. My hope, of course, was that it would open their eyes as it had mine."

"But your suggestion was not well received." Dorothy had no difficulty imagining that. This must have been the article he'd written that had inflamed Xavier's residents. She could even believe that while passions were high someone had suggested

234

Brandon leave town, but she did not see how an editorial about *Uncle Tom's Cabin* related to his father's death.

"Not well received is a major understatement." Brandon returned to the chair, his posture still tense. "People stormed the newspaper office, demanding that I print a retraction. I refused."

Of course, he had. Dorothy would have expected nothing else from Brandon. "Rightly so. The Constitution guarantees freedom of speech."

A soft scoff was his first response. "Those are simply words on a piece of paper, just like the ones on the Declaration of Independence that talk about life, liberty, and the pursuit of happiness. They have no meaning unless people agree to them. The good citizens of Xavier did not agree to my right to express my opinion."

Brandon paused for a moment, his expression leaving no doubt that he was remembering what must have been one of the most difficult parts of his life.

"Some threatened tar and feathers, but those were empty threats." His lips tightened, as if he were trying to control his emotions. "I thought the controversy had died down, but it was only seething."

He paused for a second. "Everyone in

town knew that Pa and I had supper with friends every Thursday. They counted on the house being empty when they came, but it wasn't. Pa had been having one of his dizzy spells, so he stayed home."

This was the first Dorothy had heard of Mr. Holloway suffering from dizziness, but now was not the time to ask Brandon for more details of his father's health.

"As best I can piece it together, he heard the mob breaking everything they could get their hands on. It seems they were determined to stop the paper one way or another. When Pa saw someone raise a hammer to destroy the press, he tried to stop him, but before he could reach the man, Pa fell to the floor. Doc told me it was apoplexy and that he died immediately."

Brandon recited the events that had occurred that evening as calmly as if he were discussing last week's weather, but Dorothy saw the effort that apparent calmness required.

"The crowd fled when they realized what was happening — cowards every one of them. I heard later that no one even tried to revive Pa. 'Serves him right,' someone is reported to have said."

Dorothy could not fathom such cruelty. Surely there had been one kind person in the mob, one person who was willing to be a Good Samaritan, but it seemed there had not been. Though she'd never encountered a mob, she had heard that men lost their inhibitions when they joined one. Brandon's story appeared to confirm that.

He had not yet finished. Though his eyes glistened with unshed tears, Brandon's voice was even as he said, "When I returned home, the sheriff was waiting. The press was untouched, but my father was gone. That was when I resolved I would never again do anything that might divide a town. I will never impose my beliefs on another person. I will not create controversy, and I will not do anything that might endanger others."

"So, you won't defend yourself?"

"No. People will have to weigh the evidence and make up their minds."

"But they don't have the facts."

"They've seen the kind of paper I produce. That should be enough."

Perhaps Brandon was right. The complaints about Pastor Coleman had petered out. Perhaps this would too. But Dorothy didn't want to take that chance. Even if he wouldn't defend himself, she would do everything she could to counteract Miss Jacobs's lies. Perhaps she could learn who'd started the story and why, but right now all

237

that mattered was helping Brandon.

Dorothy reached out and laid her hand on his. It might be forward, but she had to do something to show him that someone cared — that she cared. The people in Xavier may have stood by and watched an innocent man die, but she would not let this innocent man believe he was alone.

Poor Brandon. Though she had grieved when her father had been the victim of a senseless killing, Dorothy had never blamed herself for Pa's murder. Brandon, however, was haunted by a misplaced belief that he was responsible for his father's death.

She might not agree, but Dorothy understood why he refused to write an editorial or take a stand on a controversial issue. Brandon's sorrow was deeper than she'd realized, leaving him with unhealed wounds, and though she wished she could heal them, she could not. All she could do was try to offer comfort.

"Oh, Brandon, I'm so sorry. I don't know what else to say. It's a horrible story."

He looked at her hand, as if suddenly aware that she had placed it on his, but he did not draw his away. "There's nothing to say. If I hadn't been so pigheaded, so sure I was helping the town by presenting another view on an important issue, my father would still be alive."

And that was the crux of the problem. Brandon believed that, and until he could forgive himself for what he believed he'd done, he would find no peace.

"You don't know that, Brandon. Apoplexy can strike at any time."

He shook his head slowly, his lips contorted with pain. "That's what the doctor said, but I know better. God was punishing me for my pride. That's why he let Pa die."

CHAPTER SEVENTEEN

She hadn't run away. She hadn't showered him with pity. She hadn't spouted platitudes. Instead, she had tried to make sense of what he'd endured. *Endured* had been her word. Dorothy had sat there, her hand on top of his, its warmth giving him comfort he did not deserve, telling him he'd done nothing wrong.

According to Dorothy, he'd been a hero, trying to open people's minds. While it was true that that had been his goal, Brandon didn't consider it heroic. He'd believed it was his responsibility.

According to Dorothy, Pa had been proud of him. That much was true. Pa had applauded his editorial, saying the town needed to understand what was causing the increasing hostility between the North and the South.

According to Dorothy, Brandon had not been responsible for Pa's death. If anyone was responsible, it was the mob. That's where she was wrong. No matter what she said, Brandon knew that if he hadn't written that editorial, if he hadn't left Pa alone that night, his father would still be alive. He would carry that guilt for the rest of his life.

But, though regrets and recriminations still weighed on him, Brandon was buoyed by Dorothy's faith in him. It might be undeserved, but it was like a ray of light, helping to chase away the shadows.

Dorothy Clark was an extraordinary woman.

After what had been the most emotional morning she could remember, Dorothy had returned to the apartment, recognizing that her thoughts were too turbulent for her to try to interview anyone. Instead, she had planned to work on the stories she already had for the Sociable. But even that proved impossible, and so she'd spent most of the day watching Nutmeg and the puppies while she tried and failed to find new ways to convince Brandon that he had been a victim, not a villain.

Today was a new day, and despite the sleepless night, she was determined to get her final story. Ma had suggested asking Mrs. Lockhart if she would be willing to talk about her first years in Mesquite Springs and the house she and her husband built. "Until Leonard and Ida built their mansion, the Lockhart house was the finest in town," Ma had said. "We all wondered why they wanted such a big one when they had no children. Maybe Virginia will tell you."

And so, Dorothy was heading to Mrs. Lockhart's home, hoping for a story but — more importantly — hoping to clear her head. Brandon's revelation wasn't the only thing that had disturbed her sleep. Evelyn's words had been just as disturbing. "You're a woman in love" continued to echo through Dorothy's brain.

Evelyn was mistaken. That was understandable. After all, she was a newlywed, still basking in the glow of those wonderful first few months as a bride. It was only natural that Evelyn would want her friend to experience the same happiness. That was why she was imagining love where none existed.

Dorothy exhaled the breath she hadn't realized she was holding as she rounded the corner from River onto Hill. There was no need to tell Evelyn she was wrong. Dorothy would simply pretend she hadn't heard her sister-in-law's silly words. The reason she had reacted so strongly to Brandon's distress was that he was a good friend, not that she was in love with him.

Her good humor restored, Dorothy was smiling when she saw Phil emerge from Mrs. Lockhart's house.

"Good morning." Phil seemed more cheerful than normal. "I hadn't expected to see you out at this hour. Shouldn't you be at the restaurant?"

Dorothy shook her head. "Since my sister-in-law's back, I don't work there anymore." Though she didn't owe him an explanation, Dorothy continued. "I was on my way to see Mrs. Lockhart about an article for the *Chronicle*."

Furrows formed between Phil's eyes. "You might want to wait a day or two. I just took some mail to her, and she seemed preoccupied with it."

"Thanks for the warning." Dorothy did not want to interrupt Mrs. Lockhart if she was busy, for if there was one thing she had learned, it was the importance of choosing the right time to interview people. Instead, she would continue around the block and stop at the dressmaker's shop to see whether Mrs. Steiner had a story to recount.

Phil's next words stopped her. "May I escort you back to Polly's Place? There's something I'd like to discuss with you."

Her curiosity aroused, Dorothy nodded. "Of course."

They walked for a few yards with Phil talking about Christmas dinner at the Downeys' and the cold front that had made New Year's one of the chilliest the old-timers could recall. Those were ordinary subjects, nothing Dorothy would call a discussion.

"You said there was something you wanted to discuss," she reminded Phil as they approached the park.

"I do." He appeared abashed. "It's a bit awkward, though. I don't like asking you for a favor, especially after you gave me the idea of selling sketches to accompany the Christmas stories, but the truth is, I need your help."

His expression reminded Dorothy of Nutmeg the first day she'd seen her, hopeful and yet apprehensive. "I can't make any promises," she told Phil, "but I'll help you if I can."

"Fair enough." He took a deep breath, as if fortifying himself for what was to come. "I want to stay in Mesquite Springs, but to do that, I need more money. The only way I can think of to earn it is to sell illustrations to the *Chronicle*. I know they'd make the paper better."

Dorothy could not disagree with that. Illustrated newspapers were more visually appealing. "It's a good idea."

Phil practically preened. "I thought you'd agree. The problem is, when I mentioned it to Holloway, he refused. That's why I need your help. You're the only person who could change his mind."

But that was something Dorothy would not do. A week ago, she might have tried, but Brandon had enough turmoil in his life right now. She would not add to it.

"I'm sorry, Phil, but I can't help you with that."

Oddly, he did not seem disappointed.

Phil nodded when he received the note from Mrs. Lockhart, asking him to join her for supper. Far from being surprised, he'd expected it, just as he'd expected Dorothy's refusal to intervene with Holloway. He'd been fishing, and she'd taken the bait. The way she'd looked when he'd mentioned the newspaperman's name had confirmed Phil's suspicions: Dorothy Clark had more than a professional interest in Holloway. And, unless he was sorely mistaken, those feelings were reciprocated. Perfect. Phil had been searching for Holloway's weak point, and he'd found it. Now the only question was how to exploit it. Jealousy? Possibly. But first he had to have dinner with the lonely widow.

Half an hour later, he knocked on her front door.

"Come in, come in. The ham is almost done, and I've made scalloped potatoes." As always, Mrs. Lockhart sounded a little breathless, making Phil wonder just how long she would be walking this earth. He needed to get her to sign the papers soon, because there was no telling what might happen to the house otherwise.

"You didn't need to go to all that trouble."

"Nonsense. It's no trouble. I enjoy having you here." The widow led the way into the dining room and gestured toward the chair she'd designated as his. "Please sit down. I have so much to tell you."

When she'd placed the food on the table and waited until Phil rose to pull out her chair and help her sit, Mrs. Lockhart inclined her head. "Will you ask the blessing?"

He did, even though it made him feel like a hypocrite. It had been more years than he wanted to count since he'd trusted God and believed God would listen to him, but if it made the widow happy to hear him pray, he would.

"This is delicious," Phil said, and for once he was being honest. "It's the best food in Mesquite Springs."

His hostess and the key to making Mr. K happy blushed with pleasure. "You know I like to cook, but I've been thinking about what you said, that I ought to let someone else do the work." She cut a tiny piece of ham, leaving it on her plate as she continued. "I wasn't sure it was the right thing to do, so I prayed about it. I was looking for a sign, and at first, the letter you brought me seemed like one, but now I'm not sure."

"That dirty old letter? I almost didn't bring it. It looked so disreputable."

The letters had been the most difficult part of the plan so far. Mr. K had insisted that the ones for the ranchers and the one Mrs. Lockhart received appear to have come from different people in different parts of the country, so Phil had carefully drawn postmarks on the envelopes, then rubbed dirt on several of them, grass stains on others, all designed to make it seem that the letters had traveled a long distance. The final step had been to deliver each of the letters, pretending that he'd told the Mesquite Springs postmaster whom he'd be visiting and had offered to take any mail they might have.

The ranchers were so unaccustomed to receiving mail that they'd opened their letters in Phil's presence and asked his advice. He'd feigned reluctance to offer it but had admitted that the offers they'd received for their land seemed generous. Then, claiming that he wanted to be helpful, he'd offered to carry their responses back to the post office. Because their offers supposedly came from Mississippi, he would wait another couple weeks before crafting the final letters and delivering them along with the payments from Mr. K.

Mrs. Lockhart fixed a steely gaze on Phil. "It's a good thing you brought that letter. It was from some lawyer back East who says his client wants to build a hotel out here. I don't know how it happened, but he heard my house would be ideal, and he wants to buy it."

She paused long enough to butter a roll. "What do you think? Should I sell?"

Yes, yes, yes. But Phil knew better than to let his enthusiasm show. The widow had to believe this was her decision. He kept his expression neutral as he asked, "What do you think?"

"I'm not certain. Timothy built this house

for me when we were first married. I always thought I'd live out my life here."

Phil took another bite of the potatoes, chewing slowly, as if he were considering Mrs. Lockhart's concerns. "But it is a lot of work. You've said that."

"That's true." Doubt clouded her eyes. "I'm still not certain I should move. I don't know whether Timothy would have approved."

Phil forbore reminding Mrs. Lockhart that her husband was beyond approving or disapproving of anything she did. He forced furrows between his eyes as he pretended to concentrate on her dilemma. "Maybe this is more than an answer to prayer. Maybe it's the opportunity to leave a legacy to the town."

The spark of interest in her eyes encouraged Phil to continue with the speech he'd rehearsed. "You know Mesquite Springs needs a hotel. If the lawyer's client turns your house into one, the town will benefit. It'll bring more business to Mesquite Springs, and many people will be able to enjoy your home."

She stiffened her spine and pursed her lips, sure signs that she wasn't happy. But then she nodded. "You're right. I'll do it. I'll write to the attorney this evening."

Taking another bite of ham to hide the grin that threatened to break out, Phil felt himself relax. "I'll be happy to take your letter to the post office."

"Thank you, Phil. You're so thoughtful."

If only she knew what he was really thinking.

Chapter Eighteen

"Oh, Brandon, you ought to see them. They're so cute."

Brandon managed a smile, grateful that Dorothy's mood did not match his. "What are they doing now?" He had no need to ask who they were. Nutmeg's pups were the one thing that never failed to make Dorothy smile like that.

"They're starting to stand up. Of course, they're still so wobbly that they topple over as soon as they try to straighten their legs. When that happens, they wear the cutest expressions." Dorothy, the woman who never giggled, giggled. "Come see them."

Why not? A few minutes away from the office and the ledgers that held only bad news might be what he needed. Perhaps the sight of puppies scrambling to stand would soothe his worries.

"All right. Let's go."

When Dorothy turned to leave by the

front door, Brandon shook his head. "We'll take the shortcut." Though she looked askance at the idea of entering the private part of the building, he was quick to reassure her. "I doubt even the worst gossip in Mesquite Springs would see anything wrong with you walking through my kitchen."

The one oddity about the house was that the center hall ended in a closet, not the back door. To reach that, he had to go through part of the kitchen. Despite the minor inconvenience, leaving through the rear entrance and cutting across the yard to the alley was much faster than walking around the block.

"You ought to use the back door when you come," he told Dorothy. "I lock the front door when I'm gone, but I always leave the back open."

Once again, Dorothy appeared uncomfortable. "I'd rather come when you're here."

"And I'd hate to miss you." That was an understatement. Dorothy's visits were the bright spots of his days. "But think about using the back way. It'll save you time."

She nodded. When they reached the alley, to Brandon's surprise, Dorothy turned toward the restaurant's shed rather than the building itself. The reason was quickly apparent. Nutmeg and her brood now lived there.

"The puppies were fine in the apartment," Dorothy explained, "but Nutmeg was becoming anxious. I could see that she missed being outdoors during the day, so I decided to bring them all here." She gave the dogs, who were attempting to climb out of the crate, a fond glance. "Aren't they adorable?"

They were, but what was even more adorable was the sight of Dorothy gazing at them, love shining from her eyes. Surely Laura was mistaken. Surely this woman who had so much love to give wanted a family of her own.

"What do you think?"

Brandon frowned, realizing he'd missed something. "I'm sorry. My mind was drifting. What did you say?"

"I wondered if, now that you've seen how cute they've become, you'd reconsider taking one. I want them all to have good homes."

But a good home was not something Brandon could offer. Unless the current trend reversed itself, he would not be able to afford to stay in Mesquite Springs.

"Can you imagine the havoc a puppy could wreak in a newspaper office?" Brandon gave an exaggerated shudder. "I'm sorry, Dorothy, but I don't think I'm meant to have a dog."

His voice must have betrayed him, because Dorothy returned the puppy she'd been cuddling to the crate and turned toward him. "How many today?"

He knew what she meant. At first, she had asked whether anyone had cancelled a subscription. Now it was a question of how many. "Three, but that's not the worst part. Two shops cancelled their ads. I don't know how much longer I'll be able to print the paper if this continues."

"You could —"

The look he gave her was meant to stop her from suggesting he issue a rebuttal or at least an explanation. "You know I won't do that."

"Don't be so hasty, Brandon. You don't know what I was going to say. I thought you might expand the *Chronicle*'s reach. Ma said Grassey doesn't have a paper, but I'm sure they have news. I could go there once a week and gather stories. You'd have to deliver the papers, but it shouldn't be hard to arrange that."

Brandon was silent for a moment, considering not only the suggestion but the fact that Dorothy was as concerned about the paper's future as he was. Truly, she was an amazing woman.

"It's a good idea," he said, "but I don't like the thought of you riding that far alone. If anyone's going to go to Grassey, it will be me."

He paused as one of the puppies managed to climb out of the crate, then, apparently surprised to find himself alone, tried to climb back in. When Dorothy had returned the dog to its home, Brandon said, "Let's pray things change here. It might take a miracle."

She smiled and said, "Don't give up hope. God's in the miracle business."

A miracle. Dorothy wished she could do something so they didn't need one, but other than the Grassey suggestion, she had no ideas. Both Evelyn and Laura confirmed that the stories about Brandon's supposed sins continued to circulate.

"I don't understand it," Evelyn admitted. "It's like someone's fanning the fire."

But though the three of them had thought and thought, no one knew who that someone might be. What she needed, Dorothy decided, was a new perspective. That was why she had chosen a different route for Nutmeg's walk. Whether or not Nutmeg admitted it, the dog needed a bit of exercise and a few minutes' respite from her demanding brood.

Dorothy had gone only a few yards when she saw a solitary woman turn onto Main Street. Even from this distance, it was easy to identify Mrs. Lockhart by her petite size. She'd shrunk a couple inches in the last few years, but though her back was bowed, she kept her shoulders straight. This was definitely Mrs. Lockhart, although the slow, almost sluggish pace was not normal for her.

Dorothy increased her own pace, wanting to see if there was something she could do for the elderly woman. "Good evening," she called out.

The woman looked at her for a second before responding. "Oh, it's you, Dorothy." Though her diction was as precise as ever, the enthusiasm that typically characterized her voice was missing.

Dorothy tried not to be alarmed by the changes she was witnessing. Keeping her tone as light as she could, she said, "My dog needed some fresh air and some time away from her puppies."

"I see." Mrs. Lockhart gave Nutmeg an appraising look. "You could say I needed fresh air too, but I can assure you that the reason was far different."

Realizing that she hadn't been mistaken

in thinking something was wrong, Dorothy smiled at the woman who'd once given her a plate of fudge when she'd seen her crying after school for reasons that were long forgotten.

"Would you like to come in for a cup of coffee?" she asked. "Polly's Place isn't open, but I'd be happy to make some for you."

"Thank you, my dear. I'm feeling a mite lonely right now." The relief she heard in the former schoolteacher's voice confirmed the wisdom of Dorothy's invitation, and she escorted Mrs. Lockhart to the back entrance.

While she waited for the coffee to brew, Dorothy cut small pieces of leftover chocolate cake, darting glances at the obviously distressed woman. Perhaps talking about happier times would cheer her.

"This may not be the right time, but I wondered whether you'd like to tell a story for this month's Sociable. The theme is beginnings."

Mrs. Lockhart blanched. "How ironic that you chose that theme at the exact time that I'm facing an ending."

That wasn't the response Dorothy had expected. She gave the older woman a sharp look. "Are you ill?"

"No, it's not that. I suspect I have another

decade on this earth, but it won't be the same." Mrs. Lockhart paused to stir a teaspoon of sugar into the coffee Dorothy had poured for her. "Sometimes I wonder whether I've made a mistake. It seemed like a good idea, but now I don't know." Her eyes glistened with unshed tears as she looked up at Dorothy. "I wish I hadn't agreed."

Though the woman's sorrow and remorse were clear, the reason for them was not. "What did you agree to?"

"I'm selling my house. Some man from back East wants to build a hotel here. He's going to use my house."

Dorothy was silent for a moment, trying to make sense of what she'd just heard. Though both she and Wyatt had agreed that Mesquite Springs could benefit from a hotel, neither of them had envisioned one that would displace a resident. Mrs. Lockhart had just said that she was in good health for her age. That raised a critical question.

"Where will you live?"

"At the boardinghouse. Phil arranged everything with Martha Bayles. She promised me her best room, even if she has to evict someone." Mrs. Lockhart took a sip of coffee, then laid the cup back on the saucer

258

so carefully that Dorothy wondered if she thought that perfectly aligning the cup's handle would somehow bring her life into alignment.

"It won't be the same." The widow looked up, and this time a tear escaped to slide down her cheek. "Oh, Dorothy, I wish I hadn't agreed to this."

Dorothy shared her feelings. The situation didn't sound good for anyone other than the mysterious Eastern man.

"Are you sure you can't change your mind? I'm no lawyer, but there must be a way." If Sam Plaut were in town, he would have helped Mrs. Lockhart, but Sam was two thousand miles away.

"It's too late. I gave my word, and I won't renege on a promise." The older woman brushed the tear from her cheek and fixed her gaze on Dorothy. "You might not want advice from an old lady, but I'm going to give it anyway. Don't make any hasty decisions. Before you do anything, pray about it, and then pray again and again."

Dorothy nodded, acknowledging the good advice. She'd been praying about her situation and Brandon's, but she needed to redouble her efforts, because — despite the hours of prayer — she was still not certain what God had in store for them.

■ ■ ■ ■

"Here's the information." Leonard Downey handed Brandon a sheet of paper. "Ida said you'd know how to make it look pretty." The mercantile's owner settled back in the chair and took a long swig of the coffee Brandon had offered him. "The same thing happens every year," he continued. "Ida worries that something will go wrong, but nothing ever does. It's worse this year, because the date of the party is Valentine's Day."

When he'd first approached Brandon about placing an extra ad in the *Chronicle,* Leonard had described the annual party he and Ida held the Saturday before Lent and how they invited the whole town for an evening of dancing followed by a cold supper.

"Laura thinks you should hire Phil Blakeslee to draw hearts or a cupid or some folderol like that to make the ad elegant." Leonard winked. "Elegant was her word, not mine."

"The *Chronicle*'s not set up to handle woodcut illustrations," he told Leonard, "but there are other ways to make your ad stand out. I was thinking about centering it on a page and wording it like a formal invitation. You know, something like, 'Mr. and Mrs. Leonard Downey request the pleasure of your company at . . .'"

As Brandon let his voice trail off, Leonard grinned. "That's it. That'll do the trick." He drained his cup and rose. "One more thing. We'd better double the number of copies you bring me. I ran out last week." He chuckled. "Seems that most of those folks who cancelled their subscriptions still want to read the paper, but they're too proud to admit they made a mistake, so they spend more money to buy individual copies." Leonard's chuckle turned into a full-fledged laugh. "Serves 'em right for believing all those lies."

That night, Brandon slept better than he had in weeks.

"I should hate you. You know that, don't you?"

The teasing note in Wyatt's voice left no doubt that he wasn't serious, but Dorothy decided to play along with him. "Why?"

He looked up from the squirming mass of puppies he'd helped Dorothy deliver to the shed and grinned. "Because all Polly can talk about are these dogs. She wants to adopt every one of them."

"They are cute," Dorothy agreed, "but even I'll admit that six is too many." The pups were walking now, playing together, getting into mischief together, and growing so quickly that she couldn't imagine what it would be like when they were older. The apartment was already feeling crowded with them. If the nights weren't still so cold, she would have moved them to the shed permanently instead of bringing them inside before the sun set, but Dorothy knew she'd worry if they were outdoors, so she resigned herself to having her sleep disturbed by occasional barks.

"What about three?" she suggested.

"Don't you dare suggest that. If you do, I'll . . ." Wyatt rose, his patience for petting the puppies seemingly exhausted.

"You'll what?"

"I'll have Fletcher Engel lock you up . . . with all those puppies." Dorothy looked down the alley, as if expecting to see the sheriff, then raised her hands in mock surrender. "You wouldn't."

"If I didn't, Evelyn might. She has no experience with dogs and isn't sure we should take even one."

"But Polly's insisting."

"Loudly and constantly." A fond chuckle accompanied Wyatt's words. "I tell you,

Dorothy, she's driving both of us crazy."

"But you love her anyway."

"We do."

"And you're happy to be married." Dorothy was still amazed at the difference she'd seen in her brother since he'd made Evelyn his wife. He was calmer, but it was more than that. For the first time, he seemed to be content. In the past, Wyatt had always been searching for something new. Now he seemed to have found what he sought.

"I'm happier than I ever dreamt possible. Evelyn is the best thing that has happened to me." He dusted his hands on his pant legs, then placed them on Dorothy's shoulders and looked at her, his expression solemn. "You'll see what I mean when you get married."

His words sent a chill down her spine, and she moved backward, releasing herself from his grip. Though the alley was not the place for a discussion like this, if they went inside, Evelyn and Laura would hear them.

"I won't," Dorothy said firmly.

Confusion clouded her brother's eyes. "What do you mean, you won't?"

"I won't ever marry." She'd told him that before, but it appeared that Wyatt hadn't listened any more than Laura had.

Though Dorothy was chilled by the early

263

morning air, Wyatt appeared unaffected. "Why not? Surely it's not because you think that writing for the paper is more important."

He didn't understand. She had thought he would, but perhaps no one could understand why she felt the way she did. "Writing for the paper is important, but that's not the reason." Though it might be difficult, she knew she could juggle writing with her responsibilities as a wife and mother if she chose that route for her life. But she wouldn't. She couldn't.

"Wyatt, I saw what marriage did to Ma. I won't let that happen to me. I won't take the risk of a child having to go through what we did."

Wyatt took a step toward her, trying to breach the gap that was more than physical distance. "Are you talking about the way Ma was after Pa was killed?"

Dorothy nodded. "Even though she's better now, I'll never forget that." It had been the worst year of her life. She and Wyatt had lost their father to a Comanche's arrow and their mother to overwhelming grief.

"It wasn't marriage that caused Ma to fall apart. It was losing Pa." Wyatt was playing the older brother, trying to reason with Dorothy, but it wasn't working.

"It's the same thing. If she hadn't married Pa, she wouldn't have been like that."

"But if she hadn't married Pa, we wouldn't be here, and Ma wouldn't have had those years with him. Don't you remember how happy they were together?"

Though those memories had been overshadowed by the year Ma had retreated to the room she'd once shared with Pa, scarcely eating or speaking, they had not completely disappeared. "I do remember that," Dorothy admitted, "but it doesn't make up for the pain. I won't risk being like Ma."

Wyatt shook his head, as if in disbelief. "So, you're afraid to marry? I never thought you were a coward, Dorothy."

"If being afraid of what losing someone I love would do to me and how it could affect my children makes me a coward, then I guess I am one." She preferred to call herself a wise woman.

Her brother shook his head again. "There are no guarantees in life. I could lose Evelyn or Polly tomorrow, but I can't live in fear of that. It's a choice, Dorothy. You can choose happiness or fear."

Or she could choose between facing or avoiding pain. "It's not that simple."

"It is," Wyatt insisted. "But I'm not the

one you should be talking to about this. Ma is. Ask her. See what she says."

Dorothy shuddered at the prospect. Doing that would mean reliving that horrible year that even now had the power to bring her to tears. "I'm not ready."

"When will you be?"

"I don't know."

CHAPTER NINETEEN

Woof!

The dream that had brought a smile to Dorothy's face faded as she woke to the sound of Nutmeg's barking. This wasn't the normal stop-tussling-with-your-siblings bark or even the it's-time-to-go-outside one. This was a bark Dorothy had not heard before, one that seemed to say something was wrong.

"What is it, Nutmeg?"

The dog raced to the top of the stairs and barked again, her distress evident. Dorothy slid her feet into slippers, grabbed her wrapper, then descended the stairs behind Nutmeg. When the dog stood on her hind legs and attempted to open the outside door, Dorothy unlocked it.

Nutmeg raced out, running the few yards to the mercantile's back entrance, then stopped and barked furiously at the stack of newspapers. If he'd followed his usual schedule, Brandon would have delivered them an hour or so ago so that they'd be ready whenever the Downeys arrived at the store.

The cause of Nutmeg's distress was not difficult to find. Even though the moon was only a tiny sliver, there was enough light to see that what should have been a pile of crisp paper was now a sodden mess. Someone had obviously drenched the copies of the *Chronicle,* and Nutmeg's acute hearing had alerted her to what was happening.

Dorothy tossed the top few copies aside, hoping the ones underneath would be salvageable. They were not.

Oh, Brandon! Heedless of what Ma would call her shocking state of dishabille, Dorothy raced across the alley and into Brandon's backyard, then pounded on his door. Although she knew it was unlocked, she would not flout propriety by entering at this time of day. She pounded again.

Seconds later, Brandon appeared at the back door. "Dorothy." His shock was evident. "What's going on?"

"It's the paper." As quickly as she could, she told him what she'd found. "What can you do?"

"Print more copies," he replied without hesitation.

"Do you have enough paper and ink?" Dorothy wouldn't ask whether he could afford the loss he'd already sustained, because she knew the cancellations made him worry about the *Chronicle*'s profitability.

He nodded. "The shipment of both arrived yesterday. If I work quickly, I can have half the normal number ready before the mercantile opens and the rest finished before noon."

"I'll help." Dorothy flushed when she saw Brandon's sudden awareness of her attire. "I'll change clothes and get Wyatt. He can help."

And he did. But, though the three of them were able to replace the copies that had been destroyed, no one was able to answer the question of who might have been responsible.

"It makes no sense," Wyatt said.

"Evil never does." Pa had told her that on several occasions, and today, more than ever, Dorothy believed it.

When Laura started to lead Brandon to a table by the window, he shook his head. Spotting three men sitting at a table for four, their expressions telling him they were unhappy about something, he tipped his head in that direction. "I'd like to sit there, if they'll have me."

It had been a week since the papers had been destroyed, and Brandon was still no closer to knowing who might have wanted to harm him. This morning he'd waited until Leonard arrived before taking the mercantile's copies; then he'd reluctantly accepted Leonard's offer of a key.

"No need to wait for me," Leonard had said. "You can save me a bit of work by putting the papers on the table in front. Just be sure to lock up when you leave."

He didn't need the reminder. Ever since he'd realized that the person who meant him harm was not satisfied with rumors, Brandon had locked the back door to his house, giving Dorothy the spare key.

"You want to eat with those ranchers?" Laura sounded surprised. "Why?"

"I haven't met them, and I'd like to meet everyone who lives in or near Mesquite Springs." Sitting with strangers had started as a way to learn more about the community and possibly sell subscriptions. Now Brandon hoped to discover a clue to the man who'd become his adversary.

Laura stopped abruptly. "You'll be wasting your time. They're all leaving the area."

It was Brandon's turn to be surprised. "All the more reason for me to talk to them." In the time he'd lived here, half a dozen families had moved to Mesquite Springs, but to the best of his knowledge, no one had left.

Without waiting for Laura, Brandon headed toward the table. "Do you gentlemen mind if I join you?"

The men appeared to be around the same age, early thirties if Brandon was any judge, and their clothing left no doubt that they were ranchers. That was where the similarity ended. One was blond with blue eyes, the second a brunet with eyes almost as dark as Wyatt Clark's, and the third a green-eyed redhead.

Redhead nodded at the empty chair. "You're the newspaper fellow, aren't you?"

"I sure am."

"The wife and me like the *Chronicle*. 'Pears to me you're a straight shooter, so maybe you can help us. The sheriff said he couldn't."

Brandon's curiosity had been piqued. "What's going on?"

Tapping him on the shoulder to get his attention, Laura asked, "Are you going to order?"

"Sure. I smelled chicken. Whatever that is, I'll have it." He turned back to his dinner companions. "Now, men, what's the problem?"

The redhead, who seemed to be the spokesman, gave a short nod. "Reckon we ought to start with introductions. I'm George Link. These here are my neighbors, Ed Bosch and Henry Sattler." Ed was the blond, Henry the dark-haired man.

Ed cleared his throat before he began to speak. "Me and Henry and George got letters from some fella down in Mississippi. Said he wants to move to Texas and heard we had good land." When George nodded his agreement, Ed said, "He offered us what 'peared to be a good price fer our land."

So far, Brandon saw no reason for the men to have enlisted the sheriff's assistance. "Where exactly is your land?"

"North of town, next to the river." George took over the explanation. "The water's mighty good for cattle, but truth is, the land ain't the best for ranching."

The men remained silent while Laura placed plates of food in front of them; then Ed spoke again. "That artist fella tole us there's better grazing in Dakota Territory."

"So, me and Ed figgered we'd head out there together."

"What's the problem?" Brandon would be the last person to tell someone not to move if there was a chance to better his situation. Hadn't he done exactly that? Admittedly, these men's situations did not seem as dire as his had been.

"Henry here didn't want to leave Mesquite Springs," Ed said as he forked a piece of stew.

For the first time, the dark-haired man spoke. "The missus likes it here, especially now that she's in the family way."

"I can understand that." What Brandon didn't understand was what was wrong.

"Seems that fella in Mississippi wants all the land. Henry's place is between Ed's and mine."

The pieces were beginning to fit together. Someone wanted uninterrupted access to the river. It wasn't the first time Brandon had heard of land speculators buying up property as cheaply as they could, then reselling it at a substantial profit. That was probably what was happening here. Having contiguous land meant that the new owner could parcel it multiple ways.

"So, the guy offered Henry more money." His tone left no doubt that that did not please Ed.

Henry looked a bit sheepish. "I couldn't refuse. Even the missus agreed."

"And you two feel as if you were cheated."

Brandon made it a statement rather than a question.

"You bet we do." George answered for himself and Ed. "Iffen Henry's land is worth that much, ours is too."

Ed shook his head, his anger palpable. "The problem is, Sheriff Engel said that weren't a crime."

Though he wished he could disagree, Brandon could not. "Not a crime, but it was unfair."

"Ain't there anything we can do?" George asked.

Before Brandon could speak, Ed did. "Mebbe you could print something in the paper."

"I can't see how that would help. I doubt that the man who bought your land reads the *Chronicle.*" While it was true that papers were circulated to other newspaper offices, thanks to the post office's waiving of postage fees, it was unlikely that the *Chronicle* reached Mississippi.

"You're right." George's disappointment hung over him like a thundercloud. "But that don't change anything. It ain't fair."

Dorothy smiled as she rounded the corner. She had taken Mrs. Lockhart's advice to heart and had prayed, prayed, and prayed

274

some more about her relationship with Brandon. Today she had wakened filled with the conviction that God meant them to be together . . . as friends and colleagues.

As she climbed the steps to the *Chronicle*'s office, she exhaled slowly, reminding herself that this was nothing more than a business meeting. She had this week's Sociable for him, and she wanted to discuss ideas for next month's theme.

"Perfect timing!" Brandon grinned as he held up a sheet he'd been studying. "I need your advice." The paper displayed a dozen different type fonts, three of which Brandon had circled. "The type I've been using is showing signs of wear, and it's only a matter of time before several of the letters break. As much as I hate to spend the money right now, I need to order a new font. Which do you prefer?"

Dorothy picked up the sheet and looked at it from different angles, feeling both honored that he'd asked her opinion and a little intimidated. The font a newspaper used was more important than most subscribers realized. While readers might think that all that mattered was whether it was legible, Dorothy knew that some fonts excited readers, while others had a calming effect.

"This one." She pointed to the first one Brandon had circled.

His expression gave no clue to his reaction. Instead, he asked, "Why?"

"It's more modern than the others. It's also easier to read than the one you've been using."

"Exactly." This time he smiled. "I couldn't have said it better myself. You confirmed what I thought." He took the sheet from her, tossed it on the desk, then grabbed both of her hands and spun her around. "Thank you, Dorothy. I don't know what I ever did without you."

The world was spinning, not just because of the way he'd swung her. Even more powerful was the smile Brandon gave her, a smile that started in his eyes and turned his face into the most handsome one she'd ever seen. It was a moment unlike any they'd shared — wonderful, magical, and oh, so wrong.

"You might not say that when you see what I have for you." Dorothy tugged her hands from his and tried to still the pounding of her heart. She wasn't going to marry him or anyone, and that made her feelings totally wrong. "I don't have as many pieces as I'd hoped, because it hasn't been an exciting week in Mesquite Springs," she said as calmly as she could.

Brandon shook his head, although it wasn't clear whether that was from surprise that she'd pulled away or from what she'd said. He countered her statement. "Unless you live along the river. Did you know that the Bosches, the Sattlers, and the Links are moving to Dakota Territory?"

Dorothy didn't try to hide her shock. Though she'd spoken with the women in each family only a few weeks ago, she'd had no inkling that they were considering such a major change. "I didn't realize they were unhappy here."

Brandon gestured toward one of the chairs, waiting until Dorothy was seated before he continued his explanation. "It doesn't seem to be a case of unhappiness, just a better opportunity and more money if they leave."

"I used to think nothing changed in Mesquite Springs, but that's no longer the case. The ranchers aren't the only ones moving. Mrs. Lockhart is too." And that still bothered Dorothy.

"Mrs. Lockhart?"

As quickly as she could, Dorothy recounted what she knew. Brandon's expression, which had been neutral when she began, turned to a frown when she described how upset Mrs. Lockhart was over her decision.

"Something about this feels wrong. First someone from the East wants to open a hotel; now a family from Mississippi wants to have a lot of land by the river." Brandon stared at the far wall for a second before he added, "It may only be that the two things happened so close together."

"Do you think there's a connection between them?" As far as Dorothy could see, the only thing the ranchers and Mrs. Lockhart had in common was a Mesquite Springs address.

"Logically, no, but my instincts say yes." The furrows between his eyes told Dorothy that Brandon was more concerned than he was admitting.

"I don't see what it could be. The ranchers and their wives are young. It's not unusual for young families to move for better opportunities."

"But the impetus came from someone else."

Dorothy nodded, recognizing the truth in Brandon's statement. What the three ranchers and Mrs. Lockhart had in common was that someone wanted to buy their property. Dorothy would have to ask Ma or Mrs. Downey, but to her knowledge, that had never before happened.

"I wonder how the family in Mississippi and the man back East even knew about Mesquite Springs," she said.

Brandon's eyes were solemn as he said, "You probably won't like my idea, but I think Phil Blakeslee might be the connection. I know he spends a lot of time with Mrs. Lockhart, and the ranchers said he sketched their land."

"He sketched a lot of people and places as Christmas gifts." Dorothy wasn't certain why she felt the need to defend him other than that the idea of Phil being somehow involved in what seemed like suspicious dealings bothered her.

"That's true," Brandon admitted, "but those ranchers didn't have stories in the first Sociable. I think he was out there sketching before you and he decided to turn the articles into gifts. And I think somehow he's told the people in Mississippi and back East about what he's found."

The idea was almost preposterous. "How would he do that? He would have had to mail letters, and according to Laura, her parents said the postmaster told them Phil has never set foot in the post office."

When Brandon's frown deepened, Dorothy doubted it was because of the way gossip spread in Mesquite Springs.

"He could have mailed his letters in Grassey. I know he's gone there."

"So have you." Brandon had told her he'd bought his Christmas gifts there.

He nodded slowly. "You could be right, and I could be all wrong about this, but I don't trust Blakeslee."

Dorothy thought of the man whose sketches showed such sensitivity. Surely, he wouldn't be behind anything underhanded. And yet Brandon's instincts said Phil wasn't trustworthy. "Why not?"

"He's too glib, too quick with an easy answer. I think he's hiding something."

Dorothy nodded slowly, remembering the times she'd had the same impression. "I agree that he's hiding something, but it's probably not what you think. I believe Phil has wounds that haven't healed."

Brandon gave her a skeptical look. "Just what do you think those wounds are?"

"I'm not sure, other than that his sister died when he was young. We both know that a loved one's death is very painful."

Brandon was silent for a moment. "You're right, but be careful. I know you want to help everyone, but I don't want you to be the one who's hurt."

"Thou shalt not steal."

The minister's words echoed throughout the church, though he never raised his voice above normal level. That was one of the things that bothered Phil about Coleman — his ability to dominate a situation without appearing to do anything out of the ordinary. There was something almost menacing about that. Brother Josiah wasn't like that. He was a showman: loud, flamboyant, always entertaining. No one slept through one of Brother Josiah's camp meetings, but this wasn't a camp meeting, and the man who was speaking was not Brother Josiah.

Phil used both hands to grip the Bible that he rarely opened but carried to avoid looking out of place, wishing he could clap those hands over his ears and block out the sermon. He was not stealing, he reminded himself. Mr. K wasn't stealing, either. He'd offered a fair price to those ranchers. It wasn't Phil's fault that Sattler had balked at moving and he'd had to offer him more. There was no crime in that, and it was not stealing.

Coleman's gaze moved across the congregation as he said, "When God commanded

281

us not to steal, I believe he meant more than simple robbery. We all know that cattle rustling is stealing, but what about defrauding someone, paying them less than something is worth? What about destroying part of a man's livelihood? Aren't those stealing too?" His eyes seemed to be fixed on Phil as he answered his rhetorical question. "I believe they are."

Phil could feel every indentation in the leather's grain as he tightened his grip on the Bible. How he wished he could walk out of here. He'd seen the way the preacher looked at him, as if he knew Phil had been the one who'd emptied a rain barrel over the pile of newspapers, the one who'd told Mr. K about the properties, and the one who'd written those letters that were supposed to have come from Mississippi.

So what if he had? A man had to do whatever he could to survive. This holier-than-thou parson ought to know that. But he was like Selby, who condemned Esther for doing the only thing she could to feed them. Coleman was turning into even more of a nuisance than Phil had originally thought.

Phil relaxed his grip on what Ma had called the Good Book, forcing himself to relax as he closed his ears to the rest of the sermon. He could take care of Holloway. The man was proving harder to dislodge than he'd expected, but Phil had already planned the next step. Coleman was another matter. Though he hated to admit it, he needed help.

He needed Brother Josiah.

CHAPTER TWENTY

"I'm still surprised at how excited the town is over the Downeys' party," Brandon said as he and Dorothy began the typesetting process for tomorrow's issue of the *Chronicle.* They'd worked together to arrange the articles, interspersing short and long ones to provide variety. That had been the creative part of the afternoon; now it was time for the important but mechanical work.

She brushed an errant lock of hair from her face. "It's the last festive event before the somber season of Lent. Plus, it's an opportunity for folks to spend time together."

"And wear fancy clothes." Brandon tapped a finger on the article she'd written. By mutual consent, they set the type for each other's articles, reasoning that they'd be more critical that way and might catch missed words or grammatical errors. "Almost everything you've written seems to be about what the women will wear."

Dorothy nodded. "That might not sound exciting to you."

"Or to most of the men in town."

"But even women who don't subscribe will buy this issue, and some who do have subscriptions will want an extra copy to send to family or friends in other towns. The Downeys told me they're still selling out every week."

"So, we need a bigger print run." Brandon wondered if she realized how often they spoke like this, finishing each other's sentences. It was a new experience for him, but he had to admit that he found it exhilarating.

She nodded again. "That's what I'd suggest."

"Then we'll do it."

As they often did, they worked in silence, but something seemed different today. The silence wasn't as comfortable as it usually was, and though she hadn't said anything, Brandon sensed that Dorothy was preoccupied.

"Is something wrong?"

For a second, he thought she might deny it, but she shrugged. "It's silly."

Brandon doubted that. "Let's take a break. I'll make another pot of coffee, and you can tell me what's bothering you."

"It's the puppies," Dorothy said when they were seated in the office with cups of coffee in front of them.

Though he was tempted to laugh at the idea that six rambunctious dogs were causing her such distress, Brandon did not. Despite the fact that Dorothy had claimed it was silly, he knew it wasn't silly to her.

"What about them?"

"I almost wish I hadn't agreed to give them away, because I know I'm going to be lonely when they're gone."

Softhearted Dorothy probably worried that their new owners would not treat them as well as she did. It was up to him to convince her she'd made the right decision, the only one that made sense.

"Of course, you'll miss them. That's natural, but think about how happy the new owners will be."

She managed a weak smile. "Polly is counting the days. Evelyn said she's taken to going to bed early, because she thinks that will make the next day come faster."

Ah, the logic of a six-year-old. "The other owners will be almost as excited." Dorothy had said they ranged from the town's seamstress and former mayor to the woman whose gardening tips had become such a popular part of the *Chronicle.*

286

"They are, but . . ."

"You're still worried about being lonely."

She nodded. "Clark women don't handle loss well." Then, as if she'd revealed something she hadn't intended to, Dorothy finished her coffee and rose. "We ought to get back to work."

Brandon was still puzzling over Dorothy's words as he fed paper through George that evening. Though she'd tried to make light of it, her distress seemed out of proportion to the situation, and he'd seen fear — real fear — on her face. What had happened to make her fear of loss so strong? The only answer Brandon could imagine was her father's death.

He gripped George's lever more tightly than necessary as memories began to flood his brain. Tomorrow would mark four months since Pa had been killed. The pain had lessened, but the guilt was still as intense as ever.

"It wasn't your fault." The doctor had claimed that was the truth, and Dorothy had echoed his words, but no matter what they said or how often those words reverberated through his mind, Brandon did not believe them. It *was* his fault. Pa shouldn't have died.

"When you're troubled, talk to the Lord."

This time it was Ma's voice that made Brandon pause. She'd said that God was always listening, that God would lighten his load, if only he would ask. "You've got to ask, Brandon, and when you do, the Lord will help."

Perhaps that was where he'd gone wrong. He hadn't asked for help. It was time. Heedless of the copies still to be printed, Brandon dropped to his knees.

This was the latest he'd finished the paper, but Brandon could not regret the long night. There'd been no messages from burning bushes or talking donkeys, not even the still, small voice Ma had claimed she'd heard, but the hours on his knees had given Brandon a measure of peace that had been absent for four months.

He hadn't absolved himself for his role in Pa's death — he doubted he would ever be able to do that — but he'd accepted that he could not undo that night, and he'd realized that it was time to put the past behind him. It was time to move forward.

Laying the last copy of the *Chronicle* on the pile reserved for the mercantile, Brandon let out a sigh of relief. This part of his job was over for another week. All that remained was to deliver the papers, starting with Dorothy's copy.

He pulled out his watch and nodded. It would be like old times, seeing Dorothy at work in the kitchen. She'd mentioned that since Evelyn had been under the weather recently, she had resumed her early morning routine of preparing food for Polly's Place.

Dorothy would be there, perhaps with Nutmeg at her side. And since Laura wouldn't arrive for another hour, Brandon would have a chance to tell her of his conversation with the Lord and how he'd prayed, not simply for himself, but also that Dorothy would find peace.

He grabbed a paper, unlocked the back door, and started down the steps. It happened so quickly he could not stop himself. One moment he was walking; the next he was tumbling forward, unable to break his fall.

And then he knew no more.

He should have been here by now. Dorothy glanced at the clock for what felt like the hundredth time. It wasn't running fast. She knew that. Brandon should have been here at least fifteen minutes ago, but he — the man who believed punctuality to be one of the greatest virtues — was not. What could be keeping him?

Nutmeg whimpered, perhaps in response to Dorothy's unease. "I know, girl. I'm not happy, either." She waited another five minutes, darting looks at the clock as she chopped beef for today's stew. Instead of her usual neat, evenly sized pieces, she was making ragged cuts. That wouldn't change the flavor, but both Laura and Evelyn would be disappointed. Dorothy was too, but for a different reason.

She ripped off her apron, tossed it on the table, and opened the back door. "C'mon, Nutmeg. We're going to find Brandon."

Nutmeg shot forward, racing across the alley toward Brandon's home, then began barking furiously.

Oh, dear Lord, no. There was no mistaking that bark. It was the same one Nutmeg had used the day the papers were destroyed. Something was wrong. Very wrong.

Raising her skirts so she could move more freely, Dorothy ran toward Nutmeg, her heart pounding harder with each step she took. *Please let him be all right,* she prayed as she raced across the yard. But he wasn't all right. Brandon lay facedown on the ground, unmoving, while Nutmeg continued to bark.

"Quiet, Nutmeg." The dog's bark had

changed to a wail that sent shivers down Dorothy's spine. Surely Brandon wasn't . . . She refused to complete the sentence.

"What happened?" she asked as she knelt next to him.

There was no answer.

"You're scaring me, Brandon." In the dim light before sunrise, it was impossible to tell whether he was breathing. He had to be! She wasn't going to lose him. Not now, not if she could help it.

Dorothy wrapped her arms around Brandon and struggled to turn him onto his back. Though his eyes were open, there was no spark behind them, and for a second Dorothy feared that the worst had happened. But when she laid her finger on his lips, she felt a rush of air. Brandon was alive. Unconscious, but still alive.

Thank you, God.

"Wake up, Brandon." There was no response. Dorothy slapped his cheeks, hoping to rouse him. It had no effect. Dread so intense it threatened to choke her washed over her. She'd heard of people falling into a deep sleep like this — they called it a coma — and never wakening. *Please, God. Please don't let Brandon die.*

"You stay here," Dorothy told Nutmeg as she rose. "Keep him safe." She was going to find the doctor.

Less than a minute later, she was pounding on Doc Dawson's door. Fortunately, he'd already risen for the day.

"What's wrong?"

As quickly as she could, Dorothy explained how she'd found Brandon. "He's still alive, but he needs you."

The doctor, whose freckles made him appear younger than his thirty-five years, nodded. "Let me grab my bag." Seconds later, he was striding toward Brandon's backyard, Dorothy following in his wake.

"It was a bad fall, no doubt about it," the doctor said when he'd examined Brandon. "See this bruise?" he asked, pointing to Brandon's temple. "That's likely the reason he's unconscious. It looks like he hit his head on a rock."

The sun had risen enough that Dorothy had no trouble seeing the rock where Brandon had landed.

"He must have been in a hurry and tripped when he came out of the house." Doc continued trying to rouse Brandon, holding smelling salts beneath his nose, but Brandon did not respond.

"I'll get Fletcher, and we'll take him to my office." Dorothy knew that since the sheriff's office was close to Doc's, the doctor sometimes asked Fletcher to help him carry patients. "You should stay here. If Brandon regains consciousness, he may be disoriented. Seeing you may help him."

But Brandon did not regain consciousness, and Nutmeg, as if sensing that she was no longer needed, began to walk around the yard, sniffing at each of the trees and bushes.

Dorothy craned her neck, wanting to be sure Nutmeg was not getting into any trouble, and as she did, a ray of sunshine lit the steps. She stared, unable to believe what she was seeing, then closed her eyes, wanting to clear her brain. When she opened them again, nothing had changed. A rope was strung across the top step.

Brandon's fall had not been an accident.

CHAPTER TWENTY-ONE

"Do you recognize me?"

Brandon stared at the redheaded man whose green eyes were uncharacteristically serious. What on earth was Mesquite Springs's doctor doing in his bedroom? His gaze shifted, and confusion grew when he realized he was lying flat on his back in a room he'd never seen before. As he started to rise, the doctor pressed on his shoulder, keeping him down.

"Do you recognize me?" Andy Dawson repeated.

"Sure. You're the doctor." As the odors of antiseptic and what he guessed was some foul-smelling salve assailed him, Brandon realized he must be in the doctor's office.

"What happened?" The last thing he recalled was leaving the house to take Dorothy her copy of the *Chronicle*.

"That's what we're trying to figure out." Doc's expression remained solemn. "You've

got a lump on your forehead that will probably hurt like the dickens, and you were
unconscious for longer than I'd like."

Brandon winced as he touched his head.
Doc hadn't exaggerated about the lump or
how painful even brushing against it was.
What had he done? He must have fallen,
but why? Had he suffered a dizzy spell the
way Pa used to?

"Apoplexy." The word slipped out before
he could censor it.

Doc shook his head as he fitted the ear-
pieces of his stethoscope and listened to
Brandon's heart. "It wasn't apoplexy. What
made you think that?"

"My father died from it. The doctor in
Xavier said his dizzy spells were a precur-
sor."

"That's what I've seen. They're warnings,
but unfortunately, there's nothing we can
do to stop apoplexy. A fatal attack can happen at any time, but you needn't worry. You,
my friend, did not have apoplexy."

Doc gave Brandon an appraising look.
"Let's try sitting up now. Slowly."

Though his head ached and he was light-
headed as he moved, Brandon felt as if he'd
regained a measure of control over his life
once he was sitting.

The doctor nodded slowly before saying,

"There are two people who'll be very glad to see you've regained consciousness." He opened the door and beckoned. "You can come in now." Light footsteps were followed by heavier ones.

"Oh, Brandon, I was so worried." Dorothy rushed to his side, and though she did not touch him, she was studying him as carefully as the doctor had, the furrows between her eyes bearing witness to the depth of her concern.

"Doc says I'm going to live." Brandon tried to relieve her anxiety with a humorous tone.

"I'm glad to hear that." The man who'd followed Dorothy into the room moved to her side. "Seems someone is trying to send you a message."

Brandon knew he must look bewildered, but he couldn't help it. The sheriff's words made no sense. "What do you mean?"

Fletcher replied with a question of his own. "What do you remember?"

"I left the house with a copy of the paper for Dorothy. The next thing I knew, I was here with a bump on my head. I figured I got dizzy and fell."

Dorothy shuddered. "You didn't fall. You were tripped." Those lovely caramel-colored eyes bore the sheen of tears. "When you were late, Nutmeg and I tried to find you. You were lying facedown at the foot of the steps, and you weren't moving."

"When she couldn't waken you, she came for me." Doc continued the story.

"And since Doc didn't want to risk further injury by carrying you alone, he called me." That explained Fletcher's involvement, but it did not explain his assertion that someone was sending Brandon a message.

It was Dorothy who spoke. "Doc and I thought you'd tripped and were knocked out when you hit your head on a rock, but when the sun rose, it was clear this was no accident. Someone had strung a rope across the top step. You wouldn't have seen it in the dark, but it would have caused you to fall."

Brandon stared at Dorothy, trying to make sense of her story. If what she said was true — and he knew it was — someone had sought to harm him.

"He couldn't have known I'd hit my head on the rock."

"I agree. My guess is that he just wanted to frighten you — an escalation of the message he sent when he destroyed last week's papers."

The sheriff's theory made sense, though it did nothing to identify the person responsible. Brandon nodded, regretting the movement a second later when the throbbing of his head increased. "Let's keep this quiet."

The three looked as if he'd begun speaking Chinese.

"How will you explain that lump on your head?" Dorothy demanded. "It's not going to disappear overnight. You'll probably still have it on Saturday at the Downeys' party, and folks will want to know what happened."

"I'll say that I was clumsy and tripped and hit my head. There's no need to say it wasn't an accidental fall."

Though Doc remained silent, Fletcher nodded.

"So, we're agreed?" Brandon asked. "We're the only four who know what really happened."

Though the men nodded, Dorothy shook her head. "There's a fifth person — the guilty one."

It wasn't supposed to have happened this way.

Phil crumpled the newspaper he'd picked up at the mercantile, his anger preventing him from reading what Holloway had written this week. He hadn't meant to kill him or even to seriously injure him. All that was supposed to happen was that Holloway would fall, maybe wrench an ankle or bruise himself a bit. Who would have guessed that he'd land on a rock and need the doctor's care? That wasn't what Phil had planned.

When he'd first started working for Mr. K, he'd told him he would do everything he could to make his plans succeed, but he would never harm another person.

"I wouldn't ask you to do that," Mr. K had assured him. "Violence solves nothing. There are better ways to accomplish things."

But today, though he hadn't planned it, Phil had caused serious injury. It hadn't taken long for the story to circulate. According to the gossips, Holloway was a clumsy man who'd tripped and hit his head. Doc Dawson claimed he'd recover, though he'd have a lump on his head for a few days to remind him of his foolishness.

To Phil's annoyance, the story appeared to have sparked sympathy among the townspeople, and Leonard Downey said he'd sold more copies of the *Chronicle* today than any other week. That wasn't good. Not good at all.

Dorothy woke with a start, tears streaming down her face.

It was only a dream, she told herself, but

she'd never had one like this. In it, she stood in the doorway of the *Chronicle*'s pressroom, mute with horror at the sight before her. The room was in shambles, type strewn everywhere, paper torn to shreds, ink staining the floor. Those were disturbing enough, but what caused her to shriek, then sob as if her heart had been wrenched from her body, was the sight of the man lying on the floor, the overturned press crushing the life from him.

Dorothy slid her feet into slippers, donned her wrapper, and descended the stairs. Warm milk would help her forget the terror she'd felt when she'd seen Brandon's lifeless body and remind her that it was only a dream, a combination of what had happened to Brandon's father in Xavier and the accident that wasn't an accident. No one had tried to destroy the *Chronicle,* and though he'd been injured, Brandon was still alive.

Whoever wanted to harm him had not intended to kill him — she agreed with Fletcher about that — but he did want to stop Brandon from printing the *Chronicle.* And that perplexed Dorothy. How could anyone feel threatened by the paper? It wasn't as though Brandon had written anything incendiary. To the contrary, everything he'd published had had one goal: uniting the town. But it hadn't.

At least one person was unhappy enough to want Brandon to fail. Who? Why?

"Thanks, Nutmeg." The dog had abandoned her brood and followed Dorothy to the kitchen, staying by her side as if she knew Dorothy needed comfort. She woofed softly and nuzzled Dorothy's hand, helping the terror to fade.

As she patted Nutmeg's head, Dorothy wondered whether she had misinterpreted the dream. Perhaps it wasn't simply triggered by the fall. Perhaps there was a second significance, one that had weighed on her ever since Brandon had told her what had happened the night his father died. Perhaps the overturned press was a symbol of his guilt. Perhaps the dream was showing that unless Brandon could release that guilt, it would kill him — perhaps not physically, but emotionally. Dorothy knew the weight was preventing him from enjoying life and doing everything God had in store for him.

Though she had tried to convince Brandon he was not responsible for his father's death, he had refused to discuss it, apparently regretting that he'd confided in her. Her words had accomplished nothing, but perhaps her prayers would.

"Dear Lord, I beg you to lift the burden of guilt from Brandon's heart and bring him peace."

Her own heart lighter, Dorothy began to warm the milk and set out the ingredients for today's meals. Unless she was mistaken, Wyatt would knock on the door at six, telling her Evelyn was under the weather and asking if Dorothy could help Laura until Evelyn felt better. By nine or ten, Evelyn would arrive, looking a bit wan but with a smile that told Dorothy the reason for her daily bouts of illness was a happy one.

Oh, how she hoped her suspicions were true.

"How did you hurted yourself?"

Brandon chuckled when Polly pointed toward his forehead, her eyes filled with sympathy. A glimpse in the mirror had told him no one would miss his injury, and he'd hesitated before accepting Wyatt's invitation to supper, not wanting to be the center of attention, but the lure of good food and even better company had outweighed his concerns.

"I fell and bumped my head," he told the little girl.

"Does it hurt a lot?"

"Less every day."

"Good." Apparently satisfied, Polly turned toward Dorothy. "Does Buster hurt himself when he falls?"

"Buster?" Brandon directed the question to Polly.

"He's my puppy." A giggle accompanied her declaration. "Well, he's gonna be my puppy as soon as Aunt Dorothy says he's big enough." She gripped Dorothy's hand and gave her a pleading look. "Make it soon. Puh-leeze."

The adults were still laughing as Evelyn led them into the dining room. Unlike Brandon's home, which consisted of only one floor, the mayor's office and residence were in a two-story building similar to many on Main Street. The first floor contained Wyatt's office and three bedrooms, while the kitchen, dining room, and parlor were located above. Though the arrangement had seemed unusual to Brandon, Wyatt had explained that fear of fire was the reason the sleeping quarters were on the ground floor.

"We haven't had a major fire in Mesquite Springs," Wyatt had explained, "but the first settlers came from places where fires were common, so they're extra cautious."

Fire was the last thing on Brandon's mind as he walked home that night. It had been a pleasant supper — more than a pleasant supper. The hours he'd spent with Wyatt and his family, sharing the laughter, seeing the obvious love that flowed between Wyatt and Evelyn, watching Dorothy's gentle interaction with Polly, had filled Brandon with a longing for a family of his own.

Though he'd lived here only a few months, Mesquite Springs had become his home in ways Xavier never had. Perhaps it was because he'd chosen Mesquite Springs rather than being born there. Perhaps it was something else. All Brandon knew was that he wanted to stay here.

He wanted what Wyatt had — a respected position in the town, a loving wife, and children. There were still obstacles, but tonight the possibility of a happy future gleamed brightly.

Brandon's brain continued to whirl with memories of everything that had happened this week and everything he'd heard. There was no denying his concern that someone seemed determined to put him out of business one way or another, but though his head ached with the physical reminder of that determination, it was Doc's words that reverberated the loudest.

"There's nothing we can do to stop apoplexy. A fatal attack can happen at any time."

Though the doctor in Xavier had said the same thing, and Dorothy had told him he wasn't responsible for Pa's death, Brandon hadn't believed them. This was different. Doc Dawson's words had lodged deep in Brandon's heart, easing the pain that had weighed him down for four months, giving him the peace he'd sought for so long.

Brandon no longer doubted Ma's claim that God worked in mysterious ways. This week was the proof. It had taken a fall and a lump on his head to make him hear the truth, but now he had no doubts. He hadn't caused Pa's death. He wasn't unworthy of love. *Thank you, God.*

"Buster is the bestest puppy." Polly reached for the largest of the dogs, the one she'd chosen for herself, and cradled him in her arms until he began to squeak.

As she did each day, Polly had come to the restaurant as soon as school ended so that she could help Dorothy with the puppies. Though that help consisted of little more than admiring them, Dorothy would not deny the child the pleasure she found when she was surrounded by playful pups.

"Not so tightly, Polly." Dorothy loosened the girl's grip slightly. "Remember, he's still a baby. We need to be gentle with him."

Stricken, Polly looked down at the dog in her arms. "I'm sorry, Buster." She punctuated her words with a kiss to the dog's nose, then laughed when he responded with a vigorous lick. "See, Aunt Dorothy. He loves me, and I love him."

"I know you do." Though it was heartwarming to watch a child so obviously infatuated with her soon-to-be pet, Dorothy worried that she would lose interest and that Evelyn and Wyatt would regret agreeing that Polly could have a dog. "He's a very good puppy, and you'll be a good mama to him."

Polly nodded and gave Buster another kiss before returning him to his mother. Then, as she glanced down the alley, a smile lit her face. "Here comes Mr. Brandon. He likes puppies too."

The way Polly's lips twisted though no sound emerged told Dorothy she was thinking about something and would soon blurt out whatever thought was flitting through her brain.

A second later, Polly tugged on Dorothy's hand. "You oughta marry him, Aunt Dorothy. Mr. Brandon would be a good daddy for Nutmeg."

Dorothy rolled her eyes and hoped Brandon had not overheard Polly's comment. How embarrassing that would be for both of them.

As he approached, Brandon wore a serene expression, one that reminded Dorothy of the day he'd met Polly. Though his eyes had flitted to the birthmark that marred her cheek, he had not recoiled, nor had he made any reference to it. In that moment, he'd risen even higher in Dorothy's esteem. Today his calm demeanor told her he was unaware of Polly's matchmaking. Thank goodness.

"Will you let me hold Buster?" he asked Polly when he reached them.

She nodded but held her hand before her mouth and whispered to Dorothy, "You oughta, Aunt Dorothy. You oughta."

Dorothy tried not to squirm as the image of herself and Brandon sharing a home lodged inside her brain. It wouldn't happen. It couldn't happen. The approach of Valentine's Day must have been making everyone think about marriage.

Fortunately, she was immune.

CHAPTER TWENTY-TWO

"What do you think?" Laura twirled, giving Dorothy a full view of the skirt that boasted twenty-five yards of dark-rose silk and close to a hundred yards of lace trim. While it was far more elaborate than anything Dorothy owned or would consider wearing, she had to admit that it suited her friend.

"Very pretty, and so are the decorations." Laura had asked Dorothy to arrive half an hour before the party's official start to ensure that everything was perfect. And it was.

"Love is in the air . . . literally." Dorothy pointed at the garlands of red paper hearts draped from the chandelier to the four corners of the room, leaving no doubt that this was a Valentine's Day celebration. Across the hall, the massive dining room table covered with a tablecloth just a few shades lighter pink than Laura's gown continued the theme.

"Wait until you see the cookies I made." Laura started to lead the way to the butler's pantry, then stopped when the doorbell chimed.

"Are we too early?" Evelyn asked as she, Wyatt, and Polly entered the Downeys' mansion. "Mother Clark sends her regrets. You know she wanted to be here, but she's still sneezing and coughing on top of having an upset stomach, and she doesn't want anyone to catch that." Evelyn looked at the girl who was tugging on her hand. "As you can see, Polly was eager to come."

"Of course, you're not too early. You're right on time." Laura, ever the gracious hostess, gave them a warm smile, even though it was still five minutes before the party was scheduled to begin. "Mrs. Steiner is upstairs, waiting for you," she told Polly. The older woman had volunteered to take care of the children, leaving the adults free to enjoy the evening.

"I wanted to bring Buster," Polly announced, "but Aunt Dorothy said I couldn't."

"I'm afraid the noise would be too much for him," Dorothy said, shuddering as she imagined the havoc a puppy could raise.

When Polly showed no inclination to climb the stairs, Dorothy took her hand and started to lead the way. To her surprise, Evelyn followed, leaving Wyatt to greet the elder Downeys.

It took a few minutes to get Polly settled with Mrs. Steiner, but once she seemed happy about the promise of other playmates and cookies and sandwiches, Evelyn tipped her head toward the door, silently telling Dorothy it was time to leave.

"You look especially lovely today," Evelyn said when they'd reentered the hallway. "Every man will want to dance with you."

Dorothy shook her head. Unlike Laura, she had never been the belle of the ball. "I doubt that." Though Ma had made her a new dress and insisted she wear it tonight, Dorothy knew she could not compete with Laura. Nor did she want to. Still, she had to admit that the red and gray paisley print Ma had chosen was attractive, and the lace collar and bone buttons Laura had sent her from Charleston had turned it into one of the prettiest dresses Dorothy had ever owned.

"At least you didn't need dancing lessons." Evelyn chuckled, reminding Dorothy of the day she and Wyatt had taught Evelyn the polka. Because she'd spent most of her life in an orphanage whose matron disapproved of dancing, Evelyn had been woefully ignorant of modern dance steps.

"You were a fast learner, and look at you now — happily married to your dancing partner." If she'd been able to choose a wife for Wyatt, Dorothy knew she could not have found someone better suited to him than Evelyn.

"I am happy," her sister-in-law agreed, the secretive smile that Dorothy had seen so often over the past few weeks only increasing her natural beauty. "Happier than I thought possible. Being married is wonderful, and there's more." Though the rapidly rising noise from the floor below as guests crowded into the ballroom would have kept anyone from hearing what she said, Evelyn lowered her voice. "Wyatt and I are going to have a baby. That's why I've been sick so many mornings."

"What wonderful news!" A wave of pure joy swept over Dorothy at the realization that her suspicions had been accurate. "I'm so happy for you." She enfolded Evelyn in her arms and pressed a kiss on her forehead. "Wyatt must be thrilled."

"He is." Evelyn's smile widened. "He's like a little boy on Christmas Eve." She linked her arm with Dorothy's and headed toward the wide staircase. "We're not planning to tell anyone other than you and your mother for a few more weeks, but I couldn't wait another day to let you know you're going to be an aunt in September."

It was ten minutes later and Dorothy was still so happy over the knowledge that her brother and the woman he loved were soon to be parents that she hardly heard what Phil was saying.

"Of course," she said.

The grin that crossed his face told her she should have listened more carefully. Somehow, though it had been the furthest thing from her mind, she had agreed to be his partner for the first dance.

Brandon looked around the room as couples began to pair off for the first dance. First and last dances, his mother had told him, were significant, and he should choose his partners for them carefully. He'd planned to ask Dorothy for the first, but the sight of Blakeslee making his way toward her told him he was too late.

Odd. Brandon had expected Blakeslee to partner with Laura. Not only was she considered the most eligible young lady in Mesquite Springs, but she was also one of tonight's hostesses. Yet there she stood, alone and wearing a frown.

"May I have the honor of this dance?"

Laura nodded, her eyes filled with relief. "Yes, of course. I trust you not to mash my toes."

He did not. To his surprise, their steps were so well matched that onlookers might have thought they'd been frequent partners. It was an enjoyable dance, even though Laura wasn't the partner Brandon would have chosen.

"Has anyone acted strangely?" Dorothy asked him half an hour later as they shared a waltz.

She might have told Laura that romance had no part in her life, but she was as much the belle of the ball as her friend. Just look at her. Dorothy's dress didn't have the ruffles and lace Laura's did, but it was elegant, like its owner. And while her hair wasn't as elaborately styled as Laura's, those soft curls were oh, so appealing. They should be doing nothing more than enjoying this dance, but Dorothy — ever practical Dorothy — had reminded him of one of the things they'd hoped to accomplish tonight: unmasking whoever had strung a rope across his steps.

"No, unfortunately."

"I've heard several people mention your accident," Dorothy said. "Mostly they seemed concerned. A couple said it was a

313

good thing your writing wasn't as clumsy as your feet."

Brandon nodded. "I've gotten the same reactions. Even though I agree with Fletcher that the person is probably here tonight, he's doing nothing to draw attention to himself." The man was probably smart or at least shrewd.

"I wish we knew who was responsible."

"So do I."

Dorothy's smile was as mechanical as the movement of her feet as she danced a polka with Phil. Her brain was whirling, wishing she were mistaken. She had thought Brandon's accident would be the major topic of conversation, but she had been wrong. She'd believed that the sharp criticism of Pastor Coleman had died a natural death, and she had been wrong about that too.

Dorothy noticed the way some people had moved in the opposite direction when Pastor and Mrs. Coleman had entered the room. Others had greeted them warmly, but close to half the guests were obviously avoiding them, turning their gaze away when the Colemans approached, pretending to be so engrossed in a conversation that they didn't notice them.

The minister and his wife were being

shunned. There was no other way to describe it. The town that had seemed so united when Dorothy had written the Christmas memories articles was now deeply divided, and that worried her almost as much as the attack on Brandon. What was happening to Mesquite Springs?

"Is something wrong?" Phil's question drew her attention back to him and told her that her smile wasn't as convincing as she'd hoped. "You look upset. I hope it isn't my dancing."

"No, of course not. You're a good dancer." And while she was indeed as upset as Phil believed, she would not tell him what was bothering her. There was only one person she trusted enough to discuss this, and that was Brandon.

With a sigh of relief that the seemingly endless dance was over, Dorothy thanked Phil for his company, then headed toward the far wall where she'd seen Mrs. Coleman talking to Mrs. Lockhart. Others might shun the minister's wife, but Dorothy had every intention of making her support visible. She would stay at her side, ensuring she had companionship whenever she was not dancing.

"Good evening, ladies." A quick glance told Dorothy that, though the minister's

315

wife was trying to put on a good front, she was distressed. She needed more than casual conversation; she needed a sympathetic ear.

Dorothy turned to Mrs. Coleman. "I wonder if you could help me. I promised Laura I'd start pouring punch, and I could use an extra pair of hands."

When Mrs. Coleman nodded, Mrs. Lockhart shook her head. "I'd offer to help too, but Phil managed to convince me to dance with him. I told him he was a silly young man, but I agreed." She chuckled. "I guess that makes me a sillier old woman."

Grateful for the reprieve, Dorothy smiled. "You can't disappoint your beau."

When she and Mrs. Coleman reached the butler's pantry and were out of earshot, Dorothy turned to the minister's wife. "I don't really need help pouring punch, but I wanted to talk to you."

Mrs. Coleman nodded as she looked at the punch bowl with its single ladle. Only one person could fill the cups.

"My mother would tell me I shouldn't interfere," Dorothy explained, "but I couldn't help noticing that you seemed distraught. Is there anything I can do to help?"

Tears filled the older woman's eyes.

"There's nothing anyone other than God can do. I told Jonathan the letters might be a sign from God and that maybe it's time to listen to them."

Letters? Though she was certain there was no connection, Dorothy remembered the letters Mrs. Lockhart and the ranchers had received.

"Who's been sending you letters?"

Mrs. Coleman shrugged. "I don't know. They're all anonymous. Jonathan found some in the pulpit. There've been others slid under the door of the parsonage. I even found one in my shopping basket." The tears threatened to leak from her eyes. "I have no idea how it got there."

Unsure whether her next question would cause more distress but knowing that she had to ask it, Dorothy touched Mrs. Coleman's hand before she spoke. "What do they say?"

"That Jonathan should leave Mesquite Springs, that he's no longer an asset to the town. They say his messages come from Satan, not God, and that he's leading everyone astray by not preaching repentance."

Lies. All lies. But that didn't mean they hadn't inflicted deep wounds. Horrified by the messages and the realization that someone in Mesquite Springs was responsible for them, Dorothy didn't know what to say other than, "That's not true. They're lies."

The minister's wife nodded. "I know that, and so does Jonathan, but it seems like more and more of our parishioners believe the lies. Sometimes I wonder if there isn't a grain of truth in them."

Horror turned to outrage. "Pastor Coleman is not a tool of Satan!"

"That part's not true, but maybe it is true that he's no longer reaching hearts. If that's so, we need to leave." She brushed away the tears that had dampened her eyelashes. "You saw the way we were greeted today. It seems the town has split into two camps."

"What does Pastor Coleman say?"

The way his wife straightened her shoulders and looked directly at Dorothy reminded her of the minister himself. "He won't leave. He knows God led us here, and he says that until he hears otherwise directly from God, he's going to stay."

"I agree. Only cowards refuse to sign their names." Dorothy didn't want this good and godly couple to leave, and yet there were risks. Remembering Brandon's story of the cowards in Xavier and how they'd formed a mob made her shudder. She couldn't let that happen here. This was her home as well as the Colemans', and she wouldn't let people who were too cowardly to voice their opinions publicly destroy it.

"There must be a way to stop this," Dorothy said. The first step was to learn who was behind the attacks on the Colemans. The problem was, she had no idea how to identify that person any more than she knew how to identify Brandon's attacker. Could it be the same person? Though she hated the idea of two vicious people in Mesquite Springs, Dorothy could not imagine a connection between Brandon and the minister.

"Jonathan and I are praying for an answer, but so far we have not received one." Mrs. Coleman was silent for a moment, her eyes fixed on the ceiling as if she expected a heavenly messenger. "Like Jonathan, I want to see a sign, something that will tell me whether we should stay."

Dorothy knew what she wanted. The question was how to ensure it happened.

CHAPTER TWENTY-THREE

Holloway was proving more difficult than Phil had expected to discredit, discourage, dislodge . . . The words he used didn't matter; what did was that the man simply refused to leave, and the townspeople no longer showed any inclination to hasten his departure. Fortunately, the Coleman campaign, as Phil had named it, was proving more successful. Those letters he'd been writing and the stories he'd been spreading were taking root.

He lowered his eyes and pretended to search for a Bible verse, lest anyone see the gleam of satisfaction in them. He'd taken his usual seat in the last pew, not only because it gave him an easy exit, but because it was the perfect spot to watch the rest of the congregation.

They were all here. He'd thought attendance might be lower after the comments he'd overheard last night, but the church was as full as ever. What was different was the atmosphere. Though it wasn't a particularly cold day, he could feel the chill. Men and women who had previously leaned forward, nodding in approval when the preacher spoke, now sat with their arms folded, their expressions leaving no doubt that they were unhappy with the man who served as their shepherd. These sheep had no intention of following Coleman's lead. They were starting to follow his.

Phil bit back a smile. The way things were going, he might not need Brother Josiah for this part of the plan. It seemed that the people of Mesquite Springs were coming to their senses and realizing they needed a new preacher. If he was lucky, Coleman would be gone before the man arrived, but just in case he wasn't, Brother Josiah would show them what real preaching was while he denounced Holloway.

It would be a week no one in Mesquite Springs would forget. Certainly not Phil, whose nemesis would be gone and whose pockets would be heavier when it ended. Yes, indeed, having Brother Josiah come was a fine plan. A mighty fine plan.

This had not been Brandon's best day.

He looked at the articles he'd spread on

321

the large table, trying to decide how to arrange them for tomorrow's issue of the *Chronicle.* He should have made more progress, but his thoughts kept drifting to what had happened at lunchtime.

As usual, Laura had led him to a table with three other men. When he'd placed his order, the men returned to the subject they'd been discussing when he had joined them: Pastor Coleman.

"I heard tell I'm not the only one what falls asleep during his sermons," the first said.

The second man nodded. "Even my missus has trouble staying awake. We sure could use some Bible thumpin'." He took a bite of his stew before he continued. "I cain't remember where I heard it, but someone told me folks are wonderin' why he don't preach more about Sodom and Gomorrah and what happens to sinners. Seems to me he's ignoring a big part of the Bible. Kinda makes me ask whether he was sent here by God."

"Iffen you ask me, we could use a new preacher." The third joined the conversation.

"We sure could. Anybody know how you git rid of a preacher?"

The discussion had deteriorated from

there. While no one suggested tar and feathers, their ideas weren't far removed from that. And though Brandon urged moderation, his ideas were quickly squashed.

"You ain't been here long enough to know what real preaching is like. Preacher Harrison — he's the one what was here before Coleman — sure could keep a body awake. Not a week went by without a story of fire and brimstone."

The Bible spoke of more than that, but it was clear this trio had no interest in stories of love and forgiveness. Brandon had left Polly's Place having barely tasted the food, his head whirling with the implications of the conversation. Even now, hours later, he'd been unable to put it out of his mind. If only he could discuss it with Dorothy, but she was late — another sign that this was not a good day.

The clock was striking four when she rushed in the front door. "I'm sorry I'm late, but it took more time than I'd expected to write this week's articles." She held out the sheets covered with her neat penmanship. "They're done, but unfortunately, there's one fewer than usual. So many people are as sick as Ma was the night of the Downeys' party that they didn't have much news."

Less content than normal was not what he wanted to hear.

"We'll have to use a bigger font." Brandon hated to do that, because it felt as if he were cheating his subscribers, but he saw no alternative. He would not publish a paper with blank space. Though Dorothy nodded as if she'd expected that, something in her expression told him she was concerned about more than the shortage of content. "Is something wrong? You're not ill, are you?"

She shook her head. "It's the Colemans."

Relief flowed through Brandon along with a sense of amazement that he and Dorothy were concerned about the same people on the same day.

"I wanted to talk to you about them too," he admitted. "What have you heard?"

She settled into one of the chairs and waited until he'd taken the second before she replied. "I thought the nasty comments had died down, but they seem to be escalating. Did you notice how some people shunned the Colemans at the party?"

"I can't say that I did." Brandon had been preoccupied with the hope that he would be able to discover whoever was behind his attack.

"It seemed like half the people there went

out of their way to ignore them. And having that happen the same week someone hurt you, well . . ." Dorothy twisted her hands in an uncharacteristic gesture of worry. "I don't like it. Not one bit. This isn't the Mesquite Springs I know."

Dorothy's hands stilled, but her eyes reflected pain as she said, "It's almost ironic. There was a time when both Wyatt and I were convinced we wanted to leave Mesquite Springs. We were certain we'd have better lives somewhere else — anywhere else."

Her chuckle held little mirth, but the way she moistened her lips told Brandon Dorothy was not yet finished.

"I didn't fully understand why Wyatt decided to run for mayor. It seemed he was abandoning his dream."

This time she paused, and Brandon knew she was ready to listen. "Perhaps Wyatt's dream changed once Evelyn came to town." Brandon had no problem understanding how the right woman could make a man reevaluate his life.

"That was part of it," Dorothy agreed, "but he also wanted to make sure the town had the right leadership. Sam Plaut was one of his closest friends, but he wasn't the right man to become mayor."

Though Brandon wasn't certain where all this was leading, he would do nothing to discourage Dorothy from continuing, not when she was opening a window into her innermost feelings.

"When I first moved into town, I saw it as a step toward independence," she said, "but the longer I lived here, the more I realized that I wanted to do everything I could to make Mesquite Springs an even better place to live. Like Wyatt, I wanted to contribute to the town."

"And you have. Your articles for the *Chronicle* brought the residents together."

Dorothy shook her head. "Past tense. They were a unifying force, but they're not enough. The town I love is being torn apart. It may sound extreme, but it feels as if there's something evil at work here. Look what happened to you. I can't understand why anyone would want to hurt you any more than I can understand the cruel things people are saying about Pastor Coleman."

Brandon shared her concerns. "It worries me too. What I heard today reminds me of what it was like in Xavier after I wrote that editorial." He shuddered at the memory of the hatred that had turned normally peaceful residents into a vicious mob. "The discontent is growing, and I don't think it would take much to turn it into anger. I heard three men talking about taking action against the minister today."

And then there was his accident that wasn't an accident. Though he had yet to find a connection between that and the rumors that were circulating against Pastor Coleman, Brandon knew there must be one. Somehow, someone felt threatened by him and the minister.

"Some people have already done more than talk. They've started sending Pastor Coleman letters telling him to leave town." Dorothy wrinkled her nose in disgust. "Of course, they don't sign them."

"Cowards." Angry anonymous letters had been the first step in Xavier, but it hadn't taken long for the situation to deteriorate into violence.

"Exactly. This isn't like last year when Wyatt was running for mayor. The town was divided then, but everything was in the open. There were a lot of arguments about who would be the best mayor — I think there were even a few fistfights — but it didn't feel the same. Those were honest disagreements. This feels like someone is trying to undermine both you and Pastor Coleman."

"And I haven't even taken a stand."

Brandon was struck by the irony.

Dorothy's eyes reflected her worries. "I keep remembering a verse from the Bible — I think it's in the third chapter of Mark — where Jesus says that if a kingdom is divided against itself, it cannot stand. Mesquite Springs isn't a kingdom, but I'm afraid this division will destroy it."

Brandon, who'd seen how destructive divisions could be, shared her fear. Unless this was stopped, the damage could be irreparable. A week ago, he would have done nothing, telling himself the risks were too great, but now that he'd made peace with his father's death, he knew he could not stand aside and let the divisions grow.

He looked down at the pages Dorothy had given him and nodded. His path was clear. "I believe there's a reason you have fewer stories than usual today."

The abrupt change of subject appeared to have confused her. "What reason could that be?"

"It gives me space to print an editorial."

Dorothy stared at him, shock vying with relief to dominate her expression. "Do you want to do that?"

Want had nothing to do with Brandon's decision. "No, I don't want to, but I know I must. My conscience won't let me sleep if I don't do everything I can to heal the rift."

He sighed, remembering the men whose table he'd shared. "I don't think it will be easy. No one would listen to me when I urged moderation at lunch. They told me I was a newcomer and didn't understand."

Dorothy's soft scoff told him she didn't share the men's opinion.

"I don't believe that's true, either," he told her. "You don't have to have spent your whole life here to know the difference between right and wrong. What's happening is wrong."

She nodded. "And you're going to say that in your editorial."

"We're going to. Those men were right about one thing. I am a newcomer. I know what's right and what's wrong, but you know the people better than I do. I'm counting on you to help me."

Brandon saw both pleasure and hope on Dorothy's face. "You told me once that people might not listen to Brandon Holloway, the man, but they'd pay attention to Brandon Holloway, the editor." He rose and extended his hand, helping her up from the chair. "Let's find out whether you're right."

CHAPTER TWENTY-FOUR

Phil grabbed the paper with both hands and began to shred it. *Why now?* he demanded as he turned what had been a full sheet of news into tiny bits of paper.

Thank goodness he'd returned to his room to read this week's issue of the *Chronicle* instead of sitting on the porch as he did most days. He could vent his anger here where no one saw him, but if he'd been outside, he would have had to mask it. No one in Mesquite Springs could see the real Phil Blakeslee.

Mr. K had been adamant about that. "As far as anyone in that town knows, you're just a simple artist trying to make a living with your sketches and paintings." A simple artist wouldn't have reacted to today's paper. He wouldn't have cared, but Phil did.

He smiled in satisfaction as he tossed the last bit of paper into the stove. One match, and it would be gone. All gone. If only the other copies of that hateful editorial could be destroyed as easily.

Why? The question reverberated through his brain. Brandon Holloway had never before taken a stand. Why had he started now? The man ought to have been extra cautious after the fall he'd taken, but instead he seemed emboldened. What he'd written today reminded Phil of Robert Monroe, the wretched man who'd denounced Esther, and it reinforced Mr. K's decree that there be no newspapers in the town where he was going to open a hotel.

Mr. K.

Phil frowned at the thought of his boss's reaction if he learned that Mesquite Springs did indeed have a paper. He'd be angry, which was one thing Phil couldn't let happen. He couldn't disappoint the man who'd done so much for him. There was only one thing to do: reverse the damage and ensure nothing like this happened again. He'd been trying, but he had to do more.

He dusted his hands and grabbed his coat. Mr. K had told him to do everything behind the scenes, but that hadn't worked. He'd try a different approach today. It would be a friendly visit, and he'd use what Mr. K had called his persuasive skills to convince the man to print a retraction.

"People will do almost anything if you ask them nicely," Mr. K had explained the day he'd declared Phil's education was complete and he was ready to come to work for him. "If you order them to do something, their first reaction is to refuse — no one likes being commanded — but they'll almost always agree to a humble request from someone they've learned to trust." That had been one of many lessons Phil had learned from the man who'd given him a chance to succeed.

He buttoned his coat and descended the stairs.

He wouldn't go to the newspaper office directly from the boardinghouse. That would be too obvious. Instead, he'd walk the opposite direction, as if he were merely strolling around town. And if he just happened to chat with Brandon Holloway on the day that he'd done something out of the ordinary, well . . . . No one would find that remarkable.

Phil was heading west on Main when he saw the subject of that despicable article emerge from the parsonage.

"Morning, Parson," he said as politely as he could. "I reckon you're pleased by this week's paper."

The man whose interference had the power to derail Mr. K's plans gave him a look that said he saw behind the casual air Phil had assumed. "Why would you say that?" he asked.

"It 'pears to me that the editorial is defending you against some slurs."

Coleman's gray eyes were as warm as if he and Phil were friends, but there was a knowing glint in them that worried him.

"That's not the way I read it," the preacher said. "It seems to me that Brandon was asking people to talk to each other and to listen to others' opinions the way you and I are right now."

He knew. The thought pierced Phil's confidence and left him reeling. He wasn't sure how he'd discovered it, but this preacher man knew that Phil was behind the attacks on him. He had to be stopped.

"It's always a pleasure talkin' to you, Parson." Somehow the words came out smoothly, when all the while he wanted to throttle the man who could destroy Phil's chance at wealth.

"And listening?"

Preachers were all the same, using their power to destroy innocent people. Old Selby had joined the town's newspaperman in condemning Esther without ever considering that the truth might differ from what Monroe had printed. Like Coleman here,

Selby talked about listening, but he hadn't listened to anyone except his newspaper buddy.

Phil nodded, wanting nothing more than to end this conversation. "Why, sure. I always listen to your sermons." He didn't like them, but he heard them. "The one about lovin' one's neighbor was a mighty fine one."

This time a smile flitted across Coleman's lips. "I was thinking that next week's might be about truth and how it sets you free. What do you think about that?"

What he thought was that this conversation had gone on too long. What he said was, "I reckon that would be a fine sermon too." Phil started to walk away.

Coleman extended his hand, leaving Phil no alternative but to shake it. "You know, Phil, if you ever want to talk, I'm a good listener. Sometimes another view of a situation can help a person see what's important."

Phil nodded. What was important was ensuring that this man and Holloway didn't cause any problems for Mr. K.

Polly's Place had been closed for an hour, and Evelyn and Laura had almost finished the cleanup by the time Dorothy entered the restaurant, planning to help herself to a piece of the pie Evelyn had saved for her. Thanks to last spring's horse sale that had brought prospective buyers from across the state, Evelyn's oatmeal pecan pie had become famous not only in Mesquite Springs but throughout Texas, and she received regular requests to mail whole pies to men who'd enjoyed a piece while they were here. So far, she'd resisted, but Dorothy suspected she might change her mind once the baby was born. It would be easier to run a bakery than a restaurant.

The question of bakery vs. restaurant was clearly not the subject of this afternoon's discussion.

"Did you help write today's *Chronicle?*" Laura asked. "It's all anyone could talk about."

"If you mean the editorial, yes, I did help with it." The hours she and Brandon spent debating which words would be powerful but not incendiary had been among the most exhilarating of her life. When they'd finished, Dorothy had been convinced that the *Chronicle*'s first editorial would accomplish Brandon's goal of making people think.

She had wanted to be with him today, to experience the reaction firsthand, but he'd insisted that she not come to the office and had advised her to stay in her apartment. Unwilling to hide but recognizing the wisdom of Brandon's request, Dorothy had compromised by spending the day at the ranch.

"Brandon and I are both worried about the division we see in the town. Mesquite Springs has never been like this."

"I have the same concerns." Evelyn slid a piece of pie onto a plate and handed it to Dorothy. "Do you want a glass of milk to go with that?" When Dorothy nodded, she poured it, then gestured toward the table.

"This is much worse than during the election last year," Evelyn said, confirming what Dorothy had told Brandon less than a day ago. She turned toward Laura. "You weren't here for that, but the town was almost evenly divided. Half believed Sam should be mayor, and the other half supported Wyatt."

Even Evelyn's delicious pie could not erase the bitter taste that the election had left. "There were some ugly arguments." Dorothy had been more incensed over the attacks on her brother than Wyatt himself. "Fortunately, once the election was over, the town came back together." She frowned as she looked up at her friends. "This feels different."

Laura nodded. "I heard talk about establishing another church. Maybe that's the answer. Some towns have two or three."

Dorothy did not share her opinion. "Those towns are larger than Mesquite Springs. Besides, when there are multiple churches, isn't it normally because of doctrinal differences? I don't think that's the problem here. These are personal attacks on Pastor Coleman. Someone wants him to leave town." Someone had sown seeds of dissent, and those seeds had taken root.

Though the minister had not been attacked physically, the cruel words had done more damage than the rope on Brandon's steps. He would recover from the fall, but Pastor Coleman might not recover from the attack on his integrity and his calling.

"I agree with what you and Brandon are doing," Evelyn said.

Though she'd been about to take a sip of milk, Dorothy set the glass back on the table. "A newspaper is more than entertainment or simply reporting what happened. When an editor sees important issues, it's his responsibility to bring them to everyone's attention."

"Do you think it'll make a difference?" Laura seemed skeptical.

"I hope so." For Brandon's sake as well as Pastor Coleman's. If the editorial turned the tide and helped restore the town's faith in its minister, it would also restore Brandon's belief in himself, showing him that the risks he'd taken were worthwhile.

Brandon settled into the chair he always took when he visited Pastor Coleman. It wasn't the most comfortable one in the room, but somehow this straight-backed chair had become his, perhaps because it had the best view of the oil painting of Jesus with the children. The love he saw embodied in that painting never failed to fill his heart with peace. He hoped it would do so today.

Perhaps he should have chosen another day, one that had been filled with less drama, but the questions that had whirled through his brain, disturbing him more than ceaseless drumming, demanded answers.

"You look troubled, Brandon." The minister settled onto the settee at the opposite side of the low table, giving Brandon the space he needed but also the opportunity to look directly at him if he chose. "I trust it's not because of what you wrote. I appreciate your trying to help, but it wasn't necessary."

"I believe it was. My conscience told me I needed to take a stand, so I did." He and

Dorothy had agonized over every word in that editorial, with the result that it had taken him more than twice as long to write as anything else of that length, but when they'd finished, Brandon had known it was the best piece he'd written since he arrived in Mesquite Springs, perhaps ever.

Pastor Coleman gave him a wry smile. "I imagine you've received some complaints."

"Yes, but just as many compliments. I told everyone who came the same thing, that I welcomed their opinions and would print any letters I receive in the next issue."

"And by doing so, you encouraged a conversation. Excellent work."

Though his heart warmed at the praise, Brandon needed to turn the conversation in a different direction. "I'm glad you approve, but that's not why I'm here. I'd like your advice."

"I'm happy to help you any way I can. What's troubling you?"

"I can't stop thinking about your sermon."

"The one about love?" The minister leaned forward ever so slightly, encouraging Brandon to continue.

He nodded. "Love in all its forms."

"And, I'm guessing, not necessarily love for a neighbor." There was the faintest hint of humor in Pastor Coleman's voice, or perhaps it was pleasure. Brandon wasn't certain.

"You're right. That's why I need your advice. You and Mrs. Coleman have been married a long time."

"Almost twenty years."

That's what Brandon had assumed. While the marriage wasn't as long as his parents' had been, it had lasted long enough to qualify the minister as an expert.

"How did you know you were in love with her?"

The soft smile that lit Pastor Coleman's face told Brandon he was thinking of his wife and that those thoughts were happy ones. "Let me turn that question around," he said, surprising Brandon with his response. "How do you feel about the woman who has you so perplexed?"

He hadn't expected that, nor did he want to reply, but Brandon knew he needed to if he was going to have his question answered.

"She's the first thing I think about every morning and the last thing every night. If a day goes by without seeing her, I feel as if it was a wasted day." Brandon paused, knowing there was more to say. "I hate it when she's unhappy, so I do everything I can to make her smile."

The minister nodded, as if he understood.

"Do you find her physically attractive?"

"Oh yes." There was no doubt about that. "This may sound strange, though. I've seen other women who are more beautiful on the outside. It's what's inside her that attracts me. She's kind, thoughtful, loyal to her friends." He paused for a second. "She challenges me to be a better man, and I like that. We don't always agree, but she always listens to me." Perhaps that was why he'd stressed the need for people to listen when he'd written the editorial.

"Do you listen to her?"

"Of course. I respect her opinion, but that's not love, is it?" Instead of giving him an answer, Pastor Coleman posed another question. "When you think about your future, is she in it?"

"I want her to be. The idea of a life without her feels like . . ." Brandon struggled to find the correct analogy.

"Like a meal without seasoning?" the minister suggested.

"No. That's trivial. If I had to live without her, I feel as if I'd be nothing but an empty shell."

His face wreathed in a smile, Pastor Coleman reached forward and grasped Brandon's hand. "You, my friend, are in love."

CHAPTER TWENTY-FIVE

Phil frowned as his stomach began to rumble. It was too late to eat at Polly's Place. He should have gone there at noon, but he'd been so angry that he'd known he couldn't swallow a bite. His plan to have a polite discussion with that blasted newspaperman and convince him to print a retraction had been derailed by his conversation with Coleman.

When he'd left the preacher, he'd been in no mood to be conciliatory to anyone and had spent hours at the spring, staring at the bubbling water, his thoughts whirling. Now he'd have to eat whatever Mrs. Bayles had left, unless . . . Phil patted his stomach, his frown turning upside down. If he took Mrs. Lockhart some of the bath salts he'd seen at the mercantile, she might invite him to stay for supper, particularly if his stomach continued its noisy demands to be fed. Yes, that might work.

Minutes later, the carefully wrapped package in his hand, he left the mercantile. Rather than retrace his steps, he continued west on Main, planning to turn onto River and head for the widow's home that way. But when he reached the intersection, he stopped, the fury that had consumed him when he'd read that cursed editorial rising up again.

There he was. Brandon Holloway, the man who'd stirred up trouble, was leaving the home of the man who'd started it. Phil gripped the package in his hand so tightly that the corners of the box left grooves in his palm. He should have realized Holloway and the parson were in cahoots just like the editor and the preacher who'd killed Esther as surely as if they'd fashioned the noose. They'd probably spent the afternoon congratulating themselves on all they'd accomplished and plotting their next sermons and editorials.

Anger, deeper and stronger than any he'd felt since Esther had died, swept through Phil along with the conviction that it was time for stronger measures. Being subtle hadn't worked. Someone had to stop this madness, and he was that someone.

Brandon stared out the back window, smiling when he saw her emerge from the restaurant. It was later than usual, almost dark, but there she was, holding Nutmeg's leash, obviously ready to take the dog on a walk. Grabbing his coat and sliding his arms into it as he walked, Brandon hurried out the door. He wouldn't waste another minute. As he'd told Pastor Coleman, he was empty without her, and he wanted — no, he needed — to tell her how he felt.

"Dorothy!" Brandon was practically running as he crossed the yard toward the alley. "May I join you?"

Though dusk was approaching, there was still enough light to see the pleasure on her face, and his heart skipped a beat at the thought that she might share his tender feelings. His hopes were dashed a second later when she said, "I want to hear all about your day and what people said about the editorial."

The editorial wasn't important compared to what Brandon wanted to say to Dorothy, but he knew she was like a terrier. She wouldn't stop asking until he told her what had happened.

"Reactions were mixed, exactly as I expected. Some people cursed me soundly; others shook my hand and congratulated me."

344

"No tar and feathers?" The lilt in her voice told him Dorothy was teasing, not trying to remind him of the horrible time in Xavier.

"Not for me." Though some of Mesquite Springs's residents had been angry, Brandon had not felt the same underlying fury that had been present in Xavier. "I'm not sure anyone has changed their opinion of Pastor Coleman, but I hope they have." That had been the purpose of the editorial. "He's a good man."

"I agree. I also think he's a good minister for Mesquite Springs."

The conversation continued to veer off the track Brandon had planned. It was time to redirect it.

"My mother used to say that Romans 8:28 was one of her favorite Bible verses."

"The one about God using everything for good?" Dorothy sounded perplexed, justifiably so, since he'd changed the subject of their conversation without warning. "Do you believe something good will come from all the ugliness the Colemans have had to endure?"

"I hope so, but I was actually thinking of what happened to me." Brandon tapped his head. "I won't say I'm happy about the knock I took, but it seems like a gift from God."

He ruffled Nutmeg's ears, reveling in the dog's simple acceptance of him. If only he'd accepted the truth earlier. "I probably won't sound as if I'm making much sense, but Doc and I had a talk while he was patching me up, and what he said made sense. For the first time, I believed what the doctor in Xavier and you told me, that I wasn't responsible for my father's death."

He stopped and extended his hand, waiting until Dorothy placed her free one in his before he said, "I can't undo the past, but I can build a better future. That's what I want: a future . . . with you."

Dorothy's heart stuttered, then began to race. She must have been mistaken. Surely Brandon hadn't said what she thought he had.

"What did you say?"

His eyes were serious but radiated a warmth that dispelled the chill of the early evening. "I want a future with you." He spoke slowly, deliberately, as if trying to ensure that she understood. "You're the woman I love. You're the woman I want to marry."

Her head began to reel, and for a second, Dorothy wondered if she were about to faint. Brandon had said it twice now, so he must mean it. He wanted a future with her. And she . . . at the moment, her thoughts were so turbulent that she was not certain what she wanted. She wanted love; she wanted happiness; and yet . . .

As if she sensed Dorothy's distress, Nutmeg began to whimper. Dorothy pulled her hand from Brandon's and stroked the dog's head, trying to give her the comfort she sought for herself.

"Are you certain this isn't a passing fancy like the one you had for Laura?"

"Laura?" Brandon's shock was too strong to be feigned. "What are you talking about?"

"I was with you on Christmas Eve," she said slowly. "I saw the way you looked at her when we were talking after the service. You couldn't hide your longing, and when you told me a puppy wasn't what you wanted for Christmas, I knew Laura was."

For a moment, Brandon looked so perplexed that Dorothy wanted to tell him it didn't matter. But it did. Then he nodded.

"I'd almost forgotten that, but it wasn't what you thought. I was looking at Laura's parents and feeling more than a touch of envy. Even from a distance, it was evident that they were still deeply in love. That was what I wanted — a love like Leonard and Ida have."

That was the same kind of love Dorothy wanted, but she knew it would never be hers.

"I believe I could have that kind of love with you," he said.

Dorothy shook her head. "Once things settle down, you'll realize that you've mistaken what we share at the *Chronicle* for love. We work well together, but that's not the same as marriage."

She wouldn't tell Brandon that whenever the thought of marriage crossed her mind, she pictured herself with a man like him. There was no reason to share that with him, because it was nothing more than a fleeting fancy. The cold reality was that she could not take the risk. She had made that decision years ago and nothing — not even wonderful, loveable Brandon — would make her reverse it. An empty heart was far better than a broken one.

Brandon took a step closer to her, causing Nutmeg to utter a soft growl. With her puppies gone, Nutmeg was especially protective of Dorothy.

"You can say all you want, but I'm not mistaken," he insisted. "It wasn't chance that brought me to Mesquite Springs. It was God using your article to lead me. He knew and now I know that I'm meant to be here with you." Brandon's voice deepened with conviction. "I could search for the rest of my life, and I'd never find a woman more right for me."

They were words that would melt any woman's heart, and for a moment, Dorothy felt herself waver. Then the memory of Ma's grief resurfaced, bolstering her resolve.

"I'm not going to marry . . . ever."

Brandon shook his head. "Laura told me you said that, but I don't believe it. I believe you're the one who's mistaken." He patted Nutmeg's head, and this time the dog did not resist. "I'm giving you fair warning, Dorothy. I plan to change your mind."

Holloway was gone. Phil gloated at the way everything was fitting together. His timing had been perfect. He'd been on his way home from Mrs. Lockhart's when he passed the alley and spotted them there. Holloway was standing with Dorothy and that mutt of hers. Phil had paused long enough to see that they were setting out, not returning from their walk. Perfect. Perfect. Perfect. He'd have enough time for what he had to do.

Moving as silently as he could, he entered the boardinghouse and strode toward the pantry. If anyone saw him, they'd think he was looking for something to eat. Instead, he grabbed the hammer from the third shelf and hid it under his coat. He had never understood why Mrs. Bayles kept a hammer and nails next to bags of flour and sugar, but he didn't care. A hammer was what he needed, and now he had it.

Thank goodness for the alley that skirted the back of the boardinghouse and Holloway's home. Few traveled it at this time of day, making it unlikely anyone would see him opening the rear door of the *Chronicle.* He tested the latch and grinned, thankful that hardly anybody locked doors in this town.

Though the half-moon shone through the bare windows, providing enough light for him to see where he was going, it wasn't bright enough that anyone would spot him. No one would be looking for him, anyway. As long as he didn't light a candle or one of those lamps, he'd be safe.

When he reached the room that housed the press, Phil raised his hammer, then lowered it. He ought to destroy the press, but now that he was here and saw how sturdy it was, he doubted Mrs. Bayles's hammer was strong enough. The last thing he needed was to make so much noise that someone heard him and came to investigate, but he couldn't leave without ensuring that today's issue of the *Chronicle* would be the last.

He looked around, chuckling when he spotted shallow boxes filled with type. Not even Holloway could print a paper without type.

Still chuckling, Phil raised his hammer.

CHAPTER TWENTY-SIX

He should have realized it would not be simple. Dorothy was a determined woman. He might even call her stubborn, because once she made up her mind about something, it was difficult to get her to change it. But he would. He was as determined as she. Though Dorothy might believe that she would never marry, Brandon had no intention of abandoning their hope for future happiness without a fight.

God had brought him to Mesquite Springs for a reason, and Dorothy was a large part of that reason. Brandon no longer had any doubts about that. The challenge would be convincing her.

He glanced at the dog straining at her leash. "Nutmeg doesn't look like she's ready to go home."

After Dorothy had delivered her flat refusal, she'd turned around, clearly no longer wanting to visit the spring. And since darkness was rapidly approaching, there would be little to see at the spring anyway. But as they neared the corner of Spring and River, Brandon knew he wasn't ready for the evening to end. If he was going to win Dorothy's heart — and he was determined that he would — he needed to woo her, and wooing involved spending as much time as possible together. Nutmeg was a good excuse.

"She has a lot of energy now that the puppies are gone," Dorothy admitted. "You should see her when she spots one of them. She practically tears my arm off."

This was the Dorothy that Brandon knew and loved, the one who could laugh at her dog's antics. He gave a silent prayer of thanksgiving that she sounded so normal and that his fears that she might be reluctant to spend time with him now that he'd declared his love had not been fulfilled.

"Shall we go around the block then?"

"All right. It's a lovely night." Perhaps it was only his imagination that she sounded eager, but at least he heard no hesitation in her voice.

Brandon kept the conversation light, then stopped when they reached the walk leading to his home. "Can you wait a minute? I have something for Nutmeg."

His mother had once told him that the way to a man's heart was through his stomach. Was it possible that the way to Dorothy's heart was through her dog's stomach? It was worth a try.

"Mrs. Lockhart brought me some roast beef, and I saved the fat for Nutmeg."

"She'd love that." The pleasure in Dorothy's voice told Brandon he had not made a mistake. Even Nutmeg seemed to approve, giving a short bark, as if she understood the humans' conversation.

His spirits lighter than they'd been since Dorothy's refusal, Brandon slid the key into the lock, opened the door, and entered the hallway. A second later, he stopped abruptly as the hairs on the back of his neck rose. Something was wrong. He tipped his head to one side and listened. No unexpected sounds, no sense that someone else was here. It was probably nothing more than his imagination.

He strode into the office, lit the desk lamp, and looked around. Nothing was amiss here. Lamp in hand, he crossed the hall to the pressroom and stopped, feeling the blood draining from his face at the sight before him. Not again!

"Dorothy!" Brandon raced to the front door, gesturing for her to come inside.

"You'd better leave Nutmeg out there."

"What's wrong?" she asked as she wrapped the dog's leash around the porch rail.

Wordlessly, he led the way to the pressroom. The faint hope that he'd imagined the destruction faded as quickly as it was ignited. Overturned boxes, bottles of ink leaking their contents onto stacks of paper, and the type trays — oh, the type trays. It hadn't been his imagination.

Dorothy's horrified gasp mirrored Brandon's emotions. "First the rope on the steps. Now this. Oh, Brandon, who's responsible?" Her eyes darkened with worry as she gestured toward what remained of the type trays. The vandal had done almost everything he could to ensure that the *Chronicle* had printed its last issue.

"I don't know. It could have been any one of a dozen men who came here today. They were all angry. I thought I calmed them down, but apparently I didn't."

The scene, so reminiscent of the one in Xavier last fall, made Brandon shudder. At least no one had died tonight. That was the only good thing he could say.

Anger flickered across Dorothy's face. "I wish you hadn't written the editorial." She pressed her lips together, as if trying not to cry.

Brandon took a step closer, wanting to enfold her in his arms and ease her anguish, but he knew the time was not right. Instead, he infused his words with as much warmth as he could muster.

"You don't really mean that. You know it was the right thing to do."

Tears glistened in her eyes. "But we didn't think this would be the result."

"I knew there was a risk. There are risks to everything in life." Brandon had risked his heart when he told Dorothy of his love, but he wouldn't remind her of that. "Apparently one of the men was angrier than I realized."

"Are you certain it was a man?"

"If it had been a woman, we would smell her perfume." He made a show of sniffing the air. "I smell tobacco."

Skirting the debris that now littered the floor, Brandon walked to the press, and this time his smile was genuine. "At least George was spared."

It was an inanimate object, nothing more than pieces of metal, and yet Brandon felt a sense of satisfaction that the press his father had died protecting had survived tonight's attack. A newspaper press might not be the legacy Pa had wanted to leave Brandon, but it was the one thing that remained of their life in Xavier.

"You may have the press, but that doesn't mean you can print a paper." Dorothy pursed her lips as she surveyed the destruction. "The type is all gone. It's been smashed to smithereens." Bits of type had flown across the room, mute testimony to the intruder's fury.

"That's true, but it's not the end of the *Chronicle*. On Monday I was annoyed that the new type hadn't arrived. Now I'm grateful for whatever delayed the shipment."

Brandon thought about the supply of paper that was also scheduled to arrive this week. If it came on time, he wouldn't have to skip an issue. "Despite everything the intruder has done, we'll be able to print a paper."

Though she still seemed dubious, Dorothy nodded. "You need to report what happened to the sheriff. Do you want me to get him?"

"Would you?" Fletcher wouldn't be pleased by the second incident in a week, but he needed to be notified. "I want to see if I can figure out how the vandal got inside."

After he'd escorted Dorothy to the front

door, Brandon walked slowly through the rest of the house. When he reached the kitchen, he noticed that the back door was ajar. This must have been the path of entry, but how? A quick inspection revealed no sign of force.

Brandon clenched his fists in frustration. In his eagerness to see Dorothy, he must have forgotten to lock the back door. This was his fault.

"Do you suppose Pastor Coleman will preach about the destruction?" Dorothy asked the next Sunday morning. As had become their habit, her mother, Wyatt, Evelyn, and Polly had come to her apartment for breakfast before the service began. Though her culinary skills would never match Evelyn's, Dorothy could make an edible breakfast.

"I imagine so." Wyatt helped himself to a second helping of scrambled eggs. "It's the only thing anyone's talked about in days. Fletcher still has no idea who could be responsible, and that bothers him."

Evelyn's eyes, whose vivid blue color reminded Dorothy of the summer sky, were serious as she said, "I wonder if we'll ever know."

"I hope so. Brandon's discouraged by

what happened." Dorothy knew the destruction must have brought back memories of his father's death, but she suspected that was not his only concern. Though he'd made no reference to his proposal of marriage, she had caught him looking at her wistfully, as if trying to decide how to best woo her. There was no best way, no way at all, because — no matter that Brandon claimed that all of life involved risks — marriage was one risk she would not take.

Dorothy forced her attention back to the present. "Even though the new type and another shipment of paper arrived, Brandon talked about not printing an issue this week." And that had surprised her. The night they'd discovered the destruction, he'd seemed determined not to miss a week, but by the next morning, he'd had second thoughts, telling Dorothy he was afraid it would only inflame more people.

Though he had said no more, she wondered if he was worried about her safety. It was understandable that what had happened to his father would color his view of the situation, even though Dorothy knew it was unlikely that someone would dare to harm the mayor's sister.

Wyatt gave her an appraising look as he buttered a biscuit. "But you convinced

Brandon otherwise."

While it was true, Dorothy wondered how her brother had realized that. "What makes you say that?"

"I know you, little sister." The grin he tried to hide behind a biscuit was triumphant.

Polly, who'd been uncharacteristically silent, plopped her elbows on the table and stared at Dorothy. "Are you gonna marry Mr. Brandon? I think you should."

Dorothy almost choked on a bite of eggs. This wasn't the first time Polly had asked that question, but it was the most public.

Clearly trying to hold back a chuckle, Evelyn gave the child a stern look. "Now, Polly, you know it's not nice to ask personal questions."

"But I wanna know. I like Mr. Brandon." Polly turned back to Dorothy. "Don't you, Aunt Dorothy?"

"I do." As the words came out, Dorothy blushed at the realization of how the adults might construe them. That was not what she meant, not at all.

Undaunted, Polly plunked her glass on the table and announced, "Then you oughta marry him."

Wyatt exchanged a quick look with Evelyn before he laughed. "Take my advice, Dorothy. Don't argue with Polly. She always wins."

"Today's sermon is based on two verses, both from the twenty-third chapter of Luke."

Phil leaned back in the pew, trying to drown out the preacher's voice. He hadn't wanted to set foot inside the church today, but he knew this was not the time to be absent. If he didn't come, someone might think he had a guilty conscience. He didn't. Of course, he didn't.

"For those of you who are scrambling to find the chapter and are wondering why I chose Jesus's words from the cross when it's not Good Friday," the minister continued, "it's because I find these to be some of the most powerful words on a subject that weighs heavily on me: forgiveness."

Forgiveness. Esther had talked about that too, and look what it had gotten her. Public condemnation and burial in unconsecrated ground.

"Who needs to forgive and to be forgiven?" Though Coleman posed it as a question, Phil knew it was a rhetorical one. No one in the congregation would speak during the sermon.

"We all do, for we are all sinners." There

it was, the gospel according to Coleman. "Whether your sin is petty gossip or destruction of someone else's property, it is as much a sin as murder."

Phil wanted to believe it was his imagination that the preacher looked directly at him when he spoke of property destruction. If anyone had seen him, if there'd been any proof, he would have heard from Fletcher Engel, but when he'd bumped into the sheriff on his way into church this morning, the man had merely nodded.

"The wages of sin is death. The Bible tells us this is so, and I for one believe it. That's why I try not to sin."

Phil had tried too, but it wasn't easy. Not easy at all.

"No matter how earnestly I try, I fail because I'm human, and it's human nature to sin."

For the first time since the preacher had begun, Phil looked directly at him. Maybe the man understood after all. Maybe this sermon wasn't about condemnation but commiseration. Phil shook his head at the improbability of that. Preachers were all the same. Condemn, condemn, condemn. That's all they knew.

"So, what hope do I have?" Coleman paused after posing another of those rhetorical questions. "None by myself, but infinite hope because of Jesus and his sacrifice. And that brings us to the verses I've chosen for today. While Jesus was on the cross, Luke reports that he spoke three times. The first two times, his words were for others."

Though Phil suspected the man had everything memorized, he held up his Bible as if he were reading from it.

"Verse 34 says, 'Father, forgive them; for they know not what they do.' " Coleman laid the Bible back on the pulpit. "Was Jesus speaking only of the Romans who crucified him or the Jews who chose Barabbas over him? I don't believe so. I believe he was asking for forgiveness for each of us. Even when we sin intentionally, we do not understand the full implications, and yet Jesus pled for us to be forgiven."

The preacher paused again, his gaze moving from row to row, as if he were making certain he had everyone's attention.

"Think about it. Would you do that? *Could* you do that? Could you forgive everyone who's ever hurt you or who will ever hurt you? I couldn't, because I'm human, but Jesus is divine. He can, he did, and he always will forgive us."

It was a pretty story, a bit like the fairy tales Esther had loved so much. But like those fairy tales, it was only a story, wishful thinking. Phil hoped the preacher was done talking, because he was done listening.

"I'm overwhelmed with gratitude when I think of that, and so was one of the two criminals who was crucified alongside Jesus. Luke calls them malefactors, people who do wrong. One of them heard the way Jesus forgave others and, though he knew he was unworthy, he wanted that same forgiveness for himself. He admitted his sin and asked Jesus to remember him."

Phil's ears perked up. He must have heard this story before, but he couldn't recall what came next.

"What did Jesus say? Listen to verse 43. 'Verily I say unto thee, Today thou shalt be with me in paradise.' Today. Not sometime in the future, but today." The preacher closed his Bible and looked out at the congregation. "And that, my friends, is why I have hope."

The sermon continued, but Phil had heard enough, more than enough. Coleman could say all he wanted about forgiveness, but he knew better. If Coleman found out what Phil had done, he would do everything in his power to have him arrested. That wasn't forgiveness; that was interference. He couldn't let that happen. Phil needed

everything to be ready for Mr. K.
If only Brother Josiah were already here.

everything to be ready for Mr. K.
If only Brother Josiah were already here.

CHAPTER TWENTY-SEVEN

"Have you ever heard of Brother Josiah?" Brandon asked as Dorothy entered the office. Perhaps he should have greeted her or at least given her a chance to take off her hat and gloves, but he'd been so eager to ask what she knew that he'd let common courtesy slide. Ma would have chided him, telling him that was no way to court a woman or even to let her know how much he valued her opinion, and she'd have been right. Fortunately, Dorothy did not seem annoyed by his abrupt question.

She pulled some of those ridiculously long pins that women fancied from her hat and placed them and the hat on top of the bookcase. "I can't recall anyone in Mesquite Springs named Josiah."

"He's not from here." Brandon grabbed the letter he'd received early this morning and handed it to her. "He seems to be one of those itinerant preachers who hold camp meetings. According to this, he plans to come to Mesquite Springs and wants to buy large ads in the *Chronicle* starting this week." Brandon gave Dorothy a few seconds to read. "What do you think?"

She looked up, her expression as solemn as his had been when he'd first read the letter. "We've never had a camp meeting here, at least not as far as I know. 'Hear the real story of the Bible. Give your soul to the Almighty. Witness miraculous healings.' " She quoted part of the text that Brother Josiah wanted included in his advertisement. "He sounds like a charlatan to me. I don't like the idea of his coming here, particularly with the way some people are treating Pastor Coleman."

Brandon let out a sigh of relief as Dorothy echoed his opinions. He'd hoped she would, but a part of him had worried that she'd view Brother Josiah's plans differently. It was reassuring that she did not.

"I agree," he told her. "That's why I talked to your brother and Fletcher. They both said the man has a right to hold his meeting here. The only question is whether I should accept the ad." Brandon fixed his gaze on Dorothy. "What would you advise?"

She shook her head, clearly unwilling to answer. "What do you think? What do your instincts tell you?"

Brandon couldn't help chuckling at the fact that she'd responded exactly the way he would have if he'd been in her position. "Clever girl, turning the question around. My brain tells me the money would help replace the type that was destroyed."

"But money isn't the reason you'll do it."

His chuckle turned into a full-fledged laugh. "You sound certain that I'll agree. Why?"

"Because it's a form of free speech. You may not agree with this Brother Josiah, but you won't deny him his right to speak."

Brandon took a step toward her, his smile broadening when he saw her eyes widen in surprise. "It's almost scary. I feel as if you can read my mind." His fingers itched to touch her, to learn whether her skin was as soft as it appeared. "That's one of the things I love about you, Dorothy."

And then, before she could move, he cupped her chin in one hand, letting his fingers caress her cheek, all the while watching her reaction. It was everything he'd hoped for. Though Dorothy blushed, she did not pull away.

"Your meal is almost ready," Evelyn said when Dorothy entered the kitchen.

Though she and Brandon ate at Polly's Place each day, they never shared a table. Instead, Dorothy took her midday meal either in the main kitchen or upstairs in her apartment. They'd both agreed there was no reason to give the town's gossips any reason to speculate that their relationship was anything other than professional, which, of course, it was not, even though her face still tingled from the memory of his fingers touching her cheek. Perhaps she should have brushed his hand aside, but it had felt good — so very good that she'd actually moved a bit closer to him, not wanting the moment to end.

As Dorothy sat at the table, Evelyn gave her a quick look. Surely, she didn't know what Brandon had done. Though Dorothy felt as if her face had been branded, she'd caught a glimpse of herself in the window-pane and knew she looked normal.

"I imagine you've heard about the preacher who's coming to town next month." Evelyn's words both reassured and surprised Dorothy. Reassured her that her sister-in-law had not realized what had happened in the newspaper office and surprised her that the news had spread so quickly.

"There's going to be an ad in tomorrow's *Chronicle*," she told Evelyn. "How did you

369

hear about it?" Though Wyatt knew, it was unlikely he'd have made a special trip to Polly's Place to tell Evelyn.

Evelyn slid the plate of roast beef, mashed potatoes and gravy, and green beans in front of Dorothy, then returned to the counter to prepare a customer's meal.

"Laura told me it's all anyone's talking about. She doesn't know who started the story, but this is bigger news than what happened to Brandon's equipment. Some people are saying that if Brother Josiah is any good as a preacher, they'll ask him to stay."

A lump the size of Texas lodged in Dorothy's throat. This was worse than the shunning, worse than the criticisms she'd overheard, worse even than the anonymous letters the Colemans had received. Those had been ominous, but the threats had been vague. This was concrete. Someone — several someones, it appeared — had a plan for replacing Pastor Coleman.

Though the aromas were tantalizing, Dorothy's appetite fled. She pushed the plate aside and rose. "I'd better talk to the Colemans." She had planned to go there later today, but since the news was spreading rapidly, she did not want to delay.

"You need nourishment." Now that she'd

passed the early stages of pregnancy and was no longer sick every morning, Evelyn had become adamant about good nutrition for herself, her baby, and everyone she loved.

"I'm sorry, Evelyn, but I don't think I could eat now." Bile rose inside Dorothy at the thought of Pastor Coleman being replaced by this unknown man. "Can you keep it warm in the oven? Maybe I'll be hungrier when I return."

Though Evelyn let out an exasperated cluck, she slid Dorothy's plate into the oven, then patted her shoulder when she reentered the kitchen, dressed to go outside. "I'll be praying for you."

Dorothy feared they'd need more than prayers to heal the town's divisions. When she opened the door to admit Dorothy, Mrs. Coleman's red-rimmed eyes told her the grapevine had reached the parsonage.

"I think I may be too late."

"No, my dear. You're just in time to hear our good news." Mrs. Coleman ushered Dorothy inside, then called over her shoulder, "Jonathan, Dorothy's here." When he joined them in the parlor, she continued. "I was about to tell her of our trip. If there's still room in this week's paper, you might want to announce that Jonathan and I are

371

going to take a vacation. We've talked about it for years, but the time has never been right."

The speed with which she spoke and her almost mechanical tone of voice told Dorothy how hard the minister's wife was trying to pretend everything was normal.

"Believe it or not, my wife has never been to Austin. It's time to remedy that." Pastor Coleman began outlining their plans. "We'll be gone a week. No one need worry about services. We'll leave after them on Sunday and return in time for church the following Sunday."

"When exactly is this trip?" Though Dorothy was certain she knew the answer, she needed to have it confirmed if she was going to include the information in the Sociable column.

"Late March," the minister said. "We'll leave on the 29th and be back on Palm Sunday."

Precisely the dates when Brother Josiah would be in Mesquite Springs. According to the information he'd included in his letter, he would conduct a revival meeting each evening, beginning on Sunday and ending on Saturday.

"This will give us a chance to explore a new area." Mrs. Coleman's voice held no excitement, although she tried to smile. Though she did not say it, Dorothy feared they would spend the time looking for a new congregation.

"And after that?" she asked.

Pastor Coleman raised one eyebrow. "That's up to the good Lord."

"You look concerned," Wyatt said when Brandon entered his office Wednesday morning. "I imagine you're worried about what Brother Josiah's arrival will mean for Pastor Coleman."

Brandon took the chair Wyatt offered, waiting until Wyatt settled in the one next to him before he spoke. "It's true that that bothers me, but it's not the reason I'm here today."

Wyatt made no effort to mask his surprise. "Then what is the reason?"

"Your sister."

"Ah."

Brandon glared at the man he'd hoped could help him, the man who was sitting there with a self-satisfied smile on his face. "What's that supposed to mean?"

"It means I understand your problem. You're smitten with her, right?"

While he wouldn't have chosen that particular word, Brandon could not deny its accuracy. "How did you know?"

"Because you look the way I did a year ago. All I could think about was Evelyn, and I didn't know what to do."

The man might still be smirking, but he understood. That was good. "You're married now, so you must have figured it out."

"Yes and no." Wyatt rose to pour a cup of coffee, returning to his seat when Brandon refused one. "We didn't have a traditional courtship, but somehow I managed to overcome her fears."

He'd been right to come here, because it appeared that Wyatt had encountered the same problem he had. Brandon hadn't expected that. "So, Evelyn feared marriage the way Dorothy does."

"No. Evelyn was afraid for her life and Polly's. I had to convince her to trust that I would protect them."

Not the same problem. Brandon wouldn't discount the power of the threat Evelyn had feared, but he suspected Dorothy's fears might be more difficult to overcome.

"I don't know what to say to convince Dorothy that marriage is a risk worth taking."

Wyatt was silent for a moment. When he spoke, his question surprised Brandon. "Did you ever notice how smooth river rocks are?"

Brandon nodded, though he had no idea where this conversation was heading.

"They don't start out that way. It takes the river a long time to wear away the sharp edges, but eventually it does."

"So, I need to be patient?" That was not a virtue Brandon had in any measurable quantity.

Wyatt shook his head. "You need to be persistent. Gentle, but persistent." He took a long slug of coffee before he smiled at Brandon. "And, for the record, I think she's already softening. I've seen the way she looks at you, and it isn't like she's looking at her boss. It's more the way Evelyn looks at me."

That was the best news Brandon had had in days.

"I hope you're right."

CHAPTER TWENTY-EIGHT

"It's hard to believe it's March already," Dorothy said as she passed the mashed potatoes to her brother. As they did almost every Sunday, he, Evelyn, and Polly had joined her and Ma for dinner at the Circle C.

Wyatt nodded. "A new month, and a lot of changes for Mesquite Springs." Today had been the first Sunday since the announcement of Brother Josiah's camp meeting and Pastor Coleman's vacation plans. "There was less discussion after church than I'd expected."

"I thought there'd be more, but the anti-Colemanites left without any nasty comments."

"Anti-Colemanites?" Evelyn raised an eyebrow at Dorothy's term.

"That's what Brandon and I call them." As her face flushed, Dorothy reached for her glass of water, hoping to hide her reaction. It was silly, but she seemed to blush every time she mentioned his name.

Wyatt exchanged a quick glance with his wife before saying, "It's a good description."

"We think they're quiet because Brother Josiah is coming."

Oh, why had she said "we"? That made it sound as if she and Brandon were a couple. They weren't. It was true that Brandon's behavior had changed since he'd asked to court her. He didn't do any of the things Laura claimed a swain should do. He didn't bring her books, flowers, or candy. He didn't compose poetry comparing her eyebrows to a rainbow or something equally absurd. But he did compliment her more often — not just her writing but also her appearance.

Dorothy hadn't expected him to notice that she'd experimented with a new hairstyle. It wasn't as if she were trying to attract him. Of course, she wasn't. It was simply that now that she wasn't working at Polly's Place and didn't have to worry about her hair getting into food, she had more time to fuss with it.

All she had done was leave a few curls framing her face, but Brandon had commented on that the instant she removed her hat, saying he liked it. It would have been ridiculous to revert to the more severe style just because he'd complimented her. After all, she liked the curls too.

The compliments weren't the only changes. Although at first she had thought it mere coincidence that Brandon's hand brushed against hers while they were working, it happened so frequently that she knew it was deliberate. She could have pulled away. She could have told him to be more careful. But she hadn't, for though Dorothy wouldn't admit it to him, she enjoyed those brief touches, just as she enjoyed the compliments.

But now, when her face was as red as the beets Wyatt refused to eat, she wished — oh, how she wished — she hadn't used the plural pronoun. Fortunately, no one seemed to have noticed, or if they did, they said nothing.

"I'm hoping folks realize that flamboyant preachers are like very spicy food — a little bit is good, but you wouldn't want it every day." Trust Evelyn to use a food analogy.

"You're assuming that he'll be flamboyant?" Ma asked.

Evelyn nodded. "The ad certainly is."

"He's gonna thump the Bible." Though Polly had seemed engrossed in eating the pot roast and sneaking bites to Ma's puppy who, though supposedly banned from the dining room, was stationed next to Polly's chair, it appeared she had been following the conversation.

Dorothy turned to the child. "What makes you think that?"

"Melissa told me. Her daddy said preachers like him always thump the Bible. That's how they heal people."

"An interesting theory." And not one Dorothy would discuss with Pastor Coleman. She had never seen him thump a Bible, and while he believed in and had witnessed divine healing, he had never made a public show of it.

Polly turned to Wyatt, pleading in her eyes. "Are we gonna go see Brother Josiah?"

His reply was immediate. "I wouldn't miss it for anything."

"Goody! Me and Buster wanna go. We want Brother Josiah to heal Buster's foot."

This was the first Dorothy had heard of the puppy's injury. "What's wrong with his paw?"

"He hurted it. Just like I did."

Dorothy shot a questioning look at Evelyn. "Snake?" That seemed improbable, since an animal as small as Buster would most likely have died almost immediately.

"Prickly pear. Buster thought it would be

fun to bat one with his paw but found out otherwise." Evelyn rolled her eyes at the pup's foolishness. "Polly was convinced we needed a doctor, but I got the spine out."

"A bit like plucking pinfeathers from a chicken?" Dorothy could picture Evelyn brandishing her tweezers and trying to get the squirming puppy to stay still long enough for her to remove the thorns.

Evelyn laughed. "Not exactly. Chickens are a lot easier."

Turning her attention back to Polly, Dorothy said, "Buster will be healed before Brother Josiah comes. Evelyn knew exactly what to do for him."

"Okay." Polly's smile brightened. "Can we go home now? I wanna play with Buster."

Though Evelyn looked dubious, Dorothy nodded. "Go ahead. I'll help Ma with the dishes." She had ridden Guinevere rather than accompany Wyatt and his family in their wagon for precisely this possibility, knowing Polly was still in the early stages of infatuation with her pet and didn't like to be separated from him.

Once the table had been cleared, though Dorothy had expected to begin washing dishes, Ma gestured toward the parlor. "They can wait. This can't."

A wave of apprehension washed over Dorothy. Was Ma going to tell her she was ill? That was the only reason she could imagine for her mother's somber expression, and yet that made no sense. If something were wrong, she would have wanted Wyatt to know too.

"What is it?"

Ma remained silent until they were seated next to each other on the settee. When she spoke, her words surprised Dorothy. "I'm worried about you."

"Me? There's no reason to worry."

Ma shook her head. "I'm your mother, Dorothy. I know what I see. You seem . . ." She paused, searching for a word. "Confused, maybe. You're normally so sure of yourself, but now you seem to be struggling."

There was no point in denying what Ma had seen, even though Dorothy wished she could. "I didn't know it was obvious."

"Only to someone who's known you your whole life." Ma laid her hand on Dorothy's. "What's bothering you? Is it your love for Brandon?"

Dorothy jerked her hand away. "My what?"

"Your love. It's apparent when you talk about him, and when the two of you are together, I can see the connection between you. There's no need to deny it."

But there was, for as Ma had said, Dorothy was struggling with her feelings. She had tried — oh, how she'd tried — to tell herself that what she and Brandon shared was nothing more than friendship, but ever since the day he'd asked to court her, she had looked at him differently.

She had seen his compassion toward others, his dedication to making the *Chronicle* the best paper possible, and his deep integrity from a new perspective. In the past, Dorothy had viewed those as the characteristics of an honorable man, one she was proud to call a friend. Now she saw them as the building blocks of a wonderful husband and father.

It wasn't simply her impression of Brandon that had changed. She too had changed. She was more attuned to the world around her, more aware of the beauty of each day. All of her senses were heightened. Food tasted better; her perfume smelled sweeter; even Nutmeg's barks seemed more melodic.

And then there was the way her heart beat when she was with Brandon. Dorothy had dismissed it as nothing more than a fluke that first day when he'd entered Polly's Place, but it was no fluke. Her heartbeat accelerated every time she saw him, every time

382

she thought about him.

Laura would say it was love. Both Evelyn and Ma believed it was. Only Dorothy was not convinced.

"What if it isn't love? What if what I feel is nothing more than infatuation?" That fear had caused more sleepless hours than she could count.

Ma raised an eyebrow. "Like Laura?"

"Exactly."

Though her eyes were filled with concern, Ma was quick to shake her head. "Oh, my dear, that's not possible. You and Laura may be best friends, but you're not alike. Laura's a hummingbird, flitting from one flower to another. You're a homing pigeon. Once you start your journey, nothing stops you from returning to the same place. Your heart is so true that you can find your way through rain, through fog, even through smoke to reach your home. Like me, when you give your heart, it's forever."

Dorothy was silent for a moment, pondering her mother's words. It was the first time Ma had been so philosophical, so poetic. It was also the first time they'd had a discussion like this. Dorothy had kept her deepest feelings locked inside her, not sharing them with anyone, and Ma had never probed.

Was she right? Was Dorothy in love with

Brandon?

"I'm afraid." If they were going to have an honest discussion, Dorothy had to admit that. Though Wyatt had urged her to talk to Ma, she had been reluctant, but Ma had opened the door today by saying they were alike.

The way blood drained from Ma's face told Dorothy she was shocked. "Afraid of what?"

"Of being hurt."

Her mother's eyes, so different from Dorothy's, darkened with emotion. "I wish I could promise you that there'll never be pain, but nothing in life comes with a guarantee. I can tell you, though, that love is a precious gift. Don't squander it, or you'll regret it for the rest of your life." As often happened when she was upset, Ma's accent thickened, reminding Dorothy that English was her second language.

"I don't know, Ma. I can't forget . . ." She hesitated, not wanting to deepen her mother's distress, yet knowing that anything less than the truth would be a lie.

"Forget what?"

"What happened to you after Pa was killed."

Tears filled Ma's eyes, and she reached for Dorothy's hand, clasping it between both of hers. "I'm so sorry, so deeply sorry, for that. You must have felt as if you'd lost both parents."

Ma stroked the back of Dorothy's hand, reminding her of how she'd done that when Dorothy was a child. "I know nothing I can say will make up for the burden I put on you and Wyatt. I wish I'd been stronger, but I wasn't."

The memory of how Ma had retreated to the room she'd once shared with Pa, refusing to come out, even to eat, still haunted Dorothy. She and Wyatt had survived, but she at least bore scars. How could she risk inflicting such pain on a child of her own?

Brandon had said life was filled with risks; Ma had confirmed that there were no guarantees. Dorothy knew that even if a Comanche's arrow didn't kill them, some men died before their time. She couldn't — she wouldn't — take the risk that her husband might die, leaving her a widow unable to cope with even the simplest aspects of life, placing an impossible burden on any children she might have.

"I'm your daughter. You said that we're alike. I'm afraid that might happen to me."

"It won't." Ma's voice rang with certainty.

"How can you be so sure?" This was the

385

woman who'd said life came with no guarantees.

"Because I know you. You may have inherited my hair color, but you did not inherit my melancholy."

Dorothy blinked, trying to understand what Ma was saying. "What do you mean?"

Her mother's face contorted with pain, and her accent became more pronounced as she said, "I never told you or Wyatt. There didn't seem to be a reason to, but I suffered from bouts of melancholy when I was a child. When they'd strike me, I felt like I was surrounded by a dark cloud. All the color was drained out of the world, and I could hardly move, because I felt weighed down by some invisible force. All I wanted to do was curl up on my bed and hide. It was terrible."

A chill raced down Dorothy's spine as she tried to make sense of what she'd heard. How terrible it must have been to be caught in such a powerful snare. Though Dorothy had heard of melancholy, she had never known anyone who suffered from it, nor had she realized how debilitating it could be. Until now. She looked at her mother through new eyes. The feelings she'd had of walking through smoke, unsure where she was going or what she was supposed to do, were nothing like what Ma was describing.

"My parents didn't know what to do," Ma continued, "and the doctors in Germany were no help. Fortunately, the bouts went away when I married Wilson." Her voice softened as she pronounced her husband's name. "He and I both prayed they were gone forever."

But they hadn't disappeared completely. They'd been waiting to pounce on her when she was most vulnerable.

Ma nodded as if she'd heard Dorothy's thoughts. "One doctor told my parents I might outgrow the melancholy, so I clung to that hope. For a long time, it seemed he was right, but then your father was killed, and I sank into the worst darkness of my life."

Her eyes filled with tears, proof that the memory still brought pain. "You know how long it took me to recover. Fortunately, the few times since then have not been as severe. I don't know whether the melancholy will recur, but I pray that it won't."

"So do I." Dorothy squeezed her mother's hand, wanting to comfort her, wishing she had been able to comfort her during that terrible dark year. "It was horrible, seeing you unable to do anything."

As Ma had said, it had been almost like

losing both parents, perhaps even more difficult than if they'd both died. It was natural
to grieve for Pa. Wyatt and Dorothy had had
a grave to visit, but Ma had still been
breathing, even though she had been an
empty shell.

Before Dorothy could say more, her
mother spoke. "I wish you and Wyatt hadn't
had to endure that, but you don't need to
fear that the same thing will happen to you.
Both Wilson and I watched you two carefully to see if you had the same tendencies.
You don't." Again, Ma spoke with great
certainty.

"Don't be afraid of love. If you love
Brandon and he loves you, there's nothing
to keep you apart. Be happy, my dear. Enjoy
every minute of the life you've been given."

Dorothy was silent, trying to absorb all
that she'd heard. Was it possible that what
had happened to Ma was an illness? It
seemed that melancholy wasn't like measles
or chicken pox. It wasn't contagious, and it
didn't make its presence known through
external signs, but it was no less serious, its
effects lasting far longer than a rash and
fever.

Her heart ached over what her mother had
suffered, but at the same time, a glimmer of
hope took root deep inside her. If Ma was

correct and Dorothy did not suffer from the same illness, perhaps there was no reason to fear. No reason not to love.

She reached out with her free hand, touching her mother's, wanting to reassure her as much as Ma had sought to comfort her. "I'll try."

"Do you think I'm a meddler?" Brandon asked the question as casually as he could, hoping the fact that Dorothy was trying to restrain an exuberant Nutmeg would keep her from realizing how important her answer was.

She tugged on the leash, forcing Nutmeg to stop, then turned her attention to Brandon, her eyes reflecting her surprise. "No. Why would you even ask?"

"Because some people believe my editorials are meddling. I had a man stop me on the street today and thank me for not putting an editorial in this week's paper. He said he hoped I was done meddling."

And that had made Brandon once again question the purpose of editorials. He had thought he was doing the right thing, bringing important issues to his subscribers' attention, but after what had happened in Xavier and now here, he wondered if there

389

wasn't an aspect of meddling in what he'd done.

"Who said that?"

"Phil Blakeslee." The man rarely spoke to him, which was fine with Brandon, but today the man whose sketches had impressed so many in Mesquite Springs had sought Brandon's company.

Dorothy tipped her head to one side, reminding Brandon of a bird listening for the sound of worms or bugs underground. It was an endearing gesture, but then again, almost everything Dorothy did was endearing. Brandon might not have liked the word Wyatt had used, but he couldn't deny that he was smitten. Even a conversation about Blakeslee was more pleasant when that conversation was with Dorothy.

"I always feel sorry for Phil," Dorothy said when she acceded to Nutmeg's demands and began to walk again. "I keep thinking about how his older sister died and imagining how painful that must have been."

"And so you want to heal him, the same way you try to help everyone." Dorothy was an optimist, always looking for the good side to a situation or a person, while Brandon considered himself a realist.

"It sounds like you think I'm the one who's a meddler."

The hint of pain he heard in her voice made Brandon cringe. He hadn't meant to hurt her, but the discussion had taken an unexpected turn. Perhaps he should have anticipated that, considering how unpredictable the direction of their conversations often was. That unpredictability was one of the things he loved about Dorothy.

"That isn't what I meant. A meddler interferes where he's not wanted. You don't do that. You try to make the world a better place, and you're succeeding."

Obvious pleasure sent a glow to her face, banishing her earlier concern. "Do you really believe that?"

"I do. Your monthly themed columns are bringing the town together in new ways. That's important." It was time to redirect the conversation. "I wish my editorials were having the same effect."

Brandon couldn't help wondering if Brother Josiah's coming to Mesquite Springs was somehow the result of his first editorial. If so, he might have made a bad situation worse.

"I worry that my editorial about Pastor Coleman has stirred up hatred rather than helping to resolve it. I wanted it to have a positive effect."

It was Dorothy's turn to reassure him. "I

believe it will eventually. You're asking people to think about things in ways they may not have considered before. It's only natural that not everyone is pleased by that."

"That's an understatement if I ever heard one. Fortunately, no one has tried to destroy my equipment again."

"Now, that was meddling. Definite unwanted interference." Brandon knew her use of his own words was intentional, a deliberate attempt to lighten the conversation. He responded in kind, infusing his own words with heavy sarcasm. "On a grand scale."

He laid his hand on top of hers and gave it a quick squeeze before lacing his fingers with hers. "Thank you, Dorothy. I don't know what I'd do without you."

The words might sound extravagant, but they were nothing more than the truth.

CHAPTER TWENTY-NINE

Dorothy stared out the window. She was supposed to be writing another article, but her thoughts refused to focus on a rancher's newborn baby. She kept remembering Brandon's words and the touch of his hand on hers. It wasn't accidental that his fingers kept brushing hers and that he reached for her hand while they were walking and kept it clasped in his. Having their fingers linked together had sent tingles up her arm, and when he looked at her as if she were something priceless, those tingles spread throughout her whole body.

Brandon made her feel important. He made her believe that what she was doing was making a difference, and that made her want to continue. The fear that she was like Ma and that her world might collapse under the weight of unrelenting grief was gone, replaced by bubbles of hope that buoyed her, freeing her to dream of future happiness.

Brandon was right. Dorothy wanted everyone to be happy, especially Laura, who'd been in the doldrums recently.

She closed her eyes for a moment of silent prayer. There had to be something she could do to help her friend. As she opened her eyes and glanced at the clock, Dorothy knew she'd been given the answer.

She hurried downstairs and into the kitchen, Nutmeg at her heels.

"Laura, I need your help."

Laura, who'd been taking inventory in the pantry, turned in surprise. "I'm not going to care for that dog of yours."

"I wouldn't ask you to do that." Dorothy wouldn't mention that what she wanted her to do might include seeing a puppy. "I wondered if you would deliver Mrs. Plaut's copy of the *Chronicle*. I promised to do it, but I'm running out of time." When she saw Laura's hesitation, Dorothy added, "It's a nice day for a ride."

"All right."

"You can take Mrs. Plaut a couple pieces of pie," Evelyn offered when Laura and Dorothy returned to the kitchen. "I know she has a cook, but she likes my oatmeal pecan pie. And don't worry about the rest of the inventory. I can finish it if you want to leave now."

Laura did.

When Dorothy started toward the stairs, intending to finish the article, Evelyn stopped her. "Have you been to the bluebonnet field this year?"

Though fields of bluebonnets were common in this part of the Hill Country, Dorothy knew which one Evelyn meant. It was a spot Dorothy had found years ago and one where her family picnicked each spring. Last year Evelyn and Polly had joined them for an afternoon no one would forget.

"I've been so busy that I haven't gotten there."

One of those secretive smiles that seemed to have become common crossed Evelyn's face. "Do you think they've started to bloom?"

It was the middle of March, around the time the field began to come alive with the vibrant color of flowering bluebonnets. "It's possible. Why?"

"I thought we might have another picnic there on Sunday."

Evelyn's answer surprised Dorothy. "You want to do that after what happened last year?" Polly had almost died on that picnic.

"I thought your mother could keep Polly

395

on the ranch." Evelyn touched her midsection, smiling as she said, "I can't run as fast as I did then. I don't want to take any chances, but I would like to see the flowers again." Her smile told Dorothy that despite the way the day had ended, Evelyn had happy memories of the picnic.

With that in mind, Dorothy asked, "Wouldn't you rather be alone with Wyatt?" She suspected they didn't have a lot of time without interruptions from either Polly or Buster, and once the baby was born, their time as a couple would be even more limited.

Evelyn's smile widened. "I thought we'd invite Brandon."

A picnic with Brandon. What a great idea! Though Dorothy's pulse raced at the idea of sharing one of her favorite spots with him, she tried to keep her voice neutral as she asked, "Are you playing matchmaker?"

The smile turned into a chuckle. "Maybe."

The day was everything Dorothy had hoped it would be. The weather was sunny, warmer than normal, with a very light breeze, and when they reached the field, the first bluebonnets had opened, creating patches of blue in the vibrant green grass. The delicious aromas emanating from the basket

Evelyn had brought and the casual conversation the four of them had shared on the drive from town were almost enough to make Dorothy forget her unexpected reaction to Pastor Coleman's sermon.

Don't think about that, she admonished herself as she accepted Brandon's help dismounting. She'd climbed out of the wagon unassisted more times than she could count, but she wouldn't refuse his gallant offer, nor would she complain when he held her closer than absolutely necessary to ensure she was safely on the ground. So what if Evelyn shot her a look that seemed to say, "I thought so."

Keeping her hand firmly clasped in his, Brandon made his way to the closest patch of bluebonnets, then knelt next to them. "They're beautiful," he said as he fingered the delicate blue petals and bent closer to sniff the light fragrance. "We didn't have any around Xavier."

"They mostly grow in the Hill Country. I've heard visitors say bluebonnets are one of the things that make this part of the state so special."

"This is the first time Wyatt and I've been here in almost a year."

Evelyn and Wyatt had approached so quietly that neither Dorothy nor Brandon had heard them until Evelyn spoke. Though he'd seemed on the verge of saying something, Brandon remained silent as he rose and offered Dorothy a helping hand.

"Wyatt tells me it's pretty here all year round," Evelyn continued, "but I don't believe anything can surpass this." It was almost as if she were babbling, and that was unusual for Evelyn. Dorothy wondered if she was trying to decide whether she was a matchmaker or a chaperone.

Evelyn turned to her husband. "Will you help me spread out the quilt?" Normally, Dorothy would have helped her, but Evelyn was treating her like a guest.

As he unfolded the quilt and laid it on the ground, Wyatt said, "We wouldn't have known about this place if it weren't for Dorothy. She found it once when she ran away from home."

Dorothy cringed. If Wyatt was part of Evelyn's matchmaking scheme, he ought to realize he was hurting the campaign by dredging up stories of Dorothy's childhood foolishness.

Brandon looked both amused and surprised. "You ran away?"

"Doesn't everyone?" When the others shook their heads, Dorothy knew she'd chosen the wrong response. Brandon was looking for the cause. "I don't know why I ran away." She'd done it several times, but the reasons hadn't lingered in her memory.

"She probably got tired of eating burned beans." Wyatt's suggestion could have some validity. "They were our staple for quite a while."

Preferring not to discuss that part of her life, Dorothy said, "When I discovered the bluebonnets, I wanted to share them with Wyatt and Ma, so I went home to tell them about it." That had been the last time she'd tried to run away.

"When she heard about the flowers, Ma packed a picnic and brought us back here. It was one of the best days of the year."

Dorothy stared at her brother. He wasn't lying. She knew that, but she had no memory of the picnic. What other good times had she forgotten?

Looking at the food that Evelyn had been busy arranging on one corner of the quilt, Brandon said, "There'll be no scorched beans today. Your cooking is the best I've ever eaten, Evelyn."

"Why do you think I married her?" Wyatt asked. "I was tired of burned beans and lumpy oatmeal."

Brandon's laugh came quickly. "Somehow, I don't think that was the reason."

Wyatt gave his wife a quick kiss before he said, "You're right about that. This woman swept me off my feet the minute I met her."

It was Dorothy's turn to laugh, only her laugh came out more like a hoot. "Wait until I tell Laura. We both suspected you peeked at those silly books she sent me. Now I know you did, but you got it wrong. The hero's the one who's supposed to sweep the heroine off her feet."

"And he did."

The gentle banter continued as they enjoyed the fried chicken, potato salad, and apple pie Evelyn had brought. When they'd devoured the last of the simple but delicious meal, Evelyn turned to Dorothy. "Wyatt'll help me clean up while you and Brandon look for the white bluebonnets."

As Evelyn had probably intended, Brandon appeared intrigued. "White bluebonnets? That sounds like an oxymoron."

"I assure you they exist, although they're rare." Wyatt looked at Dorothy. "You know where they grow, don't you?"

She did not. Though Wyatt had mentioned having discovered them, he had never said exactly where. Today he provided detailed directions.

"You don't want to miss them. They're special." The wink Evelyn gave Wyatt made

Dorothy suspect she was referring to more than white flowers.

Unless she was mistaken — and she doubted that she was — her brother and Evelyn had shared a tender moment among the bluebonnets. Was that why they were so insistent Dorothy and Brandon go there? Considering Evelyn's recent penchant for matchmaking, that seemed likely, but just because one couple considered the spot special didn't mean she and Brandon would. And yet, as memories of this morning's sermon flitted through her brain, Dorothy admitted how much the idea of a romantic interlude with Brandon appealed to her.

The spot Wyatt described was perhaps a ten-minute walk from their picnic site, assuming they walked straight there. But Dorothy and Brandon meandered, taking detours each time they spotted a new color of wildflower. Though it was still early in the season, the Indian paintbrush had emerged, their bright red blossoms providing a vivid contrast to the bluebonnets.

"Red, white, and blue," Brandon said as he pointed toward a white-tipped bluebonnet growing next to a paintbrush. "The flowers are patriotic."

"Or maybe they're just Texan. After all, our state flag is red, white, and blue too."

"Good point."

Dorothy knew it was silly to take such pleasure from his approval, and yet she did. No one had ever treated her the way Brandon did, as if her ideas — as simple as they sometimes were — were important, as if he were deeply interested in whatever she had to say. His attention warmed her more than the summer sun and made her dream of . . . She wouldn't think about that. Not now.

"In another couple weeks, the bluebonnets will be in full bloom," she said as they walked through a small grove of trees, heading for the spot where the elusive white bluebonnets were supposed to be. Flowers were a safer subject than her newly awakened hopes. "You'd almost believe you were seeing a lake out here, there's so much blue."

"I'd suggest we come back then, but I doubt we'll have time." The regret in Brandon's voice sounded sincere. "Daily issues of the *Chronicle* will keep us busy."

"Do you still think that's a good idea?" Dorothy had been the one to suggest they print two-page issues each day of the camp meeting.

Brandon nodded. "You were right when you said it would be important to report what happened as well as the townspeople's reactions every day. With all the excitement surrounding Brother Josiah, I expect us to sell out every issue."

And that would mean additional profits. Even though Brandon had said they'd charge only half as much for the daily issue as they did for the weekly paper, since the dailies would be half the standard length, it still meant a substantial increase in revenue.

"Have you thought about making the *Chronicle* a daily at some point?" she asked. Talking about the paper was good. It kept her mind from dwelling on other things.

"I've thought about it," Brandon admitted, "but I haven't made a decision. That part of the future's still unclear to me."

They'd reached the edge of the grove and had emerged into the next meadow. As they approached the area where Wyatt claimed the white bluebonnets might be found, Brandon slowed his pace, then stopped and turned toward Dorothy.

"I hadn't realized it, but I was so focused on the shadows of the past that I didn't spend much time thinking about the future. It's only now becoming clear."

"Shadows?" Dorothy shivered at the realization of how similar their experiences were. "For me, it was like walking into a cloud of smoke. Everything was blurry.

Sometimes it was murky, sometimes almost invisible."

Brandon seemed surprised by her admission. "You used the past tense. Does that mean something has changed?"

She nodded. "I feel as if the wind came and is chasing the smoke away. There are still a few patches, but the future is much clearer now."

As if to underscore her words, a slight breeze ruffled the flowers and made them sway.

Brandon smiled at the sight as he asked, "What do you see in your future?"

"Writing." That much was easy to share with him. "You know that I used to dream of writing a novel like *Uncle Tom's Cabin*. I now know that's not what I'm meant to do. I could never invent a story like that. My talent lies in telling real stories."

Though Brandon said nothing, his expression encouraged her to continue.

Dorothy paused, trying to gather her thoughts. Opening her heart like this was more difficult than she'd expected, but it was important to share her innermost thoughts and her most fervent dreams with Brandon. He needed to know the real Dorothy.

"The reason I thought I should write a

book was that I saw how Mrs. Stowe changed people's lives with hers. I finally realized that that's what I want to do — influence people — and I don't need to write a novel to do that."

Brandon nodded but remained silent as Dorothy continued. "I've learned that I can make a difference doing exactly what I've been doing on the *Chronicle*. My writing may not have the impact Mrs. Stowe's book did, but even a small amount of influence is valuable."

Though his expression had been encouraging, it turned inscrutable as he asked, "Does that mean you're willing to be part of the *Chronicle* for a while longer?"

"As long as you want me."

The smile that softened Brandon's face left no doubt of his feelings. "Oh, I want you. I can't imagine the *Chronicle* without you." He paused, then took a step toward her, reaching for her hand. "The truth is, I can't imagine my life without you."

He entwined his fingers with hers, making her feel as if more than their hands were joined. "When you look into the future, do you see a husband and children in it?"

The feelings that had swept over Dorothy during this morning's sermon came back, stronger than ever. Pastor Coleman had spoken of Jesus and the children, and how Jesus had told his disciples to bring the little children to him. It was a story she had heard dozens of times, and though it had warmed her heart each time, never before had she felt as if the message were directed at her.

Instead of Jesus surrounded by the children, Dorothy had seen herself and Brandon sitting on a front porch, four young children at their side. The six of them had been laughing, enjoying something Brandon had said. And in that moment, she had known that was what she wanted. She would take the risk, believing Ma was right and that Dorothy would not succumb to melancholy, trusting that God would keep her and her family safe.

"Yes, I can," she said firmly.

Brandon's eyes shone with pleasure. "Dare I hope that that means you've changed your mind about courtship?"

"I have."

"Well, then, there's only one thing to do."

Before she knew what he intended, Brandon pulled his hand free and drew her into his arms. He gazed at her for a second, then smiled and lowered his lips to hers.

CHAPTER THIRTY

Her toes were still tingling the next morning. Dorothy smiled as she pulled on her stockings and reached for the button hook to fasten her shoes. She had hardly been able to sleep, remembering how wonderful Brandon's kiss had felt.

Her smile broadened with each button that she secured. Lace-up shoes were easier to put on, but they weren't as pretty as ones that buttoned. And today she wanted to look as pretty on the outside as she felt on the inside.

She had thought that the touch of Brandon's hand was marvelous, but that paled compared to the sensation of his lips on hers. They'd been smooth, firm, and oh, so exciting. And when he'd wrapped his arms around her to draw her close enough that she could feel his heart beating as fast as hers, she'd finally understood the verses in Song of Solomon. Winter was gone, the rain had ended, flowers and birds had appeared, not only on the earth but in her heart.

As Dorothy slid her foot into the second shoe and began to button it, she remembered her mother's words. Ma had been right when she'd said that love was a precious gift. Though it was a gift she'd never expected to receive, now that she had it, Dorothy knew she would never let it go.

Never before had she felt like this, as if she'd reached the end of a long and difficult journey, never knowing where the road would take her. Now her destination was in sight, and it was more beautiful, more peaceful, more appealing than she'd dreamt possible. She and Brandon may not have found the elusive white bluebonnets, but they'd discovered something far more important. Love.

Her toilette complete, Dorothy descended the stairs in search of a cup of coffee. As she'd expected from the delicious aroma that wafted upstairs, Laura was already in the kitchen and had a pot ready.

"You look happy," Laura said as she handed Dorothy a cup of the fragrant brew. "I am."

"Because of Brandon." Laura made it a statement, not a question, and fixed her gaze on Dorothy. "You don't need to deny it. I saw you when you came back yesterday, and you both looked happier than I've ever seen you."

The wistfulness in Laura's voice wrenched Dorothy's heart. It was no surprise that she hadn't realized Laura was outside and apparently within sight of Main Street, because she hadn't been looking at anyone other than Brandon.

The time after their kiss had passed in a blur. Dorothy knew she must have spoken to Evelyn and Wyatt, but she had no recollection of it. She had sat on the back seat, her hand clasped in Brandon's, her heart soaring with the memory of the kisses they'd shared.

Laura returned to the piecrust she'd been rolling out when Dorothy entered the kitchen. "I'm glad he's making you happy." She turned around long enough to meet Dorothy's eyes. "He is, isn't he?"

"Happier than I thought possible."

"I thought so. You're practically glowing — you, the woman who said she'd never marry."

Dorothy wouldn't point out that she wasn't married or even engaged yet, because what had happened yesterday told her that she and Brandon were headed in that direction. "I feel like I'm a different woman from the one who used to say that," she said, hoping her friend would understand. They'd shared so many confidences over the years that it seemed only right for Laura to know how much Dorothy's perspective had changed. "I've learned a lot about love," she said softly.

"Thanks to Brandon."

"And my mother. Ma told me a lot of things about her life that I never would have guessed." Dorothy's heart still ached at the thought of her mother's suffering.

"Secrets?" Laura fitted the piecrust into the pan and began crimping the edges.

"Sort of." Though Ma hadn't forbidden her to speak of it, Dorothy did not want to share her mother's past with anyone, not even Brandon. She took another sip of coffee before she said, "I imagine everyone has things they don't want revealed."

"That's what Mrs. Plaut told me." Laura smiled as she slid the finished piecrust to the other end of the table and began to work on the second. "She's a wonderful woman, almost like a grandmother." Laura's smile broadened. "I'm so glad you asked me to go out there."

"I always enjoy my time with Mrs. Plaut."

Laura gave her a mischievous grin. "Believe it or not, I don't even mind playing with her puppy."

"Now, that does surprise me."

A shrug greeted Dorothy's declaration. "You're not the only one who's changing. I find it ironic that I'm likely to be the one who'll wind up a spinster."

The slightest hitch of her voice told Dorothy how much that statement hurt Laura, and she sought a way to comfort her friend. "I don't believe you will. I'm convinced the right man for you is out there."

"Where?"

Dorothy had no answer.

Brandon glanced at the clock, counting the minutes until he'd see Dorothy again. It had been twelve days and two hours since they'd shared their first kiss. That wonderful, unforgettable kiss. Brandon knew he'd never forget it or the ones that had followed.

He looked around the office. They hadn't kissed here. He hadn't so much as put his arm around her here, because to do either would be unwise. Anyone passing by might see them and start ugly gossip, since their courtship wasn't yet official. He wouldn't subject Dorothy to prying eyes and wagging tongues. But that didn't mean he was willing to forgo holding her in his arms and pressing his lips to hers.

They waited until the end of their evening walks, entering the alley that separated Polly's Place from Brandon's home. That first night, she'd opened the storage shed to see whether Evelyn had left any extra tablecloths there, and as she did, Brandon realized that the open door blocked the view from River. It might not be the perfect place for a kiss, but it was the best he could find.

Brandon chuckled, remembering how when they'd turned into the alley the next night, Nutmeg had strained at her leash, then stood on her hind legs and unlatched the door, as if telling them she knew what they were planning to do and approved of it. That was one smart dog, and Dorothy was one wonderful woman.

Satisfied that everything in the office was in its proper place, Brandon locked the front door and let himself out the back, carefully locking it behind him. In mere seconds, he'd be with Dorothy again.

Originally, he'd thought she would want a lengthy courtship, but now he suspected she was as eager as he to announce their engagement and plan their wedding. As soon as the camp meeting ended and Pastor Coleman was back in Mesquite Springs, he would ask Wyatt for Dorothy's hand.

Nine days. In nine days, their courtship

would be official. Somehow, he would manage to wait.

"I almost didn't recognize you." Phil stared at the man who'd emerged from the grove of trees halfway between Mesquite Springs and Grassey that he'd suggested for a meeting place. The last time he'd seen him, Brother Josiah had had dark brown hair and a full beard. Today blond hair topped a smooth-shaven face. Only the deep blue eyes and the crinkles at their edges were the same.

"One thing you learn mighty quickly in this business is to make it hard for folks to find you once you leave their town." Brother Josiah's normally booming voice was subdued, his words clearly audible but designed to travel no further than Phil's ears. "That's why I've called myself Jeremiah, Timothy, and Peter as well as Josiah."

"Biblical names."

"Precisely. Good honest names for a not-so-good, not-so-honest man." His chuckle invited Phil to share the joke.

Though Phil laughed along with the man who'd agreed to pay him almost a king's ransom if the camp meeting turned out as well as they expected, his stomach clenched at the realization that his sister would not have approved of this man. Preacher or no preacher, Brother Josiah was not someone Esther would have trusted.

"Let me see that map."

Phil pulled out the map of Mesquite Springs that he'd drawn this morning.

Brother Josiah was silent for a moment before he smiled. "This is good. We'll set up the tent in the park. The rest of the men can sleep there, but I want a real bed."

That had been the most difficult of Brother Josiah's demands to fulfill, because the boardinghouse had no vacancies, and the grand hotel that Mr. K envisioned was simply a dream at this point.

"You can stay in my room at the boardinghouse. It's the only place available." Though Phil didn't like the idea of sharing a room with anyone, there were no alternatives. He pointed to the location of his current home.

This time the preacher frowned. "That's further from the park than I would have liked, but we'll have to make do with it. Did you find a place to store the records and the money? I don't want to leave the trunk where anybody can find it."

Phil nodded. A secure storage spot had been one of Brother Josiah's requirements. "There's a woodshed behind this house. It's right next door to the park." He pulled out a sketch of Widow Lockhart's house. "There's not much wood in there now."

Brother Josiah studied the sketch. "Won't the owner care if he sees me putting a trunk in there?"

"It's a she, and she won't mind. I already told her you needed a place to leave your healing waters. She offered to let you put them inside her house, but I explained the meetings would last until late each night and you wouldn't want to disturb her. The woodshed will be fine."

Brother Josiah seemed mollified. "It's a mighty nice house," he said as he continued to study the sketch. "Is she an old spinster?"

"A widow woman."

With a quick nod, the preacher handed the sketch back to Phil. "Anything valuable in her house?"

The avaricious gleam in Brother Josiah's eye made the hair on the back of Phil's neck rise. He thought about Mrs. Lockhart's silver and jewelry and how defenseless she would be if a man like the preacher entered her house.

"Nothing," he lied. "She's hard-pressed to pay the taxes."

Though Brother Josiah nodded, Phil's unease did not fade. Had he made a mistake? He tried not to frown, but the thought that it was too late to undo it turned his stomach inside out.

CHAPTER THIRTY-ONE

"I give the man credit for showmanship. Those wagons are a masterful touch." Brandon nodded toward the three wagons slowly making their way along Hill Street toward the park.

He and Dorothy had seen the entourage — for that was the only word she could find to describe Brother Josiah's arrival in Mesquite Springs — when it had traveled the length of Main, apparently turning to head east on Spring, completing the circuit on Hill. They hadn't followed it but had gone directly to the park to see how many people would be there to greet the town's highly anticipated visitors.

Dorothy's gaze moved from Brother Josiah, who was an indisputably imposing figure seated on top of the whitest horse she'd ever seen, to the wagons that had caught both her and Brandon's attention. Each of the wagons was laden with some sort of cargo covered with black canvas, each driven by a man dressed all in black, a sharp contrast to Brother Josiah's white clothing. And while the preacher appeared to be of shorter than average height, the wagons' drivers were at least as tall as Brandon, with one being a few inches taller and considerably heavier.

What set these wagons apart from any Dorothy had seen was the fact that they were painted bright white, a decidedly impractical color when traveling dirty and muddy roads. The drivers must have stopped somewhere nearby to wash off the road dirt, for the wagons looked as clean as if they were freshly painted.

The color alone would have attracted attention, but the messages on the sides made them unforgettable. "Repent before it's too late!" "Are you ready for the judgment day?" "Have you been healed by the blood?" The bloodred words practically shouted at onlookers.

"I'm not sure which message is the most powerful," Dorothy told Brandon, "but the idea of Brother Josiah healing with blood bothers me."

Brandon gave her hand a quick squeeze when he finished describing the wagons on the pad he'd brought to record his impressions. "It's probably figurative."

"I hope so. It's still disturbing."

"Showmanship." Brandon's reply was succinct. "Just like the way they drove down all the main streets before coming to the park. They want to make a grand entrance."

"And they did."

"Later, folks. Later." Brother Josiah waved at the crowd gathered by the park. "My brothers and I have work to do now. We'll see you this evening."

The dismissal was clear, and to Dorothy's surprise, the crowd accepted it, beginning to disperse almost as soon as Brother Josiah finished speaking.

"I'm going to start writing the article now," Brandon told her.

Though she would have liked to accompany him back to the *Chronicle*'s office, Dorothy caught sight of Mrs. Lockhart standing near her house. She crooked her finger at Dorothy to indicate she wanted to talk.

"I'll see you after the meeting," Dorothy told Brandon. They'd agreed to go separately to avoid speculation about the state of their courtship but would return to the office to complete the article together.

"It's very exciting, isn't it?" Mrs. Lockhart asked when Dorothy was close enough that she could be heard without shouting. "I never saw anything like this. I wonder if his preaching will be as . . ." She paused, searching for a word.

"Flamboyant?" Dorothy offered Evelyn's description.

"That's the perfect word. You'd think a former schoolteacher would have it on the tip of her tongue, but I have to say that seeing Brother Josiah's entry has left me almost speechless."

Dorothy forced herself not to smile at the evidence that the widow's speechlessness had disappeared.

"Whatever he says, it's sure to be different from Pastor Coleman."

Dorothy nodded but forbore saying that whether that would be a good thing remained to be seen. Instead, she smiled at Mrs. Lockhart. "Are you planning to attend the meeting?" She wouldn't call it a service. Somehow that seemed wrong.

"Yes, I am. I want to see whether the healing waters will really heal. I have my doubts, but I've been wrong before."

"Healing waters?" That was definitely better than blood.

Mrs. Lockhart nodded. "They're keeping them in my woodshed between meetings. Phil told me they were too valuable to be left in the tent."

Though her hackles rose at the realization that Phil was somehow involved with Brother Josiah, Dorothy merely said, "Will he be escorting you to the meeting tonight?"

"Of course. He's such a fine boy."

Brandon studied the interior of the tent, taking mental notes for the article that was still forming in his mind. If anyone had wondered about what the wagons had been carrying, the answer was apparent. Rows and rows of benches arranged on either side of a central aisle filled two thirds of the large tent. A tall pulpit stood at the end of the aisle next to a table with bottles of colored liquids on top. Red, green, blue, and clear, the bottles drew his attention as he suspected they were intended to. While the rest of the tent had minimal lighting, the pulpit and table were flanked by tall candelabra, providing excellent illumination.

It seemed as if almost everyone in Mesquite Springs had come for Brother Josiah's introduction to the town. The benches were crowded, while latecomers and others — including Brandon — stood along the perimeter. Though there had been a low drone of conversation, it ceased as Brother Josiah made his way from the back of the tent toward the pulpit. Clad in white robes, his head held high, he dominated the room as he climbed the steps to the pulpit.

"Welcome, my brothers and sisters. Welcome, fellow sinners." Brother Josiah's voice boomed throughout the tent. "We are gathered here because we know that night turns to day, that light will banish darkness."

Brandon was certain it was no coincidence that Brother Josiah himself stood in the light. The darkness of the rest of the tent made sense now. No doubt about it: Brother Josiah was a showman.

"We are fortunate to live in this great country, a country that honors the one true God." The preacher spread his arms wide, as if to encompass the entire United States. "Sadly," he said, his voice now lower and apparently filled with sorrow, "others are not so fortunate. I am here tonight to plead for those lost souls."

The room remained silent as he recounted his trip to China and the starving orphans he'd met there.

"I was able to help a few of them, to give them the food and clothing they so desperately needed. Thanks to God, I was able to show them the light." He paused for a moment, his face wreathed with sorrow. "But I am only one man. Though I gave them everything I had, it was not enough."

The man was good at what he did. Very good. Brandon could almost guarantee no one slept. Instead, they leaned forward, not wanting to miss a single word. It wasn't Brandon's imagination that even men were dabbing at their eyes as Brother Josiah described the horrible conditions in which the orphans existed.

"God is calling me to return. The children I was unable to save are calling me."

Brandon wondered where Brother Josiah had studied oratory, for it was clear to him that he'd chosen his phrases carefully, delivering them as dramatically as a Shakespearean actor.

"It breaks my heart that I cannot return to China."

"Theese is awful. Why can't you go?" an unfamiliar voice demanded.

Brother Josiah's expression was woebegone. "Money," he said simply, his face registering his pain. "I spent my last penny to help those unfortunate souls who so desperately need my help."

Brandon suspected that the repetition of "desperate need" was as deliberate as everything else the preacher had said, designed to tug on the attendees' heartstrings.

"I would be on the next ship to China if

only I could."

"I can help." The man who'd posed the question raced to the front and dropped coins in the basket Brother Josiah had pulled from a shelf inside the pulpit. Grabbing the basket and raising it above his head, the man turned to face the audience. "Will anyone else help Brother Josiah?"

As cries of "yes!" filled the tent, Brother Josiah handed the man a second basket. Within seconds, the two baskets were circulating, one on each side of the aisle. By the time one reached Brandon, it was almost filled with coins.

When the baskets had been returned to Brother Josiah, he mounted the pulpit again. "Thank you, my brothers and sisters. Your generosity will be rewarded on the judgment day. Now, let us pray. And if there are any of you sinners who desire a private prayer, I will remain here for a few moments."

Though Brandon had thought others might accept the invitation, it seemed that no one was willing to admit to being a sinner. Except one woman. Dorothy. He bit back a smile at the realization that she was doing what any good reporter would — she was going directly to the source of the story.

He left the tent with the rest of the crowd

and soon found himself surrounded by townspeople, all talking about Brother Josiah.

"That was the best sermon I've ever heard," one declared.

A second man agreed. "He sure does beat Pastor Coleman. I didn't fall asleep once."

"Those poor orphans," a man whose table Brandon had once shared chimed in. "My Millie gave them the money she's been saving for a new hat. She said she could make do with her old one."

As the praise continued, Brandon took notes, wanting to be sure his quotes were accurate. Finally, when the crowd dispersed, he headed back to the *Chronicle.*

"What did you think?" he asked Dorothy when she joined him.

"He has more than his share of charisma, but I don't trust him."

"Why not?"

"It all sounded rehearsed. I had the impression I was watching a performance."

"So did I." Brandon's spirits rose at the realization that once again he and Dorothy shared the same opinion.

"Even when I talked to him afterward, his prayer did not address my sins."

"Which sins were those?" Brandon couldn't resist asking.

"I told him I was envious of others. He prayed that God would reward my generosity toward the orphans by forgiving my sins. He even held out an empty basket, but I pretended not to see it. All I wanted to do was leave that tent."

"Which was not the desired reaction." Brandon knew he would not use any of Dorothy's experience in his article, but it reinforced his belief that something was amiss. "I don't trust him, either. The problem is, Fletcher couldn't find any evidence of wrongdoing."

"Then we have to see what happens tomorrow."

CHAPTER THIRTY-TWO

"It looked like those baskets were overflowing last night." Though Phil pretended to be engrossed in tying his shoes, he darted a glance at Brother Josiah. Ever since he'd seen how generous the citizens of Mesquite Springs had been, all Phil could think about was his share of that generosity.

"You were right. This town is mighty charitable. Mighty charitable." Though Brother Josiah didn't rub his hands together, his eyes gleamed with avarice. "And that newspaperman is helping." Brother Josiah grinned as he gestured toward this morning's *Chronicle.* "Those quotes he included will increase the collection tonight."

While that might be true, Phil still needed Brother Josiah's help in driving Holloway out of Mesquite Springs. "I thought we agreed that you were going to denounce him."

Brother Josiah nodded. "I said I would, and I always keep my word, but there's no rush. He's helping us collect more money. Only a fool would stop that, and you and I are not fools."

Maybe not, but that didn't stop Phil from wanting Holloway out of town. The man and his newspaper had to be gone before Mr. K arrived.

"When do I get my share of the money?" If he couldn't get rid of Holloway, Phil would need that money to start over somewhere else. He couldn't count on Mr. K giving him another assignment if he failed this one.

"What's the matter? Don't you trust me? You'll get your 10 percent after the last meeting." Brother Josiah clapped him on the shoulder in what Phil guessed was meant to be a gesture of reassurance. "The way things are going, you'll be a mighty rich man come the end of the week."

"I'm counting on it."

"That healing was certainly dramatic," Dorothy said as she accepted the cup of coffee Brandon had offered, then took a seat at the table in the *Chronicle*'s front room. " 'Receive these healing waters, my son,' " she said, mimicking Brother Josiah. " 'Now, put down your crutch. You have no need of it.' "

"And he walked without the slightest limp. Amazing!" Brandon made no effort to hide his sarcasm.

"You don't believe it was real, do you?"

"No. It was too polished, too rehearsed, and the man sounded like the one who offered his last penny to save the orphans Sunday night. His hair was shorter, and he wore different clothes, but his voice was the same."

Dorothy thought about the two men, searching for a resemblance. "I didn't notice the similarity."

"We'll watch tomorrow and see if he has a new role. Now, tell me what you think about this article."

By the time she'd finished reading the piece and offering a few suggestions, Dorothy was yawning. "I need some sleep, and Nutmeg needs to go out. She's not happy that I've been leaving her alone at night."

The meetings ended around 8:30, but by the time the articles were written and typeset, it was after 10:30, much later than Dorothy's normal time to return home.

"Good night." Brandon rose and offered his hand to help her rise. Though they were in full view of anyone passing by, he held her hand longer than courtesy demanded, then pressed a kiss to her palm. "Dream of me."

But Dorothy's dreams were not of the handsome newspaperman who'd somehow stolen her heart. Instead, she dreamt of a troupe of faceless men changing costumes, donning wigs, and practicing lines. Though nothing they said or did seemed menacing, she was filled with deep dread and woke to the sound of Nutmeg whimpering at her bedside, perhaps trying to comfort her.

"We need a walk," Dorothy told Nutmeg as she dressed. Fresh air would clear her head more than a cup of coffee, and the normalcy of Mesquite Springs's streets would banish the remnants of her dream of a darkened theater.

Though her usual route was west on Main, then south on Sunset to Spring, north on Mesquite to Main, and back home, today neither she nor Nutmeg seemed ready to return, and so she continued on Mesquite, turning west on Hill. It was as she approached the park and the huge tent where Brother Josiah had performed his miraculous healing that she saw two men. One had his eyes closed and tapped a cane in front of him as he walked, while the other watched.

"Theese being blind ain't easy," the first one said.

A shiver made its way down Dorothy's spine. Though every instinct told her to stop and study the man, she did not. Instead, she kept walking as if she hadn't noticed anything unusual about the man with the unnaturally dark hair, the man whose voice was unmistakably the same as that of the cripple who'd thrown away his crutch after Brother Josiah had anointed him with healing water.

"Did you get a copy of the paper?" Phil had barely closed the door when Brother Josiah barked the question.

"One for you and one for me."

From his perch on the room's only chair, the chair he had appropriated as his own, Brother Josiah laughed as he read aloud. " 'I never saw anything like it. Brother Josiah is surely God's messenger.' I couldn't have said it better myself. Who's this Schneider? I want to shake his hand and thank him for understanding my mission."

Phil, who'd skipped that part of the article, shook his head. "I haven't met him. Must be one of the ranchers."

"He's a smart man. The editor was smart to open the article with that quote."

Phil doubted Brother Josiah would be as complimentary when he read the next paragraph. He waited for the preacher's reaction.

"What's this?" Brother Josiah's voice echoed off the thin walls. " 'The apparently miraculous healing of a crippled man brought the audience to its feet with cheers.' Apparently? How dare he say that? Doesn't he know a genuine miracle when he sees it?"

Phil doubted there was anything genuine about it. A genuine miracle would have been healing Mrs. Plaut's arthritis so she could walk without a cane, not getting someone no one in Mesquite Springs knew to throw down his crutch. While it looked impressive, no one in town could vouch for the man's truthfulness or whether he'd actually been crippled.

Not seeming to notice that Phil had not replied, Brother Josiah continued his rant. "Audience? That two-bit newspaperman had the audacity to call my congregation — my flock — an audience!" He jumped to his feet and headed for the door. "I think it's time I pay a call on that upstart and set him straight."

Though Phil would have paid to see that particular meeting, confrontation was the wrong approach. "I wouldn't advise that. Holloway doesn't back down from threats." He knew that all too well. "The only way to stop him is to get the whole town behind you. Denounce him from the pulpit." Just like old Selby had done.

Brother Josiah's eyes narrowed as he considered Phil's advice. "I'll do that, all right. When the time's right."

Dorothy flung the door open, her face flushed with excitement. For a second, Brandon thought he'd lost track of time, but the clock hadn't stopped. Dorothy was here much earlier than usual, and she'd brought Nutmeg with her. Though the dog whined her protest, she remained on the porch.

"You were right!" Dorothy closed the door and walked toward him, not bothering to remove her hat and gloves.

"A man never gets tired of hearing that, but what exactly was I right about?"

"The supposedly crippled man. I saw him this morning, only he looked different. He had black hair instead of blond. There were no crutches, but he had his eyes closed and was using a cane to find his way, as if he was trying to learn what it was like to be blind."

It was what Brandon had suspected. Brother Josiah's healings were as fake as his smile. "Most blind people keep their eyes open, just as we do. From what you said, this one was pretending to be blind, just as he pretended to be lame."

"Apparently." Dorothy drawled the word that had amused her when she'd read it last night.

"You liked that word, didn't you?"

"I liked it last night when you showed me the draft, and I liked it even more when I saw it in print."

The question was how the *Chronicle*'s subscribers would react to it, but that was of lesser importance than Dorothy's revelation.

"How did you know it was the same man?"

"His voice. He said 'theese' instead of 'this' just like last night. Remember how he said, 'Theese is a miracle'? That man's a fake, and Brother Josiah is a charlatan."

Brandon grinned. "Apparently." As he'd expected, Dorothy laughed, even though the situation was far from humorous. "We need to prove it. We can't let the townspeople continue to be duped."

"Or robbed," she added. "If what we believe is true, it's likely that none of the money is going to orphans in China."

"I noticed that Brother Josiah was careful not to mention the name of the town or even the region where those poor orphans lived. That makes it impossible to prove his story is fabricated."

"He must keep records of some sort."

"Why do you think that?"

"Because when he took my hand to pray, I saw he had ink stains on his middle finger."

"That could have been from the healing waters." Although, since there had been no healing on Sunday, merely the pleas to help the orphans, that seemed unlikely.

"The stains were black. There was no black water."

Brandon pictured the table with the bottles of colored water. Red, green, blue, and clear. No black. Dorothy was as observant as anyone he'd ever met. "You're right."

"A woman never gets tired of hearing that." As she volleyed his words back at him, they both laughed.

That was another thing he admired about her, her ability to find humor in even serious situations. It took a very special person to do that, and Dorothy was that very special person.

Though he wished he could take the time to tell — and show — her just how special he found her, Brandon knew that would have to wait. "We need to find those records."

She nodded. "They're probably in Mrs. Lockhart's woodshed. She told me Phil asked if Brother Josiah could store his healing waters there. I imagine he's keeping more than water safe."

Brandon's attention was snagged by one word in Dorothy's explanation. "Phil? It sounds like he's involved in this."

He saw her reluctance as she nodded and knew she was disturbed by the idea that the man she'd defended might be a criminal. "I wonder how he met Brother Josiah," she said.

"If we find the records, we may have our answer."

The meeting had begun, and the rousing sounds of the first hymn spilled into the evening as Dorothy and Brandon made their way to Mrs. Lockhart's woodshed. They'd discussed attending the first few minutes of the meeting but had not wanted to attract attention by leaving early. As it was, they were both concerned that their absence would be noticed. Still, there'd been no choice. The best time to search the woodshed was while Brother Josiah and his henchmen — that was how she'd begun to think of them — were occupied.

"It's fortunate we have clouds tonight." Although there was a sliver of a moon, the clouds were thick enough to obscure it. "If anyone's looking, they'll be less likely to see us." But Brandon had taken no chances and had pulled a dark cap over his hair.

"The sooner we're out of there, the better." Dorothy's heart was pounding with anxiety as Brandon opened the door. Though she hated the idea of snooping through someone's belongings, she knew they needed to find answers. "I've never liked dark spaces."

Once he'd closed the door behind them, Brandon pulled a candle and matches from his pocket and lit the candle. "Does this help?"

"Yes." Dorothy looked around the small building. Although wood was stacked in the back half, the front was empty except for a large trunk. She knelt next to it and fingered the sturdy padlock. "I don't believe it. Look, Brandon. They forgot to snap it closed."

He whistled softly as he knelt next to her. "That's almost a miracle." He slid the lock out of the latch, then opened the lid. As they'd hoped, in addition to several bottles of colored liquids, one of the contents was a thick ledger.

Brandon opened the book and began to read. "It's all here, everything we suspected. Look."

He held it open so Dorothy could see what had caught his eye. She glanced at several pages, then sighed at the evidence that everything they'd thought was true.

"He has records of each camp meeting — how he learned about the town, which healings were the most lucrative, how much money he collected, what expenses he incurred."

She leafed through the pages, searching for the last one filled with Brother Josiah's careful notes. Though she'd been expecting it, the entries made her heart ache. Phil had been the one who'd contacted Brother Josiah, inviting him to Mesquite Springs.

"One thing is missing," Brandon said when she handed the ledger back to him.

She'd noticed that too. "The trip to China."

"Because there was no trip, just as there are no orphans begging for Brother Josiah's aid." Brandon rose, holding the book. "Fletcher needs to see this, and all of Mesquite Springs needs to know the truth."

Dorothy agreed, but doing it now was too risky. "I'm afraid of what might happen if

Fletcher arrests him during the meeting. There's no telling what people will do."

Brandon's expression told her he had pictured the same thing she had: a mob. There was no question that the majority of Mesquite Springs believed everything Brother Josiah said and did. While she and Brandon knew better, to the townspeople, the preacher was a hero. If the sheriff arrested him in front of them, they would demand to know why, and once his crimes were revealed, they might turn on Brother Josiah and his men with the same kind of irrational fury that had motivated people in Xavier.

"You're right. Fletcher won't be happy, but we need to wait until the meeting's over. Meanwhile, we'll leave the book so Brother Josiah doesn't know anyone was here."

Brandon started to place the ledger back in the trunk, then stopped. "We need some proof for the sheriff." He pulled out his pocketknife and carefully removed a page from the middle. "I wish we could take the page for Mesquite Springs, but Brother Josiah would miss that."

"Let's go." Dorothy looked around the woodshed, assuring herself that everything looked the way it had when they'd entered. "We've got work to do."

Chapter Thirty-Three

Dorothy was almost out of breath when she climbed the steps to the *Chronicle*'s office. She hadn't run — her mother would have been appalled if anyone had seen her doing that — but she had walked as quickly as she could without attracting unwanted notice. Even though most of Mesquite Springs was in the tent listening to Brother Josiah's lies, Dorothy would take no chances.

"It's what we thought. Fletcher's at the meeting," she told Brandon. "I left him a note to come here in case we don't see him there."

"Perfect." The smile Brandon gave her warmed Dorothy's heart. Despite being in the midst of what would become the biggest scandal in Mesquite Springs's history, he managed to make her feel important. Even more than that, he made her feel cherished. This was the man she loved. This was the future she wanted, a life working with Brandon to ensure that justice would prevail.

"Just give me one more minute," he said as he dipped his pen into the inkwell, "and I'll be finished with the first part of the article. I want you to critique it." Brandon glanced at the clock and frowned. "This may be the most important piece I've ever written, but it'll have to wait. We need to get back to the tent."

They'd agreed that they should return as close to the end of the meeting as possible so they could blend with the crowd and ask questions as if they'd been there. That was what everyone including Brother Josiah expected of them.

"I never thought I wanted to be an actress, but that's what it feels like tonight," Dorothy said as Brandon locked the front door and they both descended the steps. "I'm going to have to pretend I don't know that the man some of my neighbors think should be our next minister is a fraud who's robbing them."

"You can do it." Brandon gave her hand a quick squeeze.

"At least it's dark. That helps." Which was undoubtedly one of the reasons Brother Josiah had insisted his meetings be held at night. The shadows masked many things, including the truth.

Brandon nodded and turned to walk away. As they'd planned, Dorothy arrived at the tent just as people began to emerge. Though it was unlikely anyone would notice, she and Brandon were taking no chances and had approached from opposite directions. As they had the previous two nights, he would talk to the men, she to the women. And, as had happened on each of the previous nights, it was not difficult to find people who wanted their opinions printed in the *Chronicle*.

"I never thought I'd see a real miracle." Mrs. Douglas laid her hand on her heart, as if overwhelmed with emotion. "Pastor Coleman said they happen, but I didn't believe him. I thought miracles had ended when Jesus went back to heaven." She waited until Dorothy had finished writing before she said, "Brother Josiah showed me I was wrong. First, he healed that crippled man, and tonight he made the blind man see. Wasn't it the most wonderful thing you've ever witnessed?"

Dorothy was spared from having to reply by Mrs. Spencer's interruption. "I had my doubts when I read those advertisements. I didn't believe anyone could do what he claimed, but now I know I was wrong.

Brother Josiah is the minister Mesquite Springs needs." She glanced over her shoulder, as if looking for someone, then turned back to Dorothy. "I told my Amos we have to do everything we can to get him to stay."

Mrs. Douglas nodded. "You're right. Pastor Coleman never worked miracles."

Nor did Brother Josiah, as these women would learn in less than twelve hours.

"Thank you, ladies." Dorothy slid the paper into her reticule. "You won't want to miss tomorrow's issue of the *Chronicle*."

When she reached the office, Brandon was already there. He'd lit the lamps in the front two rooms and, since the night was unusually warm, had opened a window in each.

"You were right. Tonight's apparent miracle was healing a blind man." As Dorothy had expected, he emphasized the word *apparent*.

"People were convinced it was genuine. They won't be happy when they learn the truth, because no one likes to learn that their heroes are only human."

"Or that they've been tricked."

After a perfunctory knock on the door, Fletcher entered the office, concern etched on his face. "What's so important that it can't wait until tomorrow?"

"This." Brandon held out the page he'd

443

taken from Brother Josiah's ledger.

The sheriff scanned the entries, his frown deepening with each line he read. "I wish I'd known about this earlier. I could have arrested him before he stole any more money."

When Dorothy heard a note of anger in his voice, she said quickly, "We found the evidence during the meeting."

"And we were concerned that the town might turn into a mob. I've seen what people can do when they're angry."

The way Fletcher nodded told Dorothy he'd heard the story of what had happened in Xavier. "I don't want to think our residents would form a mob," he said, "but you could be right. They seem to idolize Brother Josiah, even though he obviously doesn't deserve it."

"He's good at what he does." As she'd walked back from the park after the meeting, Dorothy had tried to make sense of the man's appeal. "He says what people want to hear."

"He puts on a good show, but it's based on lies." Brandon added his opinion. "The whole story's going to be in tomorrow morning's *Chronicle*."

Fletcher nodded. "That's all well and good, but Brother Josiah and his men need to be behind bars. If you'd told me sooner, I could have them there now. As it is, the boys have gone home, so I'll have to ride out and get them." The boys, Dorothy knew, were Fletcher's deputies, two young men who lived on their parents' ranch a few miles north of town.

"I'd like to say I could handle this alone," the sheriff continued, "but there are too many of them for one man, and while you two did a fine job of finding the evidence, I don't think either of you is ready to tackle men like Brother Josiah and his men. The only good thing I can say is that by the time we get back, everyone will be asleep. Surprise makes a good ally."

"I heard Brother Josiah is staying at the boardinghouse in Phil Blakeslee's room. The three men who came with him sleep in the tent." Though Dorothy suspected the sheriff knew that, Brandon was ensuring there was no confusion.

"I'll send the boys to the tent. I want to be the one who catches Brother Josiah." Fletcher looked at the ledger page again. "It won't be hard to get a conviction with this."

"There's more in a trunk in Mrs. Lockhart's woodshed. That's where we found that." Dorothy realized they hadn't told the sheriff where the evidence was hidden.

"We'll get that too." He gave her a wry smile. "Even though I wish you'd told me about this earlier, part of me feels as if I ought to hire you. It seems you're doing my job."

Brandon was quick to contradict him. "Not at all. We're doing our job — searching for the truth and reporting it."

And, oh, how good it felt to be doing that together.

"Looks like another successful night." Phil stretched out on the bed, knowing that though Brother Josiah was currently pacing the room, he would soon settle in the chair. "Folks were even more impressed with the blind man seeing than they were when the cripple threw away his crutch."

"Wait until you see what happens tomorrow." The town's miracle worker made no effort to hide his gloating.

"Another miracle?"

"What else?" Brother Josiah shrugged, then stopped in front of the window. "Who's that? It looks like the sheriff."

Phil jumped to his feet and strode to the window. "That's who it is." The clouds had disappeared, leaving the moon bright enough to make the identification easy. It helped that the sheriff had a distinctive

446

walk, a bit like a swagger. "I wonder what he's doing. He doesn't usually come this way."

Brother Josiah swore loudly. "He could have been at that blasted newspaper office."

"Or at the livery." Although few entered it this late in the day. "I don't know why he'd be at either place. He doesn't keep his horse there, and it's not like Holloway's breaking any laws by working at night."

The preacher let out another curse, punctuating it with a thump on the bureau. "I've got a bad feeling about that newspaperman." He turned toward Phil, his face a study in fury. "It's time for you to earn your keep. Find out what's going on over there."

Phil blanched at the anger that appeared to be directed at him. He'd done nothing wrong. "How am I supposed to do that? It's not like I'm friends with Holloway."

Brother Josiah was clearly in no mood for excuses. "If you want your money, you'll figure it out. Now get out of here."

Though he didn't like being commanded, Phil recognized the wisdom of leaving. By the time he returned, Brother Josiah's anger might have dissipated.

Moving as silently as he could, Phil headed toward the newspaper office, assessing the building as he walked. Lamplight shone

447

from both front rooms. While that would make it more difficult for Holloway to see him, Phil wasn't going to take any chances. He'd try the back door. If luck was with him, Holloway would have left it open again, and he could sneak in that way.

Luck was with him, more luck than he'd expected. As he approached the building, he heard the sound of voices. Phil cursed silently at the realization that Dorothy was there. He had thought Holloway would be alone, but perhaps this was good. He might hear something he could report to Brother Josiah.

Crouching below the open window, Phil heard Dorothy say, "It's excellent, Brandon, truly excellent."

She paused for a second, and then it sounded as if she were reading. " 'With fake miracles, healings that are nothing more than a charade, and pleas for orphans he's neither met nor intends to meet, Brother Josiah has done his best to hoodwink the citizens of Mesquite Springs. He's exploited our generosity, our human kindness, and our sense of honor all so that he can line his own pockets. The man who claims to bring a message from God is nothing more than a charlatan.' "

Phil felt the bottom drop out of his stom-

448

ach. They knew what was going on. Somehow, they had proof. This was worse than he'd feared. As the memory of Brother Josiah's anger flashed before him, he cringed. What would the man do now?

"Don't change a single word." Dorothy's voice rang out clearly.

"What do you think about listing some of the other towns he's bilked recently? Should I include them?"

Dorothy was quick to answer Holloway's question. "I wouldn't include any names. Just say that records reveal Brother Josiah has a history of defrauding trusting congregations."

"That's a good idea."

What was a good idea was telling Brother Josiah it was time to leave town. Forget the rest of the week's meetings. They had to get away from here before everyone in Mesquite Springs knew what they'd been doing.

Phil had no doubt that Holloway had told the sheriff what he'd discovered. That was the only reasonable explanation for the man's presence near the boardinghouse. What he didn't know was why the sheriff hadn't done anything yet. Hard as it was to believe, maybe God really was on Brother Josiah's side.

Phil sprinted toward the boardinghouse

and raced up the stairs. When he entered his room, he found Brother Josiah talking to the biggest man in his entourage. More than six feet tall, the man had muscles to match his height, and while his blond hair and blue eyes might have been disarming, the scowl left no doubt that this was not someone to trifle with.

Though Phil had seen him from a distance, they'd never met. He wished that was still the case, because there was something so menacing about this man that Phil wanted to back away. Unfortunately, he could not.

"What did you learn?" Brother Josiah demanded. "Judging from your face, it wasn't good."

"It wasn't." That was the understatement of the day. "They were both there — Holloway and Dorothy — and they know what's going on. They're writing all about it."

Though Phil had expected Brother Josiah to explode with rage, he simply nodded, as if he'd expected that, and gave the big man a look Phil couldn't decipher.

"Did they say anything about the sheriff?" he asked.

"Not that I heard."

Another nod at the other man. "Walt, you handle the sheriff."

"Sure thing, boss."

Brother Josiah turned to Phil and tipped his head in the direction of the newspaper office. "You aren't squeamish, are you? Get back over there and take care of the problem."

"You want me to destroy the type and any of the papers they've already printed?"

The man who'd defrauded so many people let out a laugh that lacked all mirth. "I want you to make sure no one in that office lives to tell the story. Then you can take care of the type and the papers."

Killing. The supper Phil had eaten threatened to erupt. Before he could protest that he wasn't a murderer, Brother Josiah pulled a six-shooter from his pocket and pointed it at Phil. "Do as I say, or you won't live any longer than they will. Now, get out of here. Walt, you stay for a minute."

Wordlessly, Phil nodded. Brother Josiah was right. He had to get out of here.

Chapter Thirty-Four

"That looks perfect." Brandon had printed one copy of the paper and asked Dorothy to proofread it. "No mistakes."

Though she'd expected him to look pleased, lines of worry crossed Brandon's face. "I hope it wasn't a mistake not telling Fletcher until after the meeting."

"We had good reasons. If we'd tried to denounce him or if Fletcher had tried to arrest him at the meeting, the town might have supported Brother Josiah. You saw them. You heard them. They believe him."

"The question is, will they believe us?"

"They'll believe the *Chronicle.*" She infused her words with conviction. "Words have more power when they're printed than when they're spoken. Besides, Brother Josiah won't be there to refute anything."

"And people will be reading as individuals rather than listening as part of a crowd." Brandon's worry lines faded. "Your arguments make sense. I only wish I felt better about all of this. I can't help worrying that something will go wrong."

"We have to trust that it won't." Dorothy laid the paper on the table and reached for her reticule. "I'll come back to help with the printing, but I need to let Nutmeg out before she claws holes in the door."

It took only a minute to cross the alley and unlock the door to Polly's Place. As she'd expected, Nutmeg was waiting on the stairs, her tail wagging with delight when she heard the sound of the apartment door opening. She scampered down the final two steps, jumped up to put her front paws on Dorothy's shoulders, and gave her face a quick swipe with her tongue before she nosed the outside door open and raced into the alley.

Dorothy smiled at the dog's enthusiasm. It was the same every night. Nutmeg bounded outdoors as if she were a prisoner released from a tiny, windowless cell after years of incarceration. Not content to run through the alley, she'd head to River, then race around the block before returning home. Today, thanks to a brief afternoon rain, she would undoubtedly return with muddy paws. Fortunately, there was a good supply of old towels in the storage shed.

Dorothy unlatched the door and was about to step inside when a large hand grabbed her shoulder.

"There you are, missy."

She spun around, trying to break his grip, but the man was far stronger than she. Dorothy shuddered when she recognized the biggest of Brother Josiah's henchmen, the man who stood in the back of the tent each night, his size ensuring there were no disturbances during the meetings. What was he doing here?

"I knowed that coward wouldn't do it," he said, his lips curving into a sneer, "but I will. Killin's killin'. It don't much matter to me iffen it's a nosy newspaperman or a pretty gal. So long as I get paid, I do the job."

Killing. Newspaperman. As the words echoed through Dorothy's brain, a fear greater than she'd ever known swept over her. This man, this horrible man, planned to kill Brandon. That he intended to kill her seemed less frightening than the idea that the man she loved was in danger.

Mustering every ounce of courage she possessed, Dorothy resolved not to let the man see her fear. That would only fuel his intentions.

"Killing us won't stop people from learning the truth," she said as bravely as she could. "They'll catch you."

"You're wrong about that, missy. Me and Brother Josiah will be gone before anyone knows what happened, and there won't be nobody to tell."

Dorothy said a silent prayer that Fletcher had returned and had arrested Brother Josiah and the others and that only this man remained. Though she didn't know how it had happened, somehow these evil men had learned what she and Brandon had discovered and were preparing to flee once they'd killed everyone they considered a threat.

The man shoved Dorothy into the shed, then pulled his gun from the holster and pointed it at her, his finger on the trigger. A second later, he shook his head. "I got a better idea. I'm savin' you for the last. You and me's gonna have a little party before you meet yer Maker."

The laugh that accompanied his final words sent chills down Dorothy's spine. It was evil, pure evil. And then he closed the door, locking her inside the shed.

As total darkness surrounded her, fear and anger warred for dominance, with fear winning. Brandon was about to be killed, and Dorothy was powerless to help him. There was no way to open the shed from inside, yet she had to warn Brandon. She couldn't let that brute kill the man of her dreams.

"Please, God, show me how to save Brandon."

"I can't do it." Retching, Phil bent over and lost his supper in the bushes. It was bad enough that he'd already broken a commandment. He might not have done it himself, but he'd helped Brother Josiah steal, and the Bible said very clearly, "Thou shalt not steal."

At the time he'd invited the preacher to come here, the prospect of bilking people hadn't bothered him. The truth was, he hadn't thought beyond the money he stood to gain. But seeing people he knew giving money they could have used to feed and clothe their children made his stomach clench. If the parents gave away their last savings, the children might wind up like him and Esther.

Oh, God, what have I done? It had been years since Phil had spoken to God. He didn't expect an answer, but the silent cry echoed through his brain.

Stealing was wrong; killing was even worse. Though his limbs trembled, resolve filled his spirit. He wouldn't do it. Brother Josiah couldn't force him to kill, because he

456

wouldn't be able to find him. Phil rose and wiped his hand across his mouth, trying to rid himself of the terrible taste of vomit and fear.

He knew what he had to do. Even though it meant leaving the money behind, he wasn't going to stay here. He wasn't going to kill, and he wasn't going to watch someone else do it, either. Dusty was waiting. Together they'd leave Mesquite Springs, and if Mr. K wasn't happy, well . . . that was something Phil would deal with later. Right now, all that mattered was getting away from Brother Josiah and the killing.

As he'd expected, the livery was open, but since night rentals were rare, no one was working. Phil lit a lantern and made his way to Dusty's stall.

"It's okay, boy. Time for us to go." He patted the horse's flank, then turned to reach for the saddle.

"Coward!" The voice he'd heard for the first time only a few minutes ago rang through the livery. "I tole Brother Josiah he was wrong to trust you. I figgered you'd try to run, and you did. You ain't gettin' away." The big man Brother Josiah had called Walt raised his arm and pointed his gun at Phil's heart, laughing as he cocked it. "The boss'll be glad I took care of you first."

It was the end. Phil knew that. He was going to pay for his sins, and if the Bible was right, that payment would be endless. *"The wages of sin is death."* The words hit him with the force of a hammer. He deserved the pain; he'd earned those wages. But, as softly as the brush of a butterfly's wing, the rest of the verse slid into his brain. *"The gift of God is eternal life through Jesus Christ our Lord."*

Was it possible? In the instant before Walt pulled the trigger, Phil remembered Pastor Coleman's sermon about the thief who'd been crucified alongside Jesus. That man had received not death but the promise of paradise. And in that instant, Phil knew what he needed to say.

"Father, forgive me." The words were a mere whisper, drowned out by the sound of the gun firing and the bullet striking his chest. Then everything went black.

She should have been back by now. Brandon tried to tamp down his worries. He knew Nutmeg liked to run a bit at night, but Dorothy had been gone longer than the other nights. He fed more paper into the press, watching with satisfaction as George printed another copy of the *Chronicle* and trying to convince himself that nothing was wrong.

Bang!

Brandon's heart began to pound. Though it sounded like a gunshot, surely he was mistaken. It was too soon for Fletcher and his men to be back, and there was no reason for anyone in Mesquite Springs to be shooting at this time of night. He was mistaken.

A second later Brandon knew he was not mistaken in one thing. Those were footsteps. Heavy footsteps, definitely not Dorothy's. Brandon swiveled. Shock drained the blood from his face at the sight of Brother Josiah standing in the doorway, an amused expression on his face, a gun in his hand.

"I figured that sniveling coward wouldn't do his job, but maybe it's better this way." The man who'd duped so many people in so many towns smirked. "I heard you were planning a special edition of the *Chronicle*."

There was no mistaking the past tense he used or the gleam in the false preacher's eye. He was enjoying this, just as he'd enjoyed swindling compassionate people out of their savings. Somehow, he'd learned what Brandon and Dorothy had discovered and intended to stop the presses. Literally. Brother Josiah might not destroy George, but Brandon had no doubt that he planned to silence him permanently.

Though he and Dorothy had thought their

459

reasons were logical, they'd clearly made a huge mistake in not having Fletcher arrest this man and his cohorts immediately. Regret mingled with relief. At least Dorothy was not here. Brother Josiah might kill him, but the woman Brandon loved would be safe.

"It's time everyone in Mesquite Springs learns the truth behind your miracles and what really happens to the money you collect for those poor orphans in China." Brandon kept his voice even, refusing to give the man the satisfaction of seeing his fear.

"I've got to hand it to you. You're smarter than anyone in the other towns. They were easy to fleece." Brother Josiah took another step into the room. "What made you suspect me?"

Brandon looked around, seeking a way to disarm Brother Josiah. There were none. Perhaps if he kept the man talking, an idea might pop into his mind. Brandon said a silent prayer for guidance and for a way to keep Dorothy safe.

"Why should I tell you? That would only make it easier for you to dupe people in the next town. If, that is, you manage to leave Mesquite Springs."

"Oh, I will. You can be sure of that. My

460

men are taking care of all the problems."

The smirk on Brother Josiah's face when he said "problems" and the memory of the gunshot made Brandon's heart sink. He could only pray that Dorothy wasn't one of those problems Brother Josiah planned to eliminate.

"It was mighty considerate of you to leave the back door open. I would have hated to have to break down a door. That's messy."

"And you don't like messes." At least the man was talking. Unfortunately, Brandon still had no idea how to disarm him.

"No, I don't. That's why I'm here. I wanted to be sure there wasn't a mess."

As if shooting the gun he was brandishing wouldn't create a mess. Brandon said nothing, merely looked behind Brother Josiah as he heard more footsteps.

The tall man he'd seen guarding the entrance to the tent each night entered the office. "They won't be talkin'. Neither of 'em." Satisfaction oozed from the man's voice, and Brother Josiah beamed his approval.

As the words registered, Brandon's heart began to pound. No! It couldn't be! But though he tried to find another explanation, Brandon knew the man was boasting that he'd silenced both Dorothy and Fletcher.

Mesquite Springs had lost its sheriff, and he'd lost — Brandon's knees threatened to buckle at the thought of what he'd lost — the woman whose smile had brightened his days, whose insightful comments had made him a better writer, whose love had changed his life. The woman he loved more than life itself was gone.

He would be the next. Brandon had no doubt about that. An hour ago, he would have fought the idea of dying, but now, knowing that the woman he loved so dearly had been killed and the future that had once seemed so promising had turned bleak, Brandon had only one regret. When he died, these men would escape, fully intending to continue their evil game in another town. Though he wished it were otherwise, there was no way to stop them. All he could do was pray for a miracle. A genuine miracle.

Brother Josiah motioned to the big man. "Keep your gun on him, Walt. I've got something to do." He slid his revolver back into the holster, picked up a copy of the paper, and began to read, his smirk fading only slightly as he saw just how much the paper revealed.

"This could be your finest work, Mr. Newspaperman." The smirk was back in full form. "Too bad no one will have a chance to see it."

"What are we waitin' for?" the man named Walt demanded.

"Don't be so impatient. I like seeing a man sweat a bit. He might even beg me to spare him. Wouldn't that be worth watching?"

"That won't ever happen." Begging would do no good. It would merely feed the man's belief that he was omnipotent and infallible. "Never."

CHAPTER THIRTY-FIVE

At first it was only a whimper, then a short bark. Relief so intense that it threatened to make her knees buckle washed over Dorothy. Her prayer had been answered.

"I'm here, Nutmeg. Open the door." She shouted the command, not knowing whether the dog would understand the words but hoping she would want to play or simply lick Dorothy's face. Though there'd been a time when Nutmeg's ability to unlatch doors had annoyed her, tonight it could mean the difference between life and death.

"Please, Nutmeg, open the door." Brandon's life depended on both of them.

The scrabbling of claws on the door was the sweetest sound Dorothy had ever heard. Seconds later, the door was unlatched and moonlight streamed into her prison. *Thank you, Lord.*

"Good dog. Good Nutmeg." Dorothy

hugged her canine rescuer. Though she wanted to reward the dog, there was no time.

Dorothy raced into the house, grabbed her rifle, and headed back toward the *Chronicle,* praying she'd find Brandon there. Though the sound of the distant gunshot still echoed through her brain, she refused to give up hope. God had sent Nutmeg to release her. Surely he had kept Brandon safe and that shot had not come from the *Chronicle*'s office.

"Quiet now, Nutmeg. No barking." Tonight, she would not leave the dog at home. She wanted her faithful pet at her side.

As if she understood, Nutmeg ran silently next to Dorothy as they raced toward Brandon. When they reached the back of the *Chronicle,* Dorothy saw that the door was ajar, and fear assailed her again. She was certain she had left the door fully closed. Had that horrible man killed Brandon? Motioning to Nutmeg to remain quiet, she entered the building.

"Never."

It was only one word, but for Dorothy it was another answered prayer. Brandon was still alive, his voice as firm as ever. *Thank you, God. Now I ask for strength for whatever lies ahead.* The prayer was a silent one but no less fervent for not being spoken.

Dorothy picked her way toward the front of the house, scarcely daring to breathe for fear of alerting whoever was with Brandon. When she reached the doorway to the pressroom, the scene made her grip Nutmeg's muzzle, lest the dog bark. Brother Josiah was standing no more than two feet from Brandon, clearly taunting him about something, while the ruffian who'd locked her into the shed was pointing a gun at the man she loved.

It had been two against one. Now the odds were better. Dorothy raised her rifle as she entered the room. "If you shoot him, you'll be the next to die."

Though she kept her gaze and the rifle fixed on the man with the gun, from the corner of her eye, she saw Brandon nod.

The big man had more control than she had expected and did not turn to see who was threatening him, but Brother Josiah curled his lip in disdain. "Now, what does a little lady like you know about shooting? You wouldn't kill a man."

"It's messy."

Brandon's words made little sense to Dorothy, but they struck a nerve in Brother Josiah, for he clenched his fists and ad-

466

dressed the big man. "Take care of her, Walt."

The man named Walt turned, surprise etched on his face. "What you doin' here, missy?" He pointed his gun at her, then appeared to change his mind. Before Dorothy realized what he intended, he lunged toward her, reaching for her rifle.

No! Instinctively, Dorothy's finger curled around the trigger. Though she had never shot a man, she couldn't let him hurt Brandon, but before she could fire, Nutmeg catapulted into the room, the angry mass of fur and muscles knocking Dorothy's assailant to the floor.

"Arrgh!" Walt's shout of anger and fear was silenced as Nutmeg clamped her jaws on his throat, leaving the big man immobile. Dorothy was safe, but Brandon . . .

It happened so quickly that her brain scarcely registered the details. The moment Nutmeg sprang into the room, Brandon tackled Brother Josiah. Using the surprise he had on his side and his greater weight to topple the dishonest preacher, Brandon wrested the gun from Brother Josiah's holster and pinned the man's arms to the floor. Within mere seconds, Brother Josiah was no longer a threat. Dorothy's prayers had been answered.

Nutmeg looked up at her, seeking guidance. "Good girl. Keep him there." The dog needed no encouragement, and the man who'd threatened both Brandon and Dorothy whimpered in pain and fear.

Dorothy lifted her rifle and aimed it at Brother Josiah. "I wouldn't move if I were you."

Brandon rose to his feet. "I told you I wouldn't beg," he said as he pointed Brother Josiah's gun at him. "You can beg all you want, but it won't do any good."

Brother Josiah said not a word, although he flinched when Brandon asked Dorothy to retrieve rope from the cupboard. In less than a minute, Brandon had trussed both Brother Josiah and Walt, who made up for his boss's silence by yelling that the dog was more dangerous than three men put together. Though Nutmeg was no longer restraining the big man, she stood nearby, clearly ready to attack again if she thought either Dorothy or Brandon was in danger.

"I think he needs a gag." Dorothy pulled one of the rags they used to clean the press from the cupboard and ripped it in half. With Nutmeg's low growl ensuring the man's compliance, Dorothy tied the gag around his mouth.

"You wouldn't do that to a man of God."

Brother Josiah sounded confident.

"Maybe not," Dorothy agreed, "but you're no man of God. We don't need to hear any more of your lies." When he too was silenced, she turned to Brandon, who was keeping the false minister's gun pointed at him. "I'll go for Fletcher."

"Let's hope he's back."

He was just returning, accompanied by the two deputies. When he heard what had happened, Fletcher sent his deputies to arrest Brother Josiah's other two henchmen with orders to investigate the gunshot as soon as the men were in jail.

"It seems I was wrong when I said you and Brandon wouldn't be able to handle the preacher and his men. It sounds like you two have everything under control with Brother Josiah and Walt." There was more than a hint of humor in Fletcher's voice as he and Dorothy walked toward the *Chronicle.*

Though her legs were still wobbly from all that had happened, Dorothy nodded. "Thanks to Nutmeg. She can have anything she wants to eat for the rest of her life after what she did tonight."

"Maybe I should hire her."

Dorothy laughed at the idea of a dog on the police force. "Sorry, but she's mine."

469

She could hardly believe she was laughing after what had been the most terrifying night of her life. She and Brandon had been close to dying, but they'd been spared. And, thanks to what they'd discovered, Brother Josiah's days of swindling people were over.

"Nice job," Fletcher said when he surveyed the *Chronicle*'s office and saw Brandon holding the two trussed and gagged men at gunpoint with Nutmeg standing between them, her posture declaring she was ready to attack.

"When my deputy gets here, we'll escort you to jail," the sheriff told Brother Josiah and Walt. "The cell will be a mite crowded with four of you in it, but don't worry. It's only overnight. You'll be headed to the county seat tomorrow, and lest you think you'll find any leniency there, let me assure you that our judge takes the Commandments very seriously. When he hears how much you've stolen, well . . ." Fletcher paused for emphasis. "I expect you'll be looking at bars for a good long time."

Within a quarter of an hour, one of the deputies arrived, and he and Fletcher led the two prisoners to jail. As soon as the door closed behind them, Dorothy's legs gave way, and she crumpled onto a chair.

"Are you hurt?" Brandon rushed to her

side, his worry palpable.

"No. Not hurt, but scared and weak. Suddenly, everything that happened tonight hit me." Dorothy reached out to link her hand with his. Seeing him and hearing him was good, but she needed the reassurance of his touch. "I keep remembering that gunshot and how afraid I was that you'd been killed. Oh, Brandon, it was horrible. I couldn't do anything because I was locked in the shed."

Brandon blinked in surprise. "You were locked in? How did you get out?"

Dorothy gestured toward Nutmeg, who was now resting at her side. "My clever dog."

As she explained about her prayer and how quickly it had been answered, Brandon nodded, and his eyes darkened with emotion. "When I heard the shot, I thought you were killed, especially when Brother Josiah's henchman said neither one would talk again. I thought he meant you and Fletcher."

"He probably did mean me. He told me he would be back after he'd taken care of you." Dorothy paused for a second, remembering the man's menacing tone. "He didn't mention Fletcher. I wonder if he meant —"

"Phil."

"Blakeslee."

She and Brandon spoke at the same time. "I wonder where Blakeslee is. We know he was involved in what they've been doing here." Brandon's expression was grim. "Brother Josiah doesn't strike me as one to leave loose ends, and Blakeslee is a loose end."

Fear swept over Dorothy. No matter what Phil had done, he did not deserve to die. "What direction did the shot come from? I couldn't tell."

"West. Maybe the livery." Brandon went into the pressroom and looked out the west-facing window. "The light is on there. That's not normal for this late, but it could be that the deputy is searching there."

It would also be lit if someone were leaving town and had gone for his horse. A sense of urgency deepened Dorothy's fear. "We should see what's happening there."

"We?" Brandon looked skeptical. "I could go alone."

No, he couldn't. "I'd only worry every minute you were gone."

Brandon nodded, as if he shared her concerns about being separated, particularly now. "All right."

Though they held hands as they walked, they were silent, each caught up in thoughts of what they might find. When they entered the livery, Dorothy ordered Nutmeg to remain at the entrance. The dog would only make the horses restive, and they didn't need that.

"This way." Brandon gestured toward the opposite end of the building where a lantern hung from a peg on the wall.

Though their footsteps were muffled by the dirt floor, they heard a faint moan. That was good, Dorothy told herself. Dead men did not moan.

But her optimism fled when two more steps revealed Phil lying on the ground, his face ominously pale, his breathing labored, the reddish-brown straw beneath him leaving no doubt what had happened.

Oh, dear Lord, help him. Dorothy sent the prayer heavenward, then knelt next to him, urging Brandon to join her.

"We're here."

"He shot me." Phil's face contorted with the effort of speaking, and Dorothy knew he was dying. "Walt," he said, confirming the identity of his attacker. "Called me a coward. Was right." Phil closed his eyes as the pain worsened, then opened them again. "Wouldn't kill you, no matter what Brother Josiah said."

The last of the pieces fell into place. Phil was more than a loose end. He was a man who'd defied Brother Josiah's commands. Dorothy doubted any lived to repeat their disobedience.

"We'll get the doctor," she said, trying to reassure the man who had refused to shoot her and Brandon. He'd been wrong in bringing Brother Josiah to Mesquite Springs, but he'd shown courage by defying the charlatan.

"Too late. I know that." When he fell silent, Dorothy exchanged a look with Brandon, fearing the man was already dead, but then they heard his raspy breathing. "I'm sorry." Phil fixed his gaze on Brandon. "Sorry I hurt you. Sorry I destroyed your type. Sorry I brought Brother Josiah here." The words came out slowly, the pauses between them continuing to lengthen as Phil struggled to speak. With each sentence, he'd answered another question, telling them he was responsible for the horrible things that had happened in Mesquite Springs.

Phil's eyes moved from Brandon to Dorothy. "Can you forgive me?"

She reached for the dying man's hand, wanting to give him a measure of comfort. No matter what he'd done, no matter how much damage he'd inflicted, he deserved her forgiveness. But before Dorothy could respond, Brandon did. "Yes, Phil. I forgive you."

"So do I." Phil's hand was limp against hers, his strength so eroded that he could not return Dorothy's gentle pressure. "Have you asked for God's forgiveness?"

"Yes. No answer." Phil's voice was weaker now, each word seeming to leach more energy from him.

"Ask again." Brandon took the man's other hand. "Ask him now."

For a moment, Phil said nothing, and his breathing grew shallower, the intervals between each breath longer. Then he spoke, his words so faint Dorothy could barely hear them. "Father, forgive me."

Phil closed his eyes, his face so contorted with pain that Dorothy knew the end was imminent. When his eyelids flew open, he smiled, a smile filled with peace and joy, a smile that told Dorothy Phil's prayer had been answered. A second later, the smile faded, and the light in his eyes was extinguished.

"He met his Savior," Brandon said, his words breaking the silence.

As tears streamed down her cheeks, Dorothy nodded. "We'll never know why he did what he did, but I believe that beneath it all, he was a good man who took the wrong path."

"Now he's reached the end."

"And the beginning."

CHAPTER THIRTY-SIX

"I think you should open this." Fletcher held out the oilskin packet that Doc had found in Blakeslee's pocket when he'd examined the body. "You and Dorothy were probably closer to him than anyone in Mesquite Springs."

As unexpected as the thought was, Brandon could not disagree with it. He and Dorothy had heard Blakeslee's confession and witnessed his salvation. After those experiences, it seemed fitting that they be the first to see whatever it was that Phil Blakeslee had kept close to his heart.

Brandon accepted the packet and returned to his seat next to Dorothy. The two of them had followed Fletcher and Doc as they'd taken Blakeslee's body to Doc's office, where it would be prepared for burial. Brandon suspected Fletcher hoped the contents of the packet would include the name of Blakeslee's next of kin, even though

Dorothy had told him Blakeslee claimed he had no family.

"Ready?" When Dorothy nodded, Brandon opened the oilskin envelope and carefully withdrew the contents. Half a dozen clippings from a newspaper, the yellowed paper testifying to their age, lay on top of one of Blakeslee's sketches. Brandon set the articles aside unread and stared at the drawing.

"Oh no!"

Dorothy's gasp mirrored his own reaction. The sketch was a series of small drawings surrounding a larger central one. The small sketches showed a boy and an older girl, their resemblance leaving no doubt that they were siblings. In one, they were well dressed, playing a card game. In another, the girl appeared to be teaching her brother to paint. In still another, they were picking apples.

But then the mood changed from carefree to solemn. The expensive clothing was replaced by ragged, ill-fitting garments. Smiles turned to looks of quiet desperation as the girl dished out a meager meal. In the final of the small sketches, the boy was alone, his face contorted with rage.

It wasn't chance, Brandon knew, that the boy was looking directly at the central drawing, the one that had caused Dorothy's gasp. In it, the girl was alone, the noose around her neck and the overturned chair leaving no doubt that she had taken her own life.

"It's Phil and his sister. He must have found her." Dorothy paused for a second as she struggled to control her emotions. "Poor Phil. I knew she'd died, but I had no idea how. Discovering her body must have been horrible."

As memories of seeing his father lying on the *Record*'s floor flashed before him, Brandon nodded. What Blakeslee had found was even worse than what he'd endured. As Dorothy had said, poor Phil.

"Let's see what's in the clippings." Brandon handed the sketch to Fletcher and began to read aloud. With each article, his anger grew, for it appeared that the editor of the paper, a man named Robert Monroe, had used his power to denounce Blakeslee's sister, calling her a whore and a temptress whose only thought was to lead innocent men into sin.

Monroe hadn't been alone in his scurrilous attacks, for there were multiple references to the minister's condemnation of Esther Blakeslee and his demands that she be shunned by every God-fearing citizen. Together the two most influential men in the town appeared to have driven Blakeslee's sister to kill herself.

As he laid the last clipping on the pile, Brandon turned toward Dorothy. "We have our answers." Though neither Brandon nor Pastor Coleman had done anything like the other editor and preacher, Blakeslee's hostility toward them was understandable. His tortured mind must have believed that all newspapermen and all ministers were the same and deserved to be punished for what had happened to Esther.

Blakeslee had been trapped by the shadows of his past, but now he was free, and so was Brandon — free to pursue a life beyond the shadows.

"How are you feeling?" Evelyn gave Nutmeg a quick pat on the head before she turned her attention to Dorothy.

Though Dorothy had been surprised when Evelyn arrived half an hour earlier than normal, she was grateful for her sister-in-law's company. It had been a long and mostly sleepless night as her brain whirled with everything she'd seen and experienced.

"I'm angry, sad, and hopeful, all at the same time. Doesn't that sound crazy?"

Evelyn settled onto one of the chairs in the dining part of the apartment that had once been hers. "It sounds normal to me. That's how I felt when the orphanage burned and Polly and I were forced to find a new home. What seemed like the worst thing that could happen to me turned out to be the best, because it brought me here. Look at me now." She placed a protective hand on her midsection. "I'm married to the finest man in the world, we're expecting our first child, and I have the sister I always wanted."

The tears that had been on the verge of falling all night dampened Dorothy's cheeks. She'd been determined not to cry, but Evelyn's candor had unleashed her own emotions. Hearing Phil's final words, watching him die, and learning what had made him the man he was had shown her what was important and what she needed to do.

She laid her hand on Evelyn's and squeezed it. "I love you, Evelyn. I don't think I've ever told you that, but I do."

Evelyn's eyes misted, and she blinked back tears. "I know you do. Your actions have shown me that."

"But words are important too." Dorothy managed a little laugh. "Here I am, the woman who wanted to change the world with her words, but I rarely put my deepest feelings into words."

"Those are the hardest ones to express, because they're the most important." Evelyn threaded her fingers through Dorothy's, then smiled as she looked at their joined hands. "I had another reason for coming here this early. I wanted to tell you what Wyatt's been doing."

"Do we need coffee for this?"

Evelyn shook her head. "I've already had two cups."

"Did he contact Pastor Coleman?" After she and Brandon had left Doc's office, they'd gone to Wyatt and Evelyn's home to explain what had occurred. Wyatt, as the mayor of Mesquite Springs, needed to be informed of what had transpired. Wyatt, as Dorothy's brother, needed to be reassured that she was safe. They'd also suggested he let Pastor Coleman know that Brother Josiah was leaving town in the custody of the sheriff's deputies.

Evelyn nodded. "Wyatt sent a messenger last night. The poor man's been on horseback far too long, but he returned half an hour ago. The Colemans were leaving right away so that Pastor Coleman could conduct Phil's funeral."

"I wonder how the town will feel about that and how they'll treat Pastor Coleman."

"I suspect we'll have some very red-faced

citizens once they read the paper. I wouldn't be surprised if they conveniently forget they wanted a new minister."

"I hope you're right." Dorothy could not forget Mrs. Coleman's distress when she'd found the anonymous letters or the way some members of the community had shunned the Colemans at the Downeys' party. "I've hated seeing the town so divided."

Though she'd struggled with her feelings toward those who'd been so unkind to the Colemans, Dorothy knew the situation had been far more difficult for Brandon, since it mimicked the divisions he'd experienced in Xavier. And while the circumstances had been different, in both cases, they had resulted in a man's death. She managed a little smile. "It sounds as if my brother has been busy."

"You could say that. I need to warn you that he's done one more thing. He went to the ranch, because he wanted your mother to hear everything from him."

Chagrin washed over Dorothy. "I should have gone there last night."

"You were in no condition to do that. Besides, Wyatt can soothe her better than you."

"You're right, but if I know my mother,

she'll be here soon, and she'll insist that I need to move back to the Circle C."

But she did not. Once she'd assured herself that Dorothy was unharmed, Ma shocked her by saying, "I'm proud of you, Dorothy. Your father was right when he told me you would become a strong woman. You have." She tightened the arm she'd wrapped around Dorothy's waist. "As much as I hate the idea that my little girl is grown up and doesn't need me, I know it's true."

Dorothy leaned her head on her mother's shoulder, wanting to draw comfort as much as to give it. "I'll always be your daughter, and I'll always need you, Ma." She turned and pressed a kiss on her mother's cheek. "Most of all, I'll always love you."

The tears that filled Dorothy's eyes matched those in her mother's.

Brandon frowned as his stomach growled, sure evidence that it was even later than he'd realized. He'd hoped to see Dorothy this morning, but she hadn't come to the office, and he hadn't had a free moment. Within minutes of the paper's being delivered, people had begun to crowd the front room. Everyone, it seemed, had an opinion about Brother Josiah. Some claimed they'd never trusted him. Others admitted they'd been hoodwinked. All complimented Brandon on exposing the truth.

Though the praise was welcome, he suspected the residents were mostly grateful that they had a chance of getting their money back. After talking to Wyatt and the sheriff last night, Brandon and Dorothy had decided to revise this morning's paper, including a mention of Phil's death and information about the refund of the money Brother Josiah had collected under false pretenses.

Wyatt had agreed to be the coordinator and had asked everyone to tell him how much they'd placed in the offering baskets. Fletcher was keeping the money from Brother Josiah's trunk in his safe. When all the claims were submitted, Wyatt would begin the process of refunding people's gifts.

Another growl provoked a guffaw from the man who'd been vocal about what a shame it was that anyone would invite a scoundrel like Brother Josiah to their town. Apparently, the man had conveniently forgotten how he'd been more than happy to sing that same scoundrel's praises after the first miraculous healing.

"Hungry, huh?" he asked.

His question was loud enough that everyone who'd been milling around the office stopped and looked at Brandon.

"Sorry, folks, but it seems my stomach is demanding I fill it. I'll reopen in an hour."

When the last of the well-wishers had left, Brandon locked the door and escaped out the back. There'd undoubtedly be others who wanted to talk to him at Polly's Place, but he needed a minute of silence before he handled the next round.

As he'd expected, the restaurant was full when he entered it, and he braced himself for an onslaught of questions and comments.

"Would you like a table of your own? I have a feeling your ears are ringing right now."

Brandon breathed a sigh of relief. Somehow Laura had anticipated his need. "That would be good." He hadn't realized there were any single tables, but she led him to one so close to the kitchen door that only one chair would fit. Though it was clearly the least desirable table in the room, it was perfect for Brandon. He sank onto the chair and felt himself begin to relax for the first time all morning.

"Before I tell you today's specials, I have a question for you."

Brandon girded himself for the inevitable question about Brother Josiah.

"You love Dorothy, don't you?"

He hadn't expected that question, but he wouldn't lie. "Yes, I do."

"I thought so. That's why I'm going to give you some advice." Laura bent and whispered in his ear, "Today would be a good day to ask her to marry you."

Dorothy stood in front of the mirror, fussing with her hair. It was probably silly. After all, Brandon had seen her with disheveled hair, but when she'd received his note saying he hoped to join her for a walk this afternoon, she'd wanted to look her best. She'd changed into her favorite shirtwaist, a soft peach color that Ma said flattered her, and now the last of the curls was arranged to her satisfaction.

She was ready. Fortunately, Brandon had chosen a time after the restaurant was closed, so she didn't have to explain to Evelyn and Laura where she was going or why she wasn't taking Nutmeg with her.

"Where's her leash?" Brandon asked when he'd greeted her and ruffled Nutmeg's fur.

"She's already had her walk, so she's staying home." Nutmeg wouldn't be happy about being left behind, but Dorothy did not want any distractions. What she had to say needed to be said without a dog nudging her hand or whining for attention.

"Oh." Though he said nothing more, Brandon seemed pleased by the prospect of time alone with her. "Shall we go?" He crooked his arm so Dorothy could place her hand on it after she'd locked the door behind them. "I thought we might go to the spring, unless that's further than you want to walk today."

"It's not too far." Even to her ears, her voice sounded strained. When she'd thought about their walk and what she hoped would happen on it, she hadn't expected to feel this awkward. She wanted — no, she needed — to tell Brandon how she felt, but all those lessons in propriety were holding her back.

A lady wasn't supposed to be forward; she wasn't supposed to express her emotions; and she was never, ever, ever supposed to ask a man to marry her. It didn't matter what she was supposed to do. Dorothy intended to do all three.

"I imagine you had a busy day," she said to break the silence that had begun to feel uncomfortable.

"I certainly did. It seemed like everyone in Mesquite Springs stopped by the office." Brandon did not appear to be suffering from the same awkwardness that had afflicted her. "What did you do?"

"I spent time with Evelyn and my mother. Then I tried to think of a theme for next month's special Sociable column."

They'd crossed River Street, and while they remained on the opposite side of the street, Dorothy could not help glancing at the livery and remembering what had happened there. Despite the wrong he'd done, Phil had helped make last Christmas a special one for many in Mesquite Springs. His sketches were a lasting legacy and evidence of his God-given talent, and the peace he'd found in his final moments was a memory indelibly etched on Dorothy's brain, one that had strengthened her faith and renewed her resolve to leave a positive legacy of her own.

Starting today.

"Any ideas?" Brandon's question brought Dorothy back to the present.

"Not a one. I'm afraid my mind wasn't on the *Chronicle*."

He nodded as if he understood. "I'm not surprised. I imagine you're like me and can't stop thinking about last night."

"That's part of it, but mostly I kept thinking about you and the questions you asked me. The ones about the future." This wasn't how she'd meant to tell him, but the words seemed to bubble out of her unbidden.

"The future and marriage."

"Yes."

Brandon stopped and took her hands in his. "I have an idea for the next Sociable."

Dorothy blinked in surprise. Even though she'd mentioned it, she didn't want to discuss the paper.

"Don't look so shocked. Believe it or not, our minds have been traveling the same path." Brandon gave her hands a quick squeeze. "I wanted to wait until we reached the spring. A street corner is not a romantic spot. The problem is, I don't want to waste another minute. If I learned anything last night, it's that life can end without warning. That's why it's so important to live each day to the fullest and to not squander a single minute."

Dorothy's heart began to race as she realized that Brandon was right: they had traveled the same path. He was saying the words she wanted to say, words that made her almost giddy with joy.

"If you agree, I think the next Sociable should announce our engagement." Brandon's eyes turned that deep blue that never failed to thrill her. "I love you, Dorothy. I love you more than I dreamt was possible."

As she loved him. The love that filled her heart colored every aspect of her life. It made sunny days more beautiful and difficult times like last night easier to bear. Most of all, it gave her a sense of completeness. Ma was right. Love was a precious gift, one to be cherished, not squandered. Dorothy would no longer waste a single minute.

Before she could speak, Brandon lifted her hands and pressed a kiss on her knuckles. "You've brought laughter into my life. You've helped rekindle my dreams. You've shown me love can be a partnership and that together we are stronger than when we're apart." He paused for a second before he repeated the most powerful words in the English language. "I love you."

Though her heart was pounding so hard that she wasn't sure she could breathe, much less form a coherent sentence, Dorothy couldn't let him continue. She had to say those oh, so important words.

"I love you, Brandon, and I love the changes you've brought to my life. Loving you has shown me how wonderful the world is. I thought I was happy before, but now I realize that what I felt was only a pale imitation of what I experience when we're together."

When he started to speak, she shook her head. He'd had his turn; now was her chance to tell him how much he'd given her, how he'd turned her life from ordinary into spectacular.

"You've made me a better person. Before I met you, I was only half-alive, but when I'm with you, I feel complete. I love you, Brandon Holloway. I love you with all my heart."

He smiled, and in that smile, Dorothy saw all the love she felt for him reflected back at her.

"Will you marry me?" he asked, his lips continuing to curve upward.

"I will."

The smile broadened. "Soon?"

"Very soon."

"Then there's only one thing left to do."

"Announce our engagement in the next Sociable?"

"No. This." And then, though they were standing on a street corner where anyone could see them, he lowered his lips to hers. It was the sweetest of kisses, a kiss that banished the fears of the past, a kiss that promised a future filled with love and laughter, a kiss that told the world Dorothy and Brandon had begun their journey together.

Laura had been wrong. Dorothy wasn't lucky. She was blessed.

AUTHOR'S LETTER

Dear Reader,

Thanks so much for journeying to Mesquite Springs with me. I know you have many other things competing for your time, and I'm honored that you chose to spend some of that time with Dorothy and Brandon. And Nutmeg. We can't forget Nutmeg, can we? I have to admit she was one of my favorite characters.

Years ago, my friend Diane told me about her dog opening doors, which was something neither of the dogs my family had when I was growing up had done, perhaps because we had doorknobs rather than levers. At any rate, Diane's story intrigued me so much that I knew it would be part of a book one day. That day finally came.

I'm sure you noticed there were some unanswered questions in this book, including the reason Mr. K wanted land near the river and why he thought it important to have a hotel in Mesquite Springs. Those are questions both wealthy socialite Alexandra Tarkington, who just so happens to be Mr. K's daughter, and private investigator Gabriel Seymour want answered too. For a peek at the start of Alexandra and Gabe's story, turn a couple pages, and you'll find the first chapter. While the first chapter doesn't tell you why Calvin Tarkington is calling himself Calvin King or Mr. K, the answer is in the book itself, along with the suspense and romance you've come to expect from my stories.

Were you hoping Laura would finally find her true love? I was, and so I gave her another chance in the final Mesquite Springs book. I'll admit that her choice surprised me. You see, I had someone else in mind for her, but Laura has a mind of her own, and I've learned not to argue with my characters.

Meanwhile, if you haven't read Evelyn and Wyatt's story, which begins the Mesquite Springs trilogy, I invite you to do so now. *Out of the Embers* is available in print, large print, ebook, and audio book formats, so whatever your reading preference, it's there.

I also invite you to visit my website, www.amandacabot.com. You'll find information about my other books and a sign-up form for my newsletters as well as links to my social media accounts. I've also included my email address, because one of my greatest pleasures as an author is to receive notes from my readers. Don't be shy.

Blessings,
Amanda

ABOUT THE AUTHOR

Amanda Cabot's dream of selling a book before her thirtieth birthday came true, and she's now the author of more than thirty-five novels as well as eight novellas, four nonfiction books, and what she describes as enough technical articles to cure insomnia in a medium-sized city. Her stories have appeared on the CBA and ECPA bestseller lists, have garnered a starred review from *Publishers Weekly,* and have been nominated for the ACFW Carol, the HOLT Medallion, and the Booksellers Best awards.

Amanda married her high school sweetheart, who shares her love of travel and who's driven thousands of miles to help her research her books. After years as Easterners, they fulfilled a longtime dream when Amanda retired from her job as director of information technology for a major corporation and now live in the American West.